POISONERS

AND

SLOW POISONING.

A NARRATIVE OF

THE MOST REMARKABLE CASES OF POISONING.

BEAUTIFULLY ILLUSTRATED

BY W. G. STANDFAST, ESQ.

LONDON:

PUBLISHED BY JOHN DICKS, AT THE OFFICE, 313, STRAND.

POISONERS
AND SLOW POISONING.

POPE ALEXANDER THE SIXTH.

CHAPTER I.

INTRODUCTION—TOPHANIA—AQUA TOPHANA, ETC., ETC.

"TRUTH is stranger than fiction." History has horrors blacker than any which the imagination of the romancist has conceived. In the human soul are depths of depravity deeper than the plummet of the psychologist has yet sounded. "Knowledge is power." So it is ; but it is a power for evil as well as for good. Knowledge can raise the soul of man above the stars, and make him a fit associate for the immortal gods ; but it can also degrade below the level of the brute, and make him too vile for the companionship of the infernal fiends. Doubtless "there is a soul of goodness in things evil," but the converse of this is also true, and there is a soul of evil in things good. There is not an element in the physical world, nor a passion, feeling, or faculty in the nature of man, which is not suscep-

tible of such perversion as will make it a curse instead of a blessing to the human race. The more capable a thing is of contributing to the goodness and happiness of mankind, the more liable it is to be abused, and the more prolific it is of human suffering and degradation. Death follows life, as the shadow the substance. Pleasure and pain, virtue and vice, creation and destruction, though eternally and irreconcilably antagonistic, are yet intimately and inextricably intermixed. The same science which enables man to save life, enables him also to destroy it. The identical drug which thousands of times has repelled death from the gate, has too, too frequently acted the foul part of the traitor, and admitted the fell destroyer into the sacred citadel of life. In reading the history of those beings who have availed themselves of the discoveries of the human mind to gratify, at the expense of everything that is noble, pure, and loveable in our nature, all that is vile, false, and abominable, one would almost think that it is the doings of malignant demons, and not the actions of beings in whom benevolence and a moral sense are the most distinguishing attributes, that are recorded in the crime-stained page. The soul is sickened, and the moral sensibilities shocked, at the dreary vista of human depravity that bursts upon the mental view. For this, many have argued that such studies are pernicious, and ought to be avoided; and as there is to some minds a terrible fascination in gigantic guilt, by which they are drawn as by an invisible and irresistible power into the very jaws of perdition, it has been contended that eternal oblivion ought to shroud those instances of human transgression. Such arguments, though well intentioned, are excessively silly, and based upon the most shallow acquaintance with human nature. It is to assert that in ignorance only is safety to be found. Take the following illustration in reply to this objection. In the charts of the mariner are indicated the rocks, the quicksands, the shallows, and whirlpools which lie between him and the haven at which he wishes to arrive. Now, suppose a captain of a ship so mad or so wicked as to steer his vessel purposely upon a rock—a rock of whose existence he had no other knowledge than that derived from his chart; and that in consequence of this act of folly, or of guilt, both the ship and the cargo were lost; and suppose, also, that as soon as the news of this calamity had transpired, some solemn wiseacre had arisen to denounce the study and even the existence of charts, because the use made of the information which the madman or the villain in question received from his chart was to enable him to devote his charge to destruction,— what would be the proper answer to such an argument? Is it not that, although one ship and a few human lives had been lost by this knowledge, yet hundreds of vessels and thousands of lives had been saved by the same knowledge? It is the same with the records of human depravity—those charts on which the dangers which bestud the sea of life are marked. Some, no doubt, have wilfully or fatuously wrecked themselves upon the information imparted by history; but myriads, by the same means, have been enabled to steer their course in safety. Ignorance may have saved some, but it has destroyed millions. Knowledge has, no doubt, been the ruin of many, but it has been the salvation of an infinitely greater number. With these preliminary observations, we proceed to lay before the readers of this work an account of the most extraordinary poisoners whose gigantic villanies have startled humanity, and conferred a baleful lustre and an infamous immortality on the names of the diabolical perpetrators

Poisoning is not a modern invention; nor is an advanced civilization, or some acquaintance with science, in any degree essential to a perfect familiarity with many of the most potent and malignant poisons. From the testimony both of the sacred and profane writers, we know that in very remote times poisons and their use were familiar to the ancients. Upon the occasion of the great dearth in Samaria, the Prophet Elisha gave an entertainment to a number of the young students; and we learn that certain bitter herbs, having entered in too great a proportion into the composition of the broth, the young men, having felt its bitter taste, cried out in alarm, "There is death in the pot, O prophet!" The death of Socrates, by drinking of the hemlock juice, would have sufficed of itself to render this poison classical. We also know that many of the most savage nations are perfect adepts in the art of poisoning. Beckmann, in his history of inventions, has collected several instances of secret poisoning from the Greek and Roman writers. He refers to Aratus, of Sicyon, to whom, according to Plutarch, a poison which produced a cough, spitting of blood, a fever heat, consumption, and debility of intellect, was administered. Quintillian, in his declamations, alludes to a poison which occasioned those symptoms in such a manner as proves that it must have been well known. The American Indians are known to be acquainted with a most perfect poison of this kind, and to be able to employ it with such skill that the person to whom it is given cannot guard against the treachery by any precautions, nor counteract the deadly consequence by any antidote. Death is the infallible result, though the sufferings of the victim may extend over a series of years. Theophrastus mentions a poison which could be regulated in such a manner as to cause death in two or three months, or at the end of a year, or even two years. He remarks, that the more lingering the death the more agonizing the torments of the sufferer. This poison, he informs us, was prepared from aconitum—a plant which, on account of its owning this deadly property, people were forbidden to have in their possession upon pain of capital punishment. He relates that Thrasyas had discovered a method of extracting from other plants a poison which, given in small doses of a drachm, produced an easy but certain death, entirely painless, and which could be impeded for a long time without occasioning either weakness or corruption. This Thrasyas, whose pupil, Alexis, carried the art still further, was a native of Martinea, a city in Arcadia, and is celebrated by Theophrastus on account of his accomplishments, particularly his knowledge of botany; but those are mistaken who attribute to him the discovery of secret slow poisoning.

This poison was much used at Rome about two hundred years before the Christian era. At that period several persons of distinction died the same year, and of the same distemper. An inquiry was set on foot, and a maid-servant gave evidence against some ladies of the first families, who, she said, prepared and distributed poison, and above one hundred and fifty of them were convicted and punished. As so many had acquired this destructive art, it could not be suppressed; and we find in Roman history abundant proofs that it was continually preserved and frequently employed. Sejanus caused such a poison to be administered by an eunuch to Drusus, who gradually declined as by a consumptive disorder, and at length expired. Agrippina, being anxious to get rid of Claudius, but afraid to despatch him suddenly, and yet not wishing to allow him sufficient time to make new regulations respecting the succession to the throne, made choice of a poison which should deprive him of his reason and gradually consume him. This she caused to be prepared by an expert poisoner named Locusta, who had been condemned to death for her infamous actions, but saved, that she might be employed as a state engine. The poison was given to Claudius in a dish of mushrooms, but owing to his irregular manner of living it did not produce the desired effect. It had to be assisted by some of a stronger nature. This Locusta prepared the poison with which Nero despatched Britannicus, the son of Agrippina, whom his father, Claudius, wished to succeed to the throne. As this poison produced only a dysentery, and was too slow in its operations, the emperor compelled Locusta, by blows and menacing her with death, to prepare in his presence one more potent. It was first tried on a kid; but, as the creature did not die till the end of five hours, Locusta boiled the poison a little longer. It was next tried on a pig, which it instantaneously killed, and by this poison Britannicus was despatched. At this service Nero was delighted; he pardoned Locusta, rewarded her liberally, and gave her pupils, whom she had to instruct, in order that an art so valuable to kings and emperors might not be lost.

The art of preparing poisons must have been well understood by the Carthaginians. When M. Atillius Regulus, the Roman general who had been captured by the Carthaginians, was sent to Rome to propose to the Senate the exchange of the Carthaginian prisoners for himself, he prevented this negotiation, because he knew that he had poison administered to him, by which the Roman state would soon be deprived of his services. He returned, therefore, to Carthage, in compliance with the promise he had made to his captors, who put him to death with the most excruciating tortures.

All these poisons were prepared from plants, particularly aconite, hemlock, and poppy, or else extracted from animal substances. With the far stronger and now common mineral poisons, there is no reason to believe that the ancients were acquainted; for their arsenic was what we term orpiment, and not that pernicious metallic oxide which formed the principal ingredient in those secret poisons which in latter times were in France and Italy brought to a state of diabolical perfection No one was more famous for this art than Tophania, a female fiend of whom we shall speak hereafter.

"In the present place," says the first toxicologist of the day, "may be considered the supposed effects of the celebrated aqua Toffana, or aquetta di Napoli, or aqua della Toffana, or only aquetta, a slow poison which, in the sixteenth century, was supposed to possess the property of causing death at any determinate period, after months, for example, or even years of ill health, according to the will of the poisoners." The most authentic description of aqua Toffana ascribes its properties to arsenic. According to a letter addressed to Hoffman, by Garelli, physician to Charles VI of Austria, that emperor told Garelli that, being governor of Naples at a time when the aqua Toffana was the dread of every noble family in the city, when the subject was investigated legally he had an opportunity of examining all the documents, and that he found the poison was a solution of arsenic in aqua cymbalariæ. The dose was said to be from four to six drops; it was colourless, transparent, and tasteless, like water. Its alleged effects are thus eloquently described by Behrend, a writer in "Uden and Pyl's Magazine:"—"A certain indescribable change is felt in the whole body, which leads the person to complain to his physician. The physician examines and reflects, but finds no symptoms either external or internal—no constipation, no vomiting, no inflammation, no fever. In short, he can advise only patience, strict regimen, and laxatives. The malady, however, creeps on; and the physician again is sent for; still he cannot detect anything of note. He infers that there is some stagnation or corruption of the humours, and again advises laxatives. Meanwhile, the poison takes firm hold of the system; languor, wearisomeness, and loathing of food continues; the nobler organs gradually become torpid, and the lungs, in particular, at length begin to suffer. In a word, the malady is from the first incurable; the unhappy victim pines away insensibly, even in the hands of the physician; and thus is he brought to a miserable end, through months or years, according to his enemy's desire." An equally vigorous, and somewhat clearer, account of the symptoms, is given by Hahnemann:—"There are," says he, "a gradual sinking of the powers of life, without any violent symptom; a nameless feeling of illness, failure of the strength, slight feverishness, want of sleep, lividity of the countenance, and an aversion to food and drink, and all the other enjoyments of life. Dropsy closes the scene, along with black miliary eruptions, and convulsions, or colliquative perspiration and purging."

Whatever were its real effects, there appears no doubt that it was long used secretly in Italy to a fearful extent, the monster who gave her name to it having confessed that she was instrumental in the death of no less than six hundred persons. "It has been already stated," continues Christison, "that she owed her success rather to the ignorance of the age, than to her own dexterity. At all events, the art of secret poisoning cannot now be easily practised. Indeed, even the vulgar dread of it is almost extinct. Partly on account of the improvement in general knowledge, and chiefly in consequence of the subtlety and precision which the refinements of modern physics and chemistry have introduced into medico-legal inquiries, it is rare that the suspicious scrutiny of the world now recognises, in the accounts of the last illness of popes and princes, the effects of poison, insidiously introduced into the body."

"I may add," continues the same authority, "that I was consulted a few years ago, on the part of the crown, in a case which considerably resembled the effects ascribed in former times to the aqua Toffana, except that it was more acute in its character and swifter in its progress." As this case will probably be found to represent pretty nearly the usual effects of moderate doses frequently repeated, it is thus given in some detail.

"A woman of indifferent character married a young man in circumstances which led to a breach between him and his relations; but the pair appeared to live on good terms with one another. Eighteen months after the marriage she was attacked with sickness and faintness; and on the fourth day of this illness, while she was recovering, the symptoms unexpectedly increased, and she seemed very unwell. On the fifth day she became extremely weak, and suffered much from yellow vomiting. On the seventh, when she was first visited by a medical man, she had frequent vomiting, burning in the stomach, a yellow tongue, flushed countenance,

hot skin, and hurried pulse. On the ninth the throat was sore and red, and the expression anxious; and next day the soreness was greater, affected the nose and mouth also, and was attended with excoriation of the lips and nostrils, swelling of the glands of the throat, dimness of sight, and great exhaustion. On the eleventh day, while previously again getting better, she became much worse, and suffered greatly from excessive vomiting, pain in the stomach, and an increase of the other symptoms. On the tenth she was very hoarse, and despaired of recovery. Next day she was occasionally incoherent, and had twitches of the facial muscles; the hands and face were swelled, the eyelids dingy, the conjuctival infected, and the nails blue. On the morning of the fifteenth there was, for two hours, violent delirium and fierce maniacal excitement, which were succeeded by coma, and this by death, in the course of the evening. There was no diarrhœa or urinary complaint, and no paralysis or eruption of the skin. A variety of circumstances of a general nature, which it would be out of place to enumerate here—the detection of arsenic in various articles of which the woman had partaken, and in which the arsenic had been dissolved, sometimes simply, sometimes with the aid of an alkali—together with the fact, that the body, five months after death, was found preserved from decay, as it is now well known to be in most cases of arsenical poisoning—left little doubt that the woman died of the effects of arsenic, taken in several small doses at distant intervals, although none could be detected in the stomach and intestines. The case did not go to trial, owing to the death of an essential witness."

This infamous woman, Tophania, or Toffana, who has given her name to this poison, resided first at Palermo in Sicily, and afterwards at Naples. She sold her drops, but sometimes her preparations were distributed by way of charity to such wives as wished to have other husbands. From four to six drops were enough to destroy a man, and it has been asserted that the dose could be so proportioned as to operate in a certain time. As she was watched by the government, she fled to an ecclesiastical asylum; and when Keysler was at Naples in 1730, she was then still living, because no one could or was willing to take away her life, while under that protection. At that time she was visited by many strangers, out of curiosity.

In Labat's travels through Italy, we also find some information which may serve still further to illustrate the history of Tophania. She distributed her poison in small glass phials, with this inscription, "Manna of St. Nicholas of Bari," and ornamented with the image of the saint. A miraculous oil, employed by folly in the cure of many diseases, drops from the tomb of that saint, which is shown at Bari, in the kingdom of Naples, and on this account it is dispersed in great abundance under the like name. It was therefore the best appellation which Tophania could give to her poison, because its reputed sanctity prevented the custom-house officers from subjecting it to too close an examination. When the viceroy was informed of this, which I think was in 1709, Tophania fled from one convent to another, but was at length seized and thrown into prison. The clergy raised a loud outcry on account of this violation of ecclesiastical freedom, and endeavoured to excite the people to insurrection. But they were soon appeased, a report being spread that Tophania had confessed she had poisoned all the springs in the city and neighbourhood. Being put to the rack, she acknowledged her wickedness, and confessed to having caused the death of not less than six hundred human beings! She named those who protected her, who were immediately dragged from churches and monasteries; and declared that the day before she had absconded, she had sent two boxes of her manna to Rome, where it was found in the custom-house, but she did not accuse any person of having ordered it. She was afterwards strangled, and to appease the archbishop, her body was thrown at night into the area of the convent, from which she had been taken. Tophania, however, was not the only person at Naples who understood the making of this poison, for Keysler says, "that at the time he was there it was still secretly prepared and much employed."

In the year 1659, under the government of Pope Alexander VII, it was observed at Rome that many young married women were left widows, and that many husbands died when they became disagreeable to their wives. Several of the clergy affirmed also that for some time past various persons had declared that they had been guilty of poisoning. As the government employed the utmost vigilance to discover those poisoners, suspicion fell upon a society of young married women, whose president appeared to be an old woman who pretended to foretell future events, and who had often predicted very exactly many deaths to persons who had cause to wish for them. To ascertain the truth, a crafty female, given out to be a person of considerable distinction, was sent to this old woman, pretending that she wished to obtain her confidence, and to procure some of her drops for a cruel, tyrannical husband. By this stratagem the whole society were arrested; and all of them, except the fortune-teller, whose name was Hieronyma Spara, confessed before they were put to the torture. "Where now," cried Hieronyma, "are the Roman princes, knights, and barons who on so many occasions promised me their protection? Where are the ladies who assured me of their friendship? Where are my children, whom I have placed in so distinguised situations?" In order to deter others from the like crime, one Gratiosa, Spara's assistant, three other women, and the obstinate Spara herself, who still entertained hopes of assistance till the last moment, were hanged in the presence of an immense number of spectators. Some months after several more women were executed in the same manner; some were whipped naked through the streets of Rome, and others were banished from the country. Notwithstanding the severity of these punishments, this wickedness from time to time re-appeared. Le Bret, to whom we are indebted for the above account, says that Hieronyma Spara was a Sicilian, and acquired her knowledge from Tophania, at Palermo. If this be true, the latter must have been initiated into her villany at a very early age, and must, when very young, have become a teacher in this infamous art. Keysler calls her a little old woman.

In reference to the aqua Tophana, the Abbe Gagliani, well known as a writer, has given the following extraordinary account:—"It is certain that in Europe the preparation of those drugs renders them pernicious and mortal. For example, at Naples, the mixture of opium and cantharides, in known doses, is a slow poison, the surest of all, and the more infallible as one cannot mistrust it. At first it is given in small doses, that its effects may be incurable. In Italy we call it Aqua di Tufania—Tufania water. No one can avoid its attacks, because the liquor obtained from that composition is as limpid as rock water and without taste. Its effects are slow, and almost imperceptible. A few drops of it only are poured into tea, chocolate, or soup, &c. *There is not a lady* at Naples who has not some of it lying carelessly on her toilette with her smelling bottles. She alone knows the phial, and can distinguish it. Even the waiting-woman, who is her confidant, is not in the secret, and takes the phial for distilled water, or water obtained by precipitation, which is the purest, and which is used to moderate perfumes when they are too strong." Only think of those ladies! Verily the charms which, knowing how their toilettes were furnished, could induce one to enter boudoirs must have been powerful indeed.

After the death of Tophania, the mania for poisoning seems to have abated in Italy. Of the French people it took hold at a somewhat earlier period. So rooted had it become in France, between the years 1670 and 1680, that Madame de Sevigne, in one of her letters, expresses her fear that Frenchman and poisoner would become synonymous terms. But this part of the subject we must postpone till a future number. Our introduction has already extended beyond our original intention.

CHAPTER II.

THE BORGIAS—ALEXANDER VI.

RODERIC LEUZIOLI BORGIA—who assumed the name of Alexander VI upon his elevation to the throne of St. Peter—was born at Valentia, in Spain, in 1430, or, according to some authors, in 1431. On the mother's side, he was of a family originally of royal extraction, and who, before the tiara was the object of his ambition, had preferred a claim to the crown of Arragon and Valentia. In his youth he received an admirable education; and, when he attained the years of manhood, he was not slow to acquire for himself a very distinguished reputation as a soldier, an orator, and a man of science. He became, early in life, attached to a widow who had two children. She died, and he became the guardian of the orphans. The one he placed in a convent, and the other, the most distinguished beauty of the day, he made his mistress. This was the celebrated Rosa Vanozza, the mother of his five children—two of whom have passed to a comparative oblivion, but the others, Francesco, Lucretia, and Cæsar, have obtained, and no doubt will continue to occupy, an unenviable and imperishable niche in history. Roderic was deeply attached to his mistress. For a number of years he remained in the bosom of his family, absorbed in domestic enjoyments, a stranger alike to the schemes and the thoughts of ambition, little dreaming of the noise which he was to make in the world, or of the dark and terrible destiny which awaited him. Had it not been for an event which occurred in another land, the probability is that Roderic Borgia would have finished his earthly career in obscurity, and dropped into the grave without having left behind that foul and lurid track, upon which the student of humanity gazes with feelings of profound astonishment and unutterable detestation.

This event was the election of the uncle of Roderic Borgia, under the name of Calixtus III, to the papal throne. As soon as Roderic heard of this event, he is said to have been both grieved and afraid, lest the advancement of his relation should have the effect of drawing him from that private life to which he was deeply attached, and in which he had enjoyed so much felicity. However, as he greatly respected his uncle, by whom he was in return tenderly beloved, he felt himself in duty bound to write to the Pope congratulating him on his exalted position. Calixtus was forcibly impressed with the modesty and disinterestedness manifested in his nephew's letter, and could not help contrasting those qualities with the unbecoming eagerness and rapacity of the rest of his relations, who were incessantly pestering him for those dignities and emoluments placed at the disposal of the successor of St. Peter. Whatever might be the intent of Roderic, the effect of his letter was to make Calixtus resolve to advance him beyond any of his kinsmen. Accordingly, a letter from the Pope reached him, requesting him to repair immediately to Rome, to embrace his uncle, who was most favourably inclined towards him. Roderic hesitated whether or not to comply with this invitation; but he had no time to resolve, when a messenger arrived with express injunctions to bring him as soon as possible to the presence of his affectionate uncle. Roderic was forced to obey, and departed for Rome with the messenger, after having previously arranged that Rosa Vanozza and her children should follow him, under the protection of his friend, Don Melchioro, who afterwards passed for the husband of Vanozza, and the father of her children; and thus, by concealing her connexion with Roderic Borgia, facilitated the accomplishment of those projects of ambition in which the latter had so ardently embarked.

Roderic was most warmly welcomed by his uncle, who employed all the arguments he could think of to induce his nephew to overcome his reluctance to a public career. In this Calixtus met considerable difficulty, nor was it until he opened up to Roderic's vision the prospect of one day being pope himself, that he obtained his full consent to submit himself to his guidance. Roderic Borgia no sooner conceived the idea of one day wearing the tiara, and wielding the sceptre of

Christendom, than he became completely changed; or rather, those evil passions which till then were torpid in his soul, and of whose existence he himself was probably unconscious, sprang up at once, all armed and in full maturity, to do battle against all that was pure, and noble, and human in his nature. The demon of ambition entered into his soul, and with it that of hypocrisy.

He was formally created Archbishop of Valentia, and soon after he was made a cardinal. And now he assumed the mask, and set himself to work for the prize on which he had set his heart. Now commenced that career of dissimulation in which he may be almost said to have been unrivalled,—in which certainly he has never been surpassed. His humility and piety soon became the common talk of Rome. His reputation for sanctity outstripped that of all his competitors. The words of Scripture were constantly on his lips. The good of the Church and the welfare of the poor were the themes of his most frequent prayers and conversation. The world was deceived, the people were charmed. Cardinal Roderic, in wisdom, was compared to Solomon; in patience, to Job; in meekness and divine zeal, to Moses. One person alone could estimate the value of the pious cardinal's conversion. This person was Rosa Vanozza. She, with his children, lived in his house, in the street Della Lungarda, near the church Regina Cœli, upon the banks of the Tiber. "It was there in after years that, after a day spent in prayer and works of piety, Roderic came every evening to lay his mask of hypocrisy aside. Then it was said (although of this no one can adduce proofs) commenced the most infamous practices. It was rumoured that incestuous intercourse was carried on between the parents and their children, and between Lucretia and her brothers; and those stories were so general, that to silence them, or else to divert their current, Roderic sent Cæsar to the University of Pisa, and married Lucretia to a young noble of Arragon."

The good fortune of Roderic Borgia made him, of course, many and dangerous enemies; and upon the death of his uncle it might have fared hard with him, if his reputation for sanctity and benevolence had not been widely and deeply established. During the entire pontificate of Pius II, he remained in seclusion; nor did he reappear until Sextus IV gave him the Abbey of Liubaco, and appointed him legate to the courts of Arragon and Portugal. His return to Rome was under the pontificate of Innocent VIII. It was on the death of this pontiff that Roderic was elected to the papal throne. Of the mode of his election, and of the emotions of his family while the sacred conclave were engaged in selecting a successor to Innocent, we have the following very vivid and dramatic description :—

On the 9th of August, 1492, it seemed as if the entire population of Rome, from the Gate of the People to the Colosseum, and from the Baths of Diocletian to the Castle of St. Angelo, had assembled by appointment in the Place of St. Peter. For so dense was the multitude, that its pressure filled the streets adjacent; and, radiating from one common centre like the rays of a star, the vast mass was seen ascending the basilica, grouping themselves among the blocks of stones, clinging around the columns, winding along the broken outline of the wall, disappearing at intervals within the different houses, and reappearing at the windows in such a manner that each casement seemed walled up with heads. The eyes of all, from every quarter, were intently fixed upon one quarter of the Vatican, for the conclave was there assembled; and as Innocent VIII had been sixteen days dead, the cardinals were proceeding to the election of a new pope. Rome is truly the city of elections. From the foundation to the present day—that is, during the course of about twenty-six centuries—she has constantly elected her kings, consuls, tribunes, emperors, and popes, hence, during the sitting of the conclave, Rome seemed excited by a strange fever, urging all ranks towards the Vatican, or Monte Cavallo, according as the scarlet assembly was held in the one palace or the other. The election of a new pope is of unusual interest to Christendom: as from the days of St. Peter to those of Pius IX, the reign of every pope may be averaged at eight years, so, according to the character of the elected is this period

one of tranquillity or disorder, justice or venality, peace or war. And never, possibly, from the hour when the first successor of St. Peter ascended the throne of the pontiffs, had so much inquietude been exhibited as that which was now observable among the people. Nor was it without cause, for Innocent VIII, who had obtained the honourable title of the father of his people, arising very probably from the fact of his having increased the number of his subjects by eight sons and as many daughters, had died as has been stated, after a licentious life, exhausted by a lingering disorder, during the progress of which, if we may rely upon the statement of Stefano Juffessura, no less than two hundred and twenty murders had been committed in the streets of Rome. . . . . The eyes of the spectators were, therefore, as has been said, fixed upon the Vatican, and particularly upon a chimney from whence the first signal should issue; when suddenly at the hour when the Ave Maria ushers in the close of day, cries mixed with shouts of laughter arose from the crowd, a discordant murmur of raillery and menace; for at that moment a small column of smoke was discerned, ascending like a fleecy vapour to the sky. And this announced that Rome was yet without a ruler, the world still deprived of a pontiff; for this smoke was the sign that the ballot lists were burnt, and that the cardinals had not yet decided the election. No sooner was it seen, than the countless crowd, well aware that until the assembly of the cardinals in the morning there was nothing further to expect, retired in hurried throngs and a jesting humour, as if after the last discharge of fireworks; so that in the place where but a few minutes before a nation seemed collected, a few groups only were now idly scattered. Even those imperceptibly diminished, for at half-past nine the streets of Rome were insecure, and as the hour struck, the hurried step of some casual passer-by was alone occasionally heard, doors were successively closed, the lights in the windows gradually disappeared; until, as ten was repeated from the chimes around, except from one window of the Vatican, from whence the lamp still threw its fitful light around, houses, squares, and streets, were alike wrapped in darkness.

At this moment a man enveloped in a mantle, and whose dimly shadowed form arose against one of the unfinished columns of the basilica, glided slowly and cautiously among the blocks of stones scattered around its foundations, and advanced to the fountain which there formed the centre of the square, on the spot where the obelisk now stands, on reaching which he stopped, and, concealed by the obscurity of the night and the deeper shadows of the monument, he glanced furtively around, as if to be sure he was unobserved; then, drawing his sword, he struck three times upon the pavement, producing at each blow slight sparks from its point. This signal—for it was one—was not lost : the lamp in the Vatican was extinguished, and at the same moment a packet was thrown out, which fell at a few paces from him, and, guided by its ringing sound as it reached the pavement, he instantly seized it, in spite of the darkness, and hurried away. He had proceeded thus about halfway down the Borgo Vecchio, when he turned to the right, and entered a street, at the other extremity of which was a figure of a Madonna with its lamp. Approaching this, he took from his pocket the enclosure which he had picked up, which, in fact, was merely a Roman crown, only that it was hollow and divided, and contained in the interior a letter, which, notwithstanding the risk of being recognised, the stranger instantly read, so great was his anxiety to be acquainted with its contents. It was at the risk of being recognised : because in his eagerness this nocturnal correspondent had thrown back the hood of his mantle so as entirely to expose his features to the light of the lamp, by which it was easy to discern a handsome youth, apparently of about twenty-five or twenty-six years of age, dressed in a violet-coloured doublet, open at the shoulders and slashed at the elbows, with a cap of the same colour, the long black plume of which waved darkly around him. He stopped, however, but a short time, for hardly had he read the billet he had so mysteriously received, than he replaced it in his silver pocket-book; and, readjusting his mantle so as entirely to conceal his figure, he walked on with a rapid step, traversed Borgo

San-Spirito, and followed the Street Della Lingara, to where it opens upon the church of Regina Cœli. On reaching this, he knocked thrice quickly at the door of a large house, which was instantly opened ; then rapidly ascending a staircase, he entered a room where two ladies awaited his arrival with the utmost impatience.

On his entrance, they both exclaimed together, " Well, well, Francesco, what news ?"

" Excellent, mother !—excellent, sister !" replied the youth, embracing the one, and extending his hand to the other. " My father has gained three votes to-day, but he requires yet six to obtain the majority."

" And cannot those be purchased ?" asked the elder of the two females, while the other, in default of speech, interrogated him by a look.

" Yes, yes, mother," replied the youth, " that is precisely the point which my father has well considered. He gives to the Cardinal Orsini his palace at Rome, with his two villas of Monticello and Soriano ; to Cardinal Colonna, the abbey of Lubiaco : to Cardinal St. Angelo, the bishopric of Porto, with his furniture and wines ; to the Cardinal of Parma, the town of Nepi ; the Cardinal of Genoa, the church of Santa Maria-in-via-lata ; and to Cardinal Savelli, the church of Santa Maria Maggiore, and the town of Civita Castellana ; and as for Cardinal Ascanio Sforza, he is already aware that we sent him two days ago four mules heavily laden with money, and gold and silver plate ; and with this supply he has promised to give five thousand ducats to the Cardinal Patriarch of Venice."

" But what measures shall we adopt to intimate the intentions of Roderic to the others ?"

" My father has provided for this also, and points out to us an easy way. You know, mother, with what ceremony their dinner is now carried to the cardinals ?"

" Yes, in a basket, with the coat of arms of the individual for whom the meal is destined."

" My father has bribed the bishop who inspects this ; and to-morrow, being flesh day, chickens will be sent to the Cardinals Orsini, Colonna, Savelli, of St. Angelo, of Parma, and of Genoa, each of which will contain a formal donation, made by me in my father's name, of houses, palaces, and churches."

" Excellent !" exclaimed Vanozza ; " everything, I am now convinced, will proceed according to our wish."

" And by the grace of God," replied Lucretia, with a derisive smile, " our father will be elected Pope."

" A fortunate event for us," said Francesco.

" Oh ! and for Christianity," answered his sister, with an expression still more sarcastic.

" Lucretia ! Lucretia !" said the mother, " you are unworthy of the happiness we expect."

" What matters it if, nevertheless, it comes : moreover, you remember the proverb—' The Lord blesses the increase of families'—a blessing especially due to our own, considering that our domestic life has borne such a close resemblance to the patriarchal." As she uttered this, she cast upon her brother a glance of such meaning that even he was abashed ; but, as the pleasures of his incestuous love were for the moment of less interest, he summoned four servants, and whilst they armed themselves to accompany him, he drew up and signed the six donations which were on the morrow to be sent to the cardinals ; and not wishing to be seen at their abodes, he thought of profiting by the night, and thus delivering the papers unobserved to those who had agreed to convey them at the dinner-hour, as described. This done, and the servants ready, Francesco departed, leaving his mother and sister to indulge their golden reveries of coming greatness. The palaces, the abbeys, churches, villas, thus conveyed, determined the election of Roderic Borgia. The five cardinals who had not participated in this act of simony protested against its ratification , but, no matter by what means, Roderic had the majority, and was now the two hundred and sixteenth successor of St. Peter. " Although he had thus gained his end, Alexander VI did not yet venture to throw aside the mask so long worn by the Cardinal Borgia ; nevertheless, upon the announcement of his election, he could not conceal his joy. With hands upraised to heaven, and with the accents of satisfied ambition, he cried, ' Am I then Pope ? Am I indeed the vicar of Christ—the keystone of the arch of the Christian world ?'"

" Yes, holy father," replied the Cardinal Ascanio Sforza, the man who had sold the nine votes at his disposal in the conclave. " Yes ; and we shall trust by this election to have given glory to God, peace to the Church, and joyful satisfaction to Christendom, inasmuch as you have been chosen by the Eternal Spirit as the most worthy of your brethren."

This short reply enabled the Pope to recover the complete mastery of his emotions, which for a moment he had lost ; and having made a most meek and pious answer, he caused himself to be clothed in the pontifical robes, and the slips of paper on which his name was written in Latin to be thrown out of the window, and these, scattered by the wind, seemed to bear to the world the great event, so soon to change the political destiny of Italy.

When Cæsar Borgia received the news of his father's elevation he was at the University of Pisa : he was then a youth of two or three-and-twenty, adroit in all manly, and particularly martial, exercises, riding unsaddled horses of the highest spirit, and able to sever a bull's head from his body by a single stroke of his sword. His disposition was haughty, jealous, and dissembling ; and, according to one historian, he was great among the impious, as his brother Francesco was good among the great. As to his personal appearance, even contemporaneous authors have transmitted us the most contradictory descriptions. According to some, he was an abortion of ugliness ; while others, on the contrary, are highly laudatory of his beauty. This contradiction is easily explained. It arose from the circumstance, that at certain periods of the year, particularly in spring, his face was covered with blotches, which made him, for the time, an object of horror and disgust ; whereas, during the rest of the year, he appeared the thoughtful cavalier, with the black flowing hair, the pale complexion, and auburn beard, painted of him by Raphael. Historians, chroniclers, and painters are all agreed as to the intense expression of his eyes, describing them as emitting an incessant lustre, and investing him with the character of something unearthly or infernal. Such was the man who took for his motto, " Aut Cæsar, aut nihil :" Cæsar, or nothing.

When the news reached Cæsar that his father had been elected Pope, he started for Rome immediately ; and such was his eagerness to present himself, that, without even calling upon his mother, he proceeded direct to the Vatican. By the courtiers and attendants he was viewed with the utmost respect. He was conducted to the presence of the pontiff, who, however, contrary to Cæsar's expectations, received him with freezing politeness. Cæsar fell upon his knees and made a speech, congratulating his father on his elevation to the throne of Christendom, an eminence to which his virtues entitled him, and the duties of which he was so well qualified to discharge. Alexander thanked Cæsar in a cold and studied oration, in which he admonished him to reform his conduct, and not to expect any preferment from him on account of the relationship subsisting between them. Merit, and merit alone, would influence his holiness in bestowing the good things belonging to the patrimony of St. Peter, and the future behaviour of Cæsar himself would determine whether or not any share of his favour should be extended to him. Having said this, and a great deal more to the same effect, his holiness and his train retired, leaving Cæsar in a state of stupified indignation ; so very different proved his reception from what he had anticipated. He rushed from the Vatican to his mother, Vanozza, in whose ear he poured the story of his supposed wrong. She told him to comfort himself, not to mind what the Pope said in the presence of his court, for that she knew that he entertained very different intentions as to the disposal of the wealth and dignities of the Church. Cæsar was easily reassured. He began to see the matter in a more consoling light ; and the event proved that his father had not turned quite so impartial and austere as he had dreaded. For a long time, however, Cæsar was doomed to great mortification, in consequence of the determination of Alexander to confer the most valuable of the secular dignities in his gift upon Francesco, who was made a noble and a duke; while Cæsar, sore against his will, was compelled to don the ecclesiastical garb, to which he could not be reconciled by the archbishopric and cardinalship to which his father had appointed him. This partiality of Alexander for Francesco, if it did not absolutely originate, greatly assisted to increase the hatred which Cæsar felt for his brother,—a hatred which, as the sequel will show, contributed to the untimely end of Francesco, and to one of the foulest fratricides at which humanity ever shuddered.

No sooner did Alexander find himself firmly established on his throne, than he began to work out those designs of empire and family aggrandizement which he had so long cherished in his inmost heart. He commenced to play the temporal potentates of the day the one against the other. In this he was upon the whole successful, partly through his good fortune, but chiefly through the skill with which he availed himself of the jealousies and animosities with which the various Italian and European states regarded each other. But gold was the main instrument with which Alexander designed to extend and consolidate the greatness and permanency of the House of Borgia. Gold, then, must be obtained, and obtained too at any cost and by whatever means. To obtain gold, POISON was unscrupulously and unsparingly resorted to.

Amongst the first and most atrocious of the murders by poison committed by Alexander and his family, was that of Dijem, or Zizime, a noble and beautiful youth, the son of Mahomet II, the conqueror of Constantinople. Dijem, because he was born "in the purple," that is, since his father's accession to the empire of the East, attempted to set aside the claims of his elder brother, Bajazet, who was born before Mahomet ascended the throne. The brothers fought, Bajazet was triumphant, and Dijem was compelled to become a fugitive successively at the courts of several of the monarchs of Western Europe. Bajazet offered a large reward to any who would give him his brother, dead or alive; or, failing in that, a sum of 60,000 ducats per annum to any monarch who would detain Dijem in safe custody. One of the predecessors of Alexander, coveting the yearly stipend allowed for the detention of the royal Moslem, contrived to get him to Rome. Here Dijem was when Charles VIII of France and his army entered the Eternal City. Before the French king left Rome, it was arranged between himself and the Pope that Dijem should accompany Charles, and be entertained at Paris. But Dijem was not allowed to leave Italy. He was poisoned at a farewell banquet which the Pope had given him, and two days after the unfortunate son of Mahomet died, and was buried at Castel Nuovo, greatly to the regret of Charles and all who knew Dijem, by whom he was universally beloved. At his earliest convenience, Pope Alexander had the corpse of Dijem dug up and sent to Constantinople, for which service Bajazet remitted to his holiness the sum of 300,000 ducats.

A patent method of Alexander for filling his coffers with gold, was to make archbishops and cardinals. These preferments he sold, and then he poisoned the simoniacal purchasers. So that the pontiff had his dignities almost immediately to offer to fresh competitors. One of these was the Cardinal Cosenza, one of the secretaries of the Pope. Alexander, wishing to get rid of the cardinal, accused him falsely of having issued a forged papal rescript. The cardinal was confined in one of the deepest dungeons of the Castle of St. Angelo, where he found for furniture a crucifix of wood, a table, a chair, and a bed; for recreation, a lamp, a Bible, and a Breviary; and for nourishment, two pounds of bread and a small cask of water, which were to be renewed every three days. At the expiration of a year, the cardinal died of despair, after having gnawed his own arms in his agony. Cæsar received from the Pope the whole of the estate of the ill-fated man.

The successor of the Cardinal of Cosenza was soon after poisoned by Cæsar, who entertained him in his camp for three days. The cardinal returned to Rome. On the road, at Urbino, he was seized with indisposition. Three days afterwards he expired.

Some time previous to these murders Cæsar had succeeded in divesting himself of his ecclesiastical character; but this he had not accomplished until he had first disposed of his brother Francesco. The conception and execution of the foul deed is thus described:—Cæsar had in his service a bravo, of the name of Michelotto, who was capable of commiting any enormity in obedience to his master, to whom he was completely devoted. One evening Cæsar sent for his bravo, who found his employer "leaning against a large projecting chimney-piece, clothed no longer in the cardinal's robe and hat, but in a doublet of black velvet, the sashes of which displayed a satin vest of the same colour. One of his hands played mechanically with his gloves, whilst the other rested upon a poisoned dagger, never absent from his side. This was the costume usually worn by him upon his nocturnal adventures; it excited no surprise in Michelotto; he remarked only that Cæsar's eyes flashed more luridly than usual, and that his cheeks, generally pale, were then absolutely livid."

"Michelotto," he said, with a voice of which a slight accent of raillery betrayed the only sign of emotion, "what think you,—does this dress become me?" Habituated as the bravo was to the circumlocution with which his master most frequently prefaced his designs, this question was so unexpected that for a moment he was silent, then answered, "Admirably! and, thanks to it, your excellency has now the appearance as well as the heart of a soldier."—"I am well pleased that this is your opinion," replied Cæsar. "And now can you tell me why, instead of this dress, which I can only wear at night, I am forced to disguise myself by day beneath the robe and hat of a cardinal, and to expend my life in riding from church to church, instead of leading to the field of battle some noble army, in which you should hold the rank of a captain, in lieu of being as you are the poor chief of a band of miserable sbirri?" —"Yes, my lord," replied Michelotto, who had guessed from his first words the intentions of Cæsar. "Yes; he who is the cause of this is Francesco, Duke of Gandia, and Benevento, your elder brother."—"Know you," resumed Cæsar, giving the answer no further sign of approbation than a slight movement of his head, whilst a ghastly smile lingered upon his features,—"know you who has the wealth and not the genius? who has the casque and not the head? who has the sword and not the hand?"—"Again the Duke of Gandia," said Michelotto. "Know you, moreover, the man who is ever in the way of my ambition my power, and my love?"— "Still the Duke of Gandia."—"And what think you of it?" demanded Cæsar. "I think that he must die," coolly replied the bravo. "And your opinion is mine, Michelotto," said Cæsar, advancing towards him, and grasping his hand. "And my sole regret is that I had not thought so before; for had I last year borne but a sword instead of a crozier, I should now be the possessor of some rich domain. The Pope wishes to advance the greatness of his house. It is well: but he mistakes the means. It is I he should create the duke— it is my brother he should nominate the cardinal. Had he done this, one thing is most certain: I should have united to the authority of his power the intrepidity of a heart resolute to make that power more effective. He whose ambition would rule a state or a kingdom, must trample under foot the obstacles in his path; he must strike with the sword or the poignard, nor fear to steep his hands in his own blood. He should follow the example left by all the founders of empires from Romulus to Bajazet, who became kings by fratricide! And well have you said, Michelotto, what their position was is mine; and I am resolved never to recoil before it. You now know for what purpose you have been summoned. Was I right? Can I depend on you?" Michelotto, who saw his own advantage in the crime, was indifferent to the rest; he announced, therefore, that he was entirely at Cæsar's disposal.

On the following morning, Cæsar learnt that he would have to leave Rome for Naples on the 15th of June, and received at the same time from his mother an invitation to sup with her on the 14th. Michelotto was directed to be in readiness that night, at eleven.

The table was arranged in the open air, and in an extensive vineyard that Vanozza possessed near St. Pietro and Vincula. The guests were Cæsar Borgia; Francesco

LUCRETIA—DAUGHTER OF POPE ALEXANDER VI.

his brother, who had been created Duke of Gandia; the Prince de Squallici, Donna Sancia, his wife; the Cardinal of Monte Reall, Francisco Borgia, the son of Pope Calixtus III, Don Roderic Borgia, Don Godfredo, brother of Cardinal Giovanni Borgia; and Don Alphonso Borgia, nephew of the Pope; in fact, all the family, Lucretia excepted, who, residing still at the convent, had refused to be present. It was a splendid repast; Cæsar seemed as gay as was his wont; the Duke of Gandia more animated than usual. They were yet at table, when a man masked brought to the young duke a letter which he instantly opened, whilst his cheeks flushed with joy, and after reading it, merely said, "I will go." He then thrust it hurriedly into his pocket, but not so quickly as to elude the rapid glance of Cæsar, who thought he recognised in the address the handwriting of Lucretia.

The messenger departed without attracting the attention of any one but Cæsar, for it was then the custom for messages of assignations to be brought either by men whose features were concealed by a mask, or by females veiled. At ten o'clock the guests arose from the table; yet as the air still breathed the calm luxury of an Italian climate, they walked for some time between the beautiful pines which shaded Vanozza's palace, but without Cæsar's losing sight for one minute of his brother. At eleven the Duke of Gandia went away; Cæsar did the same, alleging as a reason that he was desirous of proceeding that evening to the Vatican to take leave of the Pope, a duty he could not discharge on the morrow, his departure for Naples being fixed at the break of day. The brothers therefore departed toge-

ther, mounted their horses, and proceeded side by side until they reached the palace Borgia, where the Cardinal Ascanio Sforza then resided, having received it as a gift from the Pope on the day of his election. The Duke of Gandia here separated from his brother, saying with a smile, "that it was not yet his intention to return home, as he must first keep an engagement he had made." Cæsar replied, "that he was in all respects the master of his own actions," and bade him good night. The Duke of Gandia turned to the right, Cæsar to the left, remarking only, that the street down which the duke proceeded led towards the monastery in which Lucretia resided; then with this slight confirmation of his suspicion, he turned his horse towards the Vatican, where having found the Pope, he took leave, and received his benediction. From that hour all is obscure as the darkness which shrouded the terrible event now to be related.

On quitting Cæsar, the Duke of Gandia appears to have dismissed his attendants and proceeded with a valet towards the Place Della Gindecca. He there found the man who had spoken to him during the banquet, and forbidding his servant to follow him any further, he desired him to await his return in the street in which they were, adding that in about two hours he would rejoin him. At the time mentioned the duke returned, dismissed his masked conductor, and was proceeding towards his palace; but scarcely had he passed the corner Del Ghetto, when he was attacked by four men on foot, directed by a man on horseback. Supposing either that he was assailed by robbers or else the victim of some mistake, the Duke of Gandia called out his name;

but instead of this arresting the daggers of the murderers, it served but to redouble their blows, and he soon fell dead by the body of his dying servant. The horseman who, passive and motionless, had hitherto witnessed the scene, now reined up his horse backwards towards the body, which was placed by the four assassins behind him, and walking by his side to conceal it and keep its position, they were soon lost in the narrow street which leads to the church Santa Maria di Montecelli. As for the servant, believing him to be dead, they left him stretched upon the pavement. But slightly recovering, his groans were heard by the inmates of a poor dwelling-house, who raised him and placed him upon a bed, when he instantly expired, without being able to give the slightest indication of the assassins or of their victim. They awaited the duke's return that night and following morning in the palace; expectation became fear, and fear soon became alarm. They sought the Pope, and acquainted him that since his departure from his mother's house the duke had not been seen. But Alexander endeavoured to dissipate their anxiety and his own, hoping that his son, overtaken by daylight in some intrigue, awaited the closing in of night to return home. But the night passed as the day: he came not; so that the following morning the Pope—a prey to the saddest forebodings—abandoned himself to grief, unable to give utterance to more than these words, a thousand times repeated, "Search for him! search for him! Ascertain how my poor son died!" A few days afterwards, the Tiber having been dragged, the body of Francesco Borgia was found stabbed in nine places; his clothes remained untouched, his purse was full of gold. It was evident that his assassins were not actuated by motives of plunder.

Alexander was for a time inconsolable for the loss of his son. He tore his hair, raved, and blasphemed in the most frightful manner. He confessed his sins, declared that the judgments of God were upon him, for his own and his family's crimes. He shut himself up in his study, refused to see anybody, and expressed his resolution to starve himself to death. For sixty hours he is said to have abstained from any food. At last the door of his room was forced open, and his daughter, Lucretia, after much entreaty, succeeded in reconciling the grief-stricken pontiff to this world. He became gradually calmed, and instituted measures for the discovery of the murderers of his son. From this undertaking, however, he very soon desisted, from, it is said, Vanozza warning him that unless he forbore from further inquiry, the fate of Francesco would soon be his own. The horrible truth now seems to have dawned upon the Pope. From that moment all that was good in his nature appears to have been utterly destroyed. The devil of ambition was now his absolute master, and thenceforward he went hand in hand with his miscreant son in working those fiendish projects which, by the most signal and righteous retribution of heaven, recoiled upon his own head—visiting him with that horrible doom which in the unfathomable depravity of his soul he had prepared for others. But, before relating the terrible death of Pope Alexander, we must first revert to some of the doings of Cæsar and Lucretia.

CHAPTER III.

LUCRETIA AND CÆSAR BORGIA—DEATH OF ALEXANDER THE SIXTH AND HIS SON CÆSAR.

LUCRETIA BORGIA was a most dutiful daughter. To accomplish the ambitious designs of her scheming father she lent herself with the utmost readiness. She was of the true Borgia blood; she lived only for power and pleasure—and power was chiefly coveted because it extended the range and multiplied the means of sensuous enjoyment. Pleasure was with her the supreme good; the gratification of the passions the chief end of existence. In her code of morality, poverty or weakness were the only crimes; in her vocabulary, pain and evil, suffering and sin, were synonymous and convertible terms. Life was with her a game of skill, in which the wise were ever the vanquishers, the fools ever the losers. Men and

women, in the mass, she regarded as the puppets and slaves with which the knowing and the powerful effected their purposes of enjoyment and ambition. Morality was but another name for agreeable sensations; vice and wickedness, terms with which the powerful and successful branded the impotent efforts of the wretched and unfortunate. And as for religion, what was it but a hook baited with a future life, in order that fools might abandon to knaves all the good things of the present? As the child of a cardinal and a pope, she, of course, professed Christianity, and this profession was exceedingly convenient, for then, as now, it served as a mask, behind which all unlawful passions might be gratified, and all unpopular projects concealed until they were fully matured, and the moment for their execution had arrived. Lucretia Borgia had a magnificent organization; her beauty was superb; her complexion was fair and transparent, as a daughter of the snowy North; her soul was fiery and passionate, as became a child of the sunny South. Her manners were polished and fascinating in the highest degree; but her conduct was licentious in the extreme, and her imagination teeming with prurient and impure ideas. She was irreligious from natural impulse, and her education was such as to foster and develop to its utmost this instinctive impiety of her character. She panted after pleasure, flattery, rank, titles, gold, jewels, splendid and costly dresses. "A Spaniard under her light hair—a courtezan under her open, guileless manner,—she had the features of one of Raphael's Madonnas, and the heart of Messalina. She was doubly dear to her father, who saw reflected in her all his passions and his vices."

To put a stop to the horrible stories which circulated respecting Lucretia and her brothers, a young Arragonese noble was procured her for a husband This, however, was the husband of necessity, not of choice. Lucretia was not greatly enamoured of him; and Alexander, after his accession to the pontificate, discovered that a more advantageous match could be found for Lucretia. Her husband was not by birth, fortune, or genius, capable of mingling with any degree of influence in the political intrigues of Alexander VI. A divorce, therefore, was determined on. Nothing, of course, could be more facile of accomplishment than this; for was not her father the vicegerent of the Almighty, and was he not entrusted with the power to bind and unloose? And should not this power be exerted for the relief of his own child? Certainly it should, and Lucretia was divorced.

Her next husband was Giovanni Sforza, brother of the Duke of Milan, and Lord of Pisaro, which, because it was situated near the sea, between Florence and Venice, was admirably adapted for those purposes of territorial aggrandizement which his holiness had so closely at heart. But the tide of politics is ever fluctuating; power was then being constantly transferred from one state to another; so the value (to the Borgias) of the husband of Lucretia was ever changing. Giovanni Sforza had lost importance, and for that reason he must also be deprived of his spouse. Lucretia was a second time separated from her husband, and at liberty to contract for the third time a matrimonial alliance, by which the power and glory of the house of Borgia might be still further augmented.

Her third husband was Don Alphonso of Arragon, Duke de Biscelli, Prince de Salerno, natural son of Alphonso II, King of Naples. This husband was greatly beloved by Lucretia; but, unfortunately for the permanency of their union, Don Alphonso did not turn out such a valuable political ally as Alexander and Cæsar had wished or anticipated. Another house—the rival of the house of Arragon—the house of Anjou, had risen in importance. The King of France, at the head of the house of Anjou, desired the dethronement of the Neapolitan monarch, in order that the sovereignty might accrue to a member of his own family. France was more powerful than Naples; the French alliance would be more profitable to the Pope. Don Alphonso, as a scion of a family hostile to France, was rather dangerous, than otherwise, to the scheming and aspiring pontiff. The union between them must be dissolved; Lucretia must be set free to form another and a more beneficial alliance. But how was this separation to be effected? Another divorce might occasion a good deal of inconvenient scandal and speculation. Besides, it was by no means certain that the parties more immediately interested would agree to a divorce. Lucretia was deeply attached to her husband, and her affection was cordially reciprocated by Don Alphonso. There was only one expedient—death. Yes, the husband of Lucretia must die. Alexander and Cæsar had so willed it.

In the meantime, Alphonso, quite conscious of the danger which he incurred by residing near his terrible father-in-law, had retired to Naples. But, with their consummate dissimulation, neither Cæsar nor Alexander had done anything towards him to justify his suspicions, so that, in a short time, they greatly abated. In this frame of mind towards his wife's relations, he received an invitation from the Pope and his son to come to Rome, and take part in a grand bull-fight, after the Spanish fashion, on the occasion of Cæsar's departure. Alphonso felt himself constrained to come. The lists were prepared in the place of St. Peter, the streets of which were barricaded, whilst the houses surrounding the arena were fitted up with galleries for the accommodation of the spectators—the Pope and his retinue occupying the balconies of the Vatican.

The combat began with professional bull-fighters. When these had displayed their strength and dexterity, the husband of Lucretia, and her brother Cæsar, entered the lists; and, as a proof of the friendly feeling which subsisted between them, it was arranged that the bull which pursued Cæsar should be slain by Alphonso, and that Cæsar should return the obligation, by slaying the bull which should pursue Alphonso. Cæsar entered the arena alone on horseback. Alphonso retired for a short distance, but held himself in readiness to come to Cæsar's aid the moment it was deemed necessary. At the same time the bull was let in, and a shower of darts and arrows, to which fireworks were attached, discharged upon him. The pain and the explosion had the desired effect—that of irritating and rousing the animal. He rolled himself upon the earth, and then arose, maddened, and rushed instantly at Cæsar, who awaited him in the arena. It was then he exhibited that consummate equestrian skill which proved him to be one of the most accomplished cavaliers of the age. But, for all that, his horsemanship, coolness, strength and skill would have been of no avail against such an adversary, in so narrow a space, where his sole resource was flight, if, at the critical moment, when the animal gained upon him, Alphonso had not suddenly appeared, shaking in his left hand a red cloak, and holding in his right a long, thin Arragonese sword. It was time to do so: the bull was but a few steps from Cæsar, and his danger seemed so imminent, that a cry of fear was heard from one of the windows; but, upon seeing Alphonso, the infuriated bull instantly halted, and, throwing up the dust with his hind feet, pawing the earth, and lashing his sides with his tail,—with bloodshot eyes, and tearing the ground with his horns, he rushed upon Alphonso, who quietly awaited his approach, and then, when within three steps of him, sprung quickly on one side, holding towards the bull his sword, which was instantly sheathed up to the hilt. Immediately the bull, arrested in his full career, remained for a moment motionless, yet quivering in every fibre, then fell upon his knees, breathed heavily, and lay dead upon the spot where he had been struck. So ably and rapidly had this been accomplished, that applauses burst from all around. As for Cæsar, he had remained unconcerned on horseback, bent only on discovering whence and from whom the cry had issued, which had evinced so marked and lively an interest in him. He very soon ascertained that it proceeded from one of the ladies of honour of Elizabeth, Duchess of Urbino, then betrothed to Giovanni Baptisti Carracciolo, Captain-General of the Venetian Republic.

Another bull was let in, and goaded to fury in the same manner as the former, with darts, arrows, and fireworks. Upon seeing the horseman, he instantly rushed upon him. A terrific race now took place, during which, so rapid were the movements, it was impossible to know whether the horse pursued the bull or the bull the horse. Nevertheless, after a few rounds, fleet as was the Andalusian steed which bore Alphonso, the bull began to gain upon him, so much so that there was scarce the distance of two lances between them, when Cæsar, in his turn, suddenly appeared, and with a two-handed sword, and striking downward with such force that the blade gleamed like a flash of lightning, at one blow struck off its head, whilst the body, still borne onwards by its impetus, fell ten steps from the head in the lists. This stroke was so unexpected, had been attended with so much skill and celerity, that it was beheld and greeted with applause so rapturous as to border upon frenzy. But Cæsar, as if amid his triumph mindful only of the fair one whose anxious cry reached him in the moment of his extreme peril, lifted up the head of the bull, and giving it to one of his squires, commanded him to lay it, as an act of homage on his part, at the feet of the beautiful Venetian who had displayed so lively an interest in his behalf. This festival, beside the triumph which it had won for the combatants, gained for the Borgias another object. It had shown to Rome the interest and the kindly feeling which mutually animated Cæsar and Alphonso, so that whatever evil might happen to the one, the other would be held blameless.

This same evening the Pope gave a splendid supper in the Vatican. Alphonso, elegantly dressed, was prepared to proceed to the room where the entertainment was laid out. Towards the tenth hour he quitted the detached wing in which he resided, to enter that in which the Pope's apartments were situated; but the door dividing the two courts was closed, and remained unopened to his repeated knockings. He then determined to go round by the Place of St. Peter, and, unattended, he succeeded along the dark street which led to the staircase ascending to the Vatican; when, hardly had his foot rested on the first step, ere he was attacked by a troop of armed men. Before he could draw his sword he had received five wounds in different parts of his body, and falling senseless on the ground, the assassins, believing him dead, re-ascended the steps, and, finding in the Place St. Peter a guard of fifty horsemen who awaited them, quietly left the city under their protection. Cæsar and his father, as a matter of course, were greatly afflicted. Next morning, to show their determination to bring the murderers to justice, they arrested an innocent man, Francesco Gazella, the uncle of Alphonso, and ordered him to be beheaded. Lucretia was really grieved, and, as soon as she heard of the attack upon her husband, hastened to his lodgings, where he had been conveyed, to nurse him herself. The physicians called imagined, from the very demonstrative sorrow of Cæsar and his father, that they really desired the recovery of Alphonso; and thus their exertions, combined with his excellent constitution, put the wounded man in a fair way of baffling his assassins. Alphonso was fast approaching to convalescence. This would never do for the male Borgias; so one night Cæsar commanded the attendance of the ever faithful Michelotto, who received certain instructions. Next morning, Don Alphonso was found strangled in his bed. The Pope had the hand of Lucretia to dispose of once again.

A short time after the atrocious crimes just related, Cæsar Borgia, accompanied by his courtiers and titled courtezans (for he had a harem stocked with the finest women in Italy, which the Sultan himself might envy) was making one of his customary excursions in the environs of the city. He saw advancing from the road to Rimini a cortege sufficiently numerous to make him believe that it belonged to a person of rank. And soon discovering that it was the escort of a lady, he advanced, and immediately recognised in her the attendant of the Duchess of Urbino—the same who had attracted his attention by her cry when Cæsar was in danger of being gored by the bull. She was, as we before observed, the betrothed of Giovanni Carracciolo, Captain-General of the Venetian Republic. She had been staying with Elizabeth of Gonzagna, her patroness and godmother, by whom she was now sent with a fitting escort to Venice, where her betrothed impatiently waited for her, and where their nuptials were immediately to be solemnized. At Rome Cæsar had been struck by her surpassing beauty, but then he was too busy to devote himself to her. For this involuntary neglect he now reproached himself. He spoke to her as an old acquaintance, inquiring if she was to remain any time at Cesena.

She told him that she was not; that she would merely rest there, pass through, and sleep at Forli that night. This was all the information Cæsar required. He called Michelotto, and whispered something in his ear. The cortege proceeded as the fair betrothed had stated, only halting for a short time at Cesena, and setting out again for Forli, which place, however, the beautiful Venetian was destined never to see. Hardly had the cortege advanced a mile from Cesena, when it was surrounded by a troop of horsemen. Although inferior in numbers, the soldiers of the escort made a gallant defence; but they were overcome; some of them were cut down, and others fled. The lady meanwhile descended from her litter and attempted to escape—the leader of the horsemen seized her in his arms, placed her before him on his saddle, ordered the soldiers to return to Cesena, and rode instantly across the country, and was soon lost in the obscurity of the night.

The evil tidings speedily sped to Venice. Carracciolo was for some time stunned, as if smitten by a thunderstroke, so intense was his grief for the loss which he had sustained. When he had regained sufficient composure to listen to the particulars of the sad mishap, he immediately recognised the hand of Cæsar Borgia in the foul outrage. The description which he had received of the uniform of the soldiers enabled him to come to this conclusion. Carracciolo lost no time in rushing to the ducal palace, where the Doge and the Council of Ten were already assembled. He related the story of his wrongs, and demanded redress and vengeance on the wicked authors of the crime. This was readily promised him; The outrage was regarded as an insult to the Republic. Inquiry was instantly set on foot. Cæsar and the Pope were at once appealed to by envoys from Venice. Both, however, declared their utter ignorance of the perpetrators of the affair, and their perfect innocence of any participation in it. Louis XII, the King of France, was solicited to exert his influence with Cæsar to restore the abducted Venetian, or, failing in that, to bring the criminals to justice. The French monarch complied, but all his endeavours proved abortive. Cæsar was constant in the protestations of his innocence. No one believed, but neither could any one convict him. No witness could or dared testify against the remorseless son of Alexander. The only person courageous or indiscreet enough to volunteer information concerning the affair was an old woman, who declared that on the evening in question she saw a horseman alight, with a lady, whom he conveyed in his arms into a lonely house, the locality of which she indicated to her interrogators. It was resolved that next day parties should proceed to the house in order to assist the investigation. But in that night the house had utterly vanished, and ere the morning the plough had passed over and obliterated every trace of the site on which it stood. The old woman also had disappeared, nor could any one tell what had become of her. What although every one believed Cæsar guilty?—he could afford to defy suspicion, since he knew full well that no one would have the temerity to accuse him. As for Carracciolo he had no alternative but submission to his wrongs. The Venetians were then engaged in a war with the Turks, and therefore could not afford to go to war with Cæsar for justice to their general, whom they forbade to seek for further redress.

A year after this, in the Tiber, a little above the Castle of St. Angelo, the body of a beautiful female, whose hands were tied behind her back, and also the body of a handsome youth, around whose neck still hung the bowstring with which he had been strangled, were found. The woman was the beautiful betrothed of Carracciolo; the youth was Astor—both sacrificed to Borgia's fiendish passions, who, when his lusts were sated, had his unfortunate victims thrown into the Tiber.

It would be both tedious and disgusting to dwell in detail on the numerous murders, rapes, and nameless infamies perpetrated by this monster of iniquity. We therefore pass them over and hasten to the narrative of the concluding actions in the lives of these stupendous miscreants.

The retribution of Heaven was fast approaching. Cæsar arrived at Rome to divide with Alexander the inheritance of Cardinal Giovanni Michele, who had just died, poisoned by a cup he had received from the hand of the Pope.

"Cæsar found his father preoccupied by an important speculation. He had decided upon creating nine cardinals upon the approaching solemnity of St. Peter, from which the following advantages would accrue:—First, the benefices of the cardinals would revert to the Pope, who would sell them; next, the nine selected would purchase the dignity, more or less dear, according to their means: the price, left to the Pope's discretion, would vary from ten thousand to forty thousand ducats. Lastly, as cardinals, having lost the right of bequest, the Pope became their successor: he had only to poison them, and to become their heir, placing himself thus in the situation of the butcher, who, in want of money, has only to slaughter the fattest sheep of the flock. The nomination took place—the nine cardinals were elected—the price of their simony paid, and their vacant benefices sold. The Pope now selected those it was requisite to poison; the number was fixed at three —Cardinals Cassa Nova, Melchiore Copis, and Adriano Castellense, who had taken the title of Adrien de Corneto, and who, by his numerous offices, had amassed an immense fortune. When these points were settled between Cæsar and the Pope, they invited their select party of guests to sup with them at a villa near the Vatican, belonging to the Cardinal de Corneto, and early in the morning they sent thither their maitre d'hotel to make the requisite arrangements; and Cæsar at the same time gave the Pope's butler two bottles of wine, prepared with a white powder resembling sugar, whose fatal properties he had so often tested, desiring him, at the same time, not to serve it but upon his orders, nor to any but those whom he should especially mention. On this account, the butler had placed the wine upon the side-board apart from the rest, and particularly desired the servants not to touch it, being especially reserved for the Pope's use.

"Towards evening, Alexander quitted the Vatican on foot, leaning upon Cæsar's arm, and accompanied by the Cardinal Caraffa; but as the heat was great, and the ascent was somewhat steep, upon reaching its height, he stopped for a few minutes to recover himself, which he had hardly done, when, putting his hand to his breast, he found he had forgotten a gold chain and a medallion, which latter contained consecrated wafers. It was his custom to wear this suspended to his neck, owing to an astrologer's prediction, that so long as he wore the consecrated host, neither steel nor poison could affect him. Deprived, therefore, of his talisman, he desired Caraffa to return immediately to the Vatican and bring it him without delay. Then, as the walk had made him thirsty, still making signs to the cardinal to haste, he turned towards a servant, and desired him to bring him some wine, and Cæsar gave a similar order. Now, by a strange fatality, it happened that the butler had returned to the Vatican for some peaches that had been sent as a present to the Pope, and which he had forgotten; the servant, upon this, spoke to the under butler, saying that his holiness and the duke being thirsty, had desired some wine. Whereupon, having observed two bottles apart from the rest, and having heard they were reserved for the Pope, he gave one to the servant, with two glasses, upon a salver; and this wine the Pope and his son took without the slightest suspicion that it was the vintage reserved for their guests.

"In the meantime Caraffa had reached the palace, and, familiar with its interior, entered the apartments of the Pope, a candle in his hand, but unaccompanied by any domestic. On entering a corridor, the wind extinguished the light; but directed, as he had been, where to find the medallion, he advanced; but, upon opening the door of the room, he fell back with a cry of terror; for before him he saw Alexander VI stretched motionless and livid on a bier, at the four corners of which were lighted flambeaux. He stood for a moment petrified by fear, unable to advance or to retire; but thinking it probably the effect of his imagination, or caused by the agency of the Evil One, he made the sign of the cross, whereupon all disappeared; and then, though a cold sweat burst from every pore, he advanced to the table and returned with the medallion. He found the guests assembled, and the Pope, extremely pale, the moment he appeared, advanced to meet him; but upon stretching out his hand to receive the medallion, he fell back and uttered a loud cry, which was instantly followed by the most violent convulsions, whilst a few moments afterwards, as he advanced to his assistance, Cæsar was seized with the same symptoms. They were carried, side by side, to the Vatican, each to their separate apartments; and from that moment they never met again. The Pope was now attacked by a violent fever, which defied all the resources of medical skill, and rendered requisite the administration of the last sacraments of the church. Yet, owing to the excellence of his constitution, he struggled for eight days against death—eight days of agony, at the expiration of which he died without once mentioning either Cæsar or Lucretia, the two pivots upon which had revolved both his affections and his crimes. He died at sixty-two, after a reign of eleven years.

"As for Cæsar, whether he had taken less of the fatal liquid, or whether the strength of his youth overcame the strength of the poison,—or whether, according to some, he had, immediately on reaching the Vatican, swallowed an antidote known only to himself,—he was less violently affected. He did not for a moment, however, lose sight of his dangerous situation, but summoned his faithful Michelotto, with those of his men upon whom he could chiefly rely, and distributed them throughout the ante-rooms, and ordered their chief not to quit the foot of his bed, but to sleep upon his coverlid, with his hand upon the hilt of his sword. The remedies adopted for Cæsar were the same as those for the Pope, except that they added extraordinary baths, which Cæsar himself directed to be prepared, having heard that in a similar case he cured King Ladislaus, of Naples. Four posts were erected in his room, firmly fixed in the floor and ceiling, similar to the machine used for shoeing horses; every day a bull was brought in, thrown upon its back, and tied by its limbs to the posts; an incision was then made in its stomach, about one foot and a half in length, through which the intestines were extracted, and Cæsar then entering while the body yet palpitated with life, enjoyed a bath of warm blood. He was then wrapped in warm cloths, by which, after profuse perspiration, he in general felt relieved. Every two hours, notwithstanding his own state, he sent to inquire about the Pope, and immediately he heard that he was dead, resuming that energy and presence of mind which were habitual to him, he desired Michelotto to close the doors of the Vatican, and to allow no one admission to the Pope's apartments until he was master of his gold, and the papers he had left. Michelotto obeyed, and sought instantly the Cardinal Cassa Nova, placed a dagger at his throat, and made him surrender the keys of the rooms and the cabinets of the Pope; and, guided by him, they took away two chests of gold, to the value of two hundred thousand Roman crowns, and a great quantity of jewels, silver plate, and precious vases, all of which were carried into Cæsar's apartments; his guards were then doubled, and the gates of the Vatican being reopened, the death of the Pope was announced. This, although expected, was nevertheless a matter of extreme dread to the whole city, for Cæsar's state of health kept every one in a fearful suspense. Had he, indeed, been sitting sword in hand upon his war-horse, events would never have appeared uncertain or indecisive; but he was confined to his bed, and although the thought to plan remained, the power to execute was gone, and he was obliged to submit and follow the course of events, instead of governing circumstances by his will. The enemies he had most to fear were the Orsini and Colonnas: the one he had robbed of life, the other of possessions. He addressed himself, therefore, to those to whom he could restore what he had taken, and opened negotiations with the Colonnas. In the meantime arrangements were made for the papal obsequies; the vice-chancellor had summoned the different superiors, and minor orders of the clergy, on pain of being deprived of their dignities, to repair in their respective costumes to the Vatican, where from whence the body was to be conveyed to St. Peter's for interment. They found upon their arrival the body abandoned by every retainer,—for every Borgia, except Cæsar, had concealed himself, and wisely; for shortly after Fabio

Orsino meeting one by chance, instantly stabbed him; and in sign of the mortal hatred which he had sworn, washed his hands and mouth with the blood of his victim."

Cæsar Borgia survived his father for some years, during which he had made several skilful and determined efforts to retrieve his fortunes; but though often on the verge of success, he was invariably doomed to failure. The curse clung too closely to him to be shaken off. His cruelties to man, his blasphemies of God, his outrages on nature, and his insults to religion, were too great to be expiated but by a life of disappointments, and a death of which the violence was embittered by its obscurity—to a man of his aspiring spirit, the most intolerable of all the terrors of dissolution. After divers dangers and adventures in Italy and France, he was for two years imprisoned in Spain, in the Castle of Medino-del-Compo. The mode of his escape and death is thus related:—

"The Duke of Valentenois (Cæsar Borgia) remained two years in prison, always hoping that, as a peer of France, Louis XII would reclaim him from his captors; but the monarch, paralysed by the loss of the battle of Garighano, which deprived him of the kingdom of Naples, was too much occupied with his own to think of the interests of Cæsar. The captive began to despair, when breaking one morning the loaf supplied for his breakfast, he found therein a file, a phial containing a narcotic liquid, and a note from Michelotto, to acquaint him that, having escaped from prison, he had followed him into Spain, and was now concealed, with the Count of Beneventuni, in the adjoining village. He added that from the next day the count and he would await his arrival every night upon the road from the fortress to the village, with three fleet horses, and that therefore it was for him to avail himself of the means placed at his disposal. Thus, when the world had abandoned Cæsar, a sbirri was faithful in misfortune. Freedom was too great a boon for Cæsar to neglect. The same day he used the file upon the iron bars of the window, which opened upon an inner court, and had soon so loosened it that it required but a slight blow to detach it. But besides that this was seventy feet from the ground, the entrance to the court was by a private door reserved for the governor, of which he alone kept the key, which never quitted his possession; here was then the principal difficulty. But prisoner though he was, he was always treated with the respect due to his rank, —dining every day with the commandant, who received him at his table with the manners of a noble and courteous gentleman. Don Manuel being also an old captain, having honourably served King Ferdinand, whilst still obeying his orders, yet felt a great respect for his prisoner, whose stories of his battles he listened to with pleasure. He insisted that Cæsar should sup as well as dine at his table, which hitherto he had refused; fortunately, as, owing to this, he had been enabled to obtain the tools supplied by Michelotto. Now it happened on the day they were received, Cæsar, going up to his room, made a false step and sprained his foot; at the dinner hour he tried to come down, but pretended to suffer so much that he gave up the attempt. In the evening, not being better, the governor visited him as before, but finding his prisoner low-spirited and weary, he offered to come and sup with him. Cæsar accepted this offer very gratefully. It was now for the prisoner to act the part of host; Cæsar's manner therefore was animated and courteous; and the governor, profiting by this circumstance, spoke to him on the subject of his arrest, as an old Castilian for whom honour had still some charms, and inquired as to the truth of the imputed breach of faith of Ferdinand and Gonzalvo. Cæsar showed every willingness to explain the matter, but indicated by a sign that the servants should retire. This precaution appeared so natural, that the governor desired them to withdraw; Cæsar filled his glass, and that of the governor, and proposed the health of the king. He then commenced his narrative, but hardly had he done so, when the eyes of his host became fixed, as by magic, and he fell into a profound sleep. Upon the return of the servants, they found the two guests, one upon the other, beneath the table; which, not being an event sufficiently extraordinary to induce them to pay any particular attention to it, they contented themselves by carrying Don Manuel to his chamber, and placing Cæsar upon his bed. Then, closing the door with the greatest care, they left the prisoner alone. For a moment he remained motionless, as if placed in the profoundest sleep; then, as he heard the steps echo in the distance, he raised his head, glided from the bed, walked towards the door, slowly, it is true, but without appearing to suffer from the injury to his foot; then, raising his head proudly, he seemed to breathe freely for the first time since the departure of his keepers. There was no time to lose; he fastened the door as firmly within as it was secured without; he put out his lamp, opened the window, and removed its bars. This done, he took off the bandage from his limb, tore the curtains from the window and from his bed, and cut them into slips, adding to this his sheets, table-cloth, and napkins. By these he formed a kind of rope, of about sixty feet in length, with knots at intervals, tied it firmly to the bar yet remaining in the window, and then descended, grasping it firmly, by his feet and hands. He reached its extremity without an accident, but as he hung by his last knot he sought in vain for the earth with his feet—the rope was too short. His situation was fearful; the darkness of the night rendered it impossible for him to ascertain the distance from the ground, and his fatigue cut off all hope of his being able to reascend. He hesitated for a moment, let the cord go, and fell, from about fifteen feet, to the ground. His peril was too great to permit his noticing a few contusions he received; he arose immediately, and, guiding himself by the direction of his window, went direct to the door opening from the court; here he stopped, a cold sweat stood upon his brow, for, whether he had forgotten it in his room, or whether he had lost it in his fall he knew not—he had not the key. Recollecting himself, he was soon convinced that the latter was the only probable cause of his loss; he, therefore, traversed the court, endeavouring to find the place where it had fallen, but the key was so small, and the night so dark, that he almost despaired of success; but, nevertheless, as upon this now depended his safety, he redoubled every effort he had made. A door suddenly opened, and a patrol advanced, preceded by torches: he now thought escape impossible; but recollecting a cistern, which was behind him, he instantly plunged into it, leaving his head only above the water, and anxiously followed the movements of the soldiers, who passed within a few yards of him, crossed the courtyard, and disappeared through another door. Short as was the interval, Cæsar's eye had espied by the light of their torches the key so long desired; and hardly had the door closed upon the soldiers when he was master of his liberty. Half-way from the castle to the village, two men on horseback, with another horse ready saddled, met him; these were the Count and Michelotto. Cæsar grasped the hands of both, and immediately galloped towards the frontiers of Navarre, which he reached in three days, and where he was warmly welcomed by the king, Jean d'Albret the brother of his wife. From Navarre Cæsar thought of passing into France, and thence, with the aid of Louis XII, on making an attempt for the recovery of his Italian estates; but during his captivity the king had made peace with Ferdinand of Spain; so that upon hearing of his escape, Louis, instead of assisting him, as he had a right to expect, deprived him of the duchy of Valentenois and his annuity. But there yet remained to Cæsar two hundred thousand ducats with the bankers of Genoa: he wrote to desire the transmission to him of this sum, with which he hoped to raise some troops in Spain and Navarre, and thus to attack Pisa. Five hundred men, two hundred thousand ducats, his name, and his sword, were more than requisite to justify him in hoping to regain his power. The bankers denied the deposit; Cæsar was at the mercy of his brother-in-law. One of the vassals of the King of Navarre had just then revolted; Cæsar assumed the command of the troops that Jean d'Albret sent against him, followed by Michelotto, the faithful companion of his prosperity and misfortunes. Owing to his courage and excellent arrangements, the revolted vassal was at first defeated; but rallying his forces soon after, he renewed the engagement. It was

obstinately maintained for nearly four hours, when, towards dusk, Cæsar wished to decide the battle, by charging himself at the head of a hundred men-at-arms against a corps of cavalry, which formed the main force of the enemy; but, to his great surprise, they fled in the direction of a little wood, wherein they seemed desirous to take refuge. Cæsar pursued them to its outskirts, when suddenly they faced about, and three or four hundred archers rushed from its coverts to their assistance. Cæsar's troops, perceiving they had fallen into an ambuscade, immediately fled, and basely abandoned their commander. Alone, yet he would not recoil one step; he had probably become weary of life, and his heroism was perchance as much the result of disgust as of courage. Whatever it might proceed from, he defended himself like a lion at bay; but pierced with arrows and crossbow bolts, his horse fell with him, and rolled over upon his leg. His opponents immediately rushed upon him; and one, thrusting at him with a sharp-pointed spear, pierced his corselet, and ran him through the chest. Cæsar uttered a blasphemy against heaven, and died— 'hoping nothing, believing nothing, and fearing nothing!'

"The enemy, however, owing to the courage of Michelotto, was defeated; but, upon returning to the camp, he heard from those who had deserted Cæsar that he had not since been seen. Too well assured, from the known courage of his master, that he had fallen, he wished to give the last sad proof of his attachment by not leaving his body to wolves and birds of prey: he caused torches to be lighted, and, accompanied by a dozen of those who pursued the cavalry with Cæsar to the wood, he commenced his search for his master's body. On reaching the spot, they found five men lying dead side by side: four were yet in their armour, but the fifth was entirely stripped. Michelotto alighted from his horse, raised the head upon his knee, and, by the light of the torches, recognised the countenance of Cæsar Borgia. Thus fell, on the 10th of March, 1507, upon a field of battle now unknown, near an obscure village called Viana, and in a miserable skirmish with the vassals of a petty prince, he whom Machiavelli has held up to the respect of princes as a model of address, of policy, and of valour." There can be no question that this infamous man possessed some truly magnificent qualities, and that if it were not for the want of one thing, he would be one of the most illustrious men that ever existed. That want, however, was all in all: it was goodness of which Cæsar Borgia was totally deficient. Everything with him was subservient to self-interest—and self-interest was the slave of passion He despised, alike, all human and divine laws. "He spared no man in his rage, and no woman in his lust." And, wanting this sense of moral right and wrong, implanted by the Creator to enable mankind to steer clear of all that is wicked and impure, Cæsar Borgia's splendid intellect was but as a blazing lamp shedding its radiance upon a dunghill, bringing into greater light and relief the putrescence, feculence, creeping and abhorrent creatures, that fermented, festered, spawned, and stank beneath.

As for Lucretia, who, after the murder of her third husband, Alphonso of Arragon, married the reigning Duke of Ferrara, "she died full of years and honours, adored by her subjects as a queen, and addressed by Ariosto and Bembo 'as a goddess.' " This adulation may grieve, but need not surprise, us. Poets excel in fiction rather than in truth; and an English poet, greater than Ariosto, has eulogized an Englishwoman viler than Lucretia.

CHAPTER IV.

THE MURDER OF SIR THOMAS OVERBURY

ROBERT KERR, or CARR, created, by the grace of King James, Baron Rochester, and afterwards Earl of Somerset, was indebted, in the first place, for his rapid rise, immense wealth and power, to an accident. At a tilting match, given by Lord Hay, in honour of the king, Kerr, was appointed, by Hay, to be his equerry; and, according to custom, upon him devolved the duty of presenting his shield to the king. In the performance of this honour, Kerr was thrown from his horse, and had, as it ultimately turned out, the *good* luck to break his leg in the fall. The king, in the first instance, being struck with the handsome appearance of the youth, and now in pity for his mishap, ordered him to be carried to a neighbouring apartment, sent a surgeon to attend him, and even condescended to pay him repeated visits in his own royal and ungainly person. The monarch soon discovered that Kerr was a countryman of his own, that he had formerly been one of his majesty's pages at Holyrood, and further, that he belonged to the family of Fernyherst, and was the son of a man who had suffered a great deal in the cause of his mother—the beautiful and unfortunate Mary Stuart. Thus Kerr had no mean claim, in the shape of his own and his father's services, upon the favour of King James. But if there had been no other plea for his advancement, it is probable that James—with that ingratitude which is so natural to crowned heads that it seems one of the attributes of royalty—might have left the young Scotchman to push his way, unaided, through the world; to rise, if he had the power, to wealth and eminence; or, if feeble and incapable, to sink into indigence, and die in obscurity. Happy for the fame and the innocence of Kerr, if it had been so. But, unfortunately for him, nature had endowed him with a comely and agreeable exterior. This was to James a more irresistible recommendation than either moral and intellectual merit, or any services rendered by Kerr or his family to the house of Stuart. James I., it is now incontestably proved, was addicted to the most abominable and atrocious of all vices. Robert Kerr was just the person to please so foul a monster. "This fellow" (Kerr), says a chronicler, "is straightlimbed, well-favoured, strong-shouldered, and smoothfaced." At first James pretended that he only took a paternal interest in the young man; he spoke of him as his adopted child; he actually took pains to instruct him in the Latin grammar, and what was more to the purpose, in "the craft of a courtier." "The king," says the chronicler, "leaneth on his arm, pinches his cheeks, smoothes his ruffled garments. The young man doth much study art and devices; he has changed his tailors and tiremen many times, and all to please the princes. The king teacheth him Latin every morning, and I think some one should teach him English, too; for he is a Scotch lad, and hath much need of better language." After his recovery, he was daily distinguished with signs of the royal favour; riches and honours were showered upon him; the estates which became forfeited to the Crown, and the gifts offered by those who entreated his mediation with the king, soon gave him a princely fortune; and he was successively raised to the titles of Baron Branspeth, Viscount Rochester, and Knight of the Garter. Still he pretended to take no part in public affairs until the Earl of Salisbury died, when several important offices became vacant, and the eagerness to obtain them, or the pleas of those who might be preferred to them, filled the court with a shoal of candidates. These candidates were all anxious for a patron. Some sought the favour of the two Howards, the Earl of Suffolk, Lord Chamberlain, and the Earl of Northampton, Lord Privy Seal; while the rest sued the protection of the young favourite, the Viscount Rochester. Intrigue, jealousy, rivalry, and enmity, agitated the court. It was in vain that the king, who abhorred strife, endeavoured to balance between the two parties and reconcile their conflicting pretensions. To Rochester, however, it was a fortunate period; for though he held no official appointment, he transacted business as prime minister and principal secretary of state. Unequal to the task himself, he availed himself of the aid of Sir Thomas Overbury, who, from Kerr's first introduction to the king, had been his counsellor and assistant.

Overbury, we are told, was an able and artful minister; but violent, capricious, and presuming. Having insulted the queen, he was banished from the court, but was, at the solicitation of Rochester, soon recalled. James, it appears, never was favourably disposed towards Overbury. In fact, the monarch regarded him as a rival in the affections of the favourite; and he moreover looked upon Overbury as an inveterate intriguer and fomenter of the feuds and factions which disturbed the harmony of the court. By the public, however, Overbury was courted on account of the influence of his all-powerful friend and patron. He received rich presents to secure his favour and intercession with Rochester; and on the morning of the 21st of April, 1615, he boasted to Sir Henry Wotton of his good fortune, and of the splendid prospects which stretched before him. Yet, that very day, ere the sun had gone down, he was committed, a close prisoner, to the Tower, from which prison he was destined never to have any deliverance but that afforded by one of the most painful, cruel, and atrocious deaths on the crimestained records of humanity.

The occasion of the fall and disgrace of Sir Thomas Overbury, was the guilty passion of his patron, Rochester, for the Lady Frances Howard, the daughter of the Earl of Suffolk. This beautiful, but infamous woman, was, at the early age of thirteen, married to the Earl of Essex, who was but a year older than herself. Immediately after the ceremony, the boy bridegroom was sent to the university, from which he proceeded to the continent. The bride was consigned to the charge of her mother, a vain and vicious woman, who bestowed more attention on the ornamental and superficial accomplishments of her daughter, than on her virtuous and moral education. The young Lady Essex became the belle and the boast of the court. Her conversation was sparkling, her wit poignant and polished, her principles lax, her passions impetuous, and her opportunities to indulge them ample as any wanton could desire. There was, however, one slight check on the licentiousness of the brilliant countess. She had a husband—an absent and a nominal one, it is true; but still, even in the estimation of the immoral court of King James, to him some respect was due. This slight restraint was intolerable to Lady Essex. For the innocent cause of it, she conceived a deep and ineradicable dislike. She resolved never to live with him, or if forced to do so, never to indulge him with the privileges of a husband. At the court she was surrounded with a swarm of glittering and obsequious admirers, all candidates for her favours. Amongst them were Prince Henry, the heir apparent to the throne, and the Viscount Rochester. The latter was the fortunate lover. Rochester, in this, as in other enterprises, called in the aid of Sir Thomas Overbury, who was unscrupulous enough for any undertaking where no hazard had to be encountered, and from which wealth and power were to be derived. Sir Thomas Overbury assisted Rochester in writing his passionate love-letters to the countess, and had even contrived sundry stolen interviews between the enamoured pair, in which what remained of the innocence of the lady was made a wreck.

Meantime, the Earl of Essex had returned from his travels, and at first claimed his rights as a husband. In this he was backed by the family of his wife. Her father, mother, and brother, insisted that she should live with her husband. To this she reluctantly assented, but so managed matters that her unfortunate husband soon ceased to have any desire for a very intimate connexion with his wilful spouse. Indeed, he was glad when she returned to the court; nor does it appear that afterwards he troubled himself about the conduct of his wife, but left her in all things to do as her inclination prompted her.

At one of their frequent but furtive interviews it was resolved by Rochester and Lady Essex that the latter should sue for a divorce, in order that she might be at liberty to marry her adulterous paramour. Rochester, according to his wont, took Overbury into his counsel; but though the lax morality of the latter did not prevent him from promoting the secret intercourse of the guilty lovers, he was strongly opposed to his patron committing himself any further. He well knew the odium which Rochester would bring upon himself by proclaiming his love and contracting an adulterous marriage with the countess. He moreover dreaded the decadence of his own influence by the ascendancy of Lady Essex; but his greatest fear was for the loss of the royal favour for his patron, because Overbury, having a deeper insight into the character of James, knew that the monarch could not brook a rival in the affections of his favourite. If, then, the royal favour should be lost, then would be sealed up the fountain whence flowed the honours and riches in which Overbury, as the satellite of Rochester, had so profusely shared. The king, however, was extremely well disposed to forward the marriage of Rochester and Lady Essex. As we before observed, James, from constitutional timidity, had an unconquerable aversion to strife; and from this union of the *parvenu* Rochester with the old nobility, he anticipated a termination to the contention which rent his court. But Overbury had not the same interest in peace. In fact, he enjoyed and flourished upon the storm. If the Howards should become reconciled to Rochester, he foresaw that his own occupation would be partly gone and his influence materially diminished; Rochester would have less occasion for his services for the future. He was therefore resolved to prevent, at all hazards, his union with Lady Essex. He thought he had a right to open his mind freely to the favourite. Rochester, he said, was indebted to him "more than to any soul living, both for his fortune, understanding, and reputation." He spoke his mind freely and boldly, objecting to the "baseness of the woman," the disgrace of such a marriage, and declaring that if Rochester persisted he would raise an insuperable obstacle to the divorce from the Earl of Essex, which was to precede any open talk about the new marriage. On one occasion, when Overbury and the viscount were walking in the gallery of Whitehall, Overbury was overheard to say, "Well, my lord, if you do marry that filthy and base woman, you will utterly ruin your honour and yourself. You shall never do it with my advice or consent; and if you do, you had best look to stand fast." Rochester rushed from him in a rage, exclaiming, with an oath, "I will be even with you for this!" These words were the death-warrant of the unfortunate Overbury. He had mortally wounded the pride of Rochester in insinuating that by his (Overbury's) means he might be lowered in the king's favour. And he had endeavoured to curb the burning passions of a heartless, dissolute, and reckless man.

Rochester, in his infatuation, had told all that had passed between them to his beautiful and revengeful mistress, who from that moment vowed the destruction of Sir Thomas Overbury. In the first paroxysm of her hate she offered 1,000*l.* to Sir John Wood to take his life in a duel. The risk, however, was too apparent, and the uncertainty too great, for this course to be followed out; and her friends (amongst whom was her uncle, the Earl of Northampton) suggested a more secret expedient, viz., to contrive to make the king a party to getting Overbury out of the way. In furtherance of this project the king was advised to send Sir Thomas Overbury on an embassy to the great Duke of Russia. Rochester, among others, told the monarch that Overbury was a person admirably qualified for the mission. When the matter was mentioned to Sir Thomas, he was willing enough to accept the offer. But the guile of Rochester intervened. Although the infamous favourite was strong in his recommendations to the monarch of Overbury's fitness, yet, with diabolical duplicity, he represented to Overbury that the object was to get him out of the way, in order that others might be preferred to honours to which he had the better right. He also told him that he could not well spare him; that he relied upon his integrity and talents for business; and, in short, so wrought on Sir Thomas Overbury, that the unfortunate man was induced to decline the embassy to Moscow. On the other hand, this refusal was interpreted to the king as an act of contumacy—as a slight to the royal authority; and this was enough to render James —who never liked Overbury—utterly furious against the doomed man. A royal warrant was prepared and signed, and Sir Thomas Overbury was committed to his dungeon. The countess's uncle, the Earl of Northampton, and her lover, Rochester, had so arranged matters that Sir William Wade was removed from the lieutenancy of the Tower, and Sir Jervis Elvis, or Elwes, who was their mere creature, put in his place. Acting on the instruction of his patrons, Elwes kept Sir Thomas Overbury so close a prisoner that not even his own father was permitted to visit him, nor were any of

his servants admitted within the precincts of the Tower. A few days after these wicked practices, the Countess of Essex, backed by her father, who at last was brought over to her side, sued for a divorce from her husband, upon the ground of the marriage being null and void by reason of physical incapacity. Forthwith, James appointed, under the great seal, a commission of delegates to try this delicate cause. The delegates named by the king were Abbot, Archbishop of Canterbury, the Bishops of London, Winchester, Ely, Lichfield, Coventry, and Rochester; with them were Sir Julius Cæsar, Sir John Bennett, Sir John Parry, Sir Daniel Dunne, Francis James, and Thomas Edwards, doctors of the civil law. The Earl of Essex, who had suffered enough already from the beautiful demon, made no resistance, but seems to have gone gladly into measures which would free him from such a wife.

In this case the king took a most active part. It was, indeed, a cause after his own heart. He descended into the theological arena like a practised gladiator, grappled with the bishops and doctors, and, as the head of the church, of course worsted all his antagonists. The Archbishop of Canterbury seems to have acted the part of a bold and honourable man. He stated it to be his conviction that the plea on which the divorce was claimed had not been established. As for the alleged physical incapacity, no evidence beyond the assertion of the countess, and the admission of the earl, that the marriage had not been consummated, had been adduced in support of its truth. The archbishop contended that medical men ought to have been called in, and, in the absence of such testimony, he declared that he could not give his sanction to the separation of the pair. The Mosaic law, as also the Latin and Greek fathers, were largely appealed to by the right reverend gentleman in confirmation of his view of the case. The archbishop also insinuated that the alleged impediments were not natural, but voluntary; and that the lady, and not the earl, was to blame for the non-completion of the marriage. The king replied, and contended strenuously in favour of the divorce. His majesty proved that he had studied theology as extensively as the bishop. He pelted his reverence with holy texts, and patristic quotations to his heart's content. And, as if these were not enough, he appealed to the royal prerogative, and told his sacred opponent, in unmistakable language, that when the king opened his royal lips even archbishops must not presume to bark. The result, as any one might have foretold, was that the petition of the countess was granted by a majority of the delegates—four of them, including the Archbishop of Canterbury and the Bishop of London, signing a protest against the divorce. That the view of the archbishop as to physical incapacity was the right one, may easily be inferred from the following letter from the abandoned countess to one of her accomplices in her murderous and adulterous acts:—

"Sweet Turner,—I am out of all hope of any good in this work, for my father, mother, and brother said I should lie with him; and my brother Howard was there, and said that he would not come from this place all this winter, so that all comfort is gone; and, which is worst of all, my lord has complained he has not lain with me, and I would not suffer him to use me. My father and mother are angry, but I had rather die a thousand times over; for, besides the sufferings, I shall lose his (Rochester's) love if I lie with him. I will never desire to see his face if my lord do that unto me. My lord is very well as ever he was, and so you may see in what a miserable case I am. You must send the party word of all. He sent me word all should be well; but I shall not be so happy as the lord to love me. As you have taken pains ever for me, so now do all you can, for never so unhappy as now, for I am not able to endure the miseries that are coming over me; but I cannot be happy as long as this man liveth—therefore, pray for me, for I have need; but I shall be better if I had your company to ease my mind. Let him know this ill news. If I get *this* done, you shall have as much money as you can demand, and this is fair play.

"Your sister, FRANCES ESSEX."

In the meantime, Sir Thomas Overbury was in safe

custody, and his enemies had opportunity to commence the work of vengeance. The insidious Rochester wrote the most friendly letters to the prisoner, and feigned the most anxious interest in his early deliverance. He advised him to bear his ill-fortune patiently, promising that his imprisonment should not be of long duration, for that himself and the rest of his friends were exerting themselves to appease the anger of the king. Previous to this, the prisoner had been surrounded with the creatures of Rochester and Lady Essex. Not only the Lieutenant of the Tower, but many of his subordinates, were in the confidence and pay of the guilty pair. None of Overbury's friends or servants were permitted to visit him, so that he was, from the very first moment of his entrance into the dungeon, absolutely at the mercy of those whom he had implacably offended. One of the most horrible features in this—one of the foulest tragedies which fiendish villany ever conceived or enacted—is the cool and diabolic deliberation with which everything had been prepared. When we add to this the professions of friendship under which Rochester masked his deadly designs, and which had the effect of throwing his victim completely off his guard, we shall be constrained to confess that the annals of no other nation under heaven can furnish a crime more loathsome than the murder of Sir Thomas Overbury. Rochester, still expressing the strongest sympathy for the prisoner, followed up his letters by presents of pastry and other delicacies, which could not be procured at the Tower. Every one of these articles was poisoned. Occasionally, presents of a similar description were sent to Sir John Elwes, with the understanding that when these were unaccompanied by letters, the articles were *not* poisoned, and might be used with safety by the lieutenant and his family. The poisons were prepared by Dr. Forman, of Lambeth—a wretch who, in addition to his avocation of physician, united in his person the professions of a pimp and a fortune-teller. He was in great request by the lords and ladies of the court, in whose characters and acts it is difficult to determine which most predominated—the most disgusting sensuality, or the most contemptible superstition. Forman, though professing to reveal the secrets of the future, did not deem it beneath his dignity to endeavour to make the present as agreeable as possible to his noble and wealthy patrons. He contrived assignations, composed love philters, and frequently helped to conceal or obviate the tell-tale consequence of the fair frail one's backslidings. For the gross and abandoned sensualists of the court of his "most sacred majesty," there could not be a more pleasant or convenient man than Dr. Forman. And the doctor was just the being to flourish on the impurities of the courtiers, for while he pandered to their lusts, he traded upon their follies. The viler the carrion, the deeper its putrescence; and the more offensive its stench, the more congenial to the taste, and the more conducive to the growth, of the crawling maggots which it feeds and engenders. The more folly and immorality, the more wealth and sensuality which prevail in the palaces of kings and queens, the more demand for Dr. Formans, and the more smooth and prosperous their career.

CHAPTER V.

SIR THOMAS OVERBURY (Continued).

THE rest of the miserable and criminal instruments of Lady Essex and her paramour will be best described by an abstract of their trial and confession. Overbury, after an imprisonment of six months, died in excruciating torments; and a few days after Frances Howard was married in the Chapel Royal to her lover. In order that she might not descend in the scale of the peerage, Rochester had been previously created Earl of Somerset. At the ceremony, this notorious wanton had the audacity to appear with her hair hanging in curls to her waist, this being the usual distinction of a virgin bride! This monstrous impudence on her part was but the natural consequence of the verdict delivered by the midwives appointed to make inspection of her body when the divorce was pending. These servile creatures gave

it as their conviction that "the Lady Essex is a woman apt to have copulation, to bring forth children, and that the said lady is a virgin, and uncorrupted." "Three noble ladies affirm that they believe the same, for that they were present when the midwives made their inspection, and did see them give good reason for it." The king and his nobles honoured the nuptials with their presence, and a long succession of feasts and masks, in which the city strove to equal, if not to outshine, the court, attested the gross hypocrisy and cringing servility of the men who, to ingratiate themselves with the royal favourite, could make public rejoicing in celebration of a marriage which, in private, they did not hesitate to stigmatize as infamous, adulterous, and unlawful. But the pleasures of the guilty are of short duration. Justice was fast pursuing the crime-stained paramours. The vague suspicions which floated in the public mind, that Sir Thomas Overbury had come to his end by foul means, had assumed a form and consistency which compelled the court to order the affair to be thoroughly investigated. Somerset and his countess were openly charged with being the prime authors of Overbury's murder. Elwes, the lieutenant of the Tower, made an incautious avowal, which opened the way to a discovery. At the instigation of the archbishop, who opposed the divorce of Lady Essex, and, under the promise of protection from the queen, Secretary Winwood ventured to communicate the circumstance to James; upon which the king proposed certain questions to Elwes in writing; and, from the answers of that functionary, the monarch learned sufficient to question the innocence not only of Lady Somerset, but also of his own favourite. Partly through a sense of justice, but chiefly through the fear of infamy, the king despatched an order to Sir Edward Coke, the lord chief justice, to make out a warrant for the commitment of Somerset to the Tower. With the true Stuart weakness and duplicity, the king kept the favourite in complete ignorance of his approaching fate. Somerset was permitted to accompany the king as usual; and the messenger who came to arrest him found them at Royston—the king embracing the neck and slavering with his disgusting kisses the cheeks of the wretch whom he believed guilty of the cowardly murder of a confiding friend. Somerset complained of his arrest in the royal presence, as an insult to the king's majesty, but was silenced by the ominous exclamation of James, "Nay, man; if Coke sends for *me*, I must go!" to which was added another, as soon as the back of the favourite was turned: "The deil go with thee, for I will never see thy face mair!"

The investigation of the matter was entrusted to Coke, who undertook the task with more than ordinary zeal. In this he was partly stimulated by the fear of incurring the suspicion of partiality, on account of his previous obligations to Somerset, and partly, also, by the extreme urgency of James, who went down upon his knees, in the midst of the judges, and said, "My lords the judges, it has lately come to my hearing that you have now in examination a case of poisoning. Lord! in what a miserable condition shall this kingdom be (the only famous nation for hospitality in the world) if our tables should become such a snare as that none could eat without danger of life, and that Italian customs should be introduced among us! Therefore, my lords, I charge you, as you will answer it at the great and dreadful day of judgment, that you examine it strictly, without favour, affection, or partiality. And if you shall spare any guilty of this crime, God's curse light on you and your posterity! And if I spare any that are guilty, God's curse light on me and my posterity for ever!"

After three hundred examinations, the lord chief justice presented a report to the king, stating "that Frances, Countess of Essex, had been in the habit of employing sorcery to estrange the affections of her husband, and to win those of Rochester; that, to remove Overbury, the principal objection to the projected union of the lovers, a plan was concerted between them and her uncle, the Earl of Northampton; that, by their joint contrivance, Overbury was committed to the Tower; Wade, the lieutenant, removed to make way for Elwes, and Weston recommended as warder of the prisoner; that the countess having, with the aid of Mr.

CÆSAR BORGIA.

Turner, procured three kinds of poison from Franklin, an apothecary, entrusted them to the care of Weston; that by him they were administered to Overbury, with the privacy of Elwes; and that, at last, the unfortunate gentleman perished in prison, a victim to the malice, or the precaution, of Rochester and his mistress.'

In this statement there was nothing wanting but a more satisfactory cause for the murder of Overbury. To Sir Edward Coke, who prided himself on the ease with which he could detect what was invisible to anybody else, this was no difficult task. In one of Overbury's letters, which fell into the hands of Coke, allusion was made to the dangerous secrets of Somerset. Coke contended that these must be seditious or treasonable practices; and, with the assistance of a few audacious conjectures, he boldly charged the favourite with the murder of Prince Henry. The queen immediately became, or pretended to have become, infected with apprehensions for her own and her children's safety. She asserted it to be her belief that a conspiracy had been formed by Somerset and his accomplices to poison herself, her son Charles, and her son-in-law, the Prince Palatine, in order that the Princess Elizabeth might be married to the Earl of Suffolk, the brother of the Countess of Somerset. The king would not permit himself to be influenced by the real or assumed alarm of his wife. The only charge which he entertained, was that Somer-

set had received money from Spain, in exchange for which he had promised to deliver Charles, the heir-apparent, into the hands of the Spanish monarch. As for the secrets, on which Sir Edward Coke laid so much stress, historians have all but unanimously agreed that they were much more personal to James, and infinitely more infamous than seditious or treasonable practices.

Weston, Turner, Franklin, and Elwes—the wretched tools of the earl and the countess—were first brought to the bar. In the arraignment of the first of these, it was set forth "that Richard Weston, about the age of sixty years, not having the fear of God before his eyes, but instigated by the devil, devised and contrived not only to bring upon the body of Sir Thomas Overbury great sickness and diseases, but also deprive him of his life; and to bring the same to pass the 9th of May, 1613, and in the eleventh year of his majesty's reign, at the Tower of London, in the parish of All Hallows, Barking, did obtain and get into his hands certain poisons of green and yellow colour, called rosacar (knowing the same to be a deadly poison), and the same did maliciously and feloniously compound and mingle with a kind of broth poured into a certain dish, and the same broth so infected did give and deliver to the said Sir Thomas Overbury, as good and wholesome broth, to intent to kill and poison the said Sir Thomas Overbury, which broth he took and did eat." The indictment then

No. 3.—POISONERS.

goes on to give further particulars of time, place, and circumstance; and on its being read, the prisoner was asked if he was guilty of the "felony, murdering, and poisoning," as aforesaid. Weston refused to plead either one way or the other. The only answer which the court could elicit from him was, " Lord have mercy upon me! Lord have mercy upon me!" The chief justice plainly intimated his conviction that Weston was instigated by " some great ones," who were guilty of the same crime, to stand mute, in order that they might escape punishment. However, upon being menaced with the penalty of the contumacious, Weston was induced to plead and confess. This frightful punishment, the mere threat of which had such an effect upon the accused, enacted that the contumacious should be stretched to the utmost tension, in which position weights were to be laid upon him, first as much as he could bear, which were to be by little and by little increased. If this did not produce the desired frame of mind, the prisoner was exposed naked in the open air, near the prison; and if this did not succeed in breaking his obstinacy or fortitude, he was to be fed with the coarsest bread, and water out of the next sink or puddle to the place of public execution; and " that on the day he had water he was not to have bread, and the day he had bread he was not to have water, and in this torment he was to linger as long as nature could linger out; so that ofttimes they live in this extremity eight or nine days." Weston shrunk from undergoing this frightful infliction, and made a full confession. He had, he said, during the time that she was Countess of Essex, been a procurer and pander to the said Earl Viscount Rochester and the Countess of Essex, " for the effecting of their adulterate desires, which they did divers times consummate, meeting in Mrs. Turner's house, once between the hours of eleven and twelve, at Hammersmith, and divers times elsewhere, for that purpose." That upon becoming Sir Thomas Overbury's keeper, Mrs. Turner, upon the first day, promised him a satisfactory reward if he would administer such things to the prisoner as should be sent to him; that he agreed to do this; and that he received certain yellow poison in a phial, on the 6th of May, on which night, bringing Sir Thomas Overbury's supper in one hand and the poison in the other, he met the lieutenant on the stairs, and asked him in these terms, " Sir, shall I give it him now?" to which the lieutenant replied, " What shall you give him?" upon which he (Weston) said, " As if you did not know, sir;" that Sir Thomas languished and decayed, and, with a sick man's appetite, craved for luscious meats; that tarts and jellies were procured by Mrs. Turner, with the knowledge of the said countess, of which tarts and jellies he did eat, the whole of them being poisoned with sublimate of mercury; that on the 6th of September, Mrs. Turner did procure an apothecary's boy, for the sum of 20l., to poison a glister, which was by the boy and Weston administered as good physic, on the 7th of October, and that after the receipt of the glister, he fell into great extremity of pain, which left him not till it caused his soul to leave his poisoned body. All this, and much more to the same effect, was confessed and signed by Weston.

Franklin, the apothecary, also made confession: Mrs. Turner came to me from the countess, and wished me, from her, to get the strongest poison I could for Sir Thomas Overbury. Accordingly, I brought seven sorts, aqua fortis, white arsenic, mercury, great spiders, powder of diamonds, lapis costitus, and cantharides, all of which were given to Sir Thomas at several times, and with the perfect knowledge of the lieutenant of the Tower. The alleged letters were proven to have passed from Sir Jervis Elwes to the countess, all of which he (Franklin) saw, and one of which he read to the countess, because she could not read it herself (owing, we presume, to the bad calligraphy), and in which occurred this expression,— " Madam, this scab is like the fox—the more he is cursed the better he fareth." Overbury never ate salt but there was white arsenic put into it. Once, he desired " pigge" (pork), and Mrs. Turner put into it lapis costitus; the white powder that was sent the prisoner, he (Franklin) knew to be arsenic—a very deadly poison. At another time he had two partridges sent him from the court, and water and onions being the sauce, Mrs.

Turner, instead of pepper, put in cantharides. In fact, there was scarcely anything which he took that did not contain poison. " For these poisons," continues Franklin, " the countess sent me rewards; she sent me gold many times by Mrs. Turner." On the marriage of the countess with Somerset, she sent him 20l., and he was also, in reward for his services, to receive an annuity of 200l. as long as he lived. The work, he said, was greatly against his conscience, but he was repeatedly (two hundred times at least) urged to it by the countess, who had such a bewitching way with her, that he was not able to refuse her anything.

The lieutenant of the Tower, Sir Jervis Elwes, at first denied his guilt, and made an able defence; but he was found guilty, and, when he gave up all hope of being saved through the influence of his employers, made a full confession. He had, he said, by the tricks and temptations of the Earl of Northampton and Sir Thomas Monson, been drawn into his crime. He expressed himself deeply penitent — vindicated himself from the charge of heresy with which the lord chief justice had reproached him—and requested the benefit of the prayers of the attendant clergymen. Drs. " Felton and Whiting," we are told, straining courtesy which of them should begin a public prayer for this party's condition, each of them willed the other; but at last Dr. Whiting said, " If you, Sir Jervis, can perform it yourself, you, of all men, are fittest to do it with efficacy, both of soul and spirit." Whereupon he said, " I shall do my best, then; but, my hearers, I crave your charitable constructions if, with half words, and imperfect sentences, I chatter like a crane." The prayer being ended, he asked if he might not pray privately. The doctors said " Yes." Then made he a short prayer to himself with his face covered. After that he uncovered it, and said, " Now I have prayed, now must I pay;— I mean, do the last office to justice." With that, Dr. Whiting said, " Sir Jervis, you may stand one step lower upon the ladder;" to whom the sheriff answered, " It is better for him, Mr. Doctor, to be where he is." " Stay," quoth the doctor to the executioner, " for he has given a watchword he is in private prayer again."— " Yea," quoth the executioner, " for he has given me a watchword when I shall perform my office unto him." He uncovered his face after this second short prayer, and took leave of the assembled multitude, saying, with a cheerful voice and countenance, " Pray for one who shall never more behold your faces;" then he said, with great fervency of spirit, " Lord, I desire at thy hand this bitter cup of death, as the patient receives a bitter potion, not once demanding what is in the cup, but takes and drinks it off, be it never so bitter." As soon as he had then said, audibly, " Lord Jesus, receive my soul," which, belike, was the executioner's watchword, he was turned off the ladder, and the executioner's man, catching at one of his feet, and his own man by the other, they suddenly weighed his life out of him. He remained suspended for a short time, " all which being ended, both corpse and high gibbet were from thence conveyed."

Sir Thomas Monson, a friend and creature of the Earl of Northampton, was tried soon after the execution of the lieutenant. He pleaded " not guilty," and demanded to be " tryed by God and his country." The chief justice urged him to confess, and recommended him to profit by the example of the other criminals, who had died penitent. But the prisoner was deaf to his lordship's counsel, and requested permission to write to the lord treasurer, who, he alleged, could testify to his innocence. Leave was obtained, but the answer of the lord treasurer did not render him any service. It simply stated, after " hearty commendations " to the chief justice, to whom it was directed, " I hear that Sir Thomas Monson says I can clear him, but I hear nothing of him to accuse him; and I hope he is not guilty of so great a crime."

" You hear," quoth the judge to the prisoner, " that he will neither accuse nor excuse you.

" Monson: I do not accuse the lord treasurer nor calumniate, for I know he is very honourable, but I desire to have answer to my two questions.

" Judge: You shall hear more of that when time shall serve. Do you, as a Christian, and as Joshua bid

Achan, 'My son, acknowledge thy sin, and give glory to God.'

"Monson: If I be guilty I renounce the king's mercy, and God's. I am innocent!

"Judge: There is more against you than you know of.

"Monson: If I be guilty it is of that I know not.

"Judge: You are Popish. That pulpit (bar) was the pulpit whereon Garnet and the lieutenant denied their guilt. I am not superstitious, but we will have another confession.

"Justice Doddridge: It is an atheist's words to renounce God's mercy.

"Hyde (the attorney-general): I have looked into this matter, and I protest, my lord, he is as guilty as the guiltiest.

"Monson: There never was man more innocent in this cause. I will live and die an innocent man."

After this scene certain yeomen of his majesty's guard, attending for that purpose, conducted him to the Tower, where between the yeomen and the warders there occurred some contention about his entertainment. But Monson knew too many of the Court secrets to be further punished; so he was soon after set at liberty.

On the 7th of November, Ann Turner, a widow, was arraigned at the bar of the King's Bench, at Westminster. The indictment whereupon Richard Weston took his trial being repeated verbatim, she was indicted for "comforting, aiding, and assisting the said Weston in the poisoning to death of Sir Thomas Overbury." She pleaded "not guilty." The lord chief justice told her that although women must be covered in church, they are not to be covered when arraigned at the bar of justice, and so caused her to put off her hat, which done, she covered her hair with her handkerchief, being before dressed in her hair and her hat over it.

Sir Lawrence Hyde opened the charge, much to the same effect as he did at Weston's trial. He dwelt upon the wickedness and heinousness of poisoning. He then proceeded to relate, that there was one Doctor Forman, who dwelt at Lambeth, and who died very suddenly; that just previous to his death he desired that he might be buried very deep in the grave, "or else," said he, "I shall terrify you all." It was further shown that during his lifetime the Countess of Essex and Mrs. Turner were in the habit of resorting to Forman, always calling him "father." One cause of their visits was that Forman should by force of magic procure the Earl of Somerset—then Viscount Rochester—to love the countess, and Sir Arthur Mainwaring to love Mrs. Turner, by whom, as it was then related, she had three children. Letters of the countess to Forman and Mrs. Turner were put in and read. That to the latter we have already given: the one to Forman is as follows:—

"Sweet Father,—I must still crave your love, although I hope I have it, and shall deserve it better hereafter. Remember the galls, for I fear, though I have yet no cause but to be confident in you, yet I desire to have it. As it is remaining yet well, so continue it still if it be possible, and if you can you must send me some good fortune. Alas! I have need of it. Keep the lord (Rochester) still (true) to me, for that I desire. Be careful that you name me not to anybody, for we have so many spies, that you must use all your wits, and all little enough, for the world is against me, and the heavens favour me not. Only happy in your love, I hope you will do me good, and if I be ungrateful, let all mischief come upon me. My lord is lusty and merry, and drinketh with his men; and all the content he gives me is to abuse me and use me as doggedly as before. I think I shall never be happy in this world, because he hinders my good, and will ever. So remember, I beg, for God's sake, and get me from this vile place.

"Your affectionate, loving daughter,
"Frances Essex.

"Give Turner warning of all, but not the lord. I would not have anything come out for fear of my lord treasurer; for so they may tell my father and mother, and fill their ears full of toys. F. E."

There was shown in the court, pictures made in lead, of a most obscene description. A black scarf, full of white crosses, which belonged to Mrs. Turner, was also exhibited. When these and divers other enchanted papers and disgusting pictures were produced in court, there was heard a great crack from the scaffold, which caused much fear, tumult, and consternation amongst the spectators and throughout the hall, "every one fearing hurt, as though the devil had been present, and growing angry to have his workmanship shown to such as were not his own scholars."

Dr. Forman's widow discovered several packets of letters, which threw considerable light on the quackish and wicked practices of her husband, and on the motives of his infamous visitors. She deposed that Mrs. Turner came to her house immediately after the death of Forman, and demanded certain pictures which were in her husband's study. One of these pictures was in wax, very sumptuously arrayed in silks and satins; another was that of a naked woman spreading and laying forth her hair before a looking-glass. These Mrs. Turner confidently affirmed to be in a box, the exact position of which she indicated.

Mrs. Forman further deposed that Mrs. Turner and her husband would be sometimes three or four hours locked up in his study together. She also stated that her husband had a ring which would open like a watch. A memorandum, made by Dr. Forman upon parchment, was produced in court, "signifying what ladies loved what lords" in the royal household; but the chief justice, to prevent annoyance to the titled strumpets, would not suffer it to be read in open court. It was shown that Mrs. Turner sent Margaret, her maid, to Mr. Forman, to ask for all such letters and papers as concerned the Earl of Somerset and the Countess of Essex, or else to desire that they should be burnt, as well as the letters of any other great personages that might be discovered. The reason for this request was, investigation being set on foot, council warrants for searching the deceased doctor's study might be expected, so that many parties might be inculpated. In consequence of this, Mrs. Forman burnt several papers, but preserved others, unknown to Mrs. Turner. There were also several "enchantments" displayed in court, inscribed on parchment. These, for the most part, were fantastic devices, crosses of various forms and sizes, and all the names of the blessed Trinity mentioned in the Scriptures. Upon one of those parchments, we are told, was fastened a little piece of the skin of a man. In those disgusting documents the devil was addressed by particular names and titles, by all of which his infernal majesty was conjured to torment the Lord Somerset and Sir Arthur Mainwaring, if they should prove inconstant in their loves to the countess and Mrs. Turner. After a great deal more of the same description of evidence, Mrs. Turner was found guilty, and sentenced to death by the lord chief justice. His lordship told her that "she had the seven deadly sins—that she was a whore, a bawd, a sorceress, a murderer, a witch, a *Papist*, a felon, and the daughter of the devil." She implored the chief justice to be good to her; declared that she had been brought up with the Countess of Essex, and had for a long time been her servant, and that she did not know that there was poison in any of the things sent to Sir Thomas Overbury. She became so overcome with weeping that she could not speak, only beseeching the mercy of the court.

Upon the Wednesday following she was brought from the sheriff's in a coach to Newgate, and was there put into a cart, and casting money often amongst the people on her way, she was carried to Tyburn, where she was appointed to be executed, and where many rich and noble lords and ladies of fashion came in their coaches to see her die. To the assembled spectators she made a speech, desiring them not to rejoice at her fall, but to take warning from her fate. She exhorted them to serve God, and abandon evil company and all other sins. She related her breeding with the Countess of Somerset, and that upon what she received from that lady she was entirely dependent for her own and her children's maintenance, and that when her hand was once in this business she knew the revealing of it would be her overthrow, "by which, with other like speeches and great penitence, she moved the spectators to great pity and grief for her."

CHAPTER VI.

SIR THOMAS OVERBURY (Concluded).

THE trial of the Earl and Countess of Somerset was put off as much as possible, doubtless through the reluctance of the king to push matters to too great an extent against a former favourite, who held so many of his majesty's most dangerous secrets. The monarch, we can easily conceive, expected the public indignation against the murderers of Sir Thomas Overbury would have been appeased by the sacrifice to outraged justice of the subordinate actors in the foul and atrocious tragedy. The high and influential connexions of Lady Somerset also used their power to shield the daughter of the Howards from the shame of a public trial and conviction for murder. But the crime was of so black and flagrant a description, the guilt of the earl and countess so notorious, and popular indignation so deep and violent, that the king was constrained to command that Lord and Lady Somerset should be arraigned for the murder of Sir Thomas Overbury before a high commission, composed of peers of the realm, assisted by the principal ministers of justice. Amongst these, the most conspicuous were Sir Edward Coke, Lord Chief Justice of England; Sir Henry Hobart, Lord Chief Justice of Common Pleas; Sir Francis Bacon (the great Lord Bacon), Attorney-General, Sergeant Montague, Sergeant Crew, and many others; but, as these three were the only speakers, their names are of no consequence to the detail of our narrative.

On the 24th of May, 1616—about six months after the execution of the Lieutenant of the Tower, Mrs. Turner, and the rest of their miserable accomplices—the Earl and Countess of Somerset were indicted before the high commission for the murder of Sir Thomas Overbury. The commission was opened in the following manner:—The Lord Chancellor, who was also the Lord High Steward of England, entered the court, preceded by six sergeants-at-arms, with their maces; Sir George Coppin, bearing the royal patent for the commission; Sir Richard Connisby, with his white staff; the great seal being borne by Mr. Manning, who took his seat at the upper end of the board, under a canopy of cloth of purple and gold. On either hand of him were seated the peers, beneath them the judges. At the opposite end of the table sat Finch, the Keeper of the Records of Attainder, flanked on either side by the Clerk of the Crown, the counsel for the king, the Seal Bearer, and Sir Richard Connisby. Beside the Keeper Finch, stood the crier of the court; and below, and facing the Lord Steward, was the bar where was to be placed the prisoner, Frances Howard, the Countess of Somerset. Silence being restored, Sir George Coppin rose to his feet, delivers upon his knees the patent to the Lord High Steward, who receives it, and, after having kissed it, returns it to Mr. Fanshawe to take it kneeling. Then the crier, in the name of the Lord Steward, makes proclamation to preserve silence. The indictment and conviction of Weston and others having been read, Walter Lee, Sergeant-at-Arms, is ordered to produce the precept or warrant to the peers, for the trial of Frances, Countess of Somerset. At last the Lieutenant of the Tower is ordered to return his warrant for the detention of the countess, and to bring his prisoner to the court. Upon entering the court, the countess made three reverences to the Lord Chancellor and the peers. "She was attired in black tammel, a cyprus caperoon, a cobwebb lawn ruff and cuffs." The Lord Steward then said, "My lords, the reason why you are called hither this day is to sit as peers for the trial of Frances Countess of Somerset." After which Fanshawe, Clerk of the Crown, addressing the prisoner, said, "Frances, Countess of Somerset, hold up thy hand." This she did, until the lieutenant told her she might hold it down. The indictment of Weston was again read, and then that of herself. During the reading those documents, the countess, who was compelled

to stand, looked exceedingly pale, trembled, and shed some tears. At the first mention of Weston's name, she held her face, which she kept half-concealed until the whole of the indictment was read. This done, Fanshawe said, "Frances, Countess of Somerset, what sayest thou? Art thou guilty of this felony and murder, or not guilty?" "She, making an obeisance to the Lord High Steward, answered, 'Guilty,' and with a low voice, but wonderful fearful." Sir Francis Bacon then proceeded to address the court to the following effect:—

"May it please your grace, my Lord High Steward of England, I am glad to hear the lady so free of acknowledgment, for confession is noble. Those that have formerly been indicted for this crime—Weston, Turner, Franklin, and Elwes,—persisted in denial; but you perceive this lady's humility and contrition by her pleading; and, certainly, she cannot be otherwise than a spectacle of much commiseration, if either you consider her sex—a woman—or her parentage, which is honourable. But this day and to-morrow are to crown justice. The mercy seat is the inward part of the temple —the public throne: therefore I do now only pray for a record of the confession and judgment. Since the peers be met together, it is good for honour's sake to declare the king's justice. This is the second time since the king's coming to this realm, these thirteen years, that any peers have been arraigned, and on both these occasions your grace hath had the place of Lord High Steward. The first case was that of Lords Gray and Cobham. And though they were convicted, yet execution followed not. No noble blood has been spilt since his majesty's reign.

"The first trial of peers was in revenge for treason against malcontents. This trial is for offence done to a private subject, and is against those who have been most high in the king's grace and favour, and therefore deserves to be written in a sunbeam. His (the king) being the best master in the world, hinders him not from being the best king; for he can as well level a hill as build a wall—a good lesson to my lords the peers. The king is lieutenant to Him who is no respecter of persons.

"This that I shall now speak of may be reduced to that which was enacted in the vault, and since upon the stage. The first I will not now enter into, because I will neither grieve a lady that is present, nor touch a lord that is absent; my duty requires it not, and my humility forbids it. That which hath been upon the stage, the theatre of God's justice, you shall understand hath been worthily acted by the king in this whole work of justice, and right well by his ministers. Overbury died, poisoned, the 15th of September, 1613, in the Tower of London. He was no sooner dead than there arose a certain rumour and muttering—that *vox populi*—that Overbury came strangely by his death. At the same time there was another and a contrary rumour—but that was *vox diaboli*—that he died of a foul disease, so foul a one as to be unfit for me to name; but for two years after this, though Overbury's blood cried for vengeance, *vox Dei* was not heard. It is the glory of God to conceal a thing—of a king to find it out; yet all the while God so dazzled the eyes of those two procurers (the prisoner and her paramour) and of their instruments, that the first looked not about them, the others fled not. All murders are strange in their discovery—this was miraculous. It came to pass in this wise: My Lord of Shrewsbury, who is now with God, commended Sir Jervis Elwes to a councillor of state, and told him that Sir Jervis, from the good report he had heard made of his honour and worth, desired to be made known to him. That councillor replied, 'That he took this for a compliment from Lord Shrewsbury;' but added, 'that inasmuch as Sir Jervis rested under a heavy imputation about Overbury's death, he should like him so to clear himself as to give some satisfaction on the point.' This conversation Shrewsbury related to Sir Jervis, who was impressed with it, and made a kind of discovery that some attempts were undertaken against Overbury, but took no effect, because they were checked by him. The councillor related this to the king, who commanded presently Sir Jervis should set down in writing what he knew about the matter. This he accordingly did, but always reserving himself, endeavouring rather to discover and inculpate others, so that none else should be beforehand with him, and accuse himself.

"The king persevered in his endeavour to search out the truth, instituted an investigation which he entrusted to certain councillors, who pick something out of Elwes and Weston. The rest of the inquiry was committed to Lord Coke, who in this cause was most painstaking, and conducted from two to three hundred examinations. But as soon as Coke found that it might touch upon greater persons, he desired that some others might be associated with him in the investigation. This request was granted, and the Lord Chancellor, the Lord Steward, and Lord South, were appointed to co-operate with the Lord Chief Justice in the endeavour to trace the authors of Sir Thomas Overbury's death. There were no expedients left untried for baffling the inquiry. Weston was solicited to stand mute, but at last his dumb devil was cast out. Then followed Elwes, Turner, and Franklin, all of whom were actors without malice in this tragedy, but not its authors. Now then this lady comes to her part. She meets justice in the way by confession, which is either the corner stone of mercy or judgment; yet it is said, mercy and truth are met together. Truth you have in her confession, and that may be a degree to mercy; with men it must be so, and to Him in whose power mercy resides; in the meantime this day must be reserved for judgment."

The king's instructions were then read, and Fanshawe, the Clerk of the Crown, then addressed the prisoner: "Frances, Countess of Somerset, thou hast been indited and arraigned, and hast pleaded guilty, as accessory before the fact of the wilful poisoning and murder of Sir Thomas Overbury. What canst thou say for thyself, why judgment of death should not be pronounced against thee?"

To this the countess replied: "I can much aggravate, but nothing extenuate my fault. I desire mercy, and that the lords would be pleased to entreat for me to the king."

This she spoke humblingly, tremblingly, and so low, that the Lord Steward could not hear it; but Bacon related its import in the following words: "This lady is so touched with remorse, and sense of her fault, that grief surprises her from the expressing of herself, but that which she has confusedly said is to this effect, that she cannot excuse herself, but desires mercy."

Sir R. Connisby, sitting before the Lord High Steward, rose, and upon his knees delivered him the white staff. Then the Lord High Steward said: "Frances, Countess of Somerset, whereas thou hast been indicted, arraigned, and hast pleaded guilty, and confessed that thou hast nothing to say for thyself, it is now my part to pronounce judgment. Only this much more—since my lords have heard with what humility and grief you have confessed the fact, I do not doubt but they will signify so much to the king's majesty, and mediate for his grace towards you; but in the meantime, and according to the law, the sentence of death must be thus:—Thou must go to the Tower of London from hence, and from thence to the place of execution, where you are to be hanged by the neck till you be dead, and the Lord have mercy upon your soul."

The bias of the king in favour of the noble poisoners—or rather his disinclination to inflict on them the extreme penalty of the law, as well as the gross servility, which forms one of the foulest blots on the character of the father of modern philosophy—are clearly discernible in the speech of Sir Francis Bacon. With the view of saving Somerset, who had the king in his power, the countess was induced to make confession, and to feign a contrition which she did not feel, well assured that the royal prerogative would interpose between her and the doom which the Lord Steward had pronounced.

Next day the commission proceeded with the trial of the Earl of Somerset. The preliminary ceremonies were much the same as in the trial of the countess. The earl was dressed in a plain suit of satin, laced with two satin laces in a seam; a gown of uncut velvet, the sleeves of which were laid with satin lace. He had on a pair of gloves with satin tops; about his neck he wore the ribbon of the George; his hair was elaborately

curled; his beard was long and carefully trimmed; his face was very pale; his eyes had an anxious and careworn appearance, and were deeply sunk in his head. While the indictment was being read, he whispered three or four times to the Lieutenant of the Tower. As soon as the reading of the indictment was over, he was asked by Fanshawe, "Robert, Earl of Somerset, what sayest thou, art thou guilty of this felony and murder whereof thou standest indicted, or not?" Somerset, bowing to the Lord Steward, answered, "Not guilty."

Fanshawe: "How wilt thou be tried?"

Prisoner: "By God and my country." But presently correcting himself, he said, "By God and my peers." A proclamation was then made, calling upon all who could testify the Earl of Somerset in the matter for which he stood arraigned to come forward; after which the Lord Steward addressed the prisoner thus: "Robert, Earl of Somerset, you have been arraigned, and you have pleaded 'Not guilty.' Now, whatsoever you have to say for yourself, say it boldly, without fear; and, although it be not the ordinary custom, you can have pen and ink to help your memory: but remember that God is the God of truth. A fault defended is a double crime. Hide not the verity, nor affirm an untruth—for to deny that which is true increaseth the offence. Take heed lest your wilfulness cause the gates of mercy to be shut upon you."

Sergeant Montague opened the charge against the prisoner. The evidence on which Weston, Franklin, and Mrs. Turner were convicted was put in, and the various dates on which the poison was administered to Sir Thomas Overbury were proved. It was shown that on the 14th of September, 1813, various poisons—arsenic, sublimate, &c., as well as a poisoned glyster—had been administered to the unfortunate Overbury. It was next proved that Weston and the other accomplices were instigated by Somerset and his paramour, so that these were in reality the murderers, the others their mere tools. "It is not only," said the counsel, "he that slips the dog, nor even the dog, but he that loves the toil, that kills the deer."

Somerset desired permission to answer any one of the points alluded to in the charge. But the Lord Steward told him that "The constant course of the court must be kept. You cannot," said his lordship, "interrupt the king's counsel; they must give their evidence entire before you come to your answer. You have now pen and ink to observe what they urge against you; and if you should omit anything when you come to your answer, you shall have all the help that can be afforded you."

The Attorney-General, Sir Francis Bacon, then entered into a narrative of the friendship and close intimacy which notoriously had subsisted between the prisoner and Sir Thomas Overbury. The dangerous secrets of the Earl of Somerset which Overbury held, the Attorney-General, in order to free the king from the infamy imputed to him, declared to be of a treasonable character. He said, "Now, the friendship and familiarity betwixt my Lord of Somerset and Sir Thomas Overbury was so great, if you believe him in his own letter, that the greatest matters and secrets of state which my lord (the prisoner) executed under the king were all communicated unto him (Overbury)—not whisperingly, or by piecemeal, as, sometimes, privy councillors used to do to their friends for a favour, but Overbury took copies, registers, and extracts of all that passed; thus had ciphers passed between them; and this kind of characteristical writing is now used but by princes and their ambassadors—or, if it be used by others, then by such as be practisers against princes. Yet, my lord (addressing the prisoner), I charge you with no disloyalty. You went about an unlawful love, designed by my Lord of Northampton, appugned by Overbury under pretence of friendship, though in truth that was not the reason, but his unwillingness to have any partners in your favour beside himself. For he himself writes in a letter to you, that you won her by his letters. But this impetuous, unbounded fellow, Overbury, first began his threats in respect to the divulging of secrets. Hereupon this, there grew two causes of hatred upon him—one from you, and another from my lady. But your hatred was of a nearer nature, for yourself confessed that he had such a hold of you, he might overthrow you. Then there was a third stream beside these, and that came from my Lord of Northampton, and from you three Overbury was concluded *filius mortis*—the son of death."

Three of the servants of Sir Thomas Overbury were called and examined. They proved the delivery of several letters from their master to the Earl of Somerset. One of these is as follows:—

"Sir Thomas Overbury, prisoner in the Tower, to the Earl of Somerset.

"Is this the fruit of my care and love to you? Be these the fruits of common secrets—common dangers? As a man, you cannot suffer me to lie in this misery—yet your behaviour betrays you. All that I entreat of you is, that you would free me from this place, and that we part friends. Drive me not into extremes, lest I may say something that you and I may both repent; and I pray God you repent not the omission of this my counsel in this place from whence I now write this letter."

Lord Wentworth: "How did you know these letters were sent from him to my Lord of Somerset?"

Sir Francis Bacon: "It is true that those letters were lost, but afterwards found by the servant, who knew his master's (Sir Thomas Overbury's) hand."

Coke: "The letters were found in a cabinet amongst some other things left in trust by my Lord of Somerset, with Sir Robert Cotton, who, fearing search, delivers them to a friend of his in Holborn, one Mistress Farnworth. She, to the intent that they might be safely kept, sent them to a merchant's house in Cheapside, where, some seven months before, she had lodged, and desired they might be safely kept for her, pretending they were letters which concerned her jointure. On St. Thomas's day, she herself came to have them again, saying, 'she must carry them to her counsel, that he might peruse them.'—'If,' said the merchant, 'you will suffer me to open them before you, and that there be nothing else, you shall have them!' But she by no means would consent to the breaking of them open in his presence. Then he answered, 'It is a troublesome matter. I will go to the Lord Chief Justice, and if he find no other writing but such as concern you, you shall have them again. So coming to my chamber, and not finding me within (for I was gone to Paul's, to the sermon), he went to my Lord South's, one of the appointed commissioners in this cause, but my lord would not himself break the letters open, but came to me at Paul's, and in a bye-room we brake them open, and found in them many things disadvantageous to my Lord of Somerset."

Sir Francis Bacon: "These matters being made evident, need no further be amplified; for, my lord, as it is a principle in nature *that the best things are in their corruption the worst, and the sweetest wines make the sharpest vinegar*, so it fell out with my Lord of Somerset and Sir Thomas Overbury, that this excess (as I may call it) of friendship, ended in mortal hatred on my Lord of Somerset's part."

The court found the prisoner guilty, sentence of death was pronounced, and their lordships dissolved.

Now arrived the time for testing that severe and unbending impartiality—that godlike love of justice—that immutable determination to visit with punishment the guilty heads, however exalted or ennobled their owners might happen to be—on which King James so loudly and so openly magnified himself. Shall the sentence of death be executed upon the Earl and Countess of Somerset—the authors of the foul murder of Sir Thomas Overbury, as well as upon the vulgar criminals who were nothing but infamous tools in the hands of the guilty pair? Let us recall to mind the solemn vow recorded by the king, upon his knees, in the midst of the judges: "And if you," said the monarch, "shall spare any guilty of this crime, God's curse light on you and your posterity! And if I spare any that are guilty, God's curse light on me and my posterity for ever!" Alas! for the justice of kings. Either the monarch, when he uttered this terrible imprecation, did not expect that his favourite should be inculpated, or else his courage failed, through fear of the horrible secret which

Somerset had it in his power to reveal. "Whatever," says Charles Mackay, in his "History of popular delusions," "the secret between the criminal and the king may have been, the latter, notwithstanding his terrific oath, was afraid to sign the death-warrant. It might, perchance, have been his own. The earl and countess were committed to the Tower, where they remained for nearly five years. At the end of this period, to the surprise and scandal of the community, and the disgrace of its chief magistrate, they both received the royal pardon, but were ordered to reside at a distance from the court. Having been found guilty of felony, the estates of the earl had become forfeited; but James granted him, out of their revenues, an income of 4,000*l.* per annum! Shamelessness could go no further."

Of the after life of these criminals, nothing is known, except that the love which they had formerly borne each other was changed into aversion, and that they lived under the same roof for months without the interchange of a word.

How the curse, which the king had invoked upon himself and his posterity, was fulfilled, we know. The crimes and misfortunes of the House of Stuart compose a large and a melancholy portion of the history of our country. And James himself, who violated his oath and outraged justice, by pardoning a foul murderer and poisoner, because the criminal was a royal favourite, is believed to have been poisoned himself by another royal favourite—Buckingham, the successor of Somerset in the affections of the monarch. "In the notes to 'Harris's Life and Writings,' James I, there is a good deal of information on this subject. The guilt of Buckingham, although not fully established, rests upon circumstances of suspicion stronger than have been sufficient to lead hundreds to the scaffold. His motives for committing the crime are stated to have been a desire of revenge for the coldness with which the king, in the latter years of his reign, began to regard him, and his hope that the great influence which he possessed over the mind of the heir apparent (Charles I), would last through a new reign, if the old one were brought to a close."

In the second volume of the "Harleian Miscellany" there is a tract, entitled the "Forerunner of Revenge," written by George Eglisham, Doctor of Medicine, and one of the physicians to King James. Harris, in quoting it, says that it is full of rancour and prejudices. It is evidently exaggerated, but forms, nevertheless, a link in the chain of evidence. Eglisham says, "the king being sick, the duke (Buckingham) took this opportunity, when all the king's doctors of physic were at dinner, and offered to him a white powder, to take the which he a long time refused; but, overcome with importunity, he took it in wine, and immediately became worse and worse, falling into many swoonings, and pains, and violent fluxes of the belly, so tormented, that his majesty cried out aloud of the white powder, 'Would to God I had never taken it!'" Eglisham then tells us "of the Countess of Buckingham (the duke's mother) applying the plaster to the king's heart and breast, whereupon he grew faint, and short-breathed, and in agony; that the physicians exclaimed that the king was poisoned; that Buckingham commanded them out of the room; and committed one of them a close prisoner to his own chamber, and another to be removed from court; and that, after his majesty's death, his body and head swelled above measure; his hair, with the skin of his head, stuck to the pillow, and his nails became loose on his fingers and toes." Clarendon, who was a partisan of the Duke of Buckingham, gives a totally different account of James's death; but he does not disprove the facts alleged by Eglisham. Inquiries were instituted, but they were not strict, and all the unconstitutional influence of the powerful favourite was exerted to defeat them. In the celebrated accusations brought against Buckingham by the Earl of Bristol, the poisoning of King James was placed last on the list; and the pages of history bear evidence of the summary mode in which these accusations were for the time got rid of.

The man from whom Buckingham is said to have procured his poisons, was one Dr. Lamb, a conjurer and empiric, who, besides dealing in poisons, pretended to be a fortune-teller. The popular fury, which broke out with comparative harmlessness against his patron, was directed against this man, until he could not appear with safety in the streets of London. His fate was melancholy. Walking one day in Cheapside, disguised, as he thought, from all observers, he was recognised by some idle boys, who began to hoot and pelt him with stones, calling out "The poisoner! the poisoner! Down with the wizard, down with him!" A mob very soon collected, and the doctor took to his heels and ran for his life. He was pursued and seized in Wood Street, and from thence dragged by the hair through the mire to St. Paul's Cross, the mob beating him with sticks and stones, and calling out "Kill the wizard! kill the poisoner!" Charles the First, on hearing of the riot, rode from Whitehall to quell it; but he arrived too late to save the victim. Every bone in his body was broken, and he was quite dead. Charles was excessively indignant, and fined the City six hundred pounds for its inability to deliver up the ringleaders to justice.

CHAPTER VII.

THE MARCHIONESS OF BRINVILLIERS.

MARIE MARGUERITE D'AUBRAY, was the daughter of the Sieur D'Aubray, civil lieutenant, an employment worth about 50,000 livres per annum. She was educated with great care, and her mental accomplishments were such as to set off to the very best advantage her various personal fascinations, which were of the highest order—being, in fact, unsurpassed by any, and approached but by few, women of her times. In 1651, being then not much more than nine years of age, she was married to the Marquis de Brinvilliers, who possessed an income of thirty thousand livres, to which she brought, as dowry, two hundred thousand in addition, besides expectations of what she might receive from her family. Her husband was colonel in the regiment of Normandy, and whilst in attendance on his military duties, he made the acquaintance of Gaudin de Sainte-Croix, a young officer of cavalry, in the regiment of Tracy, a native of Montauban, and, according to the best authorities, the natural son of a French nobleman. In person, St. Croix was extremely handsome; his face had a highly intellectual expression; he was a jovial companion, a brave soldier, very susceptible of the tender passion, and excessively extravagant in his habits. Unfortunately, he was extremely needy, having nothing to depend upon but his pay as an officer, which was far from being adequate to the supply of the demands of so brilliant a prodigal as Gaudin de Sainte-Croix. The acquaintance and friendship, therefore, of so affluent a personage as the Marquis de Brinvilliers, was an acquisition which the penniless Sainte-Croix learnt how to appreciate. The marquis lent him money, invited him to his mansion, and introduced him to his wife. At this time Sainte-Croix was about twenty-eight years of age. These were opportunities of which Sainte-Croix availed himself to the utmost—so much so, indeed, that in a very short time he occupied the first place in the affections of the marchioness. At the time of her introduction to Gaudin de Sainte-Croix, Marie de Brinvilliers was about eighteen years of age. She was in the full bloom of her beauty; her figure was small but exquisitely finished; her well-formed, rounded face was charmingly delicate, and her features were the more symmetrical as they were never disturbed by any internal emotion. They seemed like those of a statue of the purest Parian marble, which, by some enchantment, had been endued with life; so that the enraptured spectators might mistake for the composure of an innocent mind that congealed and callous impassibility which was only the visible expression of feelings petrified by a hopeless remorse. From the very first moment, the marchioness and Sainte-Croix became mutually attached. As for the husband, whether it might be that he was endowed with that spirit of conjugal philosophy, then deemed essential to good taste, or whether his attention was so completely absorbed by his own pursuits, he was either blind, or else seemingly indifferent to the fact of his friend's treachery, his wife's frailty, and his own dishonour. He did not exhibit the slightest symptom of jealousy at their intimacy, and continued that reckless course of extravagance by which already he was so much involved, until at length his pecuniary embarrassments were so great, that the marchioness, who had long since ceased to care for him, and who had abandoned herself thoroughly to her new passion, demanded, and obtained, a separation. She forthwith left her husband's house; and, disdaining any further restraint, lived openly in the society of Sainte-Croix.

Her family, whose honour was unimpeached, was grievously offended at this open and notorious shame of the marchioness. Her father and brothers used every endeavour to induce her to abandon her adulterous intercourse with Sainte-Croix; but all their efforts were in vain. At length the Sieur D'Aubray had recourse to an expedient, then very common in France, for terminating the scandalous career of his daughter. This expedient was to obtain a *lettre de cachet* for the committal of her paramour to the Bastile. The arrest of Gaudin de Sainte-Croix is thus graphically described by a distinguished French writer:—

It was upon a fine autumnal morning, towards the close of 1665, that a considerable crowd had assembled upon that part of Pont Neuf which descends toward the Rue Dauphine. The object of their attention was a close carriage, the door of which a sub-officer endeavoured to open, whilst, of the four sergeants who were with him, two stopped the horses as the others seized the coachman, who had only replied to their orders to draw up by driving forwards at full gallop. They continued this struggle for some time, when suddenly one of the doors was violently opened, and a young officer in a cavalry uniform jumped out upon the pavement, closing the carriage immediately, though not so quickly as to hinder those who were nearest at the time from distinguishing a female upon the back seat, who seemed, by the extreme care taken to hide her face and figure, to have the greatest interest in concealment.

"Sir," said the young man, addressing himself in a haughty and imperious tone to the officer, "as I presume that, unless by mistake, your business relates to me alone, I request you will acquaint me who and what it is that has empowered you to stop the carriage in which I was, and which, since I have left it, I demand may be allowed to continue on its progress unmolested."

"And, first," replied the officer, without suffering himself to be intimidated by this tone and manner of the great lord—and intimating at the same time to his men to detain the carriage—"first have the goodness to answer me these questions."

"I am all attention," replied the youth, evidently retaining with the greatest difficulty his *sang froid*.

"Are not you the Chevalier Gaudin de Sainte-Croix?"

"I am captain in the regiment of Tracy."

"The same. Then I arrest you in the king's name."

"And upon what authority?"

"By that of this *lettre de cachet*."

Sainte-Croix glanced rapidly over the paper, and recognising immediately the signature of the Minister of Police, seemed now to be mindful only of the lady who had remained in the carriage, and renewed, therefore, his first demand.

"Be it so, sir," he replied to the officer; "but observe, this *lettre de cachet* bears my name alone, and, I repeat, gives you no authority to expose, as you have done, the person with whom I was to the gaze of public curiosity. I request, then, you will no longer permit the detention of my carriage. As for myself, conduct me where you wish; I am prepared to follow."

This reasonable request was complied with: the officers were ordered to release the carriage. Sainte-Croix was straightway conducted to the Bastile, and placed in a cell, into which he had barely entered when the door closed upon him.

While the bolts grated harshly upon his ear, Sainte-Croix turned round as the silvery beams of the moon streamed through the iron bars of a window, which was placed at a height of about eight or ten feet from the ground. The pale moonlight fell upon a wretched bed, leaving the rest of the gloomy apartment steeped in the blackest darkness. For a second he stood anxiously listening to the hollow reverberations of the retreating footsteps; then the overwhelming feeling of utter loneliness came over him; and as if longer restraint would have been his death, he flung himself upon his bed with a cry like that of a wild beast, cursing society for tearing him from his pleasures, and blasting the Deity by whom it was suffered. He appealed to every power—whatever might be its attributes—to come to assist him in his extremity, to restore him to liberty, and to endow him with the means of revenge. In an instant, as if his words had conjured him from the depths of the earth, a form, tall, thin, and attenuated, with long dark hair, and clothed in a black doublet, slowly entered the circle of the sickly bluish light which fell around the window, and approached the bed on which Sainte-Croix was prostrate. Naturally brave though he was, yet, so instantaneous was the apparition, so immediately consequent upon his impious prayer, that, at a period of belief in supernatural agencies and visitations, Sainte-Croix did not for one moment doubt but that the Evil One, who perpetually haunts the paths of men, had heard his wish, and appeared at his supplication. He raised himself upon his bed, feeling mechanically with his hand for his sword, whilst at every step of the mysterious being towards him, his hair stood on end, and a cold sweat hung in heavy drops upon his brow. At last this awe-inspiring apparition stopped, and fixed his eyes upon the prisoner's, who returned his gaze; then, in a deep tone of voice, thus addressed him :—

"Young man, thou hast asked for the power to revenge thyself upon man who proscribes, and defy the God who abandons, thee. This power I possess, and offer. Darest thou accept it?"

"First," demanded Sainte-Croix, "who are you?"

"Why askest thou to know who I may be, since I am here at the moment thou invokest me, and bring thee what thou hast demanded?"

"It matters nothing," replied Sainte-Croix, still under the impression that he was in the presence of a preternatural being: "when one enters into such a compact, it is immaterial with whom one acts."

"Well, then, since thou wishest to know me, I am the Italian, Exili."

Sainte-Croix shuddered. He had awoke from an infernal dream to a terrible reality; for the name he had just heard had a fearful celebrity, not only throughout France, but throughout all Italy.

In his native land, Exili was suspected of having effected numerous murders by means of the most subtle and deadly poisons. On this suspicion he was sentenced to expatriation. From Rome he came to Paris, and here, as in Italy, he soon attracted the attention of the police; but, as before, they were unable to procure the evidence which could convict the disciple of Renato and La Tofano. But though the proof was wanting, the moral evidence was amply sufficient to justify his confinement. A *lettre de cachet* was issued: Exili was consigned to the Bastile, where he had been kept for six months prior to the arrival of Sainte-Croix, who, on account of the crowded state of the prison, had been by the governor introduced into the cell of Exili. The governor was not aware that he had thus yoked together two demons.

In the dreadful gloom of the Bastile those two dark and evil natures matured their schemes of avarice and revenge. In Sainte-Croix the Italian discovered an instrument; in Exili, the Frenchman found the fiendish inspiration for which he prayed. The lover of Marie Brinvilliers desired three things—liberty, wealth, and revenge—revenge on those who had snatched him from the sensual enjoyments for which he possessed so keen a relish. All these Exili promised him, on condition that he would submit himself entirely to his instructions. Exili was no ordinary practitioner in the science of poisoning; he was an adept—equal, indeed, to the Medici and the Borgias. Murder had become to him an art which he had reduced to determinate rules; and such was the perfection at which he had arrived, that he followed it less from sordid interest, than from an uncontrollable love of experiment. To create is the peculiar attribute of Deity; the power to destroy He has delegated to man, who desires therefore to rival the Deity by destroying. This was the pride of Exili, the pale and

sombre alchemist of the unseen void, who, leaving to others the investigation into the mysteries of life, had discovered the most potent agents of death.

Before finally yielding himself to the influence of his terrible companion, Sainte-Croix for some time hesitated. At length, the bitter jesting of the Italian demolished whatever scruples were left in his soul. Exili represented the French as fools in their mode of accomplishing their revenge—perishing themselves along with the enemy whom they sought to destroy; whereas, they might, by deferring more to science and less to prejudice, survive, and enjoy life after they had transferred the object of their hatred to the silent and shadowy realms of the tomb. He sneered at the bold and inconsiderate act which exposes the murderer to a death more painful than he himself inflicts. He eulogized the wisdom of the Italian, which presents the deadly poison with a smile. The various powders and fluids of some of which it is the property to destroy by slow degrees, of others to strike down with the rapidity of the lightning, he enumerated and described to his fascinated listener. He very soon succeeded in inspiring Sainte-Croix with an interest in this terrible game by which the lives of many are placed in the power of one. He at first overlooked the experiments of Exili; next he performed them himself; and at the expiration of his year of imprisonment, when he quitted the Bastile, the pupil was well nigh the equal of his master. He re-entered the society which had expelled him, possessed of a fatal secret, by which he could inflict upon others a misery more terrible than he himself had endured. Shortly after, Exili was also set at liberty, and the Italian immediately sought and found Sainte-Croix, who, in the name of his attendant, Martin de Breuilli, hired an apartment for his instructor from a woman named Brunet, in a narrow street close to the Place Maubert. It is not known whether or not the Marchioness de Brinvilliers visited her paramour during the period of his imprisonment, but it is certain that upon obtaining his liberty, their intercourse became more intimate than before. The lady was speedily initiated into the secrets of this dreadful art which Sainte-Croix had acquired in the Bastile; she proved an apt pupil, and all at once became so enthusiastic a devotee of the diabolical science of poisoning, that she permitted neither human nor divine laws to stand in the way of her murderous and adulterous intents. She selected her own father, M. D'Aubray, as the first victim on which the skill of her lover was to be immediately exercised. This choice was determined by a variety of reasons. In the first place, M. D'Aubray was the severe censor of his daughter's infamous life; in the next place, he was a great obstacle to the undisturbed enjoyment of her criminal pleasures; thirdly, he had mortally offended Sainte-Croix by procuring his incarceration; and fourthly, his death would bring her an increase of fortune, and consequently enlarge the sphere of her sensual indulgences. The blow must be decisive. It behoved, therefore, that the strength of the poison should be tested before trying it on her father. One morning, Francois Roussell, the maid of Madame de Brinvilliers, entered the room after breakfast. Her mistress gave her a slice of ham and some preserved gooseberries. The poor girl, without a particle of suspicion, ate of what had thus been given her; but scarcely had she done so than she felt a great pain in her stomach, and as if her heart were pricked with pins; she recovered, however, and the poison being thus proved defective, the marchioness received from Sainte-Croix, after a few days, another and a more efficacious poison.

M. D'Aubray had a villa at Offemont, whither he went to pass the vacation. His daughter offered to accompany him, and the old man, believing her connexion with Sainte-Croix to be at an end, agreed to this arrangement with pleasure. Offemont was a place well adapted for the crime. Situated amid the forest of Aigne, about four leagues from Compeigne, poison might do its work before succour could arrive. M. D'Aubray set out with his daughter and a single servant. Never before had the marchioness paid such sedulous attention to her father as she now did; and for his part her repentance seemed to have increased his affection. It was then, too, the marchioness availed herself of her fearful power over her emotions, of which her features never

EARL OF SOMERSET.

indicated a trace; ever by her father's side, sleeping in the room adjoining, taking her meals with him, incessant in the most affectionate and the kindliest offices, allowing none to wait upon him but herself; and amid these cares, with her infamous project still resting upon her mind, yet maintaining a countenance so open and smiling, that not the most suspicious eye could have yet marked a lineament but that of tenderness and devotion. It was thus she presented to her father a poisoned soup. He received it from her hands, she watched him as he partook of it, and upon her face of bronze no sign appeared of the awful anxiety that must have compressed her heart. Then, when it was finished, she received, without the slightest emotion, the cup from his hand, and retired to her chamber, listening and awaiting the result. The effect was prompt; she heard her father utter some complaints and groan heavily—then, unable to endure the pain, call loudly upon his daughter. The marchioness entered.

But now her features betrayed the deepest anxiety, which M. D'Aubray sought to alleviate, considering it merely a slight indisposition, for which he was unwilling to procure medical skill. At last, however, his symptoms became so violent, the pain so unendurable, that he yielded to his daughter's entreaties, and gave orders to send for a physician. He came at eight the following morning, but only enabled to judge by the statement of the sick man, he considered this ailment to be a fit of indigestion, and prescribed accordingly, and then returned to Compeigne. The marchioness now never quitted her father. Her bed was removed to his room; she declared that she alone would tend him, and thus she could watch the progress and final conflict

No. 4.—POISONERS.

now displayed in the agonies of her father. The physician returned in the morning. M. D'Aubray was worse; his vomiting had ceased, but the pains in the stomach had become more acute, and an unaccountable heat consumed his bowels. He was advised to have recourse to a certain method of treatment which would necessitate his return to Paris. His weakness, however, was so great that it was doubtful whether it would not be preferable to stop at Compeigne; but the marchioness urged so earnestly the necessity of obtaining better assistance and advice than he could elsewhere receive, that M. D'Aubray decided upon returning home. He journeyed, reclining in his carriage, his head resting upon his daughter's bosom, for not for one moment did a word or a look betray the falsehood of her affected devotion. At last they reached Paris. Everything had proceeded according to her wish: the scene was changed; the physician, who had observed the first symptoms, would not witness the final agonies, and in tracing the progress no one could now discover the cause of the illness, the thread of inquiry was broken, and its ends were too far asunder to permit of their being reunited. Notwithstanding every attention, M. D'Aubray gradually grew worse; his daughter never quitted him. After an agony of four days he expired in her arms, bestowing, with his last breath, a blessing upon his murderess. Her grief upon this was so violent and unrestrained, that, in comparison, her brother's sorrow seemed tame and indifferent. But as no one suspected the crime, no examination of the body took place, and the tomb closed without the slightest supposition of guilt on her part.

But she was yet far from the realization of her object.

She arrived at the infernal goal of the foulest guilt, but the horizon of enjoyment had receded from her approach. She had acquired a greater freedom of action, but her father's will did not fulfil her expectations; the greater part of his property reverted to her eldest brother, and to the second, who was a parliamentary counsellor. Thus, though she had incurred guilt, which could not be expiated, her fortune was but slightly increased. Her brothers still stood in her way—they also must be removed.

CHAPTER VIII.

THE MARCHIONESS OF BRINVILLIERS (Continued).

As long as her brothers remained, the removal of her father would but little avail the marchioness and her lover. Her fortune was but slightly increased by the foul and unnatural murder. The sphere of sensual pleasure was but very little extended, though she had stained her soul with the blackest guilt. Therefore, she must go on until her fell purpose was accomplished. More murders must be committed; horrors must accumulate on horrors! For the means of carrying on her adulterous enjoyments, she had poisoned a tender and confiding father. Her brothers still stand in her path; —why should she spare them? Such is the logic of crime. Already, she had contracted guilt too deep and heinous to be forgiven upon earth; and as for another life, she either did not believe in its existence, or else she expected to be able to appease the Eternal Judge by the performance of those penances which the Church has prescribed for the restoration of her erring children.

The brothers D'Aubray inherited all the disgust and indignation which their father entertained at the dishonourable commerce of their sister with Sainte-Croix. They exerted themselves as strenuously to put an end to it; and consequently drew upon themselves the same measure of hatred and revenge.

Sainte-Croix still pursued the same gay and extravagant mode of living. Besides his carriages and equipages, he had other vehicles for his nocturnal excursions. The fashionable world in which he moved, marvelled at his wealth, which was a mystery. He was known to be the scion of a poor and obscure family, whose estates had long since been consumed. He had no lucrative state appointment. His pay as a military officer could not supply him with the means of so gay and prodigal a career. Whence, then, came his wealth? He was known to be addicted to chemical researches, and from this the ignorant believed that he had discovered the philosopher's stone, by which the baser metals could be transmuted into gold. The less credulous and more knowing, however, guessed the real sources of extravagance—viz., that Sainte-Croix was running into debt, and that, as a handsome man, he was supplied with money by some rich mistress. At the time of which we write, it was customary enough for good-looking men to be furnished with money in the same infamous manner. Sainte-Croix had a steward of the name of Martin, besides three footmen, George, Lapierre, and Lachaussee. This last quitted the service of Sainte-Croix; and, through the influence of the marchioness, was received into the house of M. D'Aubray, the counsellor. Had this gentleman been aware that Lachaussee had been in the employment of Sainte-Croix, it is probable that from his antipathy to the paramour of his sister, he would not have admitted him into his family. The fact, however, was kept secret from the unfortunate man, and Lachaussee was treated with the utmost confidence.

It appears that, before making any attempt on the brothers D'Aubray, Sainte-Croix had tried the effect of his poisons upon some other persons than the family of his mistress. He had formed the acquaintance, and was on terms of friendship, with many of the nobility and men of fortune. Amongst the latter, M. de Penautier, a millionaire, the receiver-general of the clergy, and treasurer of the estates of Languedoc; one of those men who succeed in every undertaking. Penautier was connected in business with his head-

clerk, D'Alibert, who died suddenly of apoplexy. This event was known to him before D'Alibert's family were acquainted with it; all papers relative to their partnership disappeared, and the wife and daughter of the deceased were ruined. His brother-in-law, the Sieur de la Magdalaine, upon some rumours as to his death, instituted an inquiry, but died suddenly whilst it was proceeding. In one instance, Penautier was doomed to failure. He was anxious to succeed the Sieur de Mannevillitte in the office of receiver-general of the clergy, which was of the yearly value of 60,000 livres; and Penautier, knowing that he wished to resign in favour of Sieur de Sainte-Laurent, had endeavoured to purchase its possession, in order to keep Sainte-Laurent from succeeding to the office. Penautier this time, however, laboured in vain. At the express desire of the clergy, Sainte-Laurent received the appointment. Penautier did not give up the chase; he offered Sainte-Laurent 40,000 crowns for the half-share of this appointment, which offer, however, was declined. Penautier did not despair, nor did he appear to be offended at the refusal of Sainte-Laurent. Penautier had Sainte-Croix for his friend. The lover of Madame Brinvilliers became acquainted with Sainte-Laurent, who, at the recommendation of the former, took George, one of the footmen of Sainte-Croix, into his service. Shortly after Sainte-Laurent was taken ill. The symptoms in every respect resembled those of M. D'Aubray, only the disease was more rapid. Sainte-Laurent died in twenty-four hours from the time of his being taken ill. Upon the day of his death an officer of the supreme court arrived, and on hearing of the circumstance attending his friend's illness, said to the notary, in presence of the servants, that it would be necessary to open the body. An hour after, George disappeared, without a word to any one, and without even asking for his wages. Suspicion increased; the body of Sainte-Laurent was opened; but the science of the faculty was baffled. The cause of death could not be determined. The general appearance of the body was the same as in that of the Messrs. D'Aubray, only that the intestines were marked with a great many red spots. In June, the perseverance of Penautier was rewarded; he succeeded Sainte-Laurent. The widow of the latter had her suspicions raised almost to a certainty by the flight of the servant George; and the following circumstance tended still more to confirm his guilt. An abbe, a particular friend of Sainte-Laurent, aware of the sudden disappearance of George, met him some days after in the Street de Macons, near the Sorbonne. They were both on the same side, and a hay-cart which was passing at the time, stopped up the way. George, as soon as he recognised the abbe, crouched beneath the waggon, and at the risk of being crushed as it proceeded, passed beneath it, and thus fled at the mere sight of a man whose presence recalled at once his crime, and made him tremble for its retribution. This affair, in regard to Sainte-Laurent, it has been deemed best to relate in this place, although the brothers D'Aubray had been previously disposed of. Their murder we now proceed to describe.

We have seen that Lachaussee, Sainte-Croix's footman, was received into the family of M. D'Aubray; but the marchioness and Sainte-Croix did not deem it prudent to proceed against their intended victim all at once. To avoid suspicion, they determined to make use of a poison less rapid in its action than that which had been used to murder the father D'Aubray. The adulterous pair commenced a new course of experiments, not upon animals, but upon human beings. And here we have to relate one of the most revolting and fiendish atrocities ever conceived or perpetrated at the instigation of hellish passion. Charity, the most god-like of the graces, was pressed into the service of the vilest and most infamous of depraved miscreants. The brightest attribute of true religion was used to mask the foulest design which ever emanated from the brain of Satan. The sick, the infirm, and the aged—those wrecks of humanity whose sufferings and helplessness ought to have rendered them sacred and safe from every harm, and who, one would almost suppose, might be exempted from the malignity of the lowest demons,—yes, the poor and agonized victims of disease and accident, the wretched and resistless inmates of the medical hospitals, were selected by Madame Brinvilliers for the performance of her abominable experiments, to test the efficacy of her own and her paramour's infernal concoctions.

We have observed before that the marchioness was one of the most consummate dissimulators that ever existed. An outward form, radiant as that of a celestial being, concealed a soul black and loathsome as that of the vilest of the spirits of Tophet. Beneath a face beaming with love as with beauty, she had a heart callous as the asp to the agonies of humanity. In her person was most terribly illustrated the potency of unbridled lust to transform a radiant and seraphic form, into the most abhorrent and repulsive incarnations. The Marchioness of Brinvilliers was known as a pious, humane, and charitable woman, who was always prompt to relieve the distressed, and sharing with the Sisters of Mercy the ministration to the sick, to whom she sent wine and medicine at the various hospitals. Thus, it caused no surprise to see her at the Hotel Dieu, distributing biscuits and preserved fruits to the convalescents; and, as before, her kindness was greatly lauded and gratefully acknowledged. One month after this, she revisited the hospital, to make inquiries concerning some patients, in whose welfare she had professed to feel a very great interest. She was informed that they had suffered a relapse; that fresh symptoms had supervened; that a deadly languor overcame them, beneath whose wasting influence they gradually declined, and died! Of the cause of this relapse, she could learn nothing. The physicians were completely puzzled; they declared the disease was unknown, and baffled their utmost skill. She inquired at the expiration of a fortnight; some of the patients still lingered in hopeless agony, reduced to the condition of animated skeletons, whose sole signs of life were the voice, sight, and breath. Within two months, every one of them was dead. As in their treatment when living, so in the *post-mortem* examinations of their bodies—medical science was equally foiled. The marchioness and Sainte-Croix deemed these results highly satisfactory and encouraging. Lachaussee was ordered to delay no longer, but to proceed at once to the accomplishment of his mission. One morning, M. D'Aubray ordered him to fetch a glass of water and some wine for himself and his secretary, Conste. Lachaussee obeyed; but hardly had D'Aubray touched it with his lips, when he pushed it away from him, exclaiming, "What is it you have brought?—I think you wish to poison me;" then, placing the glass before Conste, he bade him examine it and see what it contained. Conste poured a few drops of the liquid into a teaspoon; it had the taste and smell of vitriol.

Lachaussee now came forward, and said he knew what it was; that another servant of D'Aubray had that morning taken medicine, and that he had by accident brought the glass, which he used. On saying this, Lachaussee took the glass from Conste's hand, pretended to taste what it contained, declared that he was right in his supposition, and thereupon threw the remainder into the fire. As neither D'Aubray nor his secretary had taken enough of the liquid to do them any perceptible injury, the circumstance was soon forgotten. To the marchioness and Sainte-Croix, however, it was a failure, and at the risk of including many in their act of vengeance, they determined to have recourse to other means. The infatuated confidence which M. D'Aubray reposed in his servant, greatly facilitated the accomplishment of the fell design against his own and his brother's life. One would have thought that the warning which he had already received, might have sufficed to put him on his guard. Not so, however; and another and a more striking instance of Lachaussee's perfidy was equally passed over. One day M. D'Aubray went to dine at his brother's house; he took Lachaussee with him, to wait upon him at table. Lachaussee contrived to stay in the room when all the other servants had gone out for the second course, and having put some of his poison into a glass of wine, he gave it to M. D'Aubray, the civil lieutenant, his master's brother, to drink. The dose was so strong that the lieutenant rose at once in amazement from the table, exclaiming, "Brother, your man would poison me." It is scarcely credible, says the record, that an incident so

suspicious should not have been further examined; and we may add that it is still more incredible that they should have been satisfied with the same lame excuse that Lachaussee had made use of on the failure of his first attempt upon his own master—viz., that the glass had most likely been used to give medicine to one of the servants, who happened to be sick, and that the bitterness of which the lieutenant complained was the result of some sediment left behind.

Three months elapsed without the occurrence of any favourable opportunity for the resumption of the frustrated attempts; but about the beginning of April, 1670, the brothers D'Aubray went to spend the Easter holidays at Villequay. Lachaussee accompanied them, and the day after their arrival, he contrived to have a pigeon-pie placed on the table at dinner. Seven persons partook of this dish, and every one of them was suddenly attacked with severe indisposition. M. D'Aubray the civil lieutenant, was seized with pains more excruciating than any of the rest. Next to him, his brother, the counsellor, was the greatest sufferer. Three of the persons who formed the dinner party, but who did *not* partake of the pie, were not affected with any of the symptoms exhibited by the other seven. The two brothers D'Aubray returned to Paris five days after, so completely changed that they seemed the victims of a long and painful illness. It was on the 12th of April that they returned, and on the 17th of June following, M. D'Aubray, the civil lieutenant, died in great anguish. The counsellor D'Aubray held out longer, but at length, after lingering in a state of intermittent torment for about thirteen weeks, he expired in the same manner as his brother. So many and so strange deaths in one family, naturally enough, excited great curiosity and some suspicion. The bodies were opened, and an examination made by the most competent surgeons in Paris. According to the testimony of M. Bachot, the medical attendant of the D'Aubrays, it appears that for the last three days of the life of the civil lieutenant, his flesh rapidly decayed, that he was very dry, completely deprived of his appetite, and subject to frequent and painful vomitings; that he had a burning in his stomach; that after the opening of the body, the stomach had a totally black appearance; and that the liver was gangrened and burnt.

The last days and autopsy of the counsellor D'Aubray revealed pretty much the same symptoms; he had a violent fever, no appetite, the skin was hot and parched, and he manifested great restlessness of mind and body. Poison was believed to be the agent which accomplished those frightful results, but the science of the day was unequal to the task of proving it; and strange to relate, Lachaussee, whose conduct was so extremely suspicious, had not for a moment his innocence questioned. The counsellor D'Aubray was so well pleased with the services of his perfidious domestic, that he bequeathed him a legacy of one hundred crowns; and for the effectual manner in which he had performed his work, the marchioness and Sainte-Croix presented Lachaussee with one thousand crowns in addition.

The authors of these most atrocious crimes were not suspected. The marchioness went into mourning for her brothers. Sainte-Croix continued his usual career of extravagance, and things proceeded in their accustomed course. Sainte-Croix lived in the Street des Bernardins, and in a room which he had hired from a widow of the name of Brunet, in a bye-street of the "Place Maupert," were conducted his chemical investigations. Some of his experiments were also performed in the house of an apothecary named Glazer. By a just retribution, these experiments proved fatal to those engaged in them. The apothecary died; Martin, the steward of Sainte-Croix, after suffering violent pains, was at his last gasp; Sainte-Croix was also ill, and ignorant of the cause of his disease. He was unable to quit his own house; he ordered the furnace and apparatus of Glazer to be brought into his chamber, in order that he might continue his experiments. At this time, he was occupied with a poison so deadly and subtle, that its emanations were mortal. Sainte-Croix had heard of the poisoned napkin which the Dauphin, eldest brother of Charles the Seventh, had used whilst playing at tennis, and recent tradition had informed him of the poisoned gloves of Jeanne d'Albret. These were lost secrets, which Sainte-Croix expected to recover. In the midst of these infernal occupations, an accident occurred, so justly retributive in its results, that it seemed like the direct interference of that Heaven whose most sacred canons Sainte-Croix had so flagrantly defied. It was, surely, excellent sport to perceive this engineer of death "hoist with his own petard." All must admit it was even-handed justice which directed the ingredients of the poisoned furnace into the citadel of his own life. At a moment when bending over his furnace, eagerly watching the deadly preparation approaching its greatest intensity, the glass mask which he wore, as a protection against its fumes, detached itself from his face, fell into the fire, and Sainte-Croix dropped down as if smitten by a thunderbolt. His wife, surprised at his lengthened stay in the laboratory, knocked at the door; and aware of his secret and dangerous pursuits, alarmed her domestics, who broke open the door, and found the wretched man extended near the furnace, and around him the broken fragments of his mask. The circumstance of his death could not be concealed. The servants had seen the body, and could reveal the facts of the case. The commissioner of police was ordered to put everything under seal, and the widow contented herself with clearing away the furnace and the remains of the mask. The news spread rapidly. Sainte-Croix was a public character, and the rumour that he was about to purchase a place at court invested him with still greater notoriety. Among the first who heard of his death, was Lachaussee; and he, knowing that his rooms were in possession of the authorities, endeavoured to get hold of some money and papers which he declared to be his own property, and as such he reclaimed them by a requisition to that effect. He was informed that he must await the removal of the seals, and that all that belonged to him should be given up if his statements should turn out to be justified by the facts. Lachaussee was not the only one who was greatly alarmed by the sudden death of Sainte-Croix. The marchioness, to whom all the fearful secrets of the fatal cabinet were perfectly familiar, no sooner heard of the death of her paramour, than she rushed to the commissioner, and, though late at night, implored an immediate interview. The head clerk assured her that it was impossible, inasmuch as his master had retired for the night. She, however persisted in her entreaty, requesting that he might be awakened, and that he would give up to her a casket which she wished to receive unopened. The clerk was obdurate, and so she was constrained to retire, saying, she would send for it in the morning. Early the next day a man called upon the commissioner, and in the name of the marchioness offered the sum of fifty louis, if he would surrender to her the casket. The commissioner replied, that the customary formalities must be observed, after which, he assured her, that whatever was her's, would at once be faithfully given up. This decisive refusal determined her course; no time was to be lost. She set out immediately from her house, in the Street Neuve St. Paul, to her country house at Picpus; thence she went to Liege, where she took refuge in a convent.

On July 31, 1672, the property of Sainte-Croix was seized by the authorities; on the 8th of August they commenced their examination. Upon this, Alexandre Delamarre, an attorney, on behalf of the marchioness, put in a paper, declaring, that if in a casket her signature should be found affixed to a promissory note of thirty thousand livres, it was her intention to declare it void, as obtained in an illegal manner. After this preliminary formality, the door was opened in the presence of the commissioner, Ricard, and the widow of Sainte-Croix. Their first labour was to arrange the loose papers which they had found, and while so engaged a small roll dropped from amid them, on which was inscribed, "My Confessions:" but as the whole of those present believed Sainte-Croix to be unconnected with any infamous or criminal transaction, it was decided that the document should be destroyed unread. This done, they proceeded to draw up an inventory of the property. One of the first objects which arrested their attention, was the casket claimed by the marchioness.

Her eagerness to obtain possession of it had excited curiosity; they resolved to commence with its examination, and every one pressed round to see what it contained. This, however, it is best to describe by the mere reproduction of the *proces-verbal*—in such a case no language is so powerfully descriptive as the official document:—"In the cabinet of Sainte-Croix was found a small casket, about a foot square, the key to which was found on a shelf in the closet. At the opening of the casket, was found half a sheet of paper, written as follows: 'I humbly pray those into whose hands this casket may fall, to restore it with their own hands to Madame Brinvilliers, dwelling in the New Street of St. Paul, seeing that what it contains concerns her, and belongs to her only; and that there is nothing which can be of any use or profit to any other person whatsoever. And in case she be dead before me, to burn it, and all that is in it, without opening or stirring anything; and to the end that none may plead ignorance, I swear by the God whom I adore, and all that is most sacred, that nothing but the truth is here averred. And in case these, my just and reasonable intentions in this particular, be contravened, I charge their consciences, both in this and the world to come, with the discharge of mine, protesting this to be my last will. Done at Paris, this 25th day of May, 1672. Signed—Sainte-Croix.' Below, upon the same paper, were found these words: 'There is one packet directed to M. Penautier, which must be rendered him.' There was likewise found a packet sealed with eight several seals, on which was written, 'Papers to be burnt in case of death, not being of any consequence to any person. I humbly pray those into whose hands they may fall to burn them, and I charge their consciences to do it without opening the packet.' In this packet were found two others, filled with sublimate of mercury. The following catalogue is then given:—

"Item: Another packet with six seals, bearing the same inscription, in which was another sublimate of about half a pound.

"Item: Another packet, with six several seals, with a similar inscription, and containing three other packets, in one of which was found half an ounce of sublimate; in another, two ounces and a quarter of an ounce of vitriol; in the third, vitriol was also found in a prepared state. In the cabinet was moreover discovered a square-shaped phial, of about the size of a pint, full of clear water-like fluid, which M. Moreau, the physician, declared he could not tell the quality of, until he had submitted it to experiment.

"Item: Another phial of a quarter of a pint of clear water, with a whitish sediment at the bottom, of which M. Moreau declared the same as of the other.

"A little earthen pot, in which was three quarters of an ounce of opium.

"A paper, folded up, in which was two drachms of sublimate of mercury in powder.

"A little box, in which was a kind of stone called 'the infernal stone.' Another paper, in which was an ounce of opium. A piece of antimony weighing three ounces. A paper with powder, under cover, on which was written, 'To stop the flow of blood from women.' Moreau said that this was made from the flower of quince and of the core of dried quince.

"Item: A packet, sealed with six seals, on which was written, 'Papers to be burnt in case of death.' In these papers were found thirty-four letters written by the marchioness.

"Item: Another packet, sealed with six seals, which had the same superscription as the above, in which were found twenty-seven several pieces of paper, on each of which was written, 'Ten several curious secrets.'

"Item: Another packet, with six seals, on which was the same superscription as the rest, and in which was found seventy-five livres, directed to divers particular persons."

Besides these, they found in the cabinet two bonds, the one from the Marchioness de Brinvilliers, for thirty thousand francs, the other from M. Penautier, for ten thousand francs. The former was the price paid for the death of M. D'Aubray by his daughter; the latter, the price paid by Penautier for the death of Sainte-Laurent. This difference proved that, according to the tariff of

THE COUNTESS OF SOMERSET.

Sainte-Croix, parricide was dearer than assassination. As may be imagined, the contents of this cabinet greatly astonished the examiners. Suspicions started up unbidden in their minds. The strange preparations in this closet, coupled with the still stranger requests of Sainte-Croix, together with the flight of the marchioness, began to throw a terrible light upon the dark and mysterious fatality which had destroyed, in a few months, all the males of the D'Aubray family.

CHAPTER IX.

THE MARCHIONESS OF BRINVILLIERS (*Concluded*).

SAINTE-CROIX, as if desirous to continue his work of secret assassination from the tomb, had, at the moment of his death, bequeathed his poisons to his mistress and his friends. From the inventory of his dreadful cabinet, it will be seen that this infamous man did not hesitate to invoke the name of Heaven in order to conceal from the world his murderous preparations for the destruction of human life. But justice was not thus to be evaded: Sainte-Croix had already been cited to appear before the tribunal of the Eternal; and the Marchioness of Brinvilliers and the servant Lachaussee, the most dexterous and audacious of their instruments, were being fast enmeshed within the folds of righteous retribution. The first care of the officers was to analyze the contents of the packets, and to test the efficacy of the various preparations upon different animals. The following report,

by M. Guy Simons, give the results of those experiments.

After describing the elaborate preparations, subtle qualities, and fatal properties of a certain poison, Guy Simons adds:—"In water, the weight of the poison commonly throws it down; or the former rises, and the poison is precipitated. Fire consumes and dissipates what there is of harmless and pure, and leaves only an acid, pungent matter, which resists influence. The effect which the poison produces on animals is still more remarkable: wherever it spreads its malignity is uniform, vitiating all it touches, and devouring the intestines by a violent and unaccountable inflammation. But in animals the appearance of the poison is so carefully concealed that its detection is impossible; every part of the body is seemingly endowed with life, while death is circulating in the veins, but leaves no trace behind of its existence. Every kind of test has been tried—the first by pouring some drops of the liquid found in one of the phials in oil of tartar and sea-water: and nothing was precipitated at the bottom of the vessel into which it was poured: the second, by pouring the same liquid into a sanded vessel; and no matter dry or acrid to the tongue, nor scarcely any fixed salt, was found. The third was upon a Turkey hen, a pigeon, dog, and other animals; and, upon dissection, a small quantity of coagulated blood upon the ventricle of the heart was all that could be traced of its action. Two other experiments, made upon a cat and a pigeon, by a white powder, gave similar results; death was, in both cases, gradual, but left scarcely any trace of its cause."

These results proved the extent of Sainte-Croix's

chemical knowledge, and also engendered the suspicion that he had not gratuitously employed his art. The many sudden deaths which occurred amongst his acquaintances were recalled to mind. The bonds of the marchioness and Penautier seemed the covenants of blood. These, however, could not then be arrested; the marchioness was absent, and Penautier was too powerful. It was not so with Lachaussee; his strong and fervent opposition to the opening of Sainte-Croix's cabinet, his accurate knowledge of its contents, his attendance upon the brothers D'Aubray, all combined to produce the conviction in the minds of the authorities that he was the tool and the accomplice of the deceased murderer. The widow of the elder D'Aubray preferred an accusation against Lachaussee; he was arrested, and upon his person poison was found. The cause was brought before the chatelet. Lachaussee, at first, firmly denied the charge; but, after having been extended on the rack, he made the following confession. "He admitted that he was guilty; that Sainte-Croix had told him that Madame Brinvilliers had given him the poison to poison her brothers; that he had administered to them the poison in broths and water; that he had put a reddish water into the glass of the civil lieutenant at Paris, and limpid water into the pie at Villequay; that Sainte-Croix had promised him one hundred pistoles, and to retain him always in his service; and that he rendered Sainte-Croix a faithful account of the effect of the poisons; that Sainte-Croix had informed him that Madame Brinvilliers knew nothing of his poisonings; but that he (Lachaussee) believes, notwithstanding, that she was cognizant of them, because she always discoursed to him of his poisons; that she entreated him to fly, for which purpose she presented him with two crowns; that she questioned him as to the whereabouts and contents of the cabinet; and that if Sainte-Croix could have put anybody near Madame D'Aubray, the widow of the civil lieutenant, that she would have been poisoned, for that Sainte-Croix had a great mind to poison the said lady." This confession was extorted by the torture of the rack and the boots, the latter of which consisted in placing each leg of the condemned between two wooden boards, and then compressing these together by a wing of iron, after which wedges were driven down the centre of the wooden frames; the ordinary torture was four,—the extraordinary, eight wedges. The third wedge was sufficient to conquer the obstinacy of Lachaussee, he declaring his readiness to confess, upon which the torture was remitted, and the wretch, placed on a mattress, made an acknowledgment of guilt, as above detailed. In consequence of Lachaussee's statement, Penautier, Martin, and Belleguise were examined on the 21st, 22nd, and 24th of March, 1673. On the 26th, Penautier was released, Belleguise was remanded and the arrest of Martin ordered. On the 24th of March, Lachaussee was broken upon the wheel. Exili, the terrible and mysterious Italian, the principal in those crimes, disappeared, like Mephistopheles after the destruction of Faust, and he was never more heard of. Martin, at the end of the year, was released, owing to the insufficiency of the evidence against him.

It will be seen that in the declaration of Lachaussee there occurs an apparent contradiction; it is that in which Sainte-Croix is alleged to have said that he received the poison destined for her brothers from the marchioness, and yet that she knew nothing of his poisonings. As an explanation of this, it is suggested that she was cognizant only of the poisoning of her two brothers, and that Sainte-Croix kept her in ignorance of the various other murders in which he had been engaged. It is even possible that the infamous man was ashamed to let his guilty paramour know the full extent of his horrible iniquities. Be this, however, as it may, the conviction that she had contributed to the murder of her brothers was so strongly fixed in the minds of the authorities, that her arrest was determined on; and of the mode in which this was effected, we have the following very graphic account from the fluent pen of Alexandre Dumas:—

During the proceedings against Lachaussee and the other suspected parties, the marchioness had remained at Liege, and, although residing in a convent, had by no means renounced certain earthly indulgences. She be-

came reconciled to the death of Sainte-Croix, though she had loved him so much as to threaten suicide on his account, and had, moreover, appointed as his successor a person named Theria, of whom, beyond his name, no information can be obtained. But as every successive witness had implicated her, it was resolved to pursue her into the retreat where she believed herself to be in safety. This, however, was a commission of great difficulty, and requiring much discretion. Desgrais, one of the most active officers of the marshal's court, offered to undertake it. He was a handsome man, of about thirty-six or thirty-eight years of age, and his appearance in no degree betrayed the officer of police,—assuming all characters with equal ease, associating with every grade of society under his disguise, from the lowest beggar to the greatest lord. His offer was accepted. He departed, therefore, for Liege, escorted by a body of archers, and furnished with a letter from the king, addressed to the Municipal Council of Sixty, by which Louis XIV reclaimed the marchioness. Upon the perusal of this the council ordered her to be delivered up to Desgrais. This was much, but not sufficient for his purpose; he dared not arrest the marchioness in the convent, for two reasons—firstly, because, if made aware of his intention, she might conceal herself in some of those cloistered retreats known only to her superiors; and secondly, because an event of this kind, in so religious a city as Liege, would be considered a profanation, and lead to some popular excitement by the aid of which she might be enabled to escape.

Desgrais now considered what disguise he should assume, and thinking that of an abbe the least likely to excite suspicion, he presented himself at the convent gates as a fellow-countryman returning from Rome, who was unwilling to pass through Liege without paying his respects to a lady so eminent by her beauty and misfortunes as the marchioness. Desgrais had all the manners of a scion of a noble house; and, flattering as a courtier, venturous as a soldier, charming alike by his vivacity and his self-confidence, his first visit soon obtained for him the promised pleasure of another. This was not long delayed; he returned early the next day (such attention could not but be pleasing to the marchioness), and was more cordially received than before. Intellectual, and accustomed to good society, of which, lately, she had been deprived, she found in Desgrais the refined manners of her Parisian circles. Unfortunately, the charming abbe was obliged to leave Liege in a few days; he was consequently more urgent for another interview, and this was arranged for the next day, with all the usual forms of a rendezvous. He was punctual, and had been impatiently expected; but, by a conjunction of circumstances which Desgrais had doubtless pre-arranged, their agreeable conference was continually interrupted, and this precisely at the moment when witnesses were most inconvenient. He complained of this as a danger which might compromise them both, and he besought the marchioness to grant him a meeting beyond the city, in a place where they should neither be recognised nor followed. His request was denied only so long as was sufficient to enhance the value of the favour, and was finally accorded for the same evening. At the appointed place the marchioness met Desgrais, who, on taking her by the hand, made a signal—the archers advanced, the lover removed his mask, and the inamorata was a prisoner. Desgrais upon this returned immediately to the convent, produced his order from the Council of Sixty, by which he obtained access to her room, and beneath her bed he found a casket, which he instantly sealed up and brought away. The marchioness, upon seeing this casket in his hand, was for a moment completely overcome, but recovering herself, she claimed from him a paper it contained, entitled her Confessions. Desgrais refused it, and as he turned to give orders to set forward on the journey to Paris, she tried to choke herself by swallowing a pin, but this being observed, she was prevented by Claude Rolla, one of the archers. In the evening they halted for supper at which another archer named Barbier attended, and carefully removed the knives and forks, and everything with which self-destruction could be attempted. Upon this the marchioness bit a piece from the glass out of which she was drinking, but this she was prevented from swallowing. She then said that if Barbier would save her, she would amply reward him, and for that purpose proposed to him the assassination of Desgrais. This Barbier declined; adding, that for any other purpose he was at her disposal. Thereupon she asked for pen and paper, and wrote the following letter:—

"My dear Theria,—I am in the custody of Desgrais, who is forcibly conveying me from Liege to Paris. Come and release me."

Barbier took the letter, and promised to deliver it as directed, but instead of this he placed it in the hands of Desgrais. On the morrow she despatched another, acquainting him that as the escort consisted of only eight persons, four or five determined men might easily defeat them, and effect her rescue, and that she reckoned on his making this attempt. At last, anxious from not receiving any reply, nor observing any indication of an endeavour to comply with her requests, she sent a third, in which she besought Theria, if he were not able to attack the escort and free her, at least to slay two of the four horses which belonged to it, and to profit by the confusion which this would cause, to gain possession of the casket and destroy it; without this, she said that she was inevitably lost. Although Theria had never received any of those letters, yet, having heard of her arrest, he proceeded to Maestricht, through which the prisoner was to pass, and attempted to bribe the archers, offering them no less than ten thousand livres, but they refused it. At Rocroy the escort was met by M. le Counseiller Pallau, whom the parliament had empowered to meet the prisoner on the way, and submit her to an unexpected examination, so that being thus taken by surprise, she should not have time for preparation. Desgrais first made him acquainted with every previous fact, and then placed in his hand the casket which had been a point of such extreme solicitude to her. M. Pallau opened it, and found, amongst others, a paper entitled "My Confessions." This was comprised in seven articles, and commenced thus: "I confess myself to God and to you, my father," being a complete narration of all her crimes. In the first article she confessed to having been an incendiary; in the second, to have commenced her unchaste life at seven years of age; in the third, to have poisoned her father; in the fourth, her brothers; in the fifth, an attempt to poison her sister; and in the two last was a recital of strange and unheard-of debaucheries. Nothing recorded in the annals of antiquity could surpass the abominations of which this woman professed herself guilty.

Strengthened with this document, M. Pallau commenced his examination. She admitted her intercourse with Sainte-Croix, but denied being privy to his poisonings. She quitted France, she alleged, because of a misunderstanding she had with her sister-in-law. Her Confession, she declared, was penned when she was in a state of mental aberration; that she knew not what she had within her mind, being so discomposed by regret for her native country. Being interrogated on the first article in her "Confession," as to what house it was that she had set on fire, she replied that she had never done it—that when she wrote the statement, her mind was completely distracted, she being at the time in great pecuniary difficulties in a strange country, and reduced to the extremity of borrowing a few francs to preserve her from starvation.

Being questioned on the six other articles in the "Confession," she answered that she was perfectly ignorant of the matter, and that she had not the slightest recollection of ever having written such statements.

Being interrogated if she had not poisoned her father, she replied that she knew nothing of it, and gave the same answer to the question whether it was not Lachaussee who had poisoned her brothers.

Being asked if she did not know that her sister could not live long, for that she had been poisoned, she replied, "I foresaw it; for my sister was subject to the same infirmities as myself; but I have lost my memory since the Confession was written."

"Why did you leave France?"

"Because of the advice of my relations."

"For what reason was that advice given?"

"Because of the affair of my brothers."

"Have you been intimate with Sainte-Croix since he came out of the Bastile?"

"I have."

"Did not Sainte-Croix persuade you to do away with your father? and did he not supply you with certain powders for that purpose?"

"I do not remember; nor can I tell whether or not Sainte-Croix gave me any powders or drugs."

"Did not Sainte-Croix tell you that he knew the way to make himself rich?"

"I do not remember."

"Why did you promise to pay to Sainte-Croix the sum of thirty thousand livres?"

"I pretended to put this sum into the hands of Sainte-Croix, believing him to be my friend, and that he would not reveal the fact to my creditors, so that I might have something to rely on in the hour of need. I had an indemnity from Sainte-Croix, which I lost in the course of this journey."

"Was your husband cognizant of this promise?"

"He was not."

"Was the promise given before or after the death of your brother?"

"I do not recollect, nor had that anything to do with the purpose." (This statement she afterwards amended, by saying that Sainte-Croix had lent her the amount, and that he requested her to give him her acknowledgment.)

"Did you not frequently consult Glazer, the apothecary?"

"I have been twice in his house."

"Did you not write to M. Penautier, urging him to cause Martin to effect his escape?"

"If I did so it must have been to test the fidelity of Barbier Archer, in whom I pretended to have great confidence."

"What interest had you in asking the advice of M. Penautier?"

"Necessity. I implored him, if he had any friend who could help me, to employ him in my affairs."

"Why did you promise him that whatever he would advise you would do?"

"I do not know, except it be that the condition in which I then was rendered me entirely helpless."

"Wherefore did you write to Theria, at Maestricht, to take away the process?"

"I do not know that I have done so."

"Why, in your letter to Theria, did you say that you were a lost woman, unless he should be able to get the process into his hands?"

"I do not recollect."

"Did you not perceive that your father was ill in going to, and returning from, Offermont?"

"I did not."

The casket found in Sainte-Croix's cabinet having been shown her, she declared that she had no knowledge of it. All the pecuniary dealings she had with Penautier was for thirty thousand crowns, which he owed her; and that, on a subsequent occasion, her husband and herself had lent Penautier ten thousand crowns, which had been repaid; and since which she had no further transactions with him.

Such obstinate and complete denial was of no avail against the overwhelming testimony that was opposed to her. Besides the damning evidence discovered in Sainte-Croix's cabinet, and in her own flight and "Confession," the following witnesses were brought forward to convict her. First, Sergeant Cluet, who deposed that he had seen Lachaussee in the service of the Counsellor D'Aubray, and that he (Cluet) had told the marchioness that if her brother knew that Lachaussee had belonged to Sainte-Croix, he would be greatly offended. Upon this the marchioness answered, "Good God! do not tell it to my brothers, or else they will give Lachaussee the bastinade. He must get something or another to do." In consequence of this entreaty of the marchioness, he (Cluet) said nothing to the Messrs. D'Aubray on the matter, although he saw Lachaussee go every day to the residence of Sainte-Croix and M. Brinvilliers.

Edme Huet, wife of Briscier, deposed to the intimacy between the marchioness and Sainte-Croix. She said that she saw in a cabinet belonging to the said lady two little boxes, in which she saw sublimate of mercury, in paste and in powder, which she (Huet) knew very well, being the daughter of an apothecary. Huet further deposed that Madame Brinvilliers and herself dined one day together; and that the marchioness, having drank well, became very merry and communicative, and showed her a small box, saying, "Here is the wherewithal to avenge myself upon my enemies : this box is full of successions." That she (Huet) was permitted to handle the box; and that, shortly after, the marchioness, having recovered from her gaiety, exclaimed, "Good God! what have I been telling you? Do not, I beseech you, tell it to anybody."

Laurence Perrelli, who lived with Glazer, the apothecary, deposed that he had often seen a lady come to his master with Sainte-Croix; that the footman told him it was Madame Brinvilliers; that he was certain that it was to compose poisons that they visited his master, and that whenever they came, their carriage was left at a considerable distance from the house.

Marie de Villeray, a gentlewoman in the service of the marchioness, deposed, that since the death of M. D'Aubray, the counsellor, Lachaussee came to find the said lady, and spoke to her in private; further, that Brancourt had informed her that Madame Brinvilliers had caused the death of several honourable persons, and that the said lady designed to poison her sister-in-law and her children.

Francois de Grais testified to the attempt of Theria, the paramour of the marchioness, to bribe and corrupt the archers, in order to effect her escape; and Theria himself being cited, was compelled to own, that having left Maestricht, he was informed by La Violette that the marchioness contemplated committing suicide by swallowing a pin; that he (Theria) saw that she was very miserable; that what was urged against her was true; and that, in fact, she had poisoned her whole family; that she had confessed this much herself; adding, by way of extenuation, that she had been instigated by evil counsel,—that one had not always good moments.

Francois Roussel, the servant-maid, on whom the marchioness had experimented with one of her poisons, before operating on her father, deposed, that she had been in the service of Madame Brinvilliers; that one day her mistress gave her some preserves to eat on the point of the knife; that immediately after she was ill; that likewise she gave her a piece of bacon, which caused her much internal pain for a period of three years, and that she was convinced that she was poisoned. A great many more witnesses were examined, but their testimony was so similar to that which has been given, that it would be superfluous to give it here. Every one believed her guilty, although she still persisted in asserting her innocence. She entrusted her defence to M. Nivelle, one of the most celebrated advocates of the day. He admitted her adulterous intercourse with Sainte-Croix, but denied her participation in the death of her relations. These murders he imputed to the revengeful feelings of Sainte-Croix for his incarceration in the Bastile by the influence of the D'Aubray family. As to her Confession, he attacked its validity, and endeavoured to show that the evidence of an individual against himself ought not to be received. In support of this view of the case, he cited several instances in which the self-inculpations of criminals had been rejected by the judges. But, notwithstanding the ingenuity of M. Nivelle's defence, the marchioness was doomed. Indeed, before sentence was pronounced, it was apparent to every one that she could not be acquitted. Still, she continued to deny her guilt; nor were the admonitions of the judges, nor the endeavours of the ministers of religion, able to drive her to the acknowledgment of her guilt, until at length her obstinacy determined the court to try the effects of torture.

But the mere menace that the rack was to be applied sufficed to overcome the firmness of this infamous woman. She made a full confession of her guilt, and she was condemned to be drawn upon a hurdle, with her feet bare and a rope round her neck, and a burning torch in her hand, to the principal entrance of the Cathedral of Notre Dame, where she was to make full acknowledgment of her crimes in the sight of all the people; to be taken from thence to the Place de Greve, and there to be beheaded; her body was afterwards to be burnt, and her ashes to be scattered to the winds. In the interval between the trial and execution she contrived to make a very favourable impression on her ghostly adviser. She evinced great interest in theological topics, and engaged her confessor in very learned and abstruse disquisitions respecting the pains of purgatory and the thoughts and sensations of those subjected to its cleansing fires. She professed to have no fear of death, and no doubt of her final salvation. The probability, however, is that it was recklessness, and not genuine faith, which supported her; and her conduct to the priest was more likely the result of that profound hypocrisy in which all her lifetime she had proved herself so consummate an adept, than of deep and heartfelt contrition, which she pretended to feel. On her way to the scaffold we are informed that she entreated her confessor to exert his influence with the executioner to place himself next to her, that his body might hide from her view "that scoundrel Desgrais," who had so cleverly entrapped her. She also asked the ladies who had been attracted to their windows to witness the procession, what they were looking at; adding, "A pretty sight you have come to see, truly!" She laughed when on the scaffold, dying as she had lived, heartless and impenitent. On the morrow the populace came in crowds to collect her ashes, to preserve them as relics. "She was regarded as a martyred saint; and her ashes were supposed to be endowed, by divine grace, with the power of curing all diseases!" Popular infatuation has often canonized persons whose pretensions to sanctity were extremely equivocal; but the disgusting folly of the multitude in this instance has never been surpassed.

————

CHAPTER X.

MADAME LAFFARGE.

MARIE CAPELLE, afterwards Laffarge, was born in 1816. Her father was a colonel in the French army, and many of her friends and acquaintances moved in the most select circles of society. Every attention was paid to her education; and her mental accomplishments, which were of a very high order, combined with an elegant figure and an interesting expression of countenance, invested her person with no inconsiderable show of attractions. In her twenty-third year she became acquainted with M. Laffarge, who became her husband, and whose awful and mysterious death conferred on her the memorable celebrity which she is for ever destined to enjoy. As an illustration of the mode in which the important affairs of courtship and marriage are managed in France, we give Madame Laffarge's own account of her first introduction to her future husband. Her family were anxious that Marie should be provided with a husband; and her aunt, who resided in Paris, wrote to her niece, informing her that she had found a suitable man to become her future partner and protector, and inviting her to come to Paris in order to meet him.

"My aunt," she writes, "received me rather coldly. She had left the country and her friends for the appointed interview, and my day's delay had compelled the young man, who was away from his business, to defer a further appointment until the end of the week. Some information respecting him was accorded me, and I heard that he was rich, handsome, twenty-six years old, and the son of a posting-master living a short distance from Paris. I was far from sharing the general enthusiasm. Resigned to a marriage of convenience, of course I could not affect to be indifferent to the article of fortune; but while handsome features were not indifferent to me, my pride revolted from an alliance with a posting-master. I had always regarded the business as conducted by enriched vulgar contractors, versed in arithmetic, but ignorant of good breeding — vain, purse-proud, and silly. I ventured to make a remark or two to that effect, but they were received with displeasure. I was given to understand that, without beauty or fortune, I could aspire to no better match; and my aunt, in her anxiety to see me happily married and

SIR THOMAS OVERBURY.

settled, forgot that she not only wounded my vanity, but also my heart, in making me suspect the natural tenderness of her own.

"The next day M. de Martens rejoined us with mysterious looks; he had reflected on my objections, admitted their justice, and, upon reconsideration, offered me, instead of a posting-master, an iron-master. Unable to refrain from joining my aunt in laughter, I asked him where he had discovered his mine of husbands. He appeared not to relish our jocoseness, replying coldly, that he had made their acquaintance at a rich merchant's of his connexion. I had only known one iron-master, M. Muel. I knew him to be rich and educated, and that he passed, alternately, six months in Paris, and six in the Vosges. As I had been told that mining speculations conferred great local influence, my first impression was not unfavourable; and as the mania for discussing my prospects, and marrying me, was spreading amongst my relations and friends, and submit I must to the common lot, I resolved this time seriously to reflect, with the firm intention of not shrinking from the ordeal, if all the requisite conditions should unite.

"M. Martens was not possessed of positive information; he feared that the distance from Paris would frighten me, and my aunt Garat also shrank from the thought of this separation, which she regarded as little short of exile. The matter, however, did not trouble me: I had been at Strasburgh, and knew that civilization existed even a hundred leagues from Paris. Fortune annihilated distance; and as for country life, my head was still so filled with the pleasure of Corcy, that I did not fear it; and without anticipating that my future life would be so brilliant and diversified, I yet hoped that it would be peaceful, unrestrained, and hospitable.

"More precise information followed. M. Laffarge was twenty-eight years of age, of honourable family, of

No. 5.—POISONERS.

acknowledged good character, great intelligence, and desirous of carrying out his speculation to the utmost extent. He was owner of one of the finest estates in Limousin, with extensive smelting works and furnaces; he possessed two hundred thousand francs in land and vested capital, secured from the risk of his speculations, and received a large income from his iron-works. I was also told that he had been six months in Paris on business and pleasure; that his wish was to return home with an educated wife, to enliven him by her wit and talents. That he had no relations in Paris, but that his friend, M. Gautier, the deputy from Vizerche, and General Petit, a peer of France, would vouch for his position and character.

"My aunt almost forgot the hundred leagues which were to separate us, as she listened to the statement of M. Laffarge's circumstances; and I, likewise, was mightily pleased. As his person was not described, I had misgivings on that head; but on recalling to mind all the husbands of my acquaintance, I could remember so few handsome among the number, that I concluded a fatality prevented the alliance, in the same husband, of good looks and fortune.

"It became necessary so to arrange a first interview, that a possible objection on either part might be free and unembarrassing; so it was settled to take place in public, at Musard's concert in the Rue Vivienne. M. de Martens was to join us there accidentally, and introduce M. Laffarge as a friend; a conversation would ensue; and the impressions left by the meeting were to be made mutually known the next day. My aunt was so delighted with my smiling prospects, she predicted so much happiness, and rich wedding presents, and so charming a *trousseau*, that I tranquilly allowed myself to indulge in these golden dreams of the future; and, obedient this time to the dictates of common sense and the world's realities, fancied myself under the sway of reason, when not carried away by my own feelings. I saw M. Laffarge for the first time on a Wednesday. The week after was most lovely, the sky cloudless; and no presentiment of a dark future disturbed my mind.

"Ye plaintive breezes that sometimes murmur in unison with the sighing of the wretched in this world, why awakened your voice no echo in my heart? Oh! ye clouds, couriers of the tempest, why sent ye no warning thunderbolt to rouse me from my sleep? no lightnings to disclose the abyss yawning at my feet? And ye lovely stars that shone upon me from your azure thrones, could ye send no pale and prophetic messenger of futurity, in falling, to presage to the unhappy Marie her impending perdition?

"My aunt had dressed me in the colours which became me best. Strauss's exhilarating waltzes, played by the orchestra, lit up my eyes with recollections of balls and pleasure; and thus seen to advantage by M. Laffarge on his presentation, I felt in an instant that his impression was favourable.

"Not equally favourable was mine; for M. Laffarge was extremely ugly. His form and features were the most business-looking conceivable. He spoke to me a good deal, but the noisy harmony of the orchestra drowned his words; and I retired for the night with my head filled with German dances, and forgetful of the important interview.

"The first thing the ensuing morning, the natural consequence followed. I was summoned by my aunt, whom I found perusing in exultation a heap of letters, of all forms and sizes. She told me that I had made a conquest of M. Laffarge; that he was desperately in love; that he had written to ask me in marriage, and to transmit the most minute information respecting his fortune, position, and character. The letters seemed dictated by real affection, while the honourable character of the writers would not permit a suspicion of exaggeration.

"After the perusal of those letters, and the flattering encomia they conveyed, I could no longer object to M. Laffarge on the score of ugliness, nor weigh this against the great and noble qualities ascribed to him. I wished to commence the serious business of life reasonably—to make a good match,—and here was a rare opportunity, with, in addition, moral guarantees still more rare. I saw myself beloved by an excellent husband; an orphan, I found a second mother, who, kind and affectionate as she was described, would claim my tenderest affection."

Such is the description which she gives of her feelings prior to her marriage, an event which had not the effect of changing esteem into love. On the contrary, a revulsion of emotion was experienced by her as soon as the nuptial ceremony had been completed. She complains of the uncultivated tastes and coarse habits of Laffarge; and, as an instance of these, she relates that on their journey to her husband's residence, he behaved in a most unbecoming manner. "When we reached Orleans, I could scarcely support myself, and asked for a bath, in the hope of obtaining a little refreshment and repose. I had scarcely entered the room, when the door was violently shaken.

"'Madame is bathing,' said Clementine (her maid).

"'I know it. Open the door.'

"'Sir, the bathing-room is open, and it is impossible for madame to receive you.'

"'Madame is my wife, and to the devil with all ceremony.'

"'Pray do not speak so loud,' I exclaimed, somewhat petulantly. 'Wait ten minutes, and I shall be dressed.'

"'It is precisely because you are undressed that I want to come in now. Do you take me for a fool, or think that I am to be driven off for ever by your infernal Parisian modesty?'

"Clementine trembled violently, but continued to say firmly, 'Surely, monsieur will be polite the first day.'

"'Marie,' said Laffarge, 'I command you instantly to open the door, or I will break it open.'

"'Break it open, if you please; but it will not be opened by me—strength is powerless over my will; know that once for all.'

"After terrifying me by a storm of obscene imprecations, that I should shudder to write, my husband departed in a furious mood. I sunk insensible on the floor of the bath, my affectionate Clementine, in alarm, kissed my hand a thousand times to console me, and when I became calmer, left me, in tears, to seek M. Laffarge. In vain she attempted to persuade him that he had done wrong; but, on her telling him that I was ill, and that a repetition of scenes of the kind would kill me,—' So be it,' he said; 'I say no more at present, but I will bring her to reason when we arrive at Glandier.'"

As soon as she came to his house at Glandier, she wrote to her husband the following most extraordinary letter:—

"Charles, I crave pardon of you on my knees. I have deceived you. I do not love you—I love another. I esteem you. But let me die. I love another, also called Charles, handsome, noble. We have long loved. Last year another woman deprived me of his heart. I thought I should have died. For despite, I resolved to marry; and, ignorant of the mysteries of marriage, accepted your hand. I thought a kiss on my forehead would have contented you, and that you would have been to me a father. Comprehend, then, what I have suffered these three days. I respect you, but habits and character have put an abyss between us. Instead of the sweet words of love, trivial kindness, bursts of affection; nothing but those sensual feelings, which actuate you, disgust me. Him that I love I saw at Orleans, since our marriage. He has repented. He hid himself at Uzerche. I shall be an adulteress, despite of me. Let me depart. Get me horses, disguise—I will hasten off to Smyrna. I will live by my hands, or by giving lessons. Oh! throw my cloak on one of yon precipices, and give me arsenic. I cannot give you my affection, but you may take my life. Your caresses are odious to me. I have swallowed poison, but too little; tried to shoot myself, but was afraid. Save me from myself."

She continues: "I entered my chamber, summoned Clementine, and, giving her the letter, begged her immediately to give it to M. Laffarge. At her return I drew the bolt, and cast myself sobbing into her arms. The poor girl, dreadfully frightened, addressed a thousand questions to me, and I had scarcely strength to explain to her my despair, the letter I had written, and my resolution to leave the same evening.

"Clementine was terrified by this confidence, and supplicated me to endure all for a few days; to send for my family, and not expose myself to be killed by my husband in a moment of wrath.

"They struck loudly at the door. I refused to open it; and, kneeling by my bed, I wept. A more energetic summons restored my self-possession. I told Clementine to leave me alone—to open the door, and retired into the embrasure of a window that was open. M. Laffarge entered in a fearful state. He addressed to me the most outrageous reproaches—told me that I should not leave him—that he needed a wife—that he was not rich enough to purchase a mistress—that, lawfully his, I should be his in fact. He wished to approach and seize me. I told him, coldly, that if he touched me, I would leap from the window; that I recognised in him the power to kill, but not the power to pollute me.

"On seeing my paleness and energetic despair, he recoiled, and called his mother and sister, who were in the neighbouring chamber. They surrounded me, weeping; prayed me to pity their poor Charles, for the sake of their honour and their happiness, which I was about to destroy. M. Laffarge also cast himself at my knees; and my courage, firm enough to contend with injuries, softened into tears at the voice of this sorrow, and their prayers. My sister-in-law took me in her arms, and loaded me with caresses and questions. I related to her, in a few words, from the scene at Orleans, all which had chilled me; I allowed her to imagine how much I dreaded the first evening of my arrival, and what terrors I had felt. She drew her brother into a corner of the chamber, and spoke warmly with him. His mother came in turn to attempt to calm me. She promised to love me, assured me that she was proud of me, and that she would use the most maternal and affectionate attention to her daughter Marie. She entreated me to pardon her son, who, loving me to distraction, had deceived me to avoid the despair of losing me [the deception consisted in his not having informed her that he was a widower]; lastly, to convince me, she tried other means: she assured me that the country, which appeared so sadly gloomy under the wet torrents of the storm, was rich, gay, and animated on a fine day. She told me also that I should be the absolute mistress, and alter the new dwelling at will, according to my tastes and habits."

Such is Madame Laffarge's own account of her feelings towards her husband before and after their arrival at his house, and their insertion here will help to explain much in subsequent transactions, which otherwise would be doubtful or obscure. M. Laffarge determined to win the affections of his wife by redoubling his kindness towards her; and in this he so far succeeded, that she appeared not only to have become reconciled to her lot, but also to have grown enamoured of her husband. She encouraged him to take out a patent for an invention of his, and to raise money in order to carry it into effect. Some days before his departure for Paris for this purpose, she was afflicted with violent spasms, which gave her husband an opportunity of proving his affection for her. She then declared that she was indebted to her husband for her recovery, and said she would, in return, make a will in his favour.

M. Laffarge determined to give her a similar proof of his affection; for he handed her his will, by which he bequeathed all his property to her at his death. Madame Laffarge sent this document to M. Legris, a notary at Soissons. This fact took place on the 28th of October, 1839.

From this moment (the accusation goes on to state) she meditated the death of her husband, by which event she might succeed to his property. During M. Laffarge's stay at Paris, the most tender correspondence was continued between them. Every day letters passed between them expressive of the greatest affection. This correspondence continued until the middle of the month of December. At this period it became certain that M. Laffarge would obtain the patent so anxiously expected; and now his wife considered the moment had arrived to accomplish her design.

On the 12th of December she sent for arsenic to a druggist at Uzerche, under pretence of poisoning rats, which were troublesome. At the same time she expressed her desire to send her portrait to her husband, and some cakes made at Glandier. She wished that these cakes should be made by M. Laffarge's mother, who indulged this whim. The cakes were made, and, when baked, were left in Madame Laffarge's bed-room. She then prepared a box, in which she placed her portrait, a watch, shoes, music, and chesnuts; and in a separate box, some of the cakes prepared by her mother-in-law. She constantly affirmed that she had sent four of these cakes, but the examination of witnesses proved that she likewise sent another cake of a different size and description. The box was sent by the stage-coach to Paris; and it is remarkable that she requested her mother-in-law to write a note stating that these cakes were made by her own hands.

The letter in which she informed her husband that she had forwarded her portrait and the cakes, had not been found; but two letters, written by the unfortunate Laffarge himself, are in existence, containing proofs that his wife had strongly recommended to him a delicious cake.

From these letters it results that she recommended her husband to eat this delicious cake at midnight, on the 18th, and that she would eat a similar one on the same day and hour, at Glandier, so that she would be united to him in thought by an act common to both.

On the 18th, Laffarge went to the coach-office, and received the box, which he took to his lodgings. By a fortunate chance he did not open the box himself, but employed his servant, who has described accurately the articles contained in the box, and has declared that there was but one cake, and if there had been more he must have seen them. This declaration is a complete contradiction of Madame Laffarge's assertion that she sent no cakes except those made by the mother of her husband. The servant further declared, that his master broke a piece off the cake and ate it, saying, that it was his wife who sent it. Immediately afterwards, on the night of the 18th, Laffarge was attacked with vomiting, which continued him to his bed on the following day. The date of his indisposition is proved by the books of the hotel where he lodged, and by the remedies which were furnished to him on the 19th. On his death-bed, and during his agony, this unfortunate man related to his physician the fact of the cake having been sent to him, and his subsequent illness.

Whilst these extraordinary facts were passing at Paris, the wife was expressing singular apprehensions at Glandier. A letter from her husband having mentioned that he suffered from a headach, the news appeared to cause her serious uneasiness, and she expressed a determination to go to Paris, to attend on him. She expressed an apprehension that she should receive a letter sealed with black; and contrary to her custom, went to meet the postman, to see whether her apprehension would be realized.

Laffarge, though blessed with a robust constitution, was not quite recovered, when he received his patent, and returned to Glandier on the 3rd of January, 1840. His wife received him with the strongest marks of affection. She rose from her bed to come to meet him; she invited him to eat some cold turkey and truffles, but he had no sooner partaken of it than he was attacked with cholic and vomitings, which never afterwards entirely ceased. Madame Laffarge always exhibited marks of impatience whenever any person but herself wished to attend her husband, and had a violent dispute on the subject with his mother, in presence of the physician. In the meantime Laffarge's sickness made alarming progress; he felt a painful burning in his throat; he was tormented with violent cholics; and a complete interruption of the circulation of the blood proved that his end was fast approaching.

During this time his wife was continually procuring more poison, under the pretence of destroying rats. On the 5th of January, after her husband's return, she obtained some arsenic, by means of a note appended to a physician's prescription. At the same time, she sent for some arsenic to a druggist at Uzerche, who refused to deliver it. At a later period, she employed one of the workmen to procure her some arsenic at Brives. This man, after keeping it for some days, gave it her on the 10th of January. It was always under pretence of destroying rats that she procured the arsenic; and one day she told her husband that she had enough to kill a whole army of rats.

On the 11th of January, the day after that on which the workman handed her the arsenic, several circumstances occurred to excite the suspicion of the family of Laffarge. In the morning, whilst she was still in bed, Madame Laffarge asked for some milk whey, which was prepared for her by her sister-in-law, Madame Bassiere, and she drank of it. Laffarge himself expressed a wish to have some, which his sister prepared, and brought into her brother's room, who was at that moment asleep. His wife then sent her waiting-maid for the whey; and a Mademoiselle Brun, who was in bed in the same room, saw Madame Laffarge throw some white powder into the whey, and mix it with her finger. Mademoiselle Brun asked her what she had mixed in the whey, and she answered, some orange flowers. Mademoiselle Brun, not satisfied with this reply, repeated her question. Madame Laffarge affected not to hear her, and made no reply. The whey was then brought to Laffarge, who refused to take it, and it was placed on the mantel-piece.

Madame Bassiere, the sister of Laffarge, having thrown the greater part of the whey into the fire, a white powder remained at the bottom, which created no attention until Mademoiselle Brun mentioned what she had seen in the morning. This was told to Laffarge himself, who ordered what remained to be taken to a chemist at Uzerche, who examined it, and discovered arsenic, but merely said that Laffarge ought to be careful from whom he received any drink. At a later period the residue of this whey was analysed by some chemists, who discovered some arsenic in it. This happened on the 11th of January. On the same day another drink was prepared for Laffarge, composed of some wine diluted with water, sugar, and some bread. Madame Laffarge was in her husband's bed-room, with Mademoiselle Brun, who was employed near the fire-place. This lady saw Madame Laffarge take the glass which contained the drink to a press, and she heard the noise of a spoon against a vessel which she supposed was in the press. It appeared to her that Madame Laffarge had mixed something in the drink prepared for her husband. Having done this she handed the drink to him. Laffarge having drunk it, cried out, "Marie, what have you given me? it is burning me." "That is not surprising," said Madame Laffarge to Mademoiselle Brun: "he has an inflammation, and they have given him wine."

Mademoiselle Brun went near the press, and perceived traces of a white powder, and also a pot containing a similar powder. This powder was subsequently examined by chemists, who declared that it was arsenic. She asked Madame Laffarge what this powder was? She replied that it was gum. Mademoiselle Brun said that gum would dissolve. Madame Laffarge replied that she would drink out of this glass, which she did, after pouring a quantity of water into it. The following night Madame Laffarge was attacked with cholic and vomiting.

At another time, Laffarge's mother perceived her daughter-in-law mixing a white powder in a drink for her husband, when she did not think she was observed. Her mother-in-law asked her what she had mixed in the drink. She replied gum, and that she frequently did so, and at the same time she wiped the spoon carefully.

It was not only in the drink that she was alleged to mix the arsenic, but, with an inconceivable audacity, she rubbed the poisonous mineral on some flannel which was used for frictions. This flannel was examined by chemists, who proved that it contained arsenic.

Thus the unfortunate Laffarge perished, the victim of a horrible crime, in the presence of his mother, sister, and physicians, who were stupified with the symptoms, and still could not suspect a person so intimately connected with the victim. On the 13th of January, Dr. Lespinas was called in, but there were no hopes of saving Laffarge. The physician had no hesitation in affirming that Laffarge was expiring, the victim of poison.

It was a lamentable scene to see this unfortunate family at this moment. The afflicted mother threw herself on the almost inanimate body of her son, sprinkled it with her tears, and, at the same moment, was heard to exclaim, with an expression of horror, "My God! what do I see?" She had perceived Madame Laffarge resting on the dying man's bed, with her face pale, her hands joined, and some tears apparently dropping from her eyes; she seemed to be absorbed in a profound reflection. Laffarge, however, recovered from a syncope which seemed to have terminated his existence, and said to his mother, who was sobbing, "Go away; your affliction makes me ill." She was taken out of the room, and Dr. Lespinas and Madame Laffarge only remained. Immediately afterwards Laffarge exclaimed, "Amina, some drink!" He addressed his sister; but his wife handed him some water. Laffarge opened his eyes, and drank; but his lips immediately expressed a sardonic smile; and, by a motion of his head to Dr. Lespinas, he conveyed the frightful sentiment which animated him. From that moment his wife ceased to attend upon him. The next day Charles Laffarge drew his last breath. The autopsy was made, the stomach and the liquids it contained were carefully preserved and analysed, and the acid of arsenic was discovered in it.

CHAPTER XI.

MADAME LAFFARGE (Continued.)

On the 3rd of September, 1840, the trial of Madame Laffarge, for the murder of her husband, commenced at Tulle, into which, from the interest excited, flocked an immense number of strangers from all parts of the country. At a quarter past eight o'clock the judges entered and took their seats on the bench. M. Decous, Advocate-General of the Cour Royale of Limoges, appeared as the public prosecutor.

Madame Laffarge was then brought in. Her face was lividly pale and shrunk, and this was rendered still more striking by the blackness of her hair and the deep mourning in which she was dressed. Her eyes were for a time cast down, but when at length she raised them, they showed by their vivacity that she still retained her courage. A large box, containing the articles to be produced in evidence, was then placed upon the table of the court. After order and tranquillity had been established, and the jury selected, the President put the usual questions to Madame Laffarge as to her names, age, and position in society.

Madame Laffarge replied that her name was Marie Capelle (and adding, after a considerable pause), Laffarge, that she was twenty-four years old, and a proprietaire.

She listened to the reading of the indictment with perfect calmness; her features, though sad, evincing no painful emotion. Twice only she raised her eyes as though making an appeal to heaven. She was much disturbed by a short dry cough, and held a bottle of volatile salts in her hand, but she made little use of it. The Advocate-General, in the opening charge, detailed and commented on the facts narrated in the previous chapter. During his speech the paleness of the prisoner became more and more observable; but when he came to his peroration, she seemed to make an effort to recover her fortitude; she coughed more frequently, and made repeated use of her smelling-bottle. At the intercession of her counsel, M. Paillet, she was allowed an interval of repose from half-past twelve till two o'clock, and on her return she was provided with an arm-chair. The President then commenced the interrogatory of Madame Laffarge:—

"Was not your marriage with M. Laffarge negotiated by M. de Foy, the matrimonial agent?"

"No; it was effected under the auspices of Monsieur and Madame Garat. I affirm that M. de Foy had nothing to do with it."

"Is it true that in your journey to Glandier with M. Laffarge you had a pistol with you, as you stated in your letter to your husband?"

"No, I had no pistol."

"And is it true you had in your possession the poison to which you allude in the same letter?"

"No."

"How, then, do you explain this letter?"

"On the day following I was compelled to abandon my family and my previous habits, and was wretched during the whole of the journey. On arriving at Glandier, instead of finding the agreeable chateau which had been described to me, I found only a building in ruins. I was very unhappy in consequence of the rencontre which I had made at Orleans, and found myself in perfect solitude at Glandier. It was under the impression of my sad reflections that I wrote this letter, the expressions of which show the exasperated state of my mind."

"A few days after you wrote this letter did you not go to a fête at Uzerche with your husband, and had you not with him a violent altercation?"

"That scene was of M. Laffarge's making."

The President here asked the prisoner whether the dispute on this occasion had not arisen from her denying M. Laffarge the rights of a husband, and refusing to allow him to pass the night in her apartment, and whether she had not threatened to leave him and go to Egypt?

The prisoner replied that she held out no threat, but that she had refused to allow her husband to enter her apartment, in consequence of his extraordinary conduct; and that he had apologized for that conduct, and attributed it to the influence of wine.

"After this scene you were very attentive to your husband. How do you account for this sudden change from dislike to affection?"

"M. Laffarge was so kind to me, as was also his whole family, that he captivated my affections; and I

THE MARCHIONESS DE BRINVILLIERS.

had reflected that as I was married, it was my duty to do all in my power to make my husband happy."

The President then put a great number of questions o her respecting the invention by which M. Laffarge expected to realize a large fortune; the making of his will; his journey to Paris; her purchases of arsenic; the making and transmission of the cakes; the illness of M. Laffarge; her conduct to him, and his feelings manifested towards her just previous to his death; and to all of which interrogations she replied with great promptness and complete presence of mind. The examination lasted three hours, and at its conclusion Madame Laffarge was evidently in a state of the greatest exhaustion. It being now six o'clock, the court adjourned till the next morning.

On the 4th of September, two of the physicians who attended M. Laffarge during his illness were examined. One of these, M. Jules de Lespinas, in reply to the President, declared that he had no doubt that M. Laffarge's death was the result of poison.

The President then asked: "Could the poisoning have taken place without leaving traces in the throat?"

"Yes; for if it remained there only a short time it would cause no injury."

"Can a person be poisoned by means of friction?" (In allusion to the flannel saturated with arsenic.)

"No."

M. Massenat, a physician, was then examined, and said he had attended the deceased, but never suspected his being poisoned, as he was surrounded by his family. He assisted, however, in the post-mortem examination and in the experiments, and notwithstanding the acci-

dent to the crucible, was firmly of opinion that M. Laffarge was poisoned. He said the account of the experiments had been submitted to M. Orfila, and had been approved of by him.

By the President: "At what time did you obtain the approbation of M. Orfila?"

Massenat: "I am a pupil of M. Orfila, and having occasion to call on him I spoke of the affair of Madame Laffarge. He said, notwithstanding the accident to the crucible or tube, the experiments were conclusive, and that another analysis was not necessary. At a subsequent period, having heard that M. Orfila had expressed a different opinion, I wrote to him, and received the following reply: 'You have been misinformed, sir. I was never called upon to examine the body or the liquids which you have already analyzed. I am an utter stranger to the affair.'"

M. Paillet (counsel for the prisoner) here said: "Your letter is of the 31st. Wishing to enlighten myself, and knowing that in such affairs, M. Orfila is the prince of science, I wrote him, and here is his letter in reply, dated August 20th." The following letter from M. Orfila was then read:—

"Paris, August 20th, 1840.

"Sir,—You ask me in your letter of the 17th of this month, if it be necessary, in order to affirm that a liquid contained in the digestive canal of a dead body, or prepared by boiling a portion of this body in distilled water, contains arsenical acid, to obtain with it, and with sulphydric acid, a flaky yellow precipitate, soluble in ammonia. No, sir. (Profound sensation). All physicians who have written on medical jurisprudence prescribe the reduction by some process of the yellow precipitate, and to obtain from it metallic arsenic. I have long insisted in my works on the necessity of having recourse to such extraction, and have severely blamed those who, having neglected it, have concluded as to the presence of an arsenical compound in the yellow flakes in question. In the year 1830, Barreul and myself published in the third volume of the *Annales d'Hygiene*, a judicial affair, in which you will find the solution of the question you had addressed to me. Sworn examiners, whom it is not necessary to name, have raised great suspicion as to poison having been administered, merely because they had obtained, by operating on certain liquids with sulphydric acid, a yellow flaky precipitate, soluble in ammonia. We ascertained that this pretended yellow arsenical preparation did not contain an atom of arsenic when an attempt was made to reduce it, and that it was nothing else than animal matter contained in the bile. M. Chevalier has just published, in the last number of the 'Journal of Medical Chemistry,' a note, in which he announces that he has twice found, since the year 1830, a substance of this kind.—ORFILA."

M. Paillet added, that M. Orfila had not only furnished him with the books referred to in the letter, but had performed in his presence several experiments, all of which produced a negative result.

M. Massenat insisted on the correctness of his opinion.

The Advocate-General suggested that M. Orfila should be heard in court.

M. Paillet, on the part of the prisoner, assented to this, and expressed his desire that the experiments should be repeated.

The Advocate-General formally moved that M. Orfila should be called as a witness.

The President, after consulting the other judges, without granting the motion, declared that another chemical experiment should be made by scientific chemists, who had been summoned as witnesses.

M. Massenat repeated his conviction, that the precipitation of yellow flakes obtained from the stomach of the deceased, was a proof that it contained arsenic. He further stated, in reply to another observation of the President as to its having lately been discovered that arsenic existed naturally in the bodies of men, that the bones of adults were known to contain arsenic, but to extract it it must be calcined by means of Marsh's apparatus. But the process pursued with the entrails of M. Laffarge was not carried far enough to produce natural or human arsenic.

The court then appointed Messrs Dubois and Dupuytren to make the fresh experiments agreed upon. The box containing the various articles intended to be given in evidence was then opened, but they were found to be without any labels, and in such complete confusion that it was impossible to distinguish one thing from another. The court then adjourned.

Next day the court assembled at the same hour, Madame Laffarge entered, supported by her physician. She appeared to be less weak and indisposed. The box containing the matters on which the chemists were to operate was brought in, and the prisoner was called upon to verify that the seals had not been broken. Messrs. Dubois and Dupuytren, of Limoges, came into court. The President, upon the suggestion of the Advocate-General, asked the medical gentlemen whether they could make their experiments before the court and jury? M. Dubois replied that they were willing to perform such operations as they could in court, but that some of them would require a laboratory, and would produce a nauseous odour. After a short discussion, the chemists were allowed to retire with the stomach, the liquids it had contained at the time of death, and four bottles containing the matter which had previously been vomited.

Madame Laffarge, the mother of deceased, was then examined, and testified to the facts already stated, about the conduct of her daughter-in-law towards her son. About four o'clock, a message from Messieurs Dubois and Dupuytren was received, informing the court that the analysis entrusted to them was completed, and that they were prepared to deliver in their report. The President immediately ordered them to be introduced. Messieurs Dubois and Dupuytren made their appearance, and M. Dubois, sen., made the following declaration:—

"Gentlemen, we have come to render you an account of the experiment we have just made by order of the court. We declare, upon the oath which we have taken, that we have proceeded to make this experiment with all the care and prudence which the importance and delicacy of our charge required. In the first place, we bring back into court one-half of all the organic matter which was given to us—namely, 1st. One-half of the stomach, which weighed thirty-three grammes. We have operated upon only one part of it, for the rest of this matter was in such confusion, and so much dried up, that it was impossible for us to distinguish any of the organic matter. 2nd. One-half of the liquids contained in the stomach. 3rd. A little bottle containing liquid which had been vomited. 4th. A part of the vomited liquid. We have analyzed with the greatest exactitude and minutest care the matter of the stomach. Several different processes have been employed by us, in order to avoid a possibility of error. In the first place, we have applied the process most in use at the present day—that of M. Orfila. We have obtained no result, notwithstanding all our researches. In the second place, we have tried the matter without any chemical reaction, using only distilled water, boiling. This is the most rational means. This filtered water did not present any manifestation of arsenical acid. We afterwards turned our attention to the liquid of the stomach. We submitted it in its natural state to the apparatus of Mr. Marsh, and made it burn for upwards of an hour, but no metallic stain has been produced. We have also treated this liquid in its natural state, so that any confusion might be impossible. Still we failed in producing anything. There was in this liquid a suspension of brown matter, which disturbed its transparency. We analyzed this, and found it to contain salts of iron and carbonate of iron. The stomach did not afford us a particle of iron, whence we have concluded that, in consequence of the autopsy, it was entirely emptied. The matters vomited were colourless and mucilaginous. We subjected them to evaporation. We employed the apparatus of Mr. Marsh, and all the known reactions; but all without effect, as we have not in the result obtained any arsenical matter. We wish that a scientific man of the highest celebrity may be called in to confirm our opinion, which is unanimous."

These conclusions produced the strongest impression upon the audience, and half-stifled expressions of satisfaction were heard. The prisoner was in a state of the deepest emotion, and tears fell from her eyes, whilst an indescribable smile played on her lips. Her counsel was compelled to request permission for her to withdraw for an instant. M. Violene, her brother-in-law, had a violent nervous attack; and her sister, Madame Violene, directed alternately to her husband and sister looks in which delight was mingled with still remaining fear. The sitting resumed at a quarter-past five o'clock, when M. Dubois entered into a long and learned explanation of the experiments to which he had resorted. After this evidence, the Advocate-General said, that in consequence of what had occurred, it would be necessary to have a new investigation. He did not demand an adjournment of the trial, but the requirements of justice rendered the disinterment of the body of M. Laffarge necessary. The court, after a short deliberation, decided that the chemists of Limoges should, on the following day, operate on the substances which had not yet been examined by them.

Next day the Advocate-General renewed his application for the exhumation of the body, which was interred at Beyssac. To this M. Paillet, the prisoner's counsel, consented, on the condition that there should be no delay in the trial. The court consequently ordered that the exhumation should take place, and that the body be submitted to experiment. All the surgeons and chemists who had previously been engaged in the affair were formed into a commission for analyzing such of the viscera as should be found remaining in the body.

While the exhumation was going on, some witnesses were examined as to the arsenic purchased by orders of the prisoner; and some letters which passed between her and her husband during his stay in Paris were put in and read; but as these contain nothing beyond what the reader already knows, we omit them.

On the 8th of September the commissioners appointed by the Court at Tulle, after having effected the exhumation of the body of M. Laffarge, reported that on their arrival at the burying ground, they were met by the justice of the peace of Lubernac, and surrounded by an immense crowd. Large quantities of chlorate were poured out around the grave before it was opened. The coffin was a little more than three feet below the surface, and when opened the body presented a most hideous spectacle, and was so much decomposed, that, instead of the usual instruments, it was necessary, in order to take from it what was wanted, to use a spoon, which was sent for from a neighbouring village. This species of paste rather than flesh was put into earthen pots to be brought to Tulle. On their arrival, the chemists placed their alembics on the road which surrounded the Palais de Justice. Five or six furnaces were ranged in a circle, and supplied with charcoal from an enormous brazier which was kept constantly at a red heat. The heights which commanded this extraordinary scene were crowded with eager spectators, gazing on the operation of this laboratory in the open air, but they were hindered by a dense and fetid vapour from seeing much of what was going on. The odour emitted was so powerful that at the afternoon sitting it was thought it would be impossible to remain in court. The ladies, however, sustained the annoyance with astonishing resolution. Two of them were said to have applied for permission to witness the operations of the chemists, but were refused. At half-past one o'clock the court presented a most singular aspect. Every one was holding a handkerchief to the nose with one hand, and a smelling-bottle with the other. It is said that upwards of 500 smelling-bottles were sold in the course of the day. It was expected that in consideration of the feelings and health of Madame Laffarge, the proceedings would be postponed, but the jury expressed their desire that they should be continued, and the judge assented. At one time the smell was so dreadful that M. Paillet, on behalf of his client, solicited that the sitting might be adjourned till the next day. The Advocate-General objected. He admitted that he had at first been affected by the smell, but he had got used to it, and he supposed the prisoner would do the same. The jury, on being consulted by the President, decided on continuing the sitting, and the President gave orders for arrangements for preventing the smell from entering the court. These, however, were not productive of the desired result, for the court still continued to be filled with the fetid odour as long as the operations of the chemists lasted.

On the 9th the chemists appeared before the court to report the result of their experiments. The report, which was read by M. Dupuytren, commenced by stating that the commission had operated first on two-thirds of the liver, weighing when dried 120 grammes, 60 of which were dissolved in pure azotic acid, which was heated and evaporated until a friable spongy charcoal, weighing 21 grammes, had been obtained, which was pulverised, and placed in a glass vessel with 90 grammes of distilled water. This was allowed to macerate for a whole night, and on the following day was put into a small retort and boiled for an hour. The liquid was then filtered, and the result was a brown liquid, to which was added sulphydric acid, sharpened by a few drops of chlorydic acid, which formed a brown precipitate soluble in ammonia. When acted upon by the ammoniacal sulphate of copper, there was a green colour; by neutral nitrate of silver, there was a yellow precipitate; and the same result ensued from the action of ammoniacal nitrate of silver. All these precipitates became brown in a short time, and formed a new brown precipitate.

The report then proceeds as follows :—" We submitted this liquid to the test of Mr. Marsh. Whilst this was doing, some of the chemists fancied they recognised for an instant a slight garlic (arsenical) colour; others did not perceive it; some obtained a brilliant brown stain, infinitely slight; dissolved in azotic acid, it gave no brick-red colour by ammoniacal nitrate of silver. We operated on a portion of the stomach, heart, intestines, brain, bladder, and lungs, with distilled water; and for this purpose boiled the whole, cut into very small pieces, for six hours, renewing the water as it evaporated. When cold, it was filtered, and the filtered liquid was evaporated until dry. What remained in this state was divided into two portions, one of which, weighing seven grammes, was heated with thirty-one grammes of azotic acid, as in our first experiment. The charcoal which resulted was exposed for an hour to the action of boiling distilled water, and the filtered liquor was submitted to the same tests as for the first operation by Mr. Marsh's apparatus, *and we did not obtain any trace of arsenic.*"

Whilst M. Dupuytren was reading this report, a breathless attention was fixed upon him, every word was caught with intense eagerness, and even his looks were scrutinized; but no sooner had he pronounced the words, " We did not obtain any traces of arsenic," than loud bravos were uttered in every part of the court. It is impossible to describe the effect which they produced. Every woman present was in tears, and many of the men evinced their glad emotion in the same way. The countenance of Madame Laffarge, during the reading of the report, was constantly calm, and her emotion was not displayed by any external sign, except a melancholy sort of smile, which looked more like resignation than joy. M. Dupuytren then proceeded :—" We formed a new precipitate with sulphydric acid, sharpened with a few drops of chlorydic acid, and filtered. The precipitate which remained was dissolved in water, slightly ammoniacal, and then evaporated to dryness. The result was mixed with an equal weight of black flux, and placed in a reducing tube. We heated this to a red heat without obtaining any incrustation of metallic arsenic." The report was signed by the whole of the commissioners.

The Advocate-General, who appeared to be greatly disappointed at the conclusion at which the chemists had arrived, exclaimed that the prisoner might have occasion to repent the applauses she had excited, and reproved, with great acrimony, an advocate of Tulle, whom he observed to join in them.

M. Paillet, the prisoner's counsel, said he regretted these manifestations as much as any one, but they arose from honourable and humane feelings. It was shown by the report that there had been no poison administered, and every one naturally rejoiced.

The President declared that, if such demonstrations were repeated, he would order the court to be cleared.

The Advocate-General put some questions to the chemists.

M. Dubois, in reply, said, " Let the most celebrated chemists be employed. Enough of the body remains to convince the most incredulous."

M. Lespinas declared that, as a physician, he had believed there was a poison, but, as a chemist, he had not discovered any. He acknowledged his ignorance of the new process which had been used.

M. Paillet observed : " The liver, the bowels, the lungs, the bladder, the stomach, every matter that it contained, and had been vomited from it, have been analyzed. I cannot, therefore, comprehend how any doubt can be longer entertained as to the non-existence of poison."

The Advocate-General, nevertheless, maintained that the evidence against the prisoner was still strong, and therefore he should not abandon the prosecution. At half-past six the court adjourned. Madame Laffarge withdrew, evidently full of emotion, and smiling upon the audience with gratitude for the sympathy shown towards her. Madame de Violene, her sister, was hastening to rejoin her, but fainted on the steps leading to the prison-room. At seven in the evening, it was announced that the court had ordered that further experiments should be performed by chemists from Paris, and that Messieurs Orfila, Chevalier, and Devergie, had been named for that purpose. M. Paillet had been summoned to the Council Chamber of the tribunal to hear this decision. He said, with great energy, " Be it so, gentlemen; but, with your delays, you will have two corpses instead of one." The court then despatched a summons to Paris for M. Orfila and the other chemists, to perform the final experiments.

CHAPTER XII.

MADAME LAFFARGE (Concluded).

As the trial proceeded the excitement increased. Twice had science been baffled. Was, then, crime to be undetected and guilt unpunished? or was there crime in the case? Did Laffarge die a natural death? or was he poisoned? Here was the problem in the solution of which France was engaged, and in which all Europe felt interested. The result of the third analysis, to be performed by the most celebrated chemists in France, if not in the whole world, was waited for with the most intense eagerness and impatience.

On the 13th of September the Court of Assizes at Tulle sat at half-past nine. The expected arrival of the chemists from Paris attracted such an increased affluence of auditors, that when Messieurs Orfila, Ollivier, and Bussy entered, it became necessary for the gendarmes to compel several persons to withdraw, in order to make room for them. The Advocate-General announced that the nomination of the Parisian chemists had been left to the keeper of the seals, who had fixed upon the gentlemen then come into the court, and moved that all the matter which had been already analyzed should be placed in their hands, with unlimited power to carry their researches to the utmost extent. M. Paillet, on the part of the prisoner, assented, and the court gave orders accordingly, directing that all the chemists who had previously experimented should be present. MM. Orfila, Ollivier, and Bussy were then sworn. M. Orfila inquired if they were to make their experiments upon all the organic matter — as well that obtained at the exhumation, as that which was operated upon immediately after the autopsy? The President informed him that he and his colleagues were to operate on all the organic matter, but not upon that which was foreign to it, and informed him also that copies of the previous reports would be delivered to them. The chemists then withdrew.

On the next day, the 14th of September, the experiment was completed; and M. Orfila, amidst profound silence and the deepest attention, addressed the court for himself and his colleagues. He said :—

"We come to render an account of our labours. All the experiments have been made with the tests employed by the chemists who preceded us ; but we employed a certain quantity of potass, which we brought from Paris, and which those gentlemen did not think of using. Our experiments were made in the presence of at least eight members of the commission. The following are the results :—

"1. I will show that there was arsenic in the body of Laffarge. (General stupor amongst the audience at this announcement. The prisoner remained motionless.)

"2. That this arsenic does not result from the tests with which we have operated, nor from the earth which surrounded the coffin.

"3. That the arsenic extracted by us is not of that arsenical portion which exists naturally in the body of man.

"4. And finally, I shall show that it is not impossible to reconcile the diversity of results and opinions of other experiments when compared with our own.

"First. Arsenic exists in the body of M. Laffarge. We commenced our operations with treating one quarter of the stomach which remained, the matter vomited, and the liquids found in the stomach. These three matters united, being reduced to carbonization by means of nitric acid,—according to the process which I indicated for the first time eighteen months ago,—and the carbon produced having been treated with water, it was sufficient to introduce the liquid resulting from it into Marsh's apparatus to obtain a small quantity of arsenic, which is now deposited on a plate in our laboratory. A second experiment was made with the mass arising from the organs of the thorax, the abdomen, the liver, and the brain. We thought it right to divide this into two parts. The whole being at first mingled, we boiled it for some hours with distilled water ; the liquor from this, after being passed through linens, was reduced by a heat to a nearly dry matter. A portion remained undissolved, as in the case with meat when boiled—a part dissolves, the rest does not. The decoction being evaporated to desiccation, was carbonated by nitric acid in the same way as the first matter. We operated as we did before, and we again extracted arsenic from this liquid. The quantity of arsenic obtained from this decoction was nearly equal to that which we produced by the first experiment. We now deemed it our bounden duty to examine minutely the remaining portions which had not been dissolved. As we should have been impeded with a great quantity of mousse (foam) had we treated it with nitric acid, we did as I indicated eighteen months ago—we burnt it with nitrate of potass. It burnt seven hours ; and after treating this incinerated mass as before, we obtained a remarkable quantity of arsenic, which may be estimated at twelve times that which was produced by our first experiments. We did not feel it necessary to act on the totality of our produce ; we deemed it useless. We examined the piece of flesh taken from the left thigh of the corpse, and made it the subject of a distinct operation. We obtained nothing from these two pounds of muscular flesh, treated in the same manner as above. These, compared with the weight of the muscular flesh of the whole body, represent but a very small portion. The result upon this point therefore was negative. We examined a portion of the winding-sheet in which the body was wrapped ; we examined it with great care ; we boiled it in water of potass, and afterwards put the liquid into Marsh's apparatus, and we obtained nothing. This, therefore, was another negative result. Finally, we examined two of the three portions of earth collected. Our analysis was applied to those taken from immediately over and under the coffin. These two portions were boiled separately in distilled water for four hours, and produced a mass, which, on being submitted to Marsh's apparatus, did not give any arsenic. Thus, it results from the first part of my deposition, and the experiments which have been made, that there was arsenic in the fourth part of the stomach which remained in the liquids contained in the viscera and in the matter vomited, but there was not much. It results, in the second place, that in the decoction made with the organic fragments there was much, and in the solid residuum of this decoction a great deal more. It lastly results that we did not find any elsewhere.

"Second. The arsenic found did not come from the reactives employed ; these reactives had been already employed by the chemists from Tulle, and the proof that they do not contain arsenic is, that those chemists came to the conclusion that there was not any. If there had been any in the reactives, they would at least have ascertained the presence of such arsenic as might be found in them. We ought to observe that we never put Marsh's apparatus in action until we had made certain that it would operate during a quarter of an hour or twenty minutes without any accident happening. The nitric acid has been distilled with nitrate of silver. It is impossible in this state that it should contain any arsenic. No doubt can be entertained on this point. The arsenic found cannot have arisen from the earth, because the coffin remained whole with the exception of a small crevice at the bottom. Besides, the earth produced none on being analyzed.

"Third. Does the arsenic found come from that arsenical portion which is found naturally in the human body? It has been acknowledged from my experiments, which go back eighteen months, that there exists in the bones of man, and many other species of animals, an exceedingly small quantity of arsenic ; but it is equally well ascertained that by the means we have at our command we can never produce the least traces of arsenic, either from the stomach, the liver, the spleen, the kidneys, the heart, or the lungs of man. Now we have operated not upon the bones, but upon the internal organs. What we have exhibited therefore is not normal arsenic.

SAINTE-CROIX.

"Fourth. It is not difficult to explain the diversity of the results obtained by us, comparatively, to those which were furnished by the chemists who had previously examined the body and liquids. To prove this I will follow the series of operations which have been made. On the first report MM. Bardou, Lespinas, Tournadour, Massenat, and Lafosse, operated. They boiled the stomach, they treated the decoction with sulphuric acid, they obtained a yellow precipitate, flaky, and soluble in ammoniac, characters which belong to all arsenical acids. They then sought to reduce this sulphate of arsenic to its metallic state. Their tube burst. The matter they obtained did not sufficiently establish the presence of arsenic. As I said in the letter I had the honour of addressing to M. Paillet, 'Medical jurisprudence is not satisfied with suppositions—it requires positive proofs. The metal must be reproduced.' With the knowledge I have gained by making the experiments on the body of M. Laffarge, I am convinced that those gentlemen, if their tube had not been broken, would have found metallic arsenic. This first experiment, therefore, cannot be opposed to ours, because it was never brought to a conclusion. In the second report, M. Dubois and Dupuytren proceeded separately, and at first on a quarter of the stomach, afterwards on the liquids it contained, and lastly on a portion of the matter vomited. Thus there were three operations. Now we have united these three matters and made but one

No. 6.—POISONERS.

operation, and instead of acting separately upon each of the three, we have acted upon them altogether. Although we have thus acted the quantity of arsenic obtained is extremely minute. Is there anything extraordinary in this?—that an individual should have been unsuccessful in making experiments on one-third of a mass, while he who acts on the whole should be successful? Marsh's apparatus is of recent date. It has not yet been perfectly studied by every one, and even those who have studied it frequently find themselves embarrassed in using it. Thus, to-day, even when we were going to take out some arsenic which remained in it, all of a sudden, although we were certain it was still there, we could not obtain it. This arises either from the flame being too strong, the porcelain plate being put too near, or not near enough, or from a door being opened, and the draught turning the flame in another direction, or from some other causes. It is not then extraordinary that when quantities so small are being operated upon no result should be arrived at.

"Having now gone through all that I had to lay before the court, I am bound to add that no doubt can remain as to the nature of the matter we have obtained. Metallic arsenic has been collected on the plates; and the commission, composed of three persons, to whom were joined the other chemist who had previously experimented, will, I do not doubt, unanimously declare that this metal obtained on the capsules is arsenic. But this is not sufficient: it must be stated by what means we are assured it is arsenic. The stains are brown and shining; they do not attract the moisture of the air; they do not become volatilized by the cold, but the instant heat is applied, they disappear. They dissolve and detach themselves instantly, on the application of nitric acid; and this dissolution being complete, if it is evaporated into dryness, it gives a white residuum with a light yellow tint, which nitrate of silver converts into a brick red. No other substance unites in itself these characters, and therefore I am bound to conclude that the matter is arsenic."

The other chemists signified their full concurrence in all that M. Orfila had stated. The court then adjourned. Madame Laffarge shook hands with her counsel. The public withdrew in a feeling of stupor and amazement.

The evidence of M. Orfila was deemed conclusive by the jury; and, in spite of a most eloquent and ingenious defence by M. Paillet, Madame Laffarge was found guilty of the murder of her husband, and sentenced by the court to hard labour for life.

On the night following her conviction, she sank into the most abject state of lethargy; but towards morning she recovered her wonted energy, and exclaimed, "All is not over between me and my enemies; and I hope to live long enough to prove my innocence in the face of the world."

It was remarked, as a singular circumstance, that M. Raspail, the celebrated chemist and Socialist, who was summoned for the defence, was detained by an accident on his way to Tulle. It was thought that, had he arrived in time, he might in all probability have influenced the minds of the jury to return a verdict of acquittal. M. Raspail, after he heard of the result of M. Orfila's experiment, declared that " he could extract as much arsenic from any piece of old furniture as was found in Laffarge's body." And such a bold statement, it was thought, might have determined the jury, considering their previous disposition, to have disregarded M. Orfila's investigations.

M. Raspail, since he could not arrive in time enough to be of service to the accused, addressed a letter to the Parisian journals, explanatory of the part he took in the affair. He stated that he set off immediately for Tulle on receiving the following letter from Madame Laffarge :—

"I am innocent, and very wretched, sir. I suffer, and call to my aid your science and your art. Chemical experiments had restored to me a portion of that opinion by which I have been tortured for the last eight months. M. Orfila arrived, and I again fell into the abyss. I hope in you, sir, to lend to a poor calumniated woman the aid of your science. Come, and save me, now that everything abandons me.

"MARIE LAFFARGE."

M. Raspail states that he refused at first to go to Tulle, as his name was offensive to certain tribunals, and his former discussions with M. Orfila were calculated to irritate the prosecution. He requested, therefore, that some other chemist should be applied to; but, on its being observed that it was too late to do so, and the account of M. Orfila's experiments not appearing satisfactory to him, he no longer hesitated a moment, but set off at two o'clock on the morning of the 18th. On his way to Tulle, his carriage broke down no less than three times, so that it was half-past eleven at night before he arrived. All the persons at the hotel at which M. Raspail and the gentleman who fetched him alighted, came to them in tears, and, addressing his companion, said, "You have killed her. She is condemned to hard labour for life. She has counted even the seconds. You will never find consolation for it. It is your fault."

M. Raspail gives the following description of Madame Laffarge's appearance and manner:—"I saw her on the truckle bed of the prison. She is a woman devoured by grief, but which has not much effaced the regularity of her features, which must have made her a beautiful young girl, when she was in possession of for-

tune and health. Her countenance is not livid, but pale. Her black hair bound up, and her night head-dress of common calico, remind me of the gaol-dress of the female prisoners at Versailles, who frequently came under my window to thank me for services which I had rendered them. Her conversation, which is mild and captivating, retains, in humiliation and misfortune, the character of benevolence which rendered her so interesting in her prosperity. It would be difficult to find a woman who adapts her language with more discretion and goodness to the intelligence of the person with whom she converses. She always seeks to please, and never to eclipse. She plays, I understand, excellently well on the piano, and has a delightful voice. Her singing is said to be of a very superior kind. She is also well versed in more than one science, reads and translates Goethe with great facility, speaks several languages, and improvises in Italian verse with the same grace and pureness of style as in French verse."

After giving an account of the kind reception which he met with at Tulle from all classes, and of the deep sympathy exhibited in favour of Madame Laffarge, M. Raspail says, "I saw in the office of the Registrar three plates which had been deposited by M. Orfila, and took a minute description of them, and there consulted other chemists as to their mode of operation. The first two plates were the result of the action of nitric acid, but the stains they exhibited were so very small and undefined, and the indications produced by the tests were so equivocal, that I should hesitate to declare them to be arsenical stains. As to the third plate, the stains may be declared to be arsenical, but I have many serious observations to make on this point. The stains of the two first plates are small, of a yellowish grey; each of them appears like a mere breath. Those of the third plate are large, blue, and shining in the centre, and of a violet yellow at the edges. But—and pray attend carefully to this—they were only made so by the use of nitrate of potass, which M. Orfila had the precaution to bring from Paris. Upon the observation made to Orfila by some of the chemists, and particularly those of Limoges, that perhaps the nitrate of potass was not pure, he replied that he had tested its purity. But as the chemists persisted in demanding an analysis, M. Orfila, driven to his last entrenchments, said that if this experiment appeared doubtful to them, he would abandon it. Then, said M. Bussy, we must also abandon the two first plates; for they, alone, cannot constitute the basis of an accusation for poisoning. These admissions appeared to the hearers to be so grave and extraordinary, that I have been authorized to publish them. I told the chemists from whom I had these disclosures, that it would be necessary to push our investigations further, and I asked them if I might examine the tests left by M. Orfila at Tulle, in presence of an officer of justice. They replied that M. Orfila had left all his tests in the hands of M. Beries, the chemist, except his potass, his zinc, and the nitrate of potass, by means of which he had obtained the stains upon the third plate. Now, shall I tell you candidly what I think? Suppose, in the interest of the defence, I had adopted the process of M. Orfila, and had brought with me from Paris some nitrate of potass, as the only test to discover the existence of poison, where not an atom would have been discovered by any other test, what would the Advocate-General have said? He would have said, 'We require the court to order that the bottle of nitrate of potass may be immediately deposited in the hands of justice, in order that it may be examined.' And if I had refused, the Advocate-General would have demanded the record of my refusal, in order that I might be proceeded against as a false witness. Now, nothing of the kind has been done with respect to M. Orfila, and upon this single operation, which would have been suspected in me, but which has been accepted without observation in M. Orfila, Marie Laffarge has been devoted to infamy. The jury thought that the imponderable quantity of arsenic which appeared upon the plates necessarily proved the existence of arsenic in the body of the deceased. This quantity was estimated by M. Orfila at half a milligramme; but I estimate it at less than the hundredth part of a milligramme. Now, if the jury had been able to comprehend, first, that this quantity was too small to denote that Laffarge had been poisoned; and secondly, that it might have proceeded from the tests which had been brought from Paris, they could not have condemned Marie Laffarge as guilty of poisoning by arsenic."

Notwithstanding the ingenious testimony of M. Raspail, the Court of Cassation confirmed the sentence pronounced by the Court of Assizes—viz., that Madame Laffarge be exposed once in the pillory, and imprisoned for life, but the former part of this sentence was not carried into effect.

One of the circumstances which told most injuriously against this miserable woman, was some notes which she had written to young Guyet, her former lover, who, shortly after her sentence, committed suicide. The purport of these notes was to beg of him not to compromise her honour, but to save her by his silence.

Madame Laffarge suffered her sentence for a period of twelve years. In 1852, her health, which had been gradually declining, became so feeble, that the authorities granted her permission to try the baths of Ussat, in the south of France; and here, in the September of that year, in the thirty-seventh year of her age, died the woman whose name, twelve years before, had attained a world-wide notoriety.

CHAPTER XIII.

GILLES DE RETZ, THE ORIGINAL OF "BLUE-BEARD."

ON the 17th of July, 1429, the ancient city of Reims was in a state of intense excitement. An act was to be performed of the greatest importance and the deepest solemnity; an act in which the whole of France was profoundly interested, inasmuch as on it depended, in a great measure, whether France should be a free and independent nation, or the enslaved and degraded province of a neighbouring state. That act was the coronation of the dauphin, as Charles VII, the rightful sovereign of France. By this event, the English Henry VI, who laid claim to the crown and kingdom of France, was declared to be an usurper; and all patriotic Frenchmen who sighed for the liberty of their native land, and the expulsion of the stern and haughty islanders, were invited to rally round the newly-anointed monarch, to whom alone their allegiance was due, and who was to be regarded as the centre of the national unity and independence. It was not surprising, then, that the inhabitants of Reims, and the tens of thousands of nobles, knights, and soldiers, and ecclesiastics, who followed the dauphin to be present at the ceremony, should have been pervaded with feelings of exultation and awe—exultation for the novel and recent good fortune which had encouraged them to venture on so decisive a step as the coronation of the king—awe at the marvellous, and, we might almost say, miraculous agency by which that good fortune had been brought about. In any age, however mechanical and unbelieving, that agency would have been deemed astonishing in the highest degree. In the fifteenth century, it is not surprising that it should have been regarded as preternatural. We, of course, allude to Jehanne d'Arc, the world-renowned Maid of Orleans. This brave and beautiful girl, the child of two poor and simple peasants of Lorraine, by her pure and sublime faith, expelled the doubts and the despondency which had prostrated the king, the nobles, and the people of France, before their fierce invaders. Her own heroic courage she communicated to all who came within the sphere of her influence; and the timid, who before trembled at the very name of the English, demanded to be led against them. The fruits of this new-born feeling were soon manifested in the English being compelled to raise the siege of Orleans. This reverse was shortly followed by another; for Jargeau, where Suffolk had thrown himself, was attacked, and carried by the French. Beaugency was next taken; and a few days after was fought the battle of Patay, where the victorious Maid of Orleans defeated the English, who left two thousand dead upon the field, and had their great commander, Talbot, taken prisoner. After this battle of Patay (June 28th or 29th), the Maid of Orleans in-

sisted that they should push on to the sacred city of Reims, and have the king crowned with the greatest possible celerity. On the 15th of July, the dauphin made his entry; on the 17th he was to be crowned; and, as we have before observed, the marvellous circumstances which had characterized his progress and entrance, were well calculated to produce emotions of awe and exultation in the souls of the spectators. It was not, however, the king, with his agreeable countenance, undersized person, weak, and wizened legs, with his short vest of green cloth, who formed the principal object of attraction and admiration, but the beautiful girl who seemed sent from heaven for the express purpose of delivering France from her foreign tyrants. And, in truth, it was a marvel to see Jehanne d'Arc in her white armour, and on her magnificent black horse, at her side a small axe, and the sword of Sainte-Catharine. In her hand she bore a white standard, embroidered with fleurs-de-lis. On this standard, God was represented with the world in his hands, having on his right and left two angels, each holding a fleur-de-lis.

But it is not with Charles VII, nor with the Maid of Orleans, that our narrative has to do; and, however pleasing it would be to dwell on this type of womanhood in her purest and most chivalric manifestation, we must transfer our attention to another, and a far different character. In that same procession where the Maid of Orleans appeared as woman exalted to seraphic splendour, close to her—so close, indeed, that he might touch her hand—rode a being who was destined to become a synonyme for everything that is impure, unholy, horrible, and revolting in human nature. Yet, at that time, he was pure and innocent; and, judged by externals, he would be the very last of whom one would have predicated the frightful and hateful deeds which are eternally associated with his name. We now speak of Gilles de Retz, or De Rays, or De Rais, as his name is variously spelt. He was then a young man, or rather boy, of about sixteen years of age. His person was singularly handsome, and the expression of his face, particularly his eyes, which were deeply and mystically dark, was fascinating in the highest degree. Though but young, he had already greatly distinguished himself. Under the Count de Richemont, brother of the Duke of Brittany, Gilles de Retz had fought like a young lion, and his sword had drank deeply of the blood of the English. His prowess had received the highest recognition, and as a consequence, on him was devolved, on the day of the coronation, the honour of fetching from St. Remy's the holy oil, which, ever since the crowning of Clovis, had been used to anoint the monarchs of France, and without which no kingly consecration is believed to be complete. Long after this, Gilles de Retz continued to merit the confidence of his sovereign, and the gratitude of his country. In 1430, he greatly distinguished himself at the capture of Melun, and at the raising of the siege of Lagni by the English. In 1433, he again fought against the English, and as on all previous occasions, acquitted himself like a right valiant soldier. For his splendid services, the king raised him to the dignity of a marshal of France. But, unfortunately for the soul and the fame of Gilles de Retz, he was a very great lord, of wealthy family, and he largely increased his riches by marriage into the house of Thouars. He had, besides, succeeded to the possessions of his maternal grandfather, Jean de Craon, Lord of La Suze, Champtoce, and Ingrande. His annual income was most princely, and about the largest in France; and in order that he might enjoy this, he terminated his military career, and retired to his castle at Champtoce. Here he lived with all the magnificence of an oriental caliph. He maintained a troop of two hundred horsemen for his body-guard, which was more than most of the greatest princes of that age could afford. His excursions for the purpose of hawking and hunting were the wonder of all the country round, so gorgeous were the caparisons of his steeds, and the dresses of his retainers. All the year round, his castle was open, day and night, to comers of every description. He made it a rule to entertain the poorest beggars with wine and hippocrass. Every day an ox was roasted whole in his spacious kitchens, besides which, pigs and poultry, sufficient to feed five hundred persons. He was equally magnificent in his devotions.

His private chapel at Champtoce was the most beautiful in France, and far surpassed any of those in the richly-endowed cathedrals of Notre Dame, in Paris, of Amiens, of Beauvais, or of Rouen. It was hung with cloth of gold and rich velvet. All the chandeliers were of pure gold, curiously inlaid with silver. The great crucifix over the altar was of solid silver, and the chalices and incense-burners were of pure gold. He had, besides, a fine organ, which he caused to be carried from one castle to the other, on the shoulders of six men, whenever he changed his residence. He kept up a choir of twenty-five young children of both sexes, who were instructed in singing by the first musicians of the day. The master of his chapel he called a bishop, who had under him his deans, archdeacons, and vicars, each having great salaries—the bishop four hundred crowns a-year, and the rest in proportion. At that time, it was a devotion which was all the rage to have a rich chapel, with numbers of boy choristers, who were educated at large expense; for church music at this day, encouraged by the Dukes of Burgundy, was making rapid progress, and Retz maintained in princely style a large choir, with a troop of young choristers forming part of his train wheresoever he went.

He also maintained a whole troop of players, including ten dancing girls and as many ballad singers, besides morris-dancers, jugglers, and mountebanks of every description. The theatre in which they performed was fitted up without any regard to expense, and they played "mysteries," or danced the morris every evening, for the amusement of himself and household, and such strangers as were sharing his prodigal hospitality.

At the age of twenty-three he married Catherine, the wealthy heiress of the house of Thouars, for whom he refurnished his castle at an expense of a hundred thousand crowns. His marriage was the signal for new extravagance; and he launched out more madly than ever he had done before,—sending for fine singers or celebrated dancers from foreign countries to amuse him and his spouse, and instituting tilts and tournaments in his great court-yard almost every week, for almost all the knights and nobles of the province of Brittany. The splendour of Marshal de Retz's court threw completely into the shade that of the Duke of Brittany. His utter contempt for wealth was so well known, that he was charged three times its value for everything which he purchased. Swarms of parasites and panderers to his pleasures lived in his castle, and on those unworthy and disgusting creatures he lavished rewards with an unsparing hand. But the ordinary round of sensual gratifications ceased at last to afford him delight. He had obviously exhausted his powers to extract enjoyment from the affluence of wealth, and beauty, and homage with which he was surrounded. His faculties had become paralysed by satiety. He was observed to be more abstemious in the pleasures of the table, and to be indifferent to the charming dancing girls who used formerly to occupy so large a portion of his attention. He became subject to fits of gloominess and taciturnity, and his eye sometimes had an expression of unnatural wildness which may be regarded as symptomatic of incipient insanity. Still his discourse continued to be as rational as ever, his courtesy to his guests underwent no change, and the stream of visitors to the castle of Champtoce suffered no diminution; and the erudite ecclesiastics, who delighted to converse with him, gave it as their unanimous opinion that few of the nobles of France had the mental grasp and culture of Gilles de Retz. But dark and sinister rumours spread gradually over the country; murder, and even more atrocious deeds, were hinted at; and it was remarked that many young children of both sexes disappeared, and were never afterwards heard of. An old woman, called La Meffraie, was in the habit of travelling about the district, the *iandes*, and when she met children tending cattle or begging, she flattered or caressed, but always kept her face half hid by a black scarf. She enticed them as far as the castle of the Sire de Retz, and they were never more heard of. So long as the lost ones were children of country folks who might be supposed to have lost their way and wandered from home, or poor beings deserted by their parents, no complaints were made. But growing bolder with impunity, the children of towns-men were next attacked. Retz's instruments ventured into the great city of the district, into Nantes, into the known established family of an artist, and got his young brother from his wife under pretence of bringing him up as a chorister in the chapel of Retz's castle. The child was never seen again.

But no one had the courage to accuse openly so powerful a man as the Lord of Champtoce. Whenever the subject of the lost children was mentioned in his presence, he feigned the greatest astonishment at the mystery which shrouded their fate, and indignation against those who might be guilty of kidnapping them. Still the world was not wholly deceived; his name became as great a terror to young children as that of the devouring ogre in fairy tales, and they were taught to make a circuit of miles round rather than pass under the turrets of the ill-famed Champtoce.

The result of De Retz's unbounded prodigality may be readily conceived. In the course of a few years the whole of his funds were exhausted, so that he was reduced to the necessity of alienating many of his magnificent landed estates. One of these, the valuable seignory of Ingrande, was about being purchased by the Duke of Brittany, but Charles VII, at the instance of the heirs of De Retz, interfered, and issued an edict, which was confirmed by the provincial parliament of Brittany, prohibiting the marshal from alienating any portion of his paternal inheritance. De Retz was compelled to obey. He was now so stripped of all pecuniary resources that he had nothing remaining to sustain his extravagance but his allowance as one of the marshals of France. To a man of his habits existence was intolerable in this impoverished condition. How could he maintain his princely household, his costly and splendid retinue, his body-guard of cavaliers, his mimes, his morris-dancers, his dancing-girls, his choristers, his priests, and all his other parasites, which enabled him to surpass in barbaric pomp and splendour the most of the sovereign princes of his time? The sacrifice was too great for De Retz. He had not the magnanimity which would enable him to bear himself proud and erect under the burden of misfortune. He preferred infamy to poverty. He would recover more than his vanished riches; and it was in the desperate attempt to do this that he succeeded in making his name the blackest and the most horrible in the entire annals of universal crime.

CHAPTER XIV.

GILLES DE RETZ, THE ORIGINAL OF "BLUE BEARD." *(Concluded).*

"GOLD," says Christopher Columbus, "is an excellent thing. With gold one forms treasures. With gold, one does whatever one wishes in this world; even souls can be got to paradise by it." That may be; but still we believe that this same gold has sent more souls to perdition than it has ever brought to salvation. In the age to which our story refers the passion for gold was, if possible, even more ardent and all-absorbing than in the present day. The great modern idea, that man can create wealth, had not then been realized. For eight hundred years the art of alchemy captivated many exalted intellects, and commanded the implicit faith of millions. And what were the charms of alchemy, that it could exercise so potent an influence over the pursuits and imaginations of men? This: Alchemy promised to give to its true disciples pure and unlimited gold—that is, unbounded power, pleasure, and immortality. The ultimate object of alchemy was not so much to find gold as to obtain pure gold, potable gold,—the beverage which, when quaffed, was to endow with undying life and ever-blooming youth. The wonderful tale went round of an aged Sicilian herdsman, who having found buried in the earth, in King William's time, a flask of fluid gold, drank the liquor, and to his inexpressible astonishment as well as delight, found himself restored to that vigour, freshness, and beauty which he had imagined had departed never to return. It was this belief which made alchemy the master passion and pursuit of the age, and which raised the alchemist to be

EXILI.

the equal, and more than the equal, of kings. Many were the fortunes melted away in the search for that magic solvent which was to reduce every metal to the all-desired gold. Sometimes the well-nigh exhausted pursuer had his enfeebled hopes recruited and his wearied eyes refreshed by the enchanting vision of gold in his crucible. But it invariably proved to be a mirage vision, which revealed itself only to take flight, leaving the poor alchemist parched, breathless, and ruined. The unhappy wretch, abandoning now all hope in human power, denied and renounced himself, soul and God. In his despair he evoked the Devil. King of the subterranean abysses, the Devil was beyond doubt the king of gold. This principle is developed in the art of the age. See at Notre-de-Paris, and on many churches besides, the melancholy representation of the poor man who gives his soul for gold, who enfeoffs himself to Satan, kneels before the Beast, and kisses the velvet paw.

This love of gold seems as old and as universal as the human race. Gods and men were supposed to be subject to its spell. See, in Aristophanes, how the blind and inert Plutus is worried by his worshippers. They prove to him, with the greatest facility, that he is the god of gods. All the deities give place to him. Jove himself acknowledges that if it were not for Plutus he would die of hunger. Mercury, that celestial swell, resigns his trade of god, enters the service of Plutus, turns the spit, and washes the dishes. The alchemist,

selling himself to the chief of evil, was but the enthronement of Plutus in the place of Jove.

It is not then surprising that the ruined prodigal of Champtoce should have abandoned himself to the seductions of an art from which hardly any had been able to escape. To a man of De Retz's mind, the veil of mysteries which enveloped the process of the alchemist, no less than the magnificent promise of his pursuits, possessed well-nigh irresistible attractions. Add to this his necessities—that cupidity as well as his curiosity impelled him on—and then it may be readily conceived that the temptation to embark the small residue of his fortune in the crucible of the alchemist was too powerful for the impoverished lord of Champtoce to withstand.

In spite of his now wretched resources, he resolved to live in all his accustomed luxury and splendour. He would turn alchemist, and transmute iron into gold, and contrive to be the most opulent and magnificent of the lords of Brittany. Acting upon this determination, he sent to Paris, Italy, Germany, and Spain, inviting all the adepts in the science to come to him at Champtoce. The messengers he despatched on this mission were two of the most needy and unprincipled of his dependants—Gilles de Sille and Roger de Bricqueville. The latter—the obsequious panderer to his most secret and abominable pleasures—he had entrusted with the education of his motherless daughter, a child but five years of age, with permission that he might marry her at the proper time to any person he might choose, or to himself, if he liked it better. This man entered into the new plans of his master with great zeal, and introduced to him one Prelati, an alchemist of Padua and a physician of Poitou, who was addicted to the same pursuits.

"The marshal caused a splendid laboratory to be fitted up for them, and the three commenced the search for the philosopher's stone. They were soon afterwards joined by another pretended philosopher, named Anthony Palermo, who aided in their operations for upwards of a year. They all fared sumptuously at the marshal's expense, drawing him of the ready money which he possessed, and leading him on from day to day with the hope that they would succeed in the object of their search. From time to time new aspirants from all parts of Europe arrived at his castle, and for months he had upwards of twenty alchemists at work, trying to transmute copper into gold, and wasting the gold which was still his own in drugs and elixirs.

"But Gilles de Retz was not the man to abide patiently their lingering processes. Pleased with their comfortable quarters, they jogged on from day to day, and would have done so for years had they been permitted. But he suddenly dismissed them all, with the exception of the Italian Prelati and the physician of Poitou. These he retained to aid him to discover the secret of the philosopher's stone by a bolder method. The physician had persuaded him that the Devil was the great depositary of that and all other secrets, and that he would raise him before Gilles, who might enter into any contract he pleased with him. De Retz expressed his readiness, and promised to give the Devil anything but his soul, or do any deed that the Arch-Enemy might command him. Attended solely by the physician, he proceeded at midnight to a wild-looking place in a neighbouring forest. The physician drew a magic circle around them on the sward, and muttered for half-an-hour an invocation to the evil spirit to arise at his bidding and disclose the secrets of alchemy. Gilles looked on with intense interest, and expected every moment to see the earth open and deliver to his gaze the great Enemy of Mankind. At last the eyes of the physician became fixed, his hair stood on end, and he spoke as if addressing the fiend! But De Retz saw nothing except his companion. At last the physician fell down upon the sward as if insensible; Gilles looked calmly on to see the end. After a few minutes the physician arose, and asked him if he had not seen how angry the Devil looked. Gilles replied that he had seen nothing; upon which his companion informed him that Beelzebub had appeared in the form of a wild leopard, growled at him savagely, and said nothing; and that the reason why the marshal had neither seen nor heard him, was that he hesitated in his own mind as to devoting himself entirely to his service. De Retz owned that he had indeed misgivings, and inquired what was to be done to make the Devil speak out and unfold his secret. The physician replied that some person must go to Spain and Africa to collect certain herbs which only grew in those countries, and offered to go himself, if De Retz would provide the necessary funds. De Retz at once consented; and the physician set out on the following day with all the gold that his dupe could spare him. The marshal never saw his face again.

"But the eager Lord of Champtoce could not rest. Gold was necessary for his pleasures; and, unless by supernatural aid, he had no means of procuring any further supplies. The physician was hardly twenty leagues on his journey, before Gilles resolved to make another effort to enforce the Devil to divulge the art of gold-making. He went out alone for that purpose; but all his conjurations were of no effect. Beelzebub was obstinate, and would not appear. Determined to conquer him if he could, he unbosomed himself to the Italian alchemist, Prelati. The latter offered to undertake the business, upon condition that De Retz did not interfere in the conjurations, and consented, besides, to furnish him with all the charms and talismans that might be required. He was further to open a vein in his arm, and sign with his blood a contract, that he would

work the Devil's will in all things, and offer up to him a sacrifice of the heart, lungs, hands, eyes, and blood of a young child!"

The horrible monomaniac did not for a moment hesitate, but agreed to the revolting terms proposed to him. On the following night, Prelati went out alone, and after having been absent for three or four hours, returned to Gilles, who sat anxiously waiting for him. Prelati then informed him, that he had seen the Devil in the shape of a handsome youth of twenty He further said, that the Devil desired to be called Barron in all future invocations, and had shown him a great number of ingots of pure gold buried under a large oak in the neighbouring forest, all of which, and as many more as he desired, should become the property of the Marshal de Retz, if he remained firm and broke no condition of the contract. Prelati further showed him a small casket of black dust, which would turn iron into gold; but as the process was very troublesome, he advised that they should be contented with the ingots they found under the oak-tree, and which would more than supply all the wants which the most extravagant imagination could desire. They were not, however, to attempt to look for the gold till a period of seven times seven weeks, or they would find nothing but slates and stones for their pains. Gilles expressed the utmost chagrin and disappointment, and declared at once that he could not wait for so long a period; if the Devil were not more prompt, Prelati might tell him that the Marshal de Retz was not to be trifled with, and would decline all further communication with him. Prelati at last persuaded him to wait seven times seven days. They then went at midnight with picks and shovels, to dig up the ground under the oak, where they found nothing to reward them, but a great quantity of slates, marked with hieroglyphics. It was now Prelati's turn to be angry; and he loudly swore "that the Devil was nothing but a cheat and a liar." The marshal cordially joined in the opinion, but was easily persuaded by the cunning Italian to make one more trial. He promised at the same time that he would endeavour on the following night to ascertain the reason why the Devil had broken his word. He went out alone accordingly, and on his return informed his patron that he had seen Barron, who was exceedingly angry that they had not waited the proper time ere they looked for the ingots. Barron had also said, that the Marshal de Retz could hardly expect any favours from him, at a time when he was meditating a pilgrimage to the Holy Land, to make atonement for his sins. The Italian had doubtless surmised this from some incautious expression of his patron, for De Retz frankly confessed "that there were times when, sick of the world and all its pomps and vanities, he thought of devoting himself to the service of God."

Still, the infatuated miscreant persevered in his attempts to propitiate the Devil. Besides Barron, he also invoked Orient, Beelzebub, Satan, and Belial; beseeching them to grant him "gold, knowledge, and power." He had with him a young priest of Pistoia, in Italy, who promised to show these demons; and an Englishman, who helped to conjure them. It was a difficult matter. One of the means essayed, was to chart the service for All Saints' Day, in honour of the evil spirits. But this mockery of the holy sacrifice was not enough. These enemies of the Creator required something more impious still—the derisive murder of God's living image. At times, in fulfilment of the terms of his contract, De Retz would present his magician with the blood, hands, eyes, and heart of an infant, in order that they might be offered to the fiend! This sacrifice of children was, more than any other rite, relied upon to conciliate the Devil and induce him to render up the great secret. Sometimes the children were burnt alive, at other times they were cut to pieces with knives, and at other times they were poisoned. De Retz and his accomplices, in the course of their chemical investigations, had become familiar with a great variety of poisonous preparations. Some of these had the property of producing the most intolerable heat in the mouth, throat, and entrails of those to whom they were administered. The agonized victims shrieked for water, and it was De Retz's greatest delight to refuse their heartrending entreaties, and to watch their inconceivable torments. There was this additional horror attendant on this worship of the Devil, that the worshipper had gradually lost all of human appertaining to him, changed his nature, and became devil. After having killed for his master—at first, no doubt, with repugnance—he came, at length, to kill for his own pleasure. "And the said lord took more pleasure in cutting, or seeing their throats cut, than in * * * He had their throats cut behind, that they might linger the longer." He enjoyed witnessing death, and, still more, pain. These fearfully serious spectacles had at last become his pastime, and were in the light of a farce to him. The heartrending cries, the convulsive rattle of the dying, tickled his ear, and he would roar with laughter at their countenances. During the last convulsive agony he would sit—horrible vampire!—on the heart of the palpitating victim.

Still the gold for which he sighed and toiled so eagerly, and sinned and sacrificed so fearfully, refused to come and reward its worshipper; and the infatuated De Retz was in this manner lured on by the Italian from month to month, extracting from him all the valuables which he possessed, and only waiting a favourable opportunity to decamp with his plunder. But the day of retribution was at hand; for both young girls and boys continued to disappear in the most mysterious manner; and the rumours against the owner of Champtoce grew so loud and distinct, that the Church was compelled to interfere.

The Duke of Brittany paid a visit to Nantes; and the bishop, who was his cousin, and his chancellor, emboldened by his presence, proceeded to make a charge against De Retz, telling the duke that it would be a public scandal if the accusations against the marshal were not inquired into. We cannot give the Bishop of Nantes credit for a pure and disinterested abhorrence of the crimes imputed to De Retz, in demanding this investigation; because that nobleman and his reverence had frequent and bitter quarrels on questions of disputed tithes and conflicting jurisdiction; and on these occasions the Lord of Champtoce showed but small respect for the bishop and the claims of the Church. It is, therefore, only reasonable to suppose that his reverence was slightly actuated by motives of revenge, and that the destruction of the powerful and arrogant Lord of Champtoce would be agreeable to him, not wholly on the ground that such destruction was deserved, but also because in such an event the bishop would have one enemy the less to contend against.

There cannot, however, be a doubt that the requirements of religion, justice, and humanity—all of which had been most flagrantly outraged by De Retz—were promoted by the interposition of the bishop.

The Duke of Brittany, delighted at the opportunity of smiting the Lavals—the family to which De Retz belonged—entertained the charge. A tribunal was formed of the bishop, Chancellor of Brittany, of the Vicar of the Inquisition, and of Pierre de l'Hospital grand judge of the duchy. De Retz, who could undoubtedly have saved himself by flight, thought himself too strong to fear anything, and allowed himself to be taken. It could not be denied that his judges were his enemies. He therefore refused to recognise their jurisdiction. On the first day of his trial, he behaved himself with the greatest insolence. He braved the judges on the judgment seat, calling them simoniacs and persons of impure life, and declared he would rather be hanged by the neck like a dog, without trial, than plead guilty or not guilty before such execrable miscreants. But, as the trial proceeded, his confidence gradually forsook him. It was not possible to reject a crowd of witnesses and poor folk, afflicted fathers or mothers, who flocked one after the other, sobbing and wailing, and circumstantially deposing to the abduction of their children. The wretches who had been his instruments did not spare him when they saw that he was hopelessly lost. The confession of Prelati first made the judges acquainted with the fiendish pursuits of this monster. Nearly a hundred children of the villagers around his two castles of Champtoce and Machecoue had within three years been missed, the greater part of whom were immolated to the lust or the cupidity of this incarnate demon. He imagined that he thus made the Devil his friend, and that his recom-

pense would be the secret of the philosopher's stone. The revelations of his instruments overcame his fortitude. He no longer denied the charge, but gave way to tears, and made his confession—a confession which absolutely horrified those who heard it, judges and priests habituated to hear avowals of crime. The crimes of De Retz were strange and well-nigh unexampled, and the judges crossed themselves as they heard. "All that the Neros of the empire, or the tyrants of Lombardy did, was nothing in comparison. To equal it, there must be added all the accursed crimes covered by the Dead Sea; and, besides this, the sacrifices to those execrable gods who devoured children."

In the town of Champtoce, there was found a tun-full of calcined bones—children's bones in such number, that it was supposed there must have been full forty of them. A like quantity was found in the privies of the Castle of La Suze, and in other places; in short, wherever he had been. Everywhere, he felt the necessity of killing. The number of children destroyed by this exterminating fiend was computed to be a hundred and forty.

De Retz and Prelati were both found guilty, and condemned to be burned alive. "Sad to tell," though having lost all idea of good, of evil, or of judgment, De Retz had to the last a comfortable opinion of his safety. The wretch thought that he had secured, at one and the same time, God and the Devil. He did not deny God, but strove to keep fair with Him, thinking to corrupt his Judge by masses and processions. The Devil he only trusted to discreetly, taking care to make his reservations, and offering him everything "save his life and his soul." This reassured him when, parting from Prelati, he addressed him with sobs in the following strange terms:—"Adieu, Francois, my friend. May God grant you patience and knowledge, and rest assured, provided you have patience, and hope in God, we shall meet in the joys of Paradise."

He was sentenced to be burnt, and was placed at the stake, but not burnt. Out of respect for his powerful family, and for the noblesse at large, he was strangled before the flames could touch him. His body was not reduced to ashes. "Damsels of high estate" carried him from the meadows of Nantez, where the pile had been raised,—bore off the corpse with their own noble hands, and, assisted by some nuns, gave him honourable burial in the Carmelite Church. Prelati, not having the advantage of being nobly connected, was burned alive.

Marshal de Retz had pursued his horrible career for fourteen years, without any one's daring to accuse him; and he never would have been accused or sentenced, but for the singular circumstances of three powers, ordinarily opposed to one another, seeming to have agreed together in order to get rid of him. These three powers were the Duke of Brittany, the Bishop of Nantes, and the king. The duke saw the Lavals and Retzes occupying a line of fortresses on the Marches of Maine, Brittany and Poitou; the bishop was the personal enemy of Retz, who respected neither churches nor priests; and the king, to whom he had rendered services, and on whom, perhaps, he counted, was no longer inclined to protect the brigands who had done his cause so much injury. It is melancholy to think that De Retz, though unquestionably the greatest, was not the only nobleman addicted to the unspeakable infamies which have rendered his name eternally and preeminently execrable. The historian of this dreadful epoch observes, on the punishment of De Retz, "An act of justice which depended on so rare a union of circumstances, was not likely to be repeated, and there was hardly an instance of punishment overtaking a man of similar rank. Others, perhaps, were as guilty." * * * But Retzes were found out and punished in the lower ranks. "This year (1440) a man was hung at Paris who was wont, when he saw a baby or any infant, to snatch it from its mother, and cast it into the fire without pity." It was indeed a frightful age, this fifteenth century. "The fear of God, and respect for use—these two curbs of the feudal times—were broken. The barons hated their kindred all the same as their enemies. For safety's sake, indeed, it was better to be enemy than kith or kin. At this epoch, fathers and brothers appear

MADAME LAFFARGE.

to have been unknown. The Count de Harcourt keeps his father in prison his life long; the Countess de Foix poisons her sister; the Sire de Giac, his wife,—' and when she had drunk the poison, he made her mount behind him on horseback, and rode fifteen leagues in that state; then the said lady died incontinently. He did this in order to marry Madame de Tonnerre.' The Duke of Brittany starved his brother to death, and that publicly: the passers-by heard with horror the piteous voice which implored the charity of a morsel of bread. One evening (January the 10th), the Count Adolphus of Guelders tore his aged father from his bed, dragged him on foot five leagues without shoes or stockings through the snow, and then flung him into a sewer ! ! !" These are a few samples of the crimes of the age; but, monstrous as they unquestionably were, there can be no doubt that they were all thrown into the shade by the stupendous villanies of Gilles de Retz.

CHAPTER XV

THE MARCHIONESS DE GANGES.

(Abridged from Dumas' "Celebrated Crimes.")

IT was towards the close of the year 1657, that a very plain carriage, and without any armorial bearings, stopped at a late hour in the evening before a house in the Rue Hautefeuille, where two others stood ready in waiting. The servant had his hand upon the door, which he was about to open, when he was stopped by a mild, though rather tremulous voice, intimating as to the place. A window was immediately let down, and a head appeared so completely enveloped in a black satin hood,

that no one feature was visible; and, after a close observation of the front of the house, as if expecting to discover some sign, the fair incognita seemed satisfied, for she turned to her companion, and said; "It is quite right; there is the name." The door was now opened; the two ladies got out; and, after looking at a small board nailed beneath the windows of the second floor, upon which was printed, "Madame Voisin, Midwife," glided rapidly up a little court, the door into which was but partly closed, and which was only lighted sufficiently to show the narrow winding staircase which led from it to the apartments above. The unknown visitors, however, one of whom seemed to be of superior rank, did not stop upon the floor to which the board seemed to guide them; but, as if familiar with the place, continued their ascent still higher. Upon reaching the landing-place of the second storey, they were stopped by a dwarfish-looking figure, strangely dressed after the mode of the Venetian buffoons of the sixteenth century, who extended a wand as they approached him, and demanded, at the same time, what was the object of their visit.

"To consult the spirit," replied the visitant, in the same mild and gentle tones.

"Enter, then, and wait," answered the dwarf, drawing aside a tapestry hanging, and ushering the two ladies into an ante-room.

They remained there for about half-an-hour, hearing nothing, seeing nothing; till, suddenly, a door in the tapestry was opened, and, upon a voice in the distance giving order for their admission, the ladies were instantly conducted into another room hung with black, and lighted only by a single lamp suspended from the ceiling. The door closed upon them as they entered and stood in the presence of the sibyl.

This was a woman of about twenty-six years of age,

LAFFARGE ATTENDED BY HIS WIFE.

who, contrary to the usual custom of the fair sex, evinced an inclination to appear elderly. She was dressed in black, her hair arranged and hanging in plaits, after the manner of the Egyptian statues; her neck, arms, and feet were bare; the girdle round her waist was fastened by a large garnet, which cast a lurid glare, and she had a divining rod in her hand. She was seated on a kind of platform, representing the ancient tripod, from whence a subtle pungent incense was diffused. Her features, though vulgar, were tolerably handsome, and her eyes, doubtless owing to some mystery of her toilet, seemed of an extraordinary size, and, like the garnet, to shine with a strange, unearthly light.

As they entered they observed the sibyl, her head resting upon her hand, as one absorbed in thought; and fearing to disturb her ecstatic reverie, they waited in silence her recovery from this abstraction. After an interval of ten minutes she raised her head, and, seemingly aware for the first time of the presence of her two visitors, she exclaimed, "What desire they of me again? Shall I never enjoy repose but in the tomb?"

"Forgive me," answered the applicant, "but I sought to know——"

"Silence," replied the sibyl, in a solemn voice; "I seek no knowledge of your affairs; you must address the spirit, who is a jealous spirit, forbidding all intimacy with his mysteries; for myself, I can but pray for you, and obey him."

At these words she descended from her tripod and entered an adjoining room, from whence she soon returned, apparently more pale and agitated than before, holding in one hand a chafing dish, and in the other a red paper. The lamp was at the same time gradually dimmed; so that, discernible only by the glare from the brazier, every object assumed a fantastic form, as it seemed half emerging from the gloom, to the no small terror of the two strangers, who felt, however, it was now too late to recede. The enchantress placed the burning chafing dish in the middle of the room; then, presenting the red paper to the lady who had addressed her, she said,—

"Write here what you desire to have foretold."

It was received by more firmness than might have been expected: the incognita placed herself at the table and wrote:—

"Am I young? Am I handsome? Am I a maid, wife, or widow? Thus much for the past.—Ought I to marry? Should I remarry? Shall I enjoy a long life, or meet with an early death? Thus much for the future."

Then, extending her hand towards the sibyl, she inquired where she was to place the paper.

"Roll it round this ball," she replied, giving her at the same time a small one of white wax, "both will be consumed in these flames before your eyes. The spirit already knows the secret of your destiny; within three days expect his reply."

The incognita obeyed, and the ball was thrown into the fire.

No. 7.—POISONERS.

"All that is requisite is now fulfilled," said the sibyl. "Comus,"—hereupon the dwarf entered—"conduct the lady to her carriage."

The lady laid a purse upon the table, and followed by the other, who was a confidential servant, quitted the house by a private staircase, leading to another entrance where the carriage awaited them, and bore them rapidly away in the direction of the Rue Dauphine. Three days after, the fair incognita found upon awaking, on her dressing-table, a letter thus addressed—"To the beautiful Provençale;" and expressed in these words :—

"You are young, you are beautiful, you are a widow; thus much for the present. You will remarry, you will die young, and meet with a violent death; thus much for the future.—THE SPIRIT."

The paper was similar to that on which the inquiry had been written. A tremour came over the reader of this mysterious epistle ; for the answer as concerned the past was so true that it confirmed the dread of a similar correctness with respect to the future. In fact, the fair unknown visitant was no other than the beautiful Marie de Rosseau, called, before her marriage, Mademoiselle de Chateaublanc, the name of one of the estates of her wealthy maternal grandfather, Johannis de Nocheres. At thirteen years of age she was married to the Marquis de Castellane, a nobleman of high rank, who traced his descent from John of Castile, the son of Peter the Cruel, and Joanna de Castro, his mistress. Proud of the charms of his youthful bride, the marquis, who was commandant of the king's galleys, hastened to present her at the court of Louis XIV, who, struck by her enchanting appearance, had danced with her twice during the same evening, to the great despair of the most eminent beauties of the day ; and, moreover, to crown her reputation, Christina of Sweden, then residing at the court, had declared, that in all the kingdoms she had visited, she had never seen the rival of the "fair Provençal." This praise had produced such an effect, that henceforth even the terms of its expression became the only designation of the Marchioness de Castellane. The favour of Louis XIV, and the commendation of Christina, produced the natural consequences. The marchioness was quite the rage ; and Mignard, but just ennobled, and appointed painter to the king, added still more to his celebrity, by obtaining permission to paint her portrait, which still exists ; but as the reader may desire to possess some idea of the aspect of the heroine of this tale, and may not have seen the portrait of the artist, we shall extract one from the description given in 1667, by the author of a little work, entitled, "The Authentic Narrative of the principal Circumstances connected with the lamentable Death of the Marchioness de Ganges ;" upon which, and the " Recital of the Death of the Marchioness de Ganges," published at Paris, in 1667, by Jacques Legental, this narrative is founded.

Her complexion was strikingly fair, yet relieved by a ruddy tint, which, far from predominating, seemed to blend with it in a manner art could not have reached by the most delicate gradation of its colours. The effect of this was increased by the rich jet black hair, which fell luxuriantly around a forehead of most exquisite proportions. Her eyes were large and dark, chastened in their expression, yet still so piercing as to forbid a fixed look upon them ; her teeth were the befitting ornaments to a mouth, which from its size, form, and delicately-shaped outline, was unequalled ; the nose, well-defined and regular, giving to her face an air of dignity, which commanded and blended respect with admiration. In every feature was the hue and freshness of health, grace was in all her looks, in every movement of her lips, and the slightest gesture of her head ; her figure corresponded with the rest, and her step and carriage were becoming the charms of one whom nature had so prodigally endowed. It may be readily supposed that amid the court of Louis XIV, she could not escape the calumnies of jealous rivals, but these were always pointless, so becoming, even in the absence of her husband, was the conduct of the marchioness. Her conversation, in general restrained, and at all times more sound than brilliant, offered a decided contrast to the frivolous and fantastical discourse of the *beaux esprits* of the period ; so that many who paid their court to her without success, unwilling to believe that rejection arose from any deficiency of attractive qualities on their part, industriously whispered that the marchioness was nothing but a beautiful statue. But it was to no purpose that such things were said and repeated in her absence ; the moment she entered a room, that instant the charm of her eye and smile, and the irresistible influence of words well-chosen, tersely and elegantly expressed, overcame even the most strongly predisposed against her, and all were forced, even reluctantly, to confess that they had never seen a creature approach so near to perfection. Thus, in the full enjoyment of a celebrity scandal could not diminish nor slander vilify, her days went by, when she heard of the shipwreck and loss of her husband, with the fleet which he commanded. The marchioness behaved on this, as on every former occasion, with the utmost piety and discretion. Although she could not, by reason of his long absence, or the circumstances of their early union, feel acutely for his loss, she not only retired from the court, to the house of her mother-in-law, Madame de Ampus, but withdrew entirely from society, during the time prescribed.

She determined to spend a portion of her mourning in the cloister ; and it was here that, with all the enthusiasm of the poor recluses of the convent, she first heard of the Marquis de Ganges, whose reputation for personal beauty was as great as her own. This was so much the topic of discourse, it was so constantly impressed upon her that nature seemed to have formed them for each other, that her curiosity was excited. The marquis, on his part, owing doubtless to a similar suggestion, had conceived an earnest desire to be introduced to the Marchioness de Castellane ; and availing himself of the kindness of her grandfather, M. Nocheres, arrived at the convent, and visited its beautiful recluse. She recognised him at first sight ; for never hitherto having met with so handsome a cavalier, it was impossible but that he who now stood before her should be the Marquis de Ganges, the object of so much animated conversation in the convent parlour. The natural result followed ; the marchioness and marquis met frequently, and became mutually attached. They were both young ; the marquis of noble rank and holding a high situation ; the marchioness was rich ; the union therefore was in every respect suitable, and was delayed only until the time of mourning expired ; and the marriage was finally celebrated towards the beginning of the year 1658.

The marquis was twenty, and the marchioness twenty-two. They were for a time perfectly happy ; the marchioness forgot the prediction, or thought of it only to feel surprise at the influence it had exerted upon her mind. But happiness of this kind finds not its dwelling-place in this world : it is at best a vision ever fleeting, always insecure. It was the marquis to whom it first became insipid. Two children, a son and daughter, had tended to cement their union. Yet, prompted by the remembered excitement of his former pleasures, he neglected the society of the marchioness to rejoin that of his early friends ; and the marchioness re-entered the brilliant society which she had quitted for the enjoyments of home, and where a fresh succession of triumphs awaited her. This excited the jealousy of the marquis, who, too much a man of the world to incur the ridicule attending its display, concealed the passion within his heart, from whence it again issued in the form of sneers, sarcasms, or slighted neglect. This continued until the marquis, under various pretexts, lived almost entirely separated from his wife. Notwithstanding this treatment, her conduct was uniformly patient, endearing, and discreet ; and it would be difficult to find upon any other woman so pre-eminently attractive, a similar unanimity of opinion.

They were thus situated when the marquis, to whom even the occasional society of his wife had become insupportable, invited his two brothers, the Chevalier and the Abbe de Ganges, to reside with him.

The abbe, who bore this title without belonging to the church, was a kind of "fine wit," a ready composer of madrigals and fugitive pieces, and handsome, although in moments of irritation his eyes became singularly expressive of ferocity. He was otherwise a libertine in the widest sense of the word, and as unabashed and shameless as if he had been really one of the profligate clergy of that period. The Chevalier de Ganges, who participated in the personal advantages so profusely bestowed upon his family, was one of those men who journey on from youth to age, indifferent alike to good and evil, unless their tendencies are directed by some mind more powerful than their own.

This was the position of the chevalier with respect to his brother; obeying an influence unknown, and against which he would have revolted like a self-willed child had he even possessed the capability of indulging such a suspicion. He was but a machine, regulated by the will of another mind—the tool of the bad passions of another heart—the more dangerous, as being unrestrained by the slightest ray of reason or of instinct to counteract the impulse which governed his career. To a limited degree the abbe possessed a similar power over the marquis; a younger brother, consequently portionless, and although wearing the costume of the church, without a benefice, he contrived to persuade the marquis—wealthy not only by his own inheritance, but by the property of his wife—that it was requisite, for the good management of his estates, to appoint a confidential agent, which office he himself proposed to fill.

The marquis, weary of his domestic solitude, and averse to business, willingly accepted his proposal, and the abbe arrived, bringing with him the chevalier, who followed him as his shadow, and to whom, generally, no more attention was paid than to a cipher.

The marchioness often afterwards said, that upon their first introduction, although their manners and appearance were unexceptionable, she had felt a presentiment of evil; and that the prediction of the sibyl, so long forgotten, flashed upon her mind like a gleam of lightning. But the effect was different with the brothers. The beauty of the marchioness had attracted the attention of both, though not in the same manner: the chevalier gazed in ecstacy upon her, as he would have contemplated a beautiful statue—it was unimpassioned admiration, and, if left to himself, perfectly harmless. The abbe, on the contrary, was impressed by a determined and violent desire to possess this the most beautiful woman he had ever seen; but, a perfect master of his feelings, he gave expression merely to those familiar phrases of gallantry which are understood to mean nothing, both by those who utter and by those who hear them; nevertheless, before the close of their first interview, the abbe had decided, with the firmness of his irrevocable will, that the marchioness should be his. He succeeded in rendering himself extremely agreeable; and soon after his introduction into the house the domestic happiness of the marchioness was restored to even more than its original integrity. The love of her husband was, seemingly, rekindled, and glowed with all its pristine fervour and brightness. As for her, she had never ceased to love the marquis; and now, when she found that her passion was reciprocated, her heartfelt delight invested her charms with a fresh and a dazzling radiancy.

Whilst in this hopeful and unsuspicious condition, the marchioness and her family received an invitation from a neighbouring lady to pass a few days at her house. During their residence here a hunting party was formed, and the abbe, whose manners made him agreeable at all parties of pleasure, undertook for that day to be the attendant cavalier of his sister-in-law. The marchioness, with her accustomed condescension, accepted his proffered services. It happened then as it invariably does—the dogs had the benefit of the run; two or three amateurs kept up with them, and the rest straggled in all directions. The abbe, as squire to the marchioness, had not quitted her for a single moment; but by his customary adroitness had obtained the opportunity for a *tete-a-tete*, which she had long very carefully avoided. The moment the marchioness perceived his intention of avoiding the chase, she endeavoured to frustrate it by riding in an opposite direction to the one she had first taken, but the abbe laid his hand upon her bridle. The marchioness could not, and would not, give occasion for a quarrel; she contented herself, therefore, with waiting for his explanation, assuming at the same time that proud, disdainful look and manner which women so readily adopt when they wish their suitors to understand they have nothing to hope from them.

There was a moment's silence, which the abbe was the first to break. "Madame," said he, "you will, I trust, excuse the means I have taken to secure this interview; but since, notwithstanding my relationship, you seem disposed to deny me the favour of this *tete-a-tete*, had I ventured to request it, I thought it advisable to deprive you of the power of its refusal."

"If, sir," said the marchioness, "you have hesitated so much to make so simple a request,—and have felt such precautions necessary to compel my attention,—it arises, doubtless, from your consciousness that the proposal you have to make is not one becoming me to hear; you will have the goodness to reflect, therefore, before you commence the conversation at which you hint; for I warn you that here, as elsewhere, I shall reserve to myself the right to decide the extent to which I may permit you to proceed."

"Upon that point," he answered, "be assured that whatever topic I may select, you will favour me with your attention to its close; but for the present it is useless to disturb yourself upon a matter so trifling, for I would now merely ask you, have you of late remarked any alteration in your husband's conduct towards you?"

"I have,—and daily offer my gratitude to Heaven for the happiness which I now enjoy."

"You were wrong to do so," he continued, with one of those smiles his features alone could assume; "Heaven has nothing to do with the matter: rather offer thanks for your matchless charms. Heaven will still have other claims upon you, without depriving me of the gratitude which is my due."

"I do not comprehend you," said the marchioness, in a proud and distant manner.

"Well, then, my dear sister, I will explain. I am the cause of the miracle; it is to me, therefore, that your thanks belong."

"You are right, sir: if you be really the cause to whom I owe this happiness, you have every claim upon my gratitude,—and to Heaven also it is due, for the mercy which inspired the good thought."

"Yes, madam, but the same influence exercised for good may be employed for evil, if I am deprived of the reward which I expect."

"What mean you, sir?"

"Simply this, madam, that in my family there is but one will; that will is mine—that my brother's thoughts take their direction from mine as the waves roll before the wind, and he who can blow hot can blow cold."

"I still wait your further explanation."

"Well, then, since you are unwilling to understand me, I will be at once more frank with you. My brother's jealousy had separated him from you; it was necessary to give you a proof of my influence; from the extreme of indifference, I re-awakened the ardour of first love: let me but alter my purpose, and his former estrangement will ensue. It is unnecessary for me to bring forward facts. You feel the truth of what I say."

"And for what purpose has this comedy been composed and acted?"

"To show you that your joys or your sorrows are in my power, and that I can cause you to be cherished or neglected, adored or hated, even as I will. Now, hear me—I love you!"

"This is insulting, sir," exclaimed the marchioness, endeavouring to withdraw the bridle of the horse from the abbe's hands.

"Moderate your expressions, madam," he replied; "for upon me, I again warn you, phrases of this description are entirely thrown away. A woman never yet was insulted by an avowal of love, but there are a thousand different ways of compelling or inducing its return. The fault is to mistake the means to be employed, and that is all."

"And may I be permitted to inquire the means you have selected," said the marchioness, with a look of contempt.

"The only means that could possibly be successful with a woman, calm, cold, and resolute as yourself; the conviction that your interest would counsel the return of my affection."

"Since you pretend to so accurate a knowledge of my character,"—making at the same time another fruitless

LAFFARGE.

effort to disengage her bridle—"you ought also to know in what manner a woman such as I am should receive an overture of this description; what I should say to you, and more especially to my husband."

He smiled.

"In that respect you are the mistress of your own actions," he replied. "Pray give utterance to what you please; repeat to him this conversation, word for word; add to it whatever memory or imagination can dictate, false or true, against me; but as soon as you have well schooled him, the moment you believe you have secured a defender there, in the next moment, but with two words I bend him to my purpose as this glove. I detain you no longer; you have in me a sincere friend or a bitter enemy. Take your choice." At these words he let go her horse.

CHAPTER XVI.

THE MARCHIONESS DE GANGES.

AFTER the interview recorded at the close of the preceding chapter, the abbe parted from the marchioness, and sought his brother, the chevalier, who was nothing better than a puppet in the hands of the wicked priest.

"Chevalier," said the abbe, "we both love this same woman—our brother's wife: do not let us cross each other's path. I can master my feelings and sacrifice them the more willingly, believing it is you whom she prefers. Endeavour to confirm her favourable impressions. If you are successful, I instantly retire;—if you fail, you will then honourably yield to me your position, that I in turn may try whether her heart be as impregnable as it is described."

The vanity of the weak-minded chevalier was delighted at the information imparted by the artful abbe—the idea of such an exquisitely lovely woman as the marchioness being enamoured of him was perfectly intoxicating. He resolved to enjoy her, and with that view commenced a series of attentions which, were they not so harmless and ludicrous, would be quite insulting and intolerable to this beautiful and accomplished woman. At first, the marchioness, who attributed his conduct to mere friendship and respect, treated him with much kindness; the more so because she could not help contrasting the disinterestedness of the chevalier, who had never expressed his feelings in words, with the selfish and disgusting motives which had prompted the attentions of the designing ecclesiastic.

Deceived by this, the chevalier was emboldened to explain his intentions. The marchioness, astonished,

DE RETZ.

and at first doubting the reality, suffered him to proceed, until further hesitation would be criminal, and thereupon abruptly stopped him by one of those cutting phrases a woman has recourse to, far more frequently from indifference than virtue. Upon this check the crestfallen chevalier lost all hope, and frankly told to his brother, the abbe, the unsuccessful termination of his suit. This was precisely what the abbe had anticipated, first to gratify his vanity, and, secondly, for the execution of his plans. He converted the mortification of the chevalier into a deadly hatred; and, now sure of a supporter, in fact, of an accomplice, he commenced his projects against his victim. The result was soon observable by the recurrence of the estrangement on the part of the marquis. A young man whom the marchioness had met with in general society became, if not the cause, at least the pretext for a fresh fit of jealousy.

The marchioness detected the fatal influence of her brother in-law, and was now convinced that he possessed the power to verify his menaces to the letter.

Some time after this unhappy discovery, her grandfather died, bequeathing to her his fortune, which, increased by the sum of 700,000 livres her already very handsome estate. According to the Roman laws which then prevailed, this became her own exclusive property, to be enjoyed and bequeathed in any manner she might

prefer. A few days after she sent for a notary to explain the technicalities of the will. This proceeding alarmed her husband and his brothers, as indicating an intention to deprive them of her estate in case they should happen to survive her; and from this moment they appear to have formed the determination of making themselves absolute masters of the marchioness's property.

Soon after this a strange circumstance occurred. At a dinner party given by the marquis, a cream was placed upon the table, of which all those who ate became seriously indisposed, more particularly the marchioness, who had rather freely indulged in it, whilst the marquis and his brothers, who carefully abstained, were not affected. This excited suspicion, and upon a careful analysis of the remains of the cream, the presence of arsenic was detected; but as it was unattended by any serious result, and was explained as occasioned by a servant's carelessness, who had taken up arsenic for sugar, the circumstance was passed over and apparently forgotten. The marquis now adopted a more conciliatory manner, he affected a return of his first affection, but the marchioness was not again the dupe of his dissimulations. She perceived the influence of the abbe, who had persuaded his brother that a large fortune was worth this forgiveness of a few inconsiderate and trifling actions.

The marchioness had her will drawn up, in which her mother was left residuary legatee, with remainder to the two children of the marquis, but subject to her mother's control.

Her husband was exasperated, and once again manifested his hatred. But—strange and unaccountable contradiction of woman's heart!—her love revived for the marquis, and by the intercessions of the ever busy abbe, she was induced to revoke her will and draw up a fresh one, in which her husband, instead of her mother, was named residuary legatee. This will was dated May 5th, 1667.

The abbe and the chevalier expressed very warmly the pleasure with which they witnessed this final removal of all further cause of discord, and promised, on their brother's part, the renewal of his former love. This hope she was permitted to indulge for a few days, but when these had expired, the cup of happiness was dashed from her lips, and never again restored.

About the 16th of May, the marchioness, owing to some trifling indisposition, desired the attendance of an apothecary, whom she requested to prepare some medicine according to her own prescription. He did so; but upon receiving this, it appeared so black and thick, that fearing some mistake, she put it aside, and availed herself of some trifling remedies at hand. The time had hardly elapsed for her taking her first prescription, when the abbe and the chevalier sent to make inquiries about her health. She thanked them, and invited them, in return, to partake of a small collation in the afternoon, with herself and some ladies. Her husband, it may be observed, was in another part of the country, attending to the management of some of his estates. An hour after these attentions were renewed, and the marchioness, not at the moment paying much attention to this excess of civility, replied that she was greatly better. She remained, however, in bed, to do the honours of the collation; and, soon after, the guests assembled, to whom the abbe and the chevalier were introduced. Neither of them, however, would partake of the meal; the former, indeed, seated himself at the table, whilst the chevalier remained standing at the foot of the bed. The abbe was silent and thoughtful, mingling occasionally in conversation, with the manner of one escaping from the power of some dominant idea that absorbs his attention against his will, and which, perpetually recurring to his mind, induces fits of abstraction or of unconscious reverie; and this the more excited attention from being opposed to his general habits. The chevalier, on the contrary, seemed conscious only of the presence of his sister-in-law, who, more beautiful than ever, attracted his undivided attention. The collation finished, the ladies retired, accompanied by the abbe, but no sooner had he quitted the room, than the marchioness observed the chevalier become extremely pale, and fall, as if suddenly taken ill, upon her bed. She inquired, with much anxiety, as to the cause, but before he could reply, the door opened, and her attention was drawn to another sight. It was the abbe, who, pale, and overcome by the violence of his conflicting passions, re-entered the room, holding in his hand a pistol and a glass. He next closed and locked the door, which so alarmed the marchioness that she half rose from her bed, fixing her eyes upon him, but incapable of uttering a word.

His lips quivering, his face livid, his eyes burning with fierce excitement, he approached the bed, and presenting the glass in one hand, and with the other pointing the pistol towards her—"Choose, madam," said he, after a moment's awful silence, as if struggling with some powerful feeling, "choose your death, by poison—this poison — or (turning to the chevalier) the sword."

A moment's gleam of hope encouraged the marchioness; for as the chevalier drew his sword, she trusted it was in her defence; but undeceived, and thus placed unprotected in the power of two such men, she sank in agony before them upon her bed.

"What evil have I done," she exclaimed, "that you thus sentence me to death—and after condemning me, as judges, should thus slay me as executioners? I am guiltless; my only fault is the observance of my duty towards my husband—your brother." Then at once perceiving remonstrance was in vain—for the determined looks and impatient gestures evinced the inflexible resolution of the abbe,—she turned towards the chevalier, "And you also, my brother," she said, "and you also! Have pity on me! as you hope yourself for mercy! Oh! spare me!"

But the cowardly miscreant stamping with his foot upon the floor, directed his sword's point to her breast, and replied, "Enough of this; delay your choice no longer; for if not, madam, it will be for us immediately to decide."

She turned round, as if once more to address the abbe; and as she did so, the muzzle of his pistol struck her mouth. She felt that she must die, and, selecting that which seemed the least terrible form of death— "Give me, then, the poison," she exclaimed; "and may God forgive you my death!"

Upon this she took the glass; but its contents were so repulsive, that with a look expressing a last entreaty, she put it from her; but the fearful blasphemy which burst from the lips of the abbe, and the menacing gesture of his brother, destroyed every hope, however faint, of mercy. She raised the glass to her lips, looked at her murderers, and murmuring a faint prayer to heaven, swallowed its contents. As she did so, some drops of the deadly mixture fell upon her neck and breast, and burnt it like fire; for, in fact, the execrable miscreants had composed it of arsenic and sublimate of mercury, diluted with aquafortis. Thus made the agent of their crime, she let the glass fall, believing even their cruelties could exact no further torture. She was mistaken; the abbe remarked that some of the poison was precipitated to the bottom of the glass, and this he collected and presented to her on the point of a silver bodkin, rolled together in the form and size of a small nut.

"Come, madam," said he,—"come, you must swallow this last most exquisite drop."

She apparently complied; but instead of swallowing it, retained it in her mouth, and then throwing herself upon the bed, contrived to eject it unperceived. Then, once more turning towards them, she cried, with her hands raised towards heaven, "Since you have destroyed my body, have yet some mercy upon my soul; let me at least see my confessor."

Remorseless as they were, her assassins felt possibly some slight emotion at the sight; moreover, after the poison she had taken, death could but be retarded a few hours; they therefore quitted the room to comply with her request, and closed the door after them.

Scarcely was she alone than the possibility of escape flashed across her mind. She rushed to the window, which was twenty-two feet from the ground, and which was covered with stones and rubbish. Then, seizing some clothes, she was hastily dressing herself, when the sound of approaching footsteps was heard; and believing her murderers were returning to assure themselves of her death, she rushed almost frantic to the window. The instant that her foot rested upon the sill the door opened, and she at once threw herself headlong from the height. The door was opened by M. Perrette, the chaplain of the marquis, who had been sent by her murderers to confess her. He was enabled to seize her clothes as she fell; but these, too slight to sustain her weight, were yet sufficient to change the direction of her fall; so that the grasp, although it tore them, yet broke her descent, and she reached the ground but little injured. Stunned and almost senseless, she was yet conscious of something which passed her as she fell, and which rebounded with great violence near her. This was an enormous water-jug, which the execrable priest, seeing she had escaped, dashed after her with the hope of killing her by the blow, but it broke in pieces at her feet; whereupon he immediately ran to acquaint the abbe and the chevalier their victim was escaping. In the meantime, with an admirable presence of mind, she contrived to eject the poison she had taken, and then, running towards the stables, directed by a light which was there burning, she accosted one of the grooms.

"In the name of God," she cried, "help me! I am poisoned; they wish to kill me. Open me the door leading from this court-yard, that I may save my life."

The groom very imperfectly understood her request; but perceiving a woman half naked and beseeching his protection, he took her under his arm, led her immediately across the stables, and opened the door into the street, where, meeting two women, he confided the marchioness to their care, but was unable to explain the cause of either her fear or her disordered state.

The marchioness herself seemed capable only of uttering exclamations for their aid. "Help me! I am poisoned! In the name of heaven, help me!" Suddenly darting from their hands, she rushed into the town; for but twenty feet from her, upon the threshold of the door she had just left, she saw her assassins in quick pursuit. Thus they passed through the street, she crying out that they had poisoned her, her assassins shouting she was mad, whilst the people, doubtful what course to pursue, allowed her to pass unassisted; for by her appearance and frantic cries it was hardly possible to believe but that her brothers-in-law spoke truth. The chevalier at last overtook her, instantly dragged her into the nearest house, and closed the door. Upon the threshold stood the abbe, with a pistol in his hand, threatening to blow out the brains of any one who should dare to come to her assistance The house belonged to M. Desprats, then absent from home, but whose wife was at that moment in company with several of her female friends.

Struggling against the force of her enemy, the marchioness was borne into the room; and, as many of the ladies there assembled had been admitted into her society, her appearance excited the greatest astonishment and sympathy. They arose, therefore, with offers of assistance; but the chevalier repulsed them, continually asserting she was mad; to which repeated asseverations the marchioness replied by pointing to her neck and lips, burnt and disfigured by the poisons, declaring she was dying, and urgently requesting them to give her some milk, or, at least, some water. Upon this a Madame Brunelle, the wife of a Protestant minister, slipped into her hand a box of confections, of which she hastily swallowed a small portion; whilst another, with ready kindness, gave her a glass of water; but the moment she placed it to her lips the chevalier broke it against her teeth, so that the fragments cut her lips. Upon this the woman called loudly for assistance, and surrounded the chevalier in the greatest excitement; but the marchioness, still hoping to turn his heart towards mercy, besought them to retire and to leave her with him alone—to which they acceded, and withdrew into the adjoining room. She threw herself upon her knees, and supplicated him, by the memory of her past kindness to himself and to his family, to have pity upon her, and promised him that if even now he would save her life, to forget what had occurred, and to consider and receive him always as her protector and friend. Whilst she spoke, the assassin, unperceived, had drawn a dagger: he struck her with it in the breast. This blow was followed by another, which she received near the collarbone: upon which the marchioness rose and uttered a loud shriek, rushed towards the door of the room adjoining, and cried loudly for assistance. As she did so, he repeated his attack, struck her five times more in different parts of her back, and was continuing to do so, when, at last, the sword broke in the shoulder, owing to the violence of a blow, which knocked her down, bathed in blood, which now streamed along the floor. The chevalier thought that she was dead; and hearing the women rushing to her assistance, escaped from the room, and found his brother, the abbe, still upon the threshold with his pistol ready cocked; whereupon, seizing him by the hand, he said, as the abbe seemed to hesitate, — "Let us go, brother; the business is over."

They had not proceeded but a few steps when a window was thrown up, and the ladies, who had found the marchioness expiring, called loudly upon the people who had assembled for succour; upon which the abbe, detaining his brother by the arm, said, "What means this, chevalier? If they call for succour, she is surely not dead."

"Go, then, and see to it yourself," replied the chevalier. "I have done enough for my part; it is your turn now."

"That is exactly my opinion," cried the abbe; and rushing again into the house, he pushed the ladies aside, and advancing closer to the head of the marchioness, he applied the muzzle of the pistol to her breast; but Madame Brunelle, the instant he touched the trigger, raised his hand, so that the ball, instead of taking effect, was lodged in the cornice of the ceiling. The abbe, upon this, seized the pistol by the barrel, and struck the marchioness so violent a blow with the butt-end upon the head that she reeled backwards and fell; but before he could repeat the blow, the ladies surrounded and thrust him, amid the loudest execrations, to the door, which they closed upon him. He rejoined his brother, and profiting by the night, the assassins fled from Ganges, and arrived at Aubenas, a considerable distance from it, about ten o'clock. From thence they succeeded in quitting the French territories. Meantime, the Marquis de Ganges returned, and affected the greatest astonishment and indignation at the horrible conduct of his brothers. He swore that he would search them out and slay them with his own hands, and went so far as to institute certain inquiries as to their place of retreat. But his professions imposed upon no one: that the assassins had acted with his passive connivance—if not with his active consent—was the universal conviction. The unfortunate marchioness herself was not deceived, although she expressed her forgiveness not only to her husband, but also to her cowardly and diabolical murderers. But the husband did not reap the advantage which he had expected from this atrocious crime. The last will of his wife, in which he was appointed the guardian and executor of her immense fortune, was declared invalid, and the previous will, in which his mother was made the executrix of her daughter's estates, confirmed. The marquis was furious at this result; he used every means to induce his dying wife to make another effort to get him appointed instead of her mother, but on this point she was inflexible to the last.

In spite of the effects of the poisons which she had taken, and the many frightful wounds inflicted on her, enough to have killed a lioness, this beautiful and unfortunate woman lingered on in indescribable agony for no less a period than nineteen days after the murderous attack of the abbe and his brother, so lovingly did nature defend the charming being she had taken such pains to form. She died imploring the forgiveness of Heaven on her despicable assassins.

The fate of the author and actors of this most horrible tragedy is soon told. The abbe and the Chevalier de Ganges were in their absence sentenced to death. The marquis was ordered to banish himself for ever from the French territory; and Perrette, the infamous chaplain, was sent to the galleys for life. This last was the first of the miscreants to experience the vengeance of Heaven —he was struck dead by a thunderbolt, whilst working at the oar in chains, on a passage from Toulouse to Brest. The chevalier fled to Naples, and from thence proceeded to Candia to fight against the Turks; but he had hardly landed on the island, when a bomb-shell burst at the feet of several persons, none of whom, however, were injured except the Chevalier de Ganges, who had his skull broken in fragments, and his brains scattered on the ground.

The abbe wandered about the Continent. In Germany he became, under another name, tutor in a noble family, where his great abilities and extensive erudition made him much respected. At last, however, he was found out, and obliged to quit the house. He renounced the Catholic religion, and married; and, after a life of unsurpassed guilt and hypocrisy, died at last in the odour of great sanctity in the Protestant Consistory at Amsterdam.

The Marquis de Ganges returned privily from his banishment, and took a most active part in the persecutions which then raged so fiercely against the Protestants in France. The zeal of the marquis ingratiated him with the ecclesiastics, and there was every chance of his sentence of exile being repealed; but the miscreant having attempted to ravish his daughter-in-law, his son made a complaint to Louis XIV, who ordered the marquis instantly to leave the kingdom. This he professed to do, but his daughter, Madame de Urban, and other

CATHERINE OF THOUARS.

powerful friends, concealed and entertained him. At last he retired to the little village Le Isle, near the celebrated fountains of Vaucluse, where he lived alone and died unlamented.

CHAPTER XVII.

WILLIAM PALMER.

THIS miscreant, whom crime has exalted to an equality with the Borgias, the Brinvilliers's, the Sainte-Croixs, and the other hideous and gigantic monsters, whose atrocities have insulted heaven, outraged justice, defiled, disgraced, and tortured humanity, is a member of a family of very considerable wealth, and was first ushered into the world polluted by his presence in 1824, in the village of Rugeley, in Staffordshire. During his boyhood he exhibited no striking peculiarities of character, if we except a strong predilection for that offensive species of joking termed "practical," and which consists in extracting enjoyment from the pain inflicted on our fellow-creatures. His insensibility to human suffering was mistaken by his family, blinded by their fond partiality, for that fortitude of mind which would qualify him for success in the medical profession. This, however, is not the first, and, we are afraid, will not be the last, occasion on which hardness of heart has been mistaken for greatness of intellect. Before and since the time of Palmer, beings whom nature designed for the slaughterers of wild-beasts, have, by the infatuation of parental fondness, been devoted to the divinest, the humanest, and the most beneficent of the sciences. After serving an apprenticeship to a country practitioner,

he was entered at St. Bartholomew's Hospital, London, where, without distinguishing himself in any respect from the crowd of medical students, he went through the various preparations presented for a general practitioner. If there was any branch of study for which he manifested any decided preference, it was for that of physiology, and the action of poison on the human system. In this very important department of medical science he was " well up," although by no means possessed of any uncommon degree of excellence. His habits were sensual, but at the same time economical. He was devoted to Mammon as well as to Belial; and though as partial as any of the medical students to midnight orgies and sensualistic sprees, he never indulged in these unless at the expense of others, or when the gratification could be procured by a very trifling outlay of his own money. His love of money and animal pleasures impelled him at a very early age to betting and gambling pursuits; and it is into his initiation to the dark mysteries of the gambler, together with his two master-passions, lust and cupidity, that we must look for those seedlings of vice which have blossomed and fructified into such a rank and fearful upas-crop of crime.

In 1846 he was admitted a member of the Royal College of Surgeons, and in the same year he settled permanently at Rugeley, his native place, where also the other members of his family were located. But Palmer was not dependent on his profession, and did not therefore apply himself with any degree of diligence to the obtainment of a lucrative and extensive practice. In fact, he does not seem to have cared anything about his profession; its drudgery was distasteful to him, and the property which he inherited enabled him to dispense with it. In 1847 he married Anne Brookes, the natural daughter of Colonel William Brookes, and his house-

PORTRAIT OF A LADY POISONER.

keeper, Mary Thornton. This Colonel Brookes belonged to the East India Company's service, which he quitted, and took up his residence at Stafford, where he died in 1834. To Anne Brookes, or Thornton, as one of his natural children, he bequeathed, by a will dated 27th July, 1833, nine houses at Stafford, besides land, and the interest of twenty thousand sicca rupees, for herself and children, and appointed Dr. Edward Knight, a physician of Stafford, and a Mr. Dawson, her guardians and trustees. To the mother of his daughter, Mary Thornton, he bequeathed some property, which was to pass to the daughter, Mrs. Palmer, at the death of the former.

After his marriage Palmer applied himself almost exclusively to gambling speculations on the " turf." His professional practice was confined entirely to the members of his own family. But his medical studies were by no means abandoned; he still continued to manifest the same penchant for certain branches of his profession which he had displayed during his student life in London, and many of his sporting friends, when they called to see their turf associate, discovered him poring over certain treatises on poisons! This, as was natural enough, excited neither suspicion nor surprise, although some of his visitors failed not to make the inference that Dr. Palmer was master of many potent drugs, the administration of which would prevent an undesirable horse

from winning. Thus his connexions, which were respectable,—his wealth, which was considerable,—his skill, which was presumed to be great,—and his manner, which was cold and reserved, conspired to render William Palmer—or Doctor Palmer of Rugeley—a very influential personage in sporting circles. He was generally believed to make up a "safe book," and to have a more than ordinary good luck in his adventures. In short, Palmer was supposed to be a very prosperous man; and in sporting, as in other circles, the successful man—or the man who is thought to be successful—is generally respected, and looked up to.

But "things are not what they seem," appearances are proverbially deceitful, and the sporting world had formed an exceedingly erroneous estimate of Palmer and his luck. The truth is that he was a very unlucky speculator. His book was almost invariably badly "made up." The horses which he backed were generally losers, and those against whom he gave the odds were very frequently winners. His stable information was generally unreliable. The reason for this is not difficult to discover. In the stable, as in the other world, information must be paid for; trainers and jockeys, as well as statesmen and politicians, have "itching palms" that crave to be rubbed with a golden ointment; and as William Palmer did not "tip" the trainers and jockeys to the satisfaction of those custodians of important stable secrets, they generally sent him upon a false scent by exaggerating the capacity of one horse and depreciating that of another. Every one must perceive the consequence: Palmer was losing instead of making money,—his own and his wife's fortune had either been sold or mortgaged. But money had to be found; that no sporting man can do without, and Palmer was not only a gambler, but also a very gross and coarse sensualist.

We have seen before, that by the will of Colonel Brookes the property which he had bequeathed to his mistress, Mary Thornton, was, at her decease, left to his daughter, Mrs. Palmer. In 1849, Mary Thornton paid a visit to her daughter and son-in-law, Mr. and Mrs. Palmer, at Rugeley. From that visit Mary Thornton never returned; she departed this life while a guest at Mr. Palmer's house. This event every one of his friends supposed was a very good thing for Mr. Palmer; the terms of Colonel Brookes' will were well known to them, and they all believed that the death of Mary Thornton would be a large accession to the fortunes of Palmer through his wife. Now, here again, Palmer's luck was not so good as the world had supposed; for although the will of Colonel Brookes would seem plain enough to any one not conversant with the nice subtleties and labyrinthine intricacies of English law,— and although in the present state of that law, confused and contradictory though it be, it might be deemed sufficiently explicit, yet then the Colonel's will was by the lynx-eyed gentlemen of the long robe and the curled wigs discovered and determined not to be sufficiently clear and forcible in its terms to put Mrs. Palmer in absolute and complete possession of the property of her mother; but only to give her a life interest in it. Consequently, William Palmer could not make this property available to extricate him from his pecuniary difficulties. It could not be sold—neither could it be mortgaged; inasmuch as no one would advance money upon securities which would revert to Colonel Brookes' heir-at-law, the moment Mrs. Palmer breathed her last—an event which might happen at any time. Palmer was greatly chagrined at this disappointment of his expectations. He thought himself an injured man; he was angry at Colonel Brookes and Mary Thornton, as if these had designed to deprive him of absolute control over his wife's estate; and by a not uncommon, though very unjust, process of reasoning, he transferred part of his indignation at his father and mother-in-law, to their daughter. From the day when it was ascertained that Mrs. Palmer had only a life interest in her mother's property, it was remarked by the neighbours that Palmer was more cold in his attentions to his wife than when he thought her the sole and absolute owner of her mother's property. He now professed himself uncertain of everything that belonged to his wife; if she died, the heir-at-law of Colonel Brookes might deprive her husband and child of everything which she had derived from her father. Palmer resolved to indemnify himself against this contingent calamity; if his wife could really leave him nothing he determined that her death should not be altogether valueless to him. Her property consisted of seventeen acres of land, valued at between 100l. and 300l. per acre, together with nine houses and the interest of the twenty thousand sicca rupees, of the total value of about 400l. per annum, upon which he had borrowed largely from his mother. There could not be any doubt in his having an interest in the life of his wife; and, therefore, he had sufficient reason to get that life insured. Accordingly, we find that, in January, 1854, he insured her life for 3,000l., in the Norwich Union, and in March of the same year, in the Sun, for 5,000l.; he had also an insurance in the Scottish Equitable, on the same life, for another 5,000l., making altogether an insurance of 13,000l., which would be paid to William Palmer, on the death of his wife. Nine months after the first insurance had been effected, that unfortunate lady breathed her last, and, from the circumstances attending her last illness, the symptoms of her disease, testified to by her deathbed attendants, and the conduct of her husband, there is too much reason to surmise that she came to her end by most foul and unnatural means. She left behind her a boy seven years old, her only surviving child. As if to justify Palmer

in effecting so large an insurance on his wife's life, within a month of her death, the heir-at-law of Colonel Brookes instituted an action at law against Palmer, to obtain possession of his deceased wife's property, which action was determined in his favour.

Previous to the death of his wife, Palmer was very heavily encumbered with debt. His creditors, the usurers, were becoming quite clamorous; bills were due, and some of them had been dishonoured; amongst these was one for 2,000l., which purported to be an acceptance of Palmer's mother, Sarah Palmer. She was a woman of considerable wealth, and her acceptance being believed to be genuine, was a security upon which money would be readily advanced. William Palmer had forged that acceptance, and converted it into money; and this was, if not the beginning, at least one of the earliest transactions of that nature in which this enormous criminal had been engaged. To prevent the public exposure, and the personal ruin consequent on detection, was, of course, a great object with Palmer, and in this fortune seemed really to have favoured him, for the various offices in which his wife's life had been insured paid without any demur, and the sum of 13,000l. thus so opportunely obtained, was applied to the paying of the most pressing of his liabilities. This was in September, 1854. But Palmer still remained under great liabilities, and amongst others was a bill of 2,000l. discounted to one Padwick, which still remained unpaid. This brings us to the close of the year 1854. In the course of that year Palmer had effected an insurance upon the life of his brother, Walter Palmer, or rather an insurance was effected in his brother's name. But William Palmer was a party to it, and corresponded with Pratt in effecting that insurance. This Pratt is an extensive money-lender, who accommodates gentlemen who can deposit satisfactory securities, by exacting from them sixty per cent. interest for the money which he advances. Just as in the case of his wife, Palmer had insured his brother's life for the 13,000l., and the policy was deposited with Pratt, the usurer, who, upon this and the other securities which he held in his hand, discounted at the same rate of sixty per cent. further bills amounting to 12,500l. With the proceeds of the money thus obtained, Palmer purchased a couple of race-horses, Nettle and Chicken. These transactions took place in March, 1855. The bills were renewed in June of that year, and became due on the 28th of September. Several other transactions of the same kind took place, and the account stood thus:—In the month of November, 1855, when the Shrewsbury races took place, and a severe pressure upon Palmer, there were in Pratt's hands bills amounting to 11,500l., all of them due, and every one of which was a forged acceptance in the name at Palmer's mother. Palmer was thus labouring under the pressure of liabilities which he had not a shilling to meet; and this distress was aggravated by the consciousness that the moment he could no longer go on, and his mother should be applied to for payment, the fact of his having committed these forgeries would become manifest, and bring upon him the penalties of the law for that crime.

It should here be mentioned that Palmer's brother, Walter, had died in the month of August, 1855. That life had been insured for 13,000l., and Palmer had expected that the proceeds of that insurance would relieve him from the pressure of his liabilities. In this, however, he was disappointed. The office in which it had been effected, suspecting some foul play in the transaction, refused to pay, so that by this time the affairs of Palmer were as desperate as they well could be.

It is now time to introduce another character, John Parsons Cooke, the victim of this terrible tragedy, for whose horrible end William Palmer has been doomed to die the ignominious death of the murderer. Cooke, like Palmer, was devoted to sporting pursuits. He was a young man of an amiable but weak and unsteady character. He was brought up to the legal profession; but having inherited, on the death of his father, a fortune of 12,000l., he abandoned the study of the law, and addicted himself to the more congenial pursuits of the turf. Palmer and Cooke had become acquainted, and were, to appearance, what might be termed friends. We have, however, evidence to prove that there was but little of the affection of friends between them. Indeed, Cooke appears to have been connected with Palmer more from fear than from regard; for, when advised by one of his friends to drop his intercourse with Palmer, Cooke exclaimed, "Would to God that I could; but you don't know how he has me in his power." What this occult influence might arise from—whether it was some fatal secret which placed those confederates mutually at the mercy of each other—or whether it might be nothing more criminal or important than those monetary difficulties in which they were both involved, is, perhaps, one of those mysteries which never will be explained in this world.

In the course of our narrative, we have arrived at the time of the Shrewsbury races, November, 1855. We have seen that Palmer was in a most desperate situation, by having to meet 11,500l. of forged bills, for which he had not a single shilling to account. Disgrace and destruction stared him in the face, and unless some immediate escape could be provided, he would find himself clasped in their fatal embrace! He had implored Pratt for time; but, in the words of the Attorney-General, "As well might a man appeal for mercy to a rabid tiger as to a usurer, when the securities he has advanced upon have failed." Pratt, tired of lawyers' letters, actually issued a writ for 4,000l. against Palmer and his mother. Everything, forgery and all, was on the point of immediate exposure.

In these transactions John Parsons Cooke was slightly implicated. We now come to the events connected with the Shrewsbury races, and with a crime unsurpassed for the cold-blooded and deliberate mode of its perpetration. Cooke had a horse, Polestar, entered for a race at Shrewsbury. This horse won, and the winnings of Cooke, including the stakes, amounted to 2,050l. He had been, during the previous week, at Worcester races, and was entitled to receive, besides stakes, between 700l. and 800l. The races took place on Tuesday, and he was entitled to receive on the Monday following—including stakes to be received from his racing agent in London—1,020l. Now, within a week from that time the man died. Cooke was a young man of twenty-eight; he was slightly disposed to pulmonary complaints, but was otherwise a hale, hearty man. On the night of the 14th a friend of Cooke's, a Mr. Fisher, occupied a room in the rear of his; he was agent to Cooke, and received his bets from time to time at Tattersall's. Mr. Fisher, with a person named Herring, was at Shrewsbury races; and Fisher went into a room which was occupied by Cooke and Palmer; Cooke, having before him a tumbler full of brandy-and-water, asked Fisher to take something to drink, and also asked Palmer would he not have more? "No," said Palmer, "unless you take your glass." Cooke said, "That is soon done," and tossed it off in one drink, leaving only a teaspoonful. He had hardly swallowed it when he said, "Good God, there is something in it; it burns my throat." Palmer took up the glass, and drank what was left. He said, "There is nothing in it," pushing the glass to Fisher; and to another person who came in he said, "Cooke thinks there is something in the brandy-and-water." Cooke rose and left the room, but returned in a few minutes. He called Fisher out, and told him he was taken violently ill, and Fisher went out with him. He was attacked with a violent vomiting, and was put to bed, where he vomited again in a violent manner. A medical man was called in, and he became more tranquil, and slept until the next morning. Such were the man's feelings at the time, that he gave Fisher the money he had about him, and desired him to take care of it. It amounted to 700l. or 800l. in a large number of notes. After the sickness had ceased Cooke went out on the course, and Fisher gave him back his notes. A woman of the name of Mrs. Brooke had occasion to see Palmer at the hotel at Shrewsbury, the night before his horse was to run; she is a remarkable person, being a female connected with the turf. The prisoner's horse was to run the next day, and she came to him to speak about the jockey he was to employ. She saw Palmer holding up a tumbler and looking at it with the action of a man who watches to see the condition of it. Having looked at it through the gaslight he withdrew to his own room, and returned with the glass in his hand, and then went into the room where Cooke was, and in which room Cooke drank the brandy-and-water, and where it is to be inferred his sickness was taken. Throughout the ensuing days Cooke constantly received things from the prisoner's hands, and during those days his sickness was continued; and after his death antimony was found in his body and in his blood. When Cooke arrived at Rugeley on the Thursday night, he stated that he had been poorly at Shrewsbury, but the people who saw him did not think that he was suffering from any serious disease. Next day he dined with Palmer, and returned to the hotel at about ten o'clock at night perfectly sober. He then went to bed. Next morning Palmer visited him at an early hour, and was constantly with him, in and out, during the whole of that day and of the Sunday, which was the day following. Coffee was brought up to him by the chambermaid at the inn, on the Saturday morning, at Palmer's request, and Palmer was the person by whom that coffee was handed to him. Immediately after he had drunk it he was attacked by the same illness which had seized him at Shrewsbury. Palmer continued to wait on him the whole of that day and of the day following; and even toast-and-water had been sent to him from Palmer's house, while he was still tormented with the same incessant and troublesome sickness. On the Saturday, Palmer ordered from the Albion Inn, at Rugeley, some broth, which he afterwards had sent over to Cooke at the Talbot Arms Tavern; and, as soon as the latter partook of a spoonful of it, he was taken sick and threw it off his stomach. The prisoner soon afterwards called, and having been told that Cooke was unable to use the broth, insisted on his taking some, and after Cooke had done so he began immediately to vomit again. The chambermaid at the inn, being tempted by the appearance of the broth, was induced to partake of it, and was afterwards seized, as Cooke had previously been seized, with violent vomiting. On the Saturday Dr. Bamford was called in to see the patient, who, as Palmer stated, had a bilious attack. Dr. Bamford prescribed some effervescing saline medicine; but after he had gone away the prisoner had ordered more coffee for Cooke, and after the latter had drunk that coffee he began to vomit again. Shortly afterwards he took some boiling water when Palmer was not there, and no vomiting ensued; but in about two hours more, when arrowroot had been administered to him in Palmer's presence, the vomiting had been renewed. On the Sunday Cooke still continued ill; but Dr. Bamford could find no indication that he was suffering in any way from a bilious attack. On Monday, the 19th, Palmer left Rugeley to go to London; but before leaving he called early in the morning, and ordered some coffee for Cooke, which he himself handed to the latter, who was immediately afterwards again seized with vomiting. Dr. Bamford saw Cooke on the same morning and prescribed for him some new medicine, and after Cooke had taken that medicine he began greatly to improve. He took coffee and was able to keep it on his stomach, and he continued much better the whole of that day. Palmer had, in the meantime, gone to London, where he met, according to previous appointment, at Beaufort-buildings, a person of the name of Herring, whom he commissioned to receive the money due to Cooke at Tattersall's on that day, and whom he ordered at the same time to make two payments on his (Palmer's) own account with that money of Cooke's, one of those payments being 350l. to Padwick, and another, a sum of 450l., to Pratt. He told Herring, who was not the usual agent of Cooke, to write either to himself or to Cooke upon that subject; but it subsequently appeared that he was able to intercept Cooke's correspondence through the instrumentality of Cheshire, the postmaster at Rugeley. Herring had paid the 450l. to Pratt, but he had not paid the 350l. to Padwick, in consequence of his not having been able himself to collect upon that occasion the whole of the money due to Cooke. Palmer returned to Rugeley on the Monday night about nine o'clock; and from that time until ten or eleven he was frequently in and out of Cooke's room. After arriving at Rugeley on that night he had gone to a person of the name of Newton, the assistant of a surgeon in the town, and asked him for some strychnine; and he accordingly got from Newton

THE MARCHIONESS DE GANGES.

three grains of that poison. Dr. Bamford had sent Cooke a box of pills, some of which had been taken by Cooke on the Saturday night and on the Sunday night; and he was to have taken more on the Monday night, which were to be given to him by Palmer. He left Cooke about eleven that night, apparently still cheerful and in improved health. But suddenly, at about midnight, the women in the lower part of the inn were alarmed by the most violent screams proceeding from Cooke's room; they rushed up-stairs, and one of them went into the room, and found him in a state of the greatest agony, screaming in the most frightful manner, shrieking "Murder," calling on Christ to save his soul, and suffering the most intense pain. His eyes were starting out of his head, and after violent convulsions, which lasted but a short time, his arms and legs became rigid, his mouth was closed, he was gasping for breath, and he could hardly speak. He requested that Palmer might be sent for, and when the latter came over to him, he said, "Oh, dear, doctor, I shall die;" to which the other replied, "No, my lad, you shall not." The prisoner then gave him a mixture, which smelt of opium, and two pills, which could not have produced much effect, as the patient soon threw them up. But shortly after he appeared more tranquil, and the pain subsided, although his arms still remained stiff. Cooke began to sleep; and next came the morning of Tuesday, the 20th, the day of his death. On that morning he was

apparently tranquil and comfortable. The prisoner had gone to the shop of a Mr. Hawkins, a druggist at Rugeley, with whom he had not dealt during the two preceding years. He saw the assistant, a person of the name of Roberts, and he at first asked him for two drachms of prussic acid. While the prussic acid was being got ready for him, Newton, the same man from whom he had received the strychnine the night before—if Newton's statement was to be believed—came into the shop, and thereupon, the prisoner taking him by the arm, went out with him for the purpose of talking to him upon some very unimportant matter, and one in which neither of them could feel any interest. He continued with Newton in the street until a person of the name of Brassington came up and entered into conversation with Newton; he then returned into Hawkins' shop, where he got from Roberts six grains of strychnine, as well as a certain quantity of liquor of opium. After he had gone away Newton returned to the shop, and being struck with the fact of the prisoner's having made any purchases at an establishment with which he did not usually deal, he asked what he had bought, and was then informed that he had got a certain quantity of strychnine. Newton, when examined before the coroner, had made no mention of the fact of his having sold strychnine to the prisoner on the preceding night. Cooke was entitled to receive the stakes which he had won at Shrewsbury. On the Tuesday Palmer sent for Cheshire, the postmaster, and

WILLIAM PALMER.

desired him to bring a receipt stamp in his hand. Palmer produced a paper, and desired Cheshire to draw a cheque in his (Palmer's) favour, for 353l., adding that Cooke was too ill to draw the cheque himself; and he further stated, as a reason for not drawing the cheque himself, that Messrs. Weatherby might know his handwriting. Cheshire filled up the cheque, but whether Cooke's signature was really put to it or not he could not tell. On the Tuesday afternoon a new person was introduced upon the scene. On the Monday Palmer wrote to a person of the name of Jones, desiring him to come over to Cooke. Mr. Jones was a medical man, in whose house Cooke was in the habit of occasionally residing. A letter was written by Palmer to Jones, in which he stated that Cooke was suffering from a bilious attack, and that he wished Mr. Jones to come and see him. Mr. Jones found that there was no fever in the case, and no indication of a bilious complaint. Cooke told the medical man that he would take no more pills, but Palmer insisted on their being continued, and he went himself to Dr. Bamford's to get the pills made up. Palmer was absent about half an hour or three-quarters of an hour, between the time he had left Dr. Bamford's house and the time of his arrival at the Talbot Arms Inn, and during that period he might have changed the pills. When he arrived at the inn he called the attention of Mr. Jones to the handwriting on the box of pills, observing that it was wonderful a man of eighty, like Dr. Bamford, should write so good a hand. Cooke

was induced against his will to take the pills brought by the prisoner; they made him vomit, but he did not throw them up. After that Mr. Jones went down stairs to take his supper, it having been previously arranged that he was to sleep that night in the same bed-room with Cooke. Mr. Jones went to bed, but he had not laid down more than twenty minutes, when he was roused up by a sudden scream from Cooke, who begged that a doctor might be sent for. The chambermaid went to Palmer's, and ringing the bell violently she saw him immediately at the window. He came across in less than two minutes, and he made the observation when he arrived, that he thought he had never dressed in so short a time. Cooke was sitting up gasping for breath, and screaming violently. His body was convulsed with spasms. He implored Palmer to give him the same remedy he had given him the night before, and Palmer said he would go and fetch it. On going down stairs he told the chambermaid that Cooke was not so bad as on the preceding evening; and then he added, "What a game to be at every night." He returned with two pills, which, he told Mr. Jones, contained ammonia. Cooke swallowed those pills, but immediately afterwards threw them up again. He was soon seized with the most violent convulsions in all his limbs; the body began to stiffen; and after a brief but apparently a terrible agony, all was over, and death brought his sufferings to a close. The whole period of his last attack did not extend over more than a few minutes. The breath was barely out of his body when Palmer sent for women to lay out the corpse, and these women when they arrived at the dead man's room found Palmer searching the pockets of his coat, and under his pillow, and under his bolster. Cooke had taken his betting-book with him to Rugeley, but after his death no trace of it could be found. Palmer appeared to have had no money just previously to that catastrophe, but immediately after it he seemed to have received fresh supplies, as he was known to have paid off a number of debts. He produced to Cheshire, the postmaster, a paper in which Cooke was made to declare that 4,000l. worth of bills, in which he himself (Palmer) stood debited, had been obtained on Cooke's account, and he requested Cheshire to attest the genuineness of Cooke's signature to that document, but Cheshire refused to comply with that request. On the Friday after Cooke's death, Mr. Stevens, who had married Cooke's mother, came down to Rugeley, and was informed by Palmer that Cooke owed the 4,000l. worth of bills; but he stated that there were not 4,000 shillings left by Cooke, and that any claim against him could only be substantiated by an appeal to the Court of Chancery. He further learned, very much to his surprise, that Cooke's betting-book and his papers had completely disappeared, and that no trace of them could be found. When a certificate had been required of the cause of Cooke's death, Dr. Bamford and Palmer had agreed to attribute it to apoplexy, and had made a return to that effect. The stomach of the deceased was sealed up in a jar, in order that it might be sent to London to undergo a chemical examination; and after it had been so sealed up the prisoner was seen attempting to remove it from the room, and on his being obliged to bring it back it was found that there were two cuts in the parchment at the top of the jar, while it was evident from the appearance of those cuts that nothing had been taken away through them. When Palmer learned that a post-boy at Rugeley was to drive to the railway station two gentlemen who had charge of the jar, he went to him and asked him whether he could not manage to upset the car he was to drive, and to spill or break the jar, promising him 10l. if he could effect that object; but the post-boy refused to carry out his wishes in that respect. The viscera had been sent up to Dr. Taylor and Dr. Rees, of London, for the purpose of undergoing a chemical analysis, and they gave it as their opinion that Cooke had died from the effects of poison.

The coroner's jury returned a verdict of "Wilful Murder" against William Palmer. The affair had produced indescribable excitement in the locality. The rage of the people was such that Palmer would have been torn to pieces, were it not for the protection of the prison and the police. The death of his mother-in-law, when at his house—of his wife, and of his brother, were all recalled to mind, and the general conclusion was that all these, and even others, had been sacrificed to the remorseless cupidity of Palmer. So strongly did the tide of public feeling run against him, that it was very naturally argued by his friends and legal advisers that he could not have a fair trial in Stafford. Therefore, a special Act of Parliament was passed to enable him to be tried in London, at the Central Criminal Court. And this trial, unprecedented for its duration, as well as for the intense interest it excited, commenced on Wednesday, the 14th of May, 1856, before Lord Chief Justice Campbell, Baron Alderson, and Mr. Justice Cresswell. The important legal and medical facts and principles discussed and established in the course of the trial, as well as the prisoner's bearing in the dock, his various extraordinary remarks to his counsel and friends, as well as his conduct in the prison subsequent to his conviction, with many other most interesting circumstances not hitherto published, we shall describe in the following chapter.

CHAPTER XVIII.

WILLIAM PALMER (Concluded.)

IF we would find a parallel to the excitement created by the trial of William Palmer, for the alleged murder, by poison, of his friend and companion, John Parsons Cooke, we must go back to the latter half of the past century, when, within the arena of the Old Bailey, was fought those politico-forensic battles between a liberty-hating Government, and those Englishmen who stood forward as the champions of their countrymen, demanding for them the right and the power to think freely, and speak fearlessly, on all those questions which affected their various interests, as members of a civilized community. It is interesting to observe how totally different characters, by diametrically opposite means, may attain, in certain respects, to the same situation. Hardy, and Horne Tooke, and Thelwall, for endeavouring to rid society of moral and social murderers and poisoners, were tried for their lives, at the Old Bailey; and those, for a time, absorbed and monopolized the attention of the nation. Then, we learn from the chronicles of the day, the court-house, and the streets adjacent, were crowded with an anxious multitude, eager to obtain a glance at the accused, and at all those engaged in the trial; then, as now, all classes, from the highest to the lowest—from the industrious citizen down to the lazy peer—felt the keenest interest in the process and result of the pending investigation. But though the public feeling, in its depth, extent, and intensity, might be pretty much the same in both cases, yet, in its course, it was vastly different. *Then*, all the people, with the exception of the incurably stupid, and the utterly infamous, sympathised with the arraigned, and ardently prayed for their delivery; and boundless, therefore, was the popular joy, when the glad tidings spread with electric rapidity through the dense masses, that the prisoners had escaped the fangs of those ferocious tyrants who thirsted for their blood. *Now*, the reverse of all this has been the case—now, the multitudes who thronged the Old Bailey and its adjacents, loathed the accused; and, though anxious that he should have all the fair play which law and justice require, yet equally anxious that, if his guilt should be proved, punishment should ensue.

There were many elements in the case of Palmer to create and stimulate the anxiety and curiosity. Here was a man who had, for the lust of gold, outraged all that men hold sacred and dear—murdered, in the cruellest and most cowardly manner, his bosom friend and boon companion. There was also another feeling which mingled with and gave potency to the desire to learn what manner of man this miscreant must be. There was a cold fear, which crept like the deadly cobra into the heart of society, that this most horrible crime was of extensive prevalence in the community—that secret poisoning, for the sake of gold, was practised by thousands who, with greater cleverness or better fortune than Palmer, contrived to shroud in impenetrable darkness doings which the blackest fiends might shrink from perpetrating. In addition to these incitements to public curiosity, there was the intelligence that the highest legal ability had been retained on both sides, and thus an expectation of a splendid display of intellectual gladiatorship enhanced the attractions of a trial which, of itself, possessed a fearful and well-nigh resistless fascination. Such were the principal elements which combined to make the Criminal Court of the Old Bailey, on the 14th of May, and during thirteen successive days, the most powerful centre of attraction in the metropolis of these realms.

The judges appointed to conduct this most important trial were Lord Campbell, Chief Justice of England; Baron Alderson, and Mr. Justice Cresswell. The following personages were accommodated with seats on the bench during the first day of the trial, and such was the interest they took in the case, that the greater part of them attended regularly until its conclusion:—

The Marquis of Anglesea, the Earl of Derby, Earl Grey, Lord Lucan, Lord Denbigh, Prince Edward of Saxe Weimar, Lord William Lennox, Lord G. G. Lennox, and Lord H. Lennox. The Lord Advocate of Scotland sat by the side of the Attorney-General during the trial. The chaplain of Newgate, in clerical costume, occupied a seat almost immediately facing the dock, and the remaining privileged seats were gradually filled by the aldermen.

Mr. Streight, the deputy clerk of arraigns, read the indictment that was intended to be proceeded with, which charged the prisoner with the wilful murder of John Parsons Cooke.

The prisoner pleaded "Not Guilty" in a firm voice. He was then arraigned upon the coroner's inquisition for the like offence, and to this he also pleaded "Not guilty."

The following individuals comprised the jury :—Wm. Fletcher, foreman ; Richard Dumbrell ; William Mavor, Park Street, Grosvenor Square, veterinary surgeon; Wm. Newman, Pimlico, bootmaker ; George Miller, 33, Duke Street, Grosvenor Square ; George Oakshott, West Ham, confectioner ; Charles Bates, Surrey, brewer ; William Eccleston, Ham Lane, West Ham, grocer; Samuel Mullin ; John Over, Pimlico, grocer ; William Nash, Bond Street ; Thomas Knight, Leytonstone.

When twelve jurymen had been called, Serjeant Shee, on behalf of the prisoner, expressed a hope that no gentleman would act on the jury who was connected with either of the three insurance companies involved in this trial—viz., the Prince of Wales, the Solicitors' and General, and Midland.

Mr. Mason, a juryman, said he felt a strong prejudice in the case, that he did not feel competent to act, and begged to be excused.

Lord Campbell said he had heard quite enough. The juryman must be discharged.

The Attorney-General, Mr. E. James, Q.C., Mr. Bodkin, Mr. Welsby, and Mr. Huddlestone appeared for the Crown. Mr. Serjeant Shee, Mr. Grove, Q.C., specially retained, with Mr. Gray and Mr. Kenealey, were counsel for the prisoner. All the witnesses, with the exception of the medical men, were ordered out of court.

The Attorney-General opened the case for the prosecution in a speech, which was universally acknowledged to be a perfect master-piece of forensic eloquence. The facts of that speech we have already alluded to. As the long detail of proof evolved itself, it was curious to watch how each fact seemed to fall into its proper place, till, link by link, there was substantiated in evidence that chain of circumstantial narrative which the skill of the great advocate had already wound in deadly but polished folds round the culprit's neck.

The case for the prosecution was altogether admirably got up. The interests of truth and society were in good hands. It is fortunate, indeed, that it was so. Had a single weak point been left—had there been any gap in the evidence—any break in that continuity of circumstances, each in itself unimportant, but in their aggregate effect overwhelming—instant advantage would have been taken of it by the counsel for the defence, and instead of rejoicing, as we now do, at the just doom by which this unparalleled offender has been overtaken, we should have had, in all probability, to submit to the scandal and the misfortune of witnessing his escape.

As, in a case of such absorbing interest, we may safely conclude that the generality of our readers have made themselves acquainted with the evidence, we shall only glance at a few of the more salient points. The case for the prosecution was, that Palmer had an interest in Cooke's death ; that he first practised upon him by antimony, and finally poisoned him by strychnia; that all the symptoms under which Cooke died ; were referable to poisoning by strychnia, and to nothing else ; while the admitted failure to discover any traces of strychnia in the body after death, was not in itself incompatible with guilt, and was utterly nugatory as a defence in the face of all the proved facts of the case. The defence took issue on all these points—but principally relied on the absence of motive, and the non-discovery of poison in the dead body. Neither of these grounds, though both were urged with considerable ingenuity and confidence, could give rise for a moment to any reasonable doubt. As to motive, it was abundant. On this point it is only necessary to recall the facts of Palmer's position on Tuesday, the 13th of November, when Cooke's horse, Polestar, won the Shrewsbury Handicap. He had long been in difficulties. For two years his normal state had

been that of a man who is paying constantly increasing losses by perpetually accumulating loans. His book was almost uniformly ill made up. He had repeatedly raised money at 60 per cent. on the security of life policies and forged acceptances. In 1854 he had just managed to clear himself by what no one, we suppose, will now doubt to have been the timely proceeds of an enormous crime. In September of that year his wife perished, and he obtained the 13,000l. for which he had insured her life. In 1855 he made a desperate effort to secure the same resource. In August of that year Walter Palmer, the brother, died, just in time to satisfy the pressing claims of his creditors; and if the offices had paid the 13,000l. for which the brother's life had also been insured, the Rugeley poisoning cases might never have been heard of. But the offices refused, and Palmer's case at once became desperate. The usurers rapidly grew importunate. Pratt held acceptances to the extent of 11,500l., *every one of which had been forged* by Palmer in his mother's name.

In support of the various allegations contained in the indictment and opening speech of the Attorney-General, witnesses were called, and their examination and cross-examination occupied the court for a period of six days. The interest which the public felt went on increasing day by day, until it culminated on Wednesday, the 21st of May, when Mr. Serjeant Shee rose, at twenty minutes past ten, amid the breathless silence of the court, to reply for the defence ; in doing which, however, he spoke in a voice almost inaudible to the reporters. He was, he said, oppressed by an almost overwhelming responsibility, owing to the talent arrayed against him, and the great length of the proceedings, which was enough to exhaust human energy. He was conscious that the least error of judgment on his part must consign his client to a murderer's doom, and the execrations of mankind. The jury were fully aware that however well disposed to be impartial they could not place perfect reliance on their judgment in such extraordinary circumstances. They had heard that at the voice of science the blood of John Parsons Cooke had risen up from the ground to cry for vengeance on his murderer, and they knew also that all throughout the length and breadth of the land one universal conviction that Cooke had been murdered seemed to be produced, and that this cry was met by another cry of "blood for blood." (Sensation.) The circumstances under which they met were such as to excite feelings of horror and alarm. The case was an extraordinary one. When it first burst upon the public mind the alarm it occasioned was increased by dark hints of alleged former deeds of blood committed by the prisoner, and the prejudice against him became so overwhelming that it was feared he could not possibly have a fair trial. The Crown, however, stretched out its hand, and that department of the legislature of which the noble and learned lord on the bench formed a part, interested itself in the passing of a measure which took away all doubt as to the fairness of the trial. He (Serjeant Shee) felt that immense responsibility was involved in conducting this defence ; but having carefully read over the papers laid before him, and closely and minutely examined all the facts in the case, he could not help coming to the solemn conclusion that the prisoner was innocent. He believed there never was a truer word spoken than when the prisoner said, "Not Guilty." He felt convinced that the prisoner was perfectly innocent of the charges laid against him. He would meet every difficulty set up by the prosecution step by step. The prosecution accused the prisoner of having deliberately made up his mind, for purposes of his own, to get rid of John Parsons Cooke, and that he had prepared his body by a slow poison for the rapid action of a more potent and deadly agent which he intended to administer afterwards. The next point in the prosecution was the motive for the act, and they had endeavoured to trace that to the pecuniary difficulties of the prisoner ; and having, as they thought, satisfactorily disposed of that part of the matter, the prosecution attributed death to poison by strychnia, relying for proof on that point to the symptoms presented by the deceased, and the appearance of his body after death. But strychnia was not found in the body. That was beyond all question. The learned serjeant then proceeded to say that he had three points to deal with. First, the motive for the alleged crime; secondly, the preparation of the body for the agent; and thirdly, the agent itself. The parties who felt satisfied that strychnia was administered to the deceased—although none was found in the body—relied upon the supposition that the strychnia had been absorbed into the blood. But it was only an hypothesis that poison had destroyed Cooke. There was no proof—not the slightest proof that death had been occasioned by strychnia. Dr. Taylor had done all he could to prove his theory, but he (Serjeant Shee) contended that he had proved nothing, and that the symptoms in the rabbits, poisoned twenty-five years ago by Dr. Taylor, ought not to be considered for a moment in connexion with the present occasion. He would, however, call before the jury gentlemen of the highest possible eminence, who would all of them reject Dr. Taylor's theory as unworthy the belief of scientific men. He would call before them such men as Dr. Nunnely, Dr. Wilkinson, Dr. Nicholas Parkes, Dr. Letheby, and last, Dr. Herepath, of Bristol. All these gentlemen would prove, on their oaths, and beyond all doubts, that if the smallest particle of strychnia, the ten thousandth part of a grain was taken into the human system, it must and would be found, no amount of decomposition of the body preventing the strychnia from being detected. Well, after the jury had heard the decisive evidence of these eminent men, they could but come to the conclusion that strychnia not being found in the body of John Parsons Cooke could not have been administered; and that therefore the prisoner being charged with administering it, was not guilty of the great crime imputed to him. He next came to the supposed motive for murder. What had been proved by the evidence on this head? Why, the testimony of various witnesses had clearly proved that it was not to the interest of William Palmer that Cooke should die, but it was the worst calamity that could possibly happen to the prisoner. That Palmer, after Cooke's death, was immediately ruined was admitted on all sides—not the slightest doubt hung over that fact. Well, then, where was the motive? That Palmer was in embarrassed circumstances at the time of Cooke's death was equally true, but the jury would have calmly to consider how Palmer could have been at all benefited by Cooke's decease. Could his prospects have been improved? Assuredly not. He firmly believed that in the correspondence which had been read, but not sustained by *viva voce* evidence, the innocence of the prisoner lay concealed. Rightly understood, it would prove that Palmer had no motive to kill Cooke, but that, on the contrary, the death of Cooke would be the very worst calamity that could befall him. Palmer and Cooke had been intimate as racing friends for two or three years; they were jointly interested in, at least, one race-horse—Perine; they generally stayed together at the same hotels; were seen together on almost all the race-courses of England, and were known to be connected in betting transactions and ventures on the sale of horses. Cooke, in the presence of Jones, had said to Palmer, "Palmer, we have lost a great deal of money in betting this year." Mr. Serjeant Shee here dwelt at considerable length on the different monetary transactions between Palmer and Cooke, in reference to advances on bills, &c., by Pratt and others, and also betting transactions, representing them to be for their (Palmer and Cooke's) mutual accommodation, remarking that they understood each other very wall. Every item in the case, he said, showed that it was to the interest of Palmer that Cooke should live. And here he would ask whether Palmer was safe after Cooke's death? Certainly not. Then where was the motive to kill Cooke? Now, with respect to the book found in Palmer's house, upon the title of which was written "strychnia kills by causing tetanic influence on the respiratory muscles," it was well known that Palmer had in early life studied chemistry, and that was one of many other notes on the margin of the pages. It was the usual book for young men studying for Apothecaries' Hall, and it was very certain that Palmer himself knew the effects of strychnia without asking Newton. Palmer was well aware that strychnia, if administered, would kill by causing horrible convulsions; and if such a death took place in a small neighbourhood

like Rugeley, it would be the talk for a month, and occasion a good deal of discussion as to how the death occurred. Besides, just before Cooke died Palmer's brother Walter had died, and his only hope of extrication from his pecuniary embarrassments was by getting the amount due to him by the Prince of Wales Insurance Office on the death of his brother. He refused the offer of a premium, and Pratt, Palmer's solicitor, believed the claim so good that he got the discount from very large sums. The 13,000*l.* was the only unpledged property Palmer possessed. Now, it was plain that in November the Prince of Wales Insurance Office was very much annoyed at being called upon to pay so large a sum as 13,000*l.*, and determined to do all they could to resist the claim. They accordingly sent down Field, a detective officer, who took his man Simpson to make inquiries. One went to Stafford, and the other went to Rugeley, where, by their investigations into the mode of life of Walter Palmer, they raised suspicions affecting the prisoner. Now this occurred just before the death of Cooke, when Palmer well knew he was the object of much unwarranted and unfounded suspicion; and was there anything more absurd than to suppose, that at that time, beyond all others, he should have done such acts as would destroy his character and bring upon him the suspicion of another murder. He thought the supposition could not be for a moment seriously considered. Then it must be recollected that the pressure of Pratt on Palmer to meet the 2,000*l.* bill never took place at all until the Prince of Wales Insurance Office disputed the payment of the policy. Pratt said nothing while he considered the policy good. Sergeant Shee said he would now direct the attention of the jury to the symptoms exhibited by Cooke on the Tuesday night, according to the evidence of Mr. Jones and Elizabeth Mills. He would submit to the judgment of the jury, upon authorities which could not deceive them, that these symptoms were indicative of Cooke's having suffered general convulsions, and by no means from tetanus of any kind or from strychnia.

The learned Sergeant's speech occupied eight hours in its delivery, and was admitted by all who listened to it to be the best possible defence that could have been made for the prisoner. Indeed, he was quite successful in creating in many minds doubts as to his client's guilt; but he did not succeed in disproving in a single point any one of the allegations on which the Attorney-General relied for a conviction. The great point for the defence was, that strychnia had not been found in the deceased's body, and that high medical and chemical authority declared that if the poison had been administered it ought to have been discovered. On the other hand, it was proved that Palmer had purchased that poison on the Monday (the day before) and on Tuesday, the day on which Cooke died; and that Palmer had access to him; that he administered medicines to him; that on each occasion Cooke was seized with those agonizing convulsions of which he ultimately died, and which *all* the medical witnesses admitted to be such symptoms as strychnia would produce. On the whole, the medical testimony was of a very unsatisfactory character—in many respects, indeed, quite contradictory. But the Attorney-General, in cross-examination, extorted from the most eminent and reliable medical witness for the defence the fatal admission that the symptoms manifested by Cooke before and after his death were referrable to no known cause except strychnia. This admission told severely against the accused. It was emphatically dwelt on by the Attorney-General in his reply, and by Lord Campbell in his charge to the jury, on whose minds it could not fail to produce a most important impression. This was the really weak — the vulnerable point in Sergeant Shee's defence—which, in every other respect, was as powerful and complete as it well could be.

At length, on the twelfth day of this most remarkable trial—the thirteenth since its commencement—the Lord Chief Justice concluded his charge to the jury, which occupied the best part of two days in its delivery, in the following words:—

"Above all, no explanation has been given of what became of the strychnia purchased on the Tuesday morning, which has been proved, and which stands entirely un-

PALMER'S HOUSE AT RUGELEY

contradicted. Of the purpose for which that was bought no explanation has been given. The case is now in your hands. Unless by the evidence for the prosecution a clear conviction has been brought to your minds of the guilt of the prisoner, it is your duty to acquit him. You are not to convict him on suspicion—even on strong suspicion. There must be a strong conviction in your minds that he is guilty of the offence; and if you have any reasonable doubt you will give him the benefit of that doubt. But if you come to the clear conclusion that he is guilty, you will not be deterred from doing your duty by any consideration such as has been suggested to you. You will remember the oath that you have taken, and you will act upon it. Gentlemen, I now dismiss you to consider your verdict, and may God direct you!" [At the close of his address the learned judge was sensibly affected. His voice trembled with emotion, and the concluding sentences were almost inaudible.]

Mr. Serjeant Shee: The question which your lordship has submitted to the jury is whether Cooke's symptoms were consistent with death by strychnia. I submit——

Lord Campbell: That is not the question which I have submitted to the jury. I have told them that unless they consider the symptoms consistent with death by strychnia they ought to acquit the prisoner.

Mr. Serjeant Shee: It is my duty not to be deterred by any expression of displeasure; it is my duty to a much higher tribunal than even your lordships', to sub-

mit what occurs to me to be the proper question. I submit to your lordships that the question whether Cooke's symptoms are consistent with death by strychnia is a wrong question, unless it is followed by this—" and inconsistent with death by other natural causes;" and that the question should be whether the medical evidence establishes beyond all reasonable doubt the death of Cooke by strychnia? It is my duty to submit that. It is your lordships' duty, if I am wrong, to overrule it.

Mr. Baron Alderson: It is done already. You have done it in your speech.

Lord Campbell (addressing the jury): Gentlemen, I did not submit to you that the question upon which alone your verdict was to turn was whether the symptoms of Cooke were those of strychnia, but I said that that was a most material question, and I desired you to consider it. I said that if you thought that he died from natural disease—that he did not die from poisoning by strychnia—you should acquit the prisoner; but then I went on to say that if you were of opinion that the symptoms were consistent with death from strychnia, you should consider the other evidence given in the case to see whether strychnia had been administered to him, and whether it had been administered by the prisoner at the bar. These are the questions that I again put to you. If you come to the conclusion that these symptoms were consistent with death from strychnia, do you believe that death actually resulted from the administration of strychnia, and that that strychnia was administered by the prisoner at the bar? Do not find a verdict of guilty unless you believe that the strychnia was administered to the deceased by the prisoner at the bar; but, if you believe that, it is your duty to God and man to find the prisoner guilty.

At the conclusion of this address from the Lord Chief Justice, the jury retired from the court, at eighteen minutes after two o'clock.

The jury re-entered their box at twenty-five minutes to four, after an absence of one hour and seventeen minutes, and the prisoner, who had been removed upon the retirement of the jury, was placed in the dock at the same moment.

The buzz of excitement which ran round the court on the re-appearance of the jury, was instantly hushed by the formal question of the clerk of arraigns, who asked, "Gentlemen of the jury, are you all unanimous in your verdict?"

The foreman: We are.

The clerk of arraigns: How say you, gentlemen, do you find the prisoner at the bar guilty, or not guilty?

The foreman (rising, and in a distinct and firm tone): We find the prisoner GUILTY!

The prisoner, who exhibited some slight pallor and the least possible shade of anxiety upon the return of the jury to the box, almost instantly recovered his self-possession and demeanour of comparative indifference. He maintained his firmness and perfect calmness after the delivery of the verdict; and when the sentence was being passed, he looked an interested, although utterly unmoved spectator. We think we may truly say that during the whole of this protracted trial, his nerve and calmness never for a moment forsook him.

The clerk of the arraigns: Prisoner at the bar, you stand convicted of murder; what have you to say why the court should not give you judgment to die, according to law?

The question is one of a formal nature, and the prisoner did not answer.

The learned judges then assumed the black cap; and

The Lord Chief Justice pronounced sentence in the following terms:—William Palmer, after a long and impartial trial you have been convicted by a jury of your country of the crime of wilful murder. In that verdict my two learned brothers, who have so anxiously watched this trial, and myself entirely concur, and we consider the conviction altogether satisfactory. The case is attended with such circumstances of aggravation that I will not dare to touch upon them. Whether this be the first and only offence of this sort which you have committed is certainly known only to God and your own conscience. It is seldom that such a familiarity with the means of death should be shown without long experience; but for this offence, of which you have been found guilty, your life is forfeited. You must prepare to die; and I trust that, as you can expect no mercy in this world, you will, by a repentance of your crimes, seek to obtain mercy from Almighty God. The Act of Parliament on which you have been tried, and under which you have been brought to the bar of this court, at your own request, gives leave to the court to direct that the sentence under such circumstances shall be executed either within the jurisdiction of the Central Criminal Court, or in the county where the offence was committed. We think that, for the sake of example, the sentence ought to be executed in the county of Stafford. I hope that that terrible example will deter others from committing such atrocious crimes; and that it will be seen, whatever art, or caution, or experience may accomplish, that such an offence will surely be detected and punished. However destructive poison may be, it is so ordained by Providence, for the safety of its creatures, that there are means of detecting and punishing those who administer it. I again implore you to repent, and to prepare for the awful change which awaits you. I will not seek to harrow up your feelings by any enumeration of the circumstances of this foul murder; but I will content myself now by passing upon you the sentence of the law, which is—that you be taken from hence to the gaol of Newgate, and be thence removed to the gaol of the county of Stafford, being the county in which the offence for which you stand convicted was

committed, and that you be taken thence to the place of execution, and be there hanged by the neck until you be dead, and that your body be afterwards buried within the precincts of the prison in which you shall be last confined after your conviction; and may the Lord of heaven have mercy on your soul!—Amen.

The prisoner was immediately removed from the dock, and the trial was at an end.

Mr. James, Q.C., applied that the bills bearing the acceptance of Mrs Sarah Palmer, which had been proved to have been forged, should be impounded—an application which the court without hesitation granted.

Turning then to the jury,—

The Lord Chief Justice said: I beg to return to you, gentlemen, the warm thanks of my learned brothers and myself, for the service which you have rendered to your country upon this occasion. Your conduct throughout this protracted trial, which you have attended, no doubt, at much serious inconvenience to yourselves, has been such as to merit our utmost commendation. I only hope, and I doubt not, that you will be rewarded for your patient attention, and for the sacrifices which you have made, by the approbation of your own consciences and the approving voice of your country.

Turning next to the sheriffs, his Lordship continued: We have also to thank the Sheriffs of London for the manner in which the court has been kept during the trial, for their excellent arrangements, and for the facilities which they appear to have afforded to every one who had any business to transact.

Before quitting the bench the learned judges signed the warrants for the removal of the prisoner to the gaol of Stafford, and for the execution to be carried out there by the Sheriffs of that county.

That same night the doomed criminal was removed from Newgate with as much secrecy as possible, and conveyed to the gaol of Stafford. The conduct of this wretched man during the whole of his most tedious and terrible trial resembled that of an indifferent spectator, rather than a prisoner charged with the most horrible crime which a human being can commit. Judged by his appearance, he had no more interest in the issue of the awful assize than any other individual in the court. The most acute and sedulous observation of his countenance could hardly have detected the slightest shade of anxiety, or, in fact, the smallest traces of any emotion, during the whole of the twelve days that his trial lasted. Indeed, it may be said that he evinced more anxiety to ascertain the name of the winner of the Derby than in his own acquittal or condemnation; for it was well known, and caused no inconsiderable astonishment in court, that on the very day which terminated his trial and consigned him to a felon's doom, he made more than one inquiry as to which horse was the favourite for the Derby! It would, however, be exceedingly illogical to make any inference as to his guilt or innocence from this seemingly cool and unconcerned demeanour throughout one of the most searching and painful ordeals to which a human being can be subjected; because an innocent person with a sensitive organization would exhibit more emotion, which the ignorant might interpret into proof of guilt, under the mere imputation of crime, than the strong-minded or coarse-minded villain, really guilty of the crime with which he is charged.

After the conviction of this unhappy man immense exertions were made by his friends to procure for him a new trial or else a commutation of his sentence. But the moral sense of the community was clearly against any such exercise of the prerogative vested in the Crown. His brother, who is a clergyman of the Church of England, has addressed a letter to Lord Campbell, remonstrating with his lordship on the alleged unfairness of his charge to the jury. It is but right to admit that there is some ground for this accusation. His lordship did not hold the scales of justice as evenly as might be desired; yet it would be difficult to state what one fact has been too severely pressed against the criminal. The letter of his brother does not explain away any of the damning circumstances which have immersed Palmer in the fatal folds of the murderer's doom; and now some of his friends, who until the last moment clung, or pretended to cling, to the hope of his acquittal, are constrained to admit that the jury had no alternative than to return the verdict which they did. And this also must be the verdict of all who intelligently and impartially examine the proofs which have astounded the nation, by revealing a crime not surpassed for its revolting accompaniments, by anything recorded in the annals of Slow Poisoning.

The law was allowed to take its course; and on the 14th of June, 1856, William Palmer was hanged at Stafford, amidst the execrations of about fifty thousand of his fellow-creatures.

CHAPTER XIX.

ROBERT DUDLEY, EARL OF LEICESTER.—ELIZABETH AND HER LOVERS.

THE brave and gallant Henry IV of France said that there were three things which to him were inscrutable mysteries. We forget one of them, but two of them were—"to what religion he himself belonged," and "whether Queen Elizabeth were a maid?" With reference to this last "mystery," it may safely be affirmed that if Elizabeth did not forfeit her title of "Virgin Queen," it certainly was not for lack of solicitations and opportunities. Few maidens ever were more assiduously wooed. Her suitors were numerous enough to form a powerful body-guard for her majesty; but whether she allowed herself to be really won by any of them is a question on which historians have fiercely and frequently differed. It must, however, be confessed that the balance of evidence is unfavourable to Elizabeth's claim to be considered as a "fair vestal throned in the West," against whose cold heart Cupid's fiery shafts were shot in vain. Indeed, it may be said that, as far as historical evidence can demonstrate anything, it has shown, beyond the possibility of dispute, that Elizabeth was not chaste as an icicle which frost has curded from the purest snow and hangs in Dian's temple. Neither her meditations nor her actions were always maidenly: her fancy was not free, her virtue was not impregnable; and more than one of her numerous lovers obtained all that a lover could desire, except the questionable privilege of being permitted to call her his wife.

The first wooer of Queen Elizabeth of whom we have any record was the brother of Jane Seymour, the woman for whose charms Anne Boleyn, the mother of Elizabeth, had been brought to the block by the amorous and ferocious Henry VIII. She was not then more than fourteen years of age, but she was of precocious intellect, great attainments, pleasing manners, had a considerable revenue, a contingent right to the throne, and some claims to personal beauty. She has been described as being then a well-grown girl, with a good figure, of which she made the most, and as having well-formed hands, which she always took pains to display. Thomas Seymour, the brother of Jane Seymour, and of the Lord Protector Somerset, was a handsome, ambitious, and unprincipled man. He is alleged to have been a lover of Katherine Parr before that lady became the last of Henry's many wives. And if this be true, it will be admitted that it was fair, since the king took Seymour's sweetheart, that Seymour should take the king's daughter. Be this, however, as it may, Henry died, and his widow, Katherine Parr, was married to her former admirer, Thomas Seymour. Elizabeth was in a manner the ward of her stepmother, and it is said that the life of the latter was embittered by the improper familiarities which she detected to exist between her husband and her daughter-in-law. The queen-dowager one day surprised her husband, Thomas Seymour, with Elizabeth in his arms. Shortly after the old lady died, and thus, by her opportune departure, the way was re-opened for the aspiring hopes of Thomas Seymour. He became now the open suitor for the hand of Elizabeth; he had for a long time enjoyed the high office of Lord High Admiral of England, and during the short reign of Edward VI his influence was second to no subject in the kingdom. After the death of Katherine Parr, his attentions to the Princess Elizabeth became most marked. Their familiarity was so undisguised that it afforded

ample employment to the propagators of scandal, even during the life-time of his wife, but now that that obstacle was removed his court was redoubled. The governess of Elizabeth was bribed; the princess herself was won; but, according to the terms of her father's will, a clandestine marriage would have annulled her right to the succession. The consent of the council was requisite to constitute the validity of her marriage; and means were devised to extort this consent, because it was well known to both the lovers that it would not be voluntarily given. In order to attain this object, he sought the friendship of the disaffected among the nobility, and by opposing the measures of the government (of Edward), he endeavoured to gain the applause of the people. He was at last convicted of contriving a plot which had for its object the abduction of the young king. He was attainted of high treason, and afterwards executed. His death-warrant, amongst other names, had that of his own brother, the Lord Protector Somerset, adhibited to it.

That his familiarity with Elizabeth was of the most gross and intimate description is evident from the reluctant testimony of Mrs. Ashby, her governess:—"The moment he was up," says Mrs. Ashby, "he would hasten to Elizabeth's chamber in his nightgown and bare-legged. If she was still in bed, he would open the curtains and make as though he would come at her, and she would go further in the bed so that he could not come at her. If she were up he would ask how she did, and strike her upon the back or the buttocks familiarly. Once he sent James Seymour to recommend him to her, and ask her whether her great buttocks had grown less or no."

Parry, the Cofferer, says, "She (Elizabeth) told me that the admiral loved her but too well; that the queen (Katherine Parr) was jealous on her and him; and that, suspecting the open access of the admiral to her, she came suddenly upon them where they were all alone, he having her in his arms." It was reported that Elizabeth was pregnant by Seymour, which she declared to be a "shameless slander," but also that she bore him a child. "There was bruite (rumour) of a child born and miserably destroyed—but could not be discovered whose it was—on the report of the midwife, who was brought from her house blindfolded thither, and so returned. Saw nothing in the house while she was there but candlelight; only said it was the child of a very fair young lady."

After the death of Seymour, and to stay the scandal which had been let loose, Elizabeth conducted herself in a remarkably modest manner. She henceforth became the model maiden at her brother's court. "Sweet Sister Temperance"—as the young Edward playfully called her—well merited that title as the very belle idéal of Puritan propriety. All splendour of apparel she carefully avoided; the valuable jewels which her father had bequeathed to her remained for some years quite unused. The arrival of a bevy of fine ladies from France turned the heads of the fair dames of the English court, but the Lady Elizabeth remained unmoved; every other head was "frowsed, curled, and double curled," but "the Lady Elizabeth alone kept her old maiden shamefacedness."

This change, however, was not of very lengthened duration. Edward died, and "bloody Mary" ascended the throne. Elizabeth now renounced both her puritanism and protestations. She, moreover, laid aside her "old maiden shamefacedness," and began to bedizen herself with all the pomps and vanities of this "wicked world." Queen Mary had no objection, either of taste or of conscience, against arraying herself and others in costly and magnificent apparel. The fine clothes and jewels which Elizabeth had left untouched during the sombre reign of her brother were now called into active service. It is true that her panegyrists inform us that it was only by sheer compulsion, in the character of a loyal subject and a dutiful younger sister, that she was seduced to this act of backsliding; but it is at least certain that the habit, however unwillingly commenced, afterwards reconciled itself to the conscience of the royal maiden. She never again, when she had no one to consult but herself, relapsed into her primitive simplicity. The wardrobe bequeathed by Henry VIII to the youthful princess must surely have been scanty compared with the three thousand gowns left behind her by the aged queen; and it is a sad fact, that when nature no longer allowed the processes of "frowsing, curling, and double curling" to be continued on the genuine growth of the royal head, a selection had each morning to be gone through to determine which of eighty wigs was most worthy to bear for that day the pressure of the triple diadem.

During the reign of Mary, as Elizabeth became at once of maturer age and nearer to the crown, it was only natural that the number of her wooers should increase. Edward Courtenay, the young and handsome Earl of Devonshire—a near relation to Elizabeth—was for a time supposed to have obtained the ascendancy over her heart. Their names were constantly joined together in the public voice. Every malcontent who made Elizabeth his watchword invariably coupled her with the Earl of Devonshire, as the selected partner of her throne. Whether any real passion existed on either side between Courtenay and Elizabeth, must probably remain a mystery. Both became involved in the Jane Grey rebellion against Mary, and, as a consequence, suffered a short imprisonment in the Tower; but the vengeance of Mary having been sufficiently slaked by the blood of other victims, she did not proceed to extremities against her sister and her lover, who, after a short incarceration, were restored to their liberty.

Foreign suitors were not wanting for the hand of the princess. They began to pour in from divers quarters, north and south, Protestant and Catholic; some wooed by deputy, others pressed their cause personally. King Philip of Spain, the husband of Mary, vehemently supported the cause of his kinsman, Philibert of Savoy; but neither Philip's patronage nor Philibert's own presence could prevail on the obdurate maiden. From the other end of Europe, Christian of Denmark, and Gustavus of Sweden, applied to the princess herself on behalf of their respective heirs, both of whom we shall find appearing again at a later period of her life. On the 17th of November, 1558, Mary died, and Elizabeth became Queen of England. This change in her position did not of course diminish the number of her suitors. It, as might be expected, greatly added to their number. First and foremost in the suit for the hand of the "throned vestal" was no other than Philip of Spain. The voice of scandal rumoured that he looked upon her with a desiring eye even during the lifetime of her sister. At all events, Mary could hardly have been in her grave before he was vigorously pressing his suit, whether of love or of policy. Elizabeth was flattered, but perplexed. She remembered her former obligations to Philip, and she knew that with him for her husband she had no reasons to fear the exertions of France in favour of Mary Stuart. On the other hand, her counsellors reminded her of her former disapproval of his marriage with her sister; they placed before her his suspicious temper and intolerant zeal in favour of the Catholic faith, which she designed to abolish; they urged that his power was rather nominal than real, and argued since he was related in the same degree of affinity to her as her father had been to Katherine, she could not marry him without acknowledging that her mother, Anne Boleyn, had been the mistress, and not the wife, of her father. At first, Elizabeth informed the Spanish ambassador that, if she made up her mind to marry, she would prefer Philip to any other prince; but at the second audience which she vouchsafed to him, she requested to be excused on account of the impediment arising from Philip's former marriage with her sister. Still the opponents of the match were apprehensive of the result. But they urged in parliament the projected measures for the abolition of the Catholic worship; and Philip, who had made its preservation an indispensable condition, turned his eyes from Elizabeth of England to Isabella of France, by whom his offer was accepted.

The place of Philip was supplied by his cousin, Charles of Austria, son of the Emperor Ferdinand. The family connexions of this prince promised equal support against the rivalry of Francis of France, and his wife, Mary Stuart. But here again the religion of the wooer presented an insuperable obstacle to his suit.

Her next wooer was Eric, King of Sweden, who sent his brother John, Duke of Finland, to England, to press his suit. He also sent her eighteen piebald horses and several chests of bullion, with an intimation that he would quickly follow to lay his heart and his crown at her feet. Eric was a Protestant, and therefore his religion could be no objection to the marriage; but Elizabeth put him off so long, that at last his patience was exhausted, and he consoled himself by marrying a lady, who, though unequal in rank to Elizabeth, could boast of superior beauty, and repaid his choice by the sincerity of her attachment.

Then came Adolphus, Duke of Holstein, to woo the royal virgin. This prince was young and handsome, and (which exalted him more in the eyes of Elizabeth) a soldier and a conqueror. On his arrival, he was received with honour and treated with peculiar kindness. "He loved, and was beloved." The queen made him a knight of the Garter; she granted him a pension for life; still she could not be induced to take him for her husband.

While Charles, and Eric, and Adolphus thus openly contended for the hand—or rather the crown—of Elizabeth, they were secretly opposed by a rival whose pretensions were the more formidable as they received the united support of the secretary and the secretary's wife. This rival was a Scot, the Earl of Arran, who, during the Reformation, had displayed a courage and constancy which left all his associates, with the exception perhaps of the Lord James Mory, far behind him; and as soon as the peace was concluded, he presumed to sue for the hand of Elizabeth as the expected recompense of his services. To the deputies of the Scottish Convention, who urged his suit, Elizabeth replied, with her habitual affectation, that she was content with her maiden state, and that God had given her no inclination for marriage. The ambassadors took her at her word, and suddenly returned to Scotland, at which the pride of the queen was deeply offended. She complained that while kings and princes persevered for months and years in their suit, the Scots did not deign to urge their requests a second time. As for the Earl of Arran, whether owing to disappointment, or to some other cause, he fell into a deep melancholy, which ended in the loss of his reason.

The next aspirant to her hand was an Englishman Sir William Pickering. He could not boast of noble blood; nor had he exercised any higher charge than that of a mission to some of the petty States of Germany. But the beauty of his person, his address, and his taste in the fine arts, attracted the notice of the young queen; and so lavish was she of her attentions to this unexpected favourite, that for some weeks he was considered by the courtiers as her future consort. But Pickering was soon forgotten, and another suitor in the person of the Earl of Arundel was doomed to experience a similar disappointment to that which had awaited the other wooers of the impregnable virgin.

We might also dwell upon many others who were her suitors and lovers—such as Hatton, and Raleigh, and Oxford, and Blount; but we must hasten to the man who made the deepest impression on her heart—the Lord Robert Dudley, son of the Duke of Northumberland, who, as well as his father, had been attainted for the attempt to remove Elizabeth as well as Mary from the succession. He had, however, been restored in blood, and frequently employed under the late queen. We have no certainty as to the time of his birth, or any accurate account of the manner of his education. All we can learn is that he had a competent knowledge of the Latin tongue, and was thoroughly versed in Italian. He received the honour of knighthood when he was but a youth, and entered early into the service of King Edward. It was one of his father's maxims to marry his children while they were young, as the secret means of fixing their fortunes, bringing them into a settled course of life, and giving him an opportunity of procuring for them valuable grants or places of honour and emoluments. Accordingly, on the 4th of June, 1580, being the day after the marriage of his brother Lord L'Isle to the Duke of Somerset's daughter, Sir Robert Dudley espoused Amy, daughter of Sir John Robsart, the king himself honouring their nuptials with his presence. Soon after he was made Master of the King's

ROBERT DUDLEY

Buckhounds, and throughout the reign of Edward he contrived to gain an uncommon share of the royal confidence and favour. In the first year of the reign of Queen Mary he fell into the same misfortunes as the rest of his family, who in their attempt to place the crown upon the head of the Lady Jane Grey were attainted for high treason, sentenced, and committed to the Tower. But, unlike his father and brother, Robert was pardoned, and throughout the whole of the reign of Mary continued to enjoy the smiles and bounty of his sovereign and her consort.

It was not, however, until the accession of Elizabeth to the throne that the full tide of this infamous man's brilliant fortunes had set in. He was by her immediately entertained at court as one of her principal favourites; promoted to the office of Master of the Horse; made a knight of the most honourable Order of the Garter; sworn in as member of the Privy Council; presented by the queen with the castles and manors of Kenilworth, Astel Grove, Denbigh, and Chink; made Lord High Steward of the University of Cambridge, was proposed by Elizabeth as the husband of the Queen of Scotland, created Earl of Leicester, and in the face of her whole court assigned an apartment contiguous to her own bedchamber! How deserving he was of such wealth and honours we propose to show in the following chapter.

CHAPTER XX.

ROBERT DUDLEY, EARL OF LEICESTER (Continued).

ALL his biographers, be they his friends or his foes, are unanimous in admitting, that had Queen Elizabeth been cognisant of Dudley's marriage with Amy Robsart, she would not have showered upon him honours and rewards in such profusion; and of this he himself became fully aware at a very early period. He, therefore, made up his mind to maintain his marriage a secret, and with that view he immured his young and beautiful wife in his manor-house of Cumnor, under the charge of his servant Anthony Foster. The village of Cumnor, Berkshire, is pleasantly built on a hill; and in a wooded park closely adjacent, was situated the ancient mansion, occupied at this time by Anthony Foster, of which the ruins may be still extant. The park was then full of large trees, and, in particular, of ancient and mighty oaks, which stretched their giant arms over the high wall surrounding the demesne, thus imparting to it a melancholy, secluded, and monastic appearance. The entrance to the park lay through an old fashioned gate-way in the outer wall, the door of which was formed of two huge oaken leaves, thickly studded with nails, like the gate of an old town. The mansion situated in this pleasant retreat, was splendidly and luxuriously furnished by Dudley for the reception of his wife. She, however, was far from being satisfied—she sincerely loved her husband, and anxiously and impatiently waited for the time when she should be presented to the world as his wife. She knew that her personal charms and mental accomplishments qualified her for shining in the highest and most brilliant circles in the land.

The Countess Amy—for to that rank she was exalted by her private but solemn union with England's proudest earl—was one of the loveliest women of her time; she was of the middle stature for a woman; her complexion was of exquisite and transparent purity; her cheeks were delicately tinged with the rosy hue of health; her eyes were hazel coloured, and her luxuriant curls of dark brown hair, when let loose from the wreath of brilliants in which it was generally bound, strayed over her snow-white shoulders, like the wild and fantastic tendrils of an unpruned vine. But beauty, such as Amy Robsart's, will pall on the taste of a selfish and ambitious man, and such was Robert Dudley, the Earl of Leicester. His own personal advantages had attracted the attention of the Queen of England; and Elizabeth, though as inferior to Amy in beauty as the latter was superior to the former in rank, became more desirable to the ambitious Dudley, than his own beautiful and lovely wife. Leicester, who had represented himself to the Queen as a bachelor, was in constant dread of exposure from the importunities of Amy; he therefore formed in his own dark mind, the design of ridding himself for ever of this impediment to the most exalted position in the land. He communicated his design to two of his creatures, on whom he could rely. Those were Anthony Foster, to whom we have referred, and Sir Richard Varney, a dependant of the earl's, two most remorseless and unscrupulous villains, who for what they deemed an adequate inducement, would not shrink from the commission of any crime however atrocious it might be. These ruffians, taking their cue from their employer, determined to put the unfortunate Amy to death. The Earl of Leicester had a physician of the name of Julio, who was known as one of the most skilful compounders of poisons in his time. Dr Julio furnished the assassins with a deadly mixture, which Foster and Varney prevailed upon the countess to swallow, upon her complaining of illness. But the taste was so nauseous that her stomach rejected it, and when she recollected the urgency with which they had pressed her to take it, a dark suspicion arose in her mind that their object was to murder her. This determined the murderers to accomplish the wishes of their master by shorter and surer means than the compounds of Dr. Julio. "So Sir Richard Varney, the chief projector in this design, who, by the earl's orders, remained that day of her death alone with her, with one man only, and Foster, who had that day forcibly sent away all her servants from her to Abingdon Market, they (I say whether first stifling her, or else strangling her) afterwards flung her down a pair of stairs and broke her neck." The murderers propagated the report that she had fallen down; but the inhabitants of the district were not deceived, and they used to say that the countess was conveyed from her usual chamber where she lay to another chamber, where the bed's head stood close to a secret postern door, and that in the night the assassins came and stifled her in her bed, bruised her head very much, broke her neck, and at length flung her down stairs, hoping the world would attribute her death to a mischance. "But," continues the chronicler, "behold the mercy and justice of God in revenging and discovering this lady's murder, for one of the persons was afterwards taken for felony in the marshes of Wales, and offering to publish the manner of the aforesaid murder, was privately made away with by the earl's appointment; and Sir Richard Varney (the other) dying about the same time in London, cried miserably, and said to a person of note, not long before his death, that all the devils in hell did tear him to pieces. Anthony Foster, likewise, after that fact, being a man formerly addicted to hospitality, company, mirth, and music, was afterwards observed to forsake all this with much melancholy and pensiveness—some say with madness—pined and drooped away. The wife also of Bald Butler, kinsman to the earl, gave out the whole fact a little before her death. Neither are the following passages to be forgotten—that, as soon as she was murdered, they made great haste to bury her before the coroner had given in his inquest, which the earl himself condemned, as not done advisedly, and her father, Sir John Robsart, hearing, came with all speed hither, caused her corpse to be taken up, the coroner to sit upon her, and further inquiry to be made concerning this business to the full; but it was generally thought that the earl had stopped his mouth; and, to make plain to the world the great love he bore to her while alive, and what a grief the loss of so virtuous a lady was to his outer heart, caused her body to be reburied in St. Mary's Church, Oxford, with great pomp and solemnity. It is also remarkable that Dr. Babington, the earl's chaplain, preaching the funeral sermon, tripped once or twice in his speech by recommending to their memories that virtuous lady so pitifully slain."

The accusation that Leicester was the real author, and Varney and Foster the actors, of the murder of the Countess Amy was quite current in his own time. It was alluded to in the "Yorkshire Tragedy," a play erroneously ascribed to Shakspere, when a rake, who determines to murder all his family, throws his wife down stairs, with this allusion to the murder of Leicester's lady:—

> The only way to charm a woman's tongue
> Is, break her neck—a politician did it!

The melancholy fate of Amy Robsart was made the subject of a beautiful ballad, by Mickle; a few stanzas of which we subjoin. The opening verse is very fine—

> The dews of summer night did fall,
> The moon—sweet regent of the sky—
> Silvered the walls of Cumnor Hall,
> And many an oak that there grew by.

> Now nought was heard beneath the skies;
> The sounds of busy life were still;
> Save an unhappy lady's sighs,
> That issued from that lonely pile.

> "Leicester," she cried, "is this thy love,
> That thou so oft has sworn to me?
> To leave me in this lonely grove,
> Immured to shameful privity."

She goes on to complain of his coolness, and upbraids him for visiting her so seldom; this she contrasts with the first ardour of his love:—

> "And when you first to me made suit,
> How fair I was, you oft would say!
> And proud of conquest plucked the fruit,
> Then left the blossom to decay.

> "Yes! now neglected and despised—
> The rose is pale, the lily's dead!
> But he that once their charms so prized,
> Is sure the cause those charms are fled."

She is jealous of the Court beauties:—

> At Court, I'm told, is beauty's throne,
> Where every lady's passing rare;
> That Eastern flowers that shame the sun
> Are not so glowing, not so fair!

> Then, earl, why did'st thou leave the bed,
> Where roses and where lilies vie,
> To seek a primrose, whose pale shade
> Must sicken when those gauds are by?

The lady continues her reproachful soliloquy to the faithless earl, and the ballad thus concludes:—

> Thus sore and sad the lady grand,
> In Cumnor Hall, so lone and drear;
> And many a heartfelt sigh she heaved,
> And let fall many a bitter tear.

> And ere the dawn of day appeared
> In Cumnor Hall, so lone and drear,
> Full many a piercing scream was heard,
> And many a cry of mortal fear!

> The death-bell thrice was heard to ring;
> An aerial voice was heard to call;
> And thrice the raven flapped his wing
> Around the towers of Cumnor Hall:

> The mastiff howled at village door,
> The oaks were shattered on the green;
> Woe was the hour—for never more
> That hapless countess ere was seen!

> And in that manor now no more
> Is cheerful feast and sprightly ball;
> For ever since that dreary hour
> Have spirits haunted Cumnor Hall!

The village maids, with fearful glance,
    Avoid the ancient moss-grown wall
Nor ever lead the merry dance
    Among the groves of Cumnor Hall!

Full many a traveller oft has sighed,
    And pensive wept the countess' fall,
As wandering onwards they've espied
    The haunted towers of Cumnor Hall!

The infamous instruments of Leicester in the atrocious murder came to a miserable, but richly-merited end. Scott, in his "Kenilworth," thus narrates the death of the villains, Foster and Varney:—

"On the next day, when evening approached, Varney summoned Foster to the execution of their plan. Tider and Foster's old man-servant were sent on a feigned errand down to the village, and Anthony himself, as if anxious to see that the countess suffered no want of accommodation, visited her place of confinement. He was so much staggered at the mildness and patience with which she seemed to endure her confinement, that he could not help earnestly recommending to her not to cross the threshold of her room on any account whatever, until Lord Leicester should come, 'Which,' he added, 'I trust in God, will be very soon.' Amy patiently promised that she would resign herself to her fate, and Foster returned to his hardened companion with his conscience half-eased of the perilous load that weighed on it. 'I have warned her,' he said; 'surely in vain is the snare set in sight of any bird?'

"He left, therefore, the countess's door unsecured on the outside, and, under the eye of Varney, withdrew the supports which sustained the falling trap, which, therefore, kept its level position merely by a slight adhesion. They withdrew to wait the issue on the ground floor adjoining, but they waited long in vain. At length Varney, after walking long to and fro, with his face muffled in his cloak, threw it suddenly back, and exclaimed, "Surely never was a woman fool enough to neglect so fair an opportunity of escape!'

"'Perhaps she is resolved,' said Foster, 'to await her husband's return.'

"'True—most true,' said Varney, rushing out; 'I had not thought of that before.'

"In less than two minutes Foster, who remained behind, heard the tread of a horse in the court-yard, and then a whistle similar to that which was the earl's usual signal; the instant after the door of the countess's chamber opened, and in the same moment the trap-door gave way. There was a rushing sound—a heavy fall—a faint groan, and all was over.

"At the same instant Varney called in at the window, in an accent and tone which was an indescribable mixture betwixt horror and raillery, 'Is the bird caught? is the deed done?'

"'O God, forgive us!' replied Anthony Foster.

"'Why, thou fool,' said Varney; 'thy toil is ended, and thy reward secure. Look down into the vault: what seest thou?'

"'I only see a heap of white clothes, like a snowdrift,' said Foster. 'O God! she moves her arm!'

"'Hurl something down on her. Thy gold chest, Tony, it is an heavy one.'

"'Varney, thou art an incarnate fiend!' replied Foster. 'There needs nothing more—she is gone!'

"'So pass our troubles,' said Varney, entering the room. 'I dreamed not I could have mimicked the earl's call so well.'

"'Oh, if there be judgment in heaven, thou hast deserved it,' said Foster, 'and wilt meet it! Thou hast destroyed her by means of her best affections. It is a seething of the kid in the mother's milk!'

"'Thou art a fanatical ass,' replied Varney: 'let us now think how the alarm should be given; the body is to remain where it is.'

"But their wickedness was to be permitted no longer; for, even while they were at this consultation, Tressilian and Raleigh broke in upon them, having obtained admittance by means of Tider and Foster's servant, whom they had secured at the village.

"Anthony Foster fled on their entrance; and, knowing each corner and pass of the intricate old house, escaped all search. But Varney was taken on the spot; and, instead of expressing compunction for what he had done, seemed to take a fiendish pleasure in pointing out to them the remains of the murdered countess, while at the same time he defied them to show that he had any share in her death. The despairing grief of Tressilian, on viewing the mangled and yet warm remains of what had lately been so lovely and so beloved, was such, that Raleigh was compelled to have him removed from the place by force, while he himself assumed the direction of what was to be done.

"Varney, upon a second examination, made very little mystery either of the crime or of its motives; alleging, as a reason for his frankness, that though much of what he confessed could only have attached to him by suspicion, yet such suspicion would have been sufficient to deprive him of Leicester's confidence, and to destroy all his towering plans of ambition. 'I was not born,' he said, 'to drag on the remainder of life a degraded outcast; nor will I so die, that my fate shall make a holiday to the vulgar herd.'

"From these words, it was apprehended he had some design upon himself, and he was carefully deprived of all means by which such could be carried into execution. But like some of the heroes of antiquity, he carried about his person a small quantity of strong poison, prepared probably by the celebrated Demetrius Alasco. Having swallowed this potion over night, he was found next morning dead in his cell; nor did he appear to have suffered much agony, his countenance presenting, even in death, the habitual expression of sneering sarcasm, which was predominant while he lived. 'The wicked man,' saith Scripture, 'hath no bonds in his death.'

"The fate of his colleague in wickedness was long unknown. Cumnor Place was deserted immediately after the murder; for, in the vicinity of what was called the Lady Dudley's Chamber, the domestics pretended to hear groans, and screams, and other supernatural noises. After a certain length of time, Janet, hearing no tidings of her father, became the uncontrolled mistress of his property, and conferred it with her hand upon Wayland, now a man of settled character, and holding a place in Elizabeth's household. But it was after they had been both dead for some years, that their eldest son and heir, in making some researches about Cumnor Hall, discovered a secret passage, closed by an iron door, which, opening from behind the bed in the Lady Dudley's Chamber, descended to a sort of cell, in which they found an iron chest, containing a quantity of gold, and a human skeleton stretched above it. The fate of Anthony Foster was now manifest. He had fled to this place of concealment, forgetting the key of the spring-lock; and being barred from escape, by the means he had used for preservation of that gold, for which he had sold his salvation, he had there perished miserably. Unquestionably the groans and screams heard by the domestics were not entirely imaginary, but were those of this wretch, who, in his agony, was crying for relief and succour."

CHAPTER XXII.

ROBERT DUDLEY, EARL OF LEICESTER (Concluded.)

AFTER the death of Amy Robsart, and the scandal which its sudden and mysterious character had created had been hushed, the Earl of Leicester paid most assiduous court to Queen Elizabeth. He aspired not only to be the most powerful subject in the realm, but also to the empire of the royal person herself. Elizabeth, however, though allowing him all the privileges, did not choose to confer on him the authority of a husband. She could obtain from Leicester all she wanted, and was not, therefore, very careful whether her lover might have some of his desires ungratified. At last, the earl was convinced that, legally, the queen would never consent to be his wife; he therefore, about the year 1572, married secretly the Baroness-Dowager of Sheffield, the granddaughter of the Duke of Norfolk, and the widow of Lord Sheffield, who had died suddenly shortly after Leicester became acquainted with his wife, and, as was then said, of the "Leicester cold"—a fatal and mysterious complaint to which it was remarked a great number of the friends and acquaintances of the great earl were subject. This marriage of Leicester with Lady Sheffield was kept secret, to prevent the wrath of Elizabeth from being kindled; for the Tudor lioness was extremely prone to the passion of jealousy, and against a rival her rage was known to be terrible, and her vengeance implacable. We have no desire to be severe upon the royal virgin, but, in truth, it must be owned that she was slightly imperious, if not unreasonable, in her exactions from her lovers; for while she expected to enjoy a perfect monopoly of the person and affections of every individual favourite, she was by no means inclined to adopt the same restricted policy as far as the sharing of her own queenly charms were concerned. Leicester was well aware of this inconsistence in the disposition of his royal mistress, and did all he could to accommodate himself to it. Accordingly, as we have observed, his marriage was kept secret, and his attentions to the queen were more fervent and incessant than ever. None were so fierce in denouncing her enemies, nor so alert in complying with her whims. His zeal to serve her majesty was prodigious—no considerations of honour or humanity were permitted to stand in its way. His acuteness, also, in divining the royal wishes which modesty or policy could not allow Elizabeth to express in words, was very great, and such as, even if the queen were not attached to him by more tender ties, must have rendered Leicester a highly-favoured and successful courtier.

At this time the beauteous and unfortunate Mary Stuart, having fled from her own fierce and rebellious subjects, was the guest, or, more properly speaking, the prisoner of the Queen of England. Elizabeth always hated Mary. The claim of the Queen of Scots to the throne of England,—the feelings with which she was regarded by the Popish party,—the dubious legitimacy of Elizabeth,—and, above all, the superior personal charms of Mary Stuart, had engendered and fostered in the proud soul of the daughter of Henry VIII a deep and unappeasable dislike to her charming and accomplished rival. That rival was now her captive; and as if to illustrate the universal supremacy of womanly fascinations, Mary Stuart—though crownless and sceptreless, a prisoner and an exile—vanquished and ruled the hearts of more than one of the nobles of the jealous and imperious Elizabeth. The Duke of Norfolk first sympathized with the misfortunes of Mary; he then beheld and loved her, and resolved to place her upon the throne of her ancestors. Mary Stuart, if she did not reciprocate the tender passion of the duke, at least encouraged it. It was natural for her to do so: she was a forlorn queen—Norfolk was a powerful noble; she was banished and without supporters—Norfolk was in his own country, where his ancient name and extensive domains gave him a princely following; she was a captive and sighed for deliverance—Norfolk might set her free. Add to this, that Norfolk clung to that old faith in which Mary Stuart was an ardent, if not bigoted, believer; and that the Church of Rome, for a time, had her hopes centered in the Queen of Scots for the reestablishment of that religion, which the father of Elizabeth had overthrown, and which she herself was pledged to keep down. The captive queen then smiled sweetly on the amorous Norfolk, but whether those smiles were the reflections of her soul, or the instruments of her policy, or a combination of both, is a question which we must abstain from discussing, and abandon to the industry of speculative and sentimental historians. Suffice it here to state that the suit of Norfolk proved fatal to himself and the object of his passion. There were not wanting friends to dissuade the duke from his dangerous enterprise; the immense hazard which he ran was pointed out to him; the hate which Elizabeth bore to the Queen of Scots was dwelt upon; and it was justly argued to him that that hate would be intensified into fury, if Elizabeth should discover that her lovely rival was seducing the hearts of her nobles from their own lawful sovereign. But Leicester did not join in those representations to his friend Norfolk. On the contrary, he incited that unfortunate nobleman to persevere in his suit to the Queen of Scots. He urged him to a bold and fearless pursuit of his object. He represented to Norfolk that Elizabeth had not the power, even if she had the will, to hinder or resent his marriage with Mary Stuart. And Leicester did this that Norfolk might be destroyed, and that he himself might have an opportunity of making a display of loyalty to his royal mistress. The tragic end of Norfolk is well known. Leicester was one of the peers who, in 1572, sat in judgment on the Duke of Norfolk, and condemned him to death.

Previous to this, when Elizabeth assembled her council to determine what should be done with her captive, Mary Stuart, the Earl of Leicester had the fiendish audacity to propose that she should be taken off by poison! But, savage and depraved though the nobles of Elizabeth were, they had enough of humanity to reject this most infamous proposal.

Like Amy Robsart, Lady Sheffield importuned Leicester to publish their marriage to the world, that she might free herself from the reproaches which attached to her, as the mother of the son that she had born to him while she was unrecognised as his wife. But Leicester was inflexible in his determination to conceal from Elizabeth that he was married; and the relations of Lady Sheffield, who profited by the power which they exercised over Leicester as masters of his secret, joined with him in persuading the unfortunate lady to conceal her claim, and to acquiesce in her degradation.

It was at this time remarked, that the Earl of Leicester had the singular good luck of being suddenly rid of all such persons as were his enemies, or all such as he had reason to suppose would become such. "This good chance," writes the chronicler, "had he in the death of my Lord Essex, and that in a moment most fortunate for Leicester; for when Essex was coming home from Ireland, to revenge himself upon Leicester for getting his wife with child in his absence, my Lord of Leicester hearing thereof, procured a friend or two to accompany Essex on his journey, and so he died on his way of an extreme flux, caused by an Italian recipe, as all his friends were well assured; and the maker whereof was a surgeon, as is believed, that then was newly come to my Lord Leicester from Italy, a cunning man and sure in operation."

The Earl of Leicester, immediately after the murder of Essex, married his widow, whom he had previously debauched. This marriage, like that of Lady Sheffield, was kept secret, and from the same reason, the fear of the queen. The affair, however, was well known about the court; but the earl was so powerful that for a long time no one had the courage to inform Elizabeth of the treachery of her foremost favourite. At length Monsieur Simier, "a very gallant gentleman" from France, an attendant of the Duke of Anjou, who was at that time a suitor for the hand of Elizabeth, having discovered that the Queen's partiality towards Leicester was an obstacle to the success of his master's courtship, told Elizabeth that her favourite earl was married to the Countess of Essex. At this intelligence the queen was so enraged that she commanded him not to stir from the Castle of Greenwich, designing to have committed him to the Tower, but from this she was dissuaded by the intercession of the Earl of Sussex.

Leicester resolved to be revenged on Simier for betraying his secret. On several occasions the Frenchman was waylaid by ruffians, who attempted to take his life. These, it was generally believed, were set on and rewarded by the infuriate Leicester. Simier, however, had the good fortune to escape in spite of the malice and ingenuity of his enemy, although on more than one occasion his life was placed in extreme peril. One day when Simier was in attendance on the queen, in her barge, not far from Greenwich, a gun was discharged from a neighbouring boat, and one of the royal bargemen was wounded through both his arms. It was believed that this shot was discharged to despatch Simier, but it was contrived to give the affair the appearance of being altogether accidental, and the man who had fired the gun was, after a short imprisonment, allowed to go at large.

Soon after the discovery of his marriage with Lady Essex, Leicester caused it to be publicly solemnized, and she was now received as the Countess of Leicester. The court wits, who were cognizant of the earl's pre-

THE COUNTESS OF SHEFFIELD.

vious marriage with Lady Sheffield, were in the habit of terming his two wives "Leicester's two Testaments"—Lady Sheffield the old, and Lady Essex the new. In order, however, to stifle this scandal as effectually as possible, Leicester endeavoured to induce Lady Sheffield to desist from enforcing her claim. This unfortunate lady deposed that, in the close harbour in the queen's gardens, at Greenwich, in the presence of Sir John Hubbard and George Digby, Leicester offered her several hundred a-year, on condition she would abstain from advancing any pretensions to him as her husband. At the same time he had recourse to threats; for he told her, unless she would comply with this proposal, he would never come near her, neither should she receive one penny of his money. Lady Sheffield felt that she was quite unable to contend with the all-powerful favourite, and therefore promised all he desired. But Leicester was far from satisfied with the advantage which he had gained, he wished to make assurance doubly sure. Lady Sheffield must be deprived of the power of claiming him for her husband. In order to do this he told her she must marry some other person; and the poor lady, to shelter herself from his resentment, was fain to marry Sir Edward Stafford, a man of high birth, great honour, and the Queen's ambassador in France. This marriage she always regretted, inasmuch as by it she bastardised her son to Leicester. She afterwards excused herself for the deed by affirming upon oath that Leicester administered some potions to her which had the effect of enfeebling her intellect, depriving her of the power of resistance, and also causing her hair and nails to loosen and fall off; besides, she

averred that, unless she complied, her life would be destroyed.

Elizabeth, though at first greatly exasperated at her favourite's marriage to the Countess of Essex, was soon reconciled to him, and the power of the earl was once more supreme in the English court. He was appointed ambassador extraordinary to the Low Countries, where he proceeded with a train of one hundred gentlemen and three hundred others of inferior rank. He was also made Captain General, or Commander-in-Chief of all the forces which served in the Low Countries, then asserting their independence against Spain. Here he acquired considerable military distinction—the Spaniards were defeated in more than one engagement. At one of these—the battle of Zutphen—the renowned Sir Philip Sydney received the wound of which he died. The English in this engagement greatly distinguished themselves, but the victory was not their's, for the Duke of Parma advanced to the assistance of the Spaniards, and Leicester found himself forced to retreat. Soon after he returned to the Hague, where he found the States-General greatly dissatisfied with the results of the campaign against the Spaniards. Leicester, presuming on his influence with the army, attempted to dissolve them; in this, however, he failed, and in his anger he declared his intention to return to England.

Upon his arrival in this country, he was warmly welcomed by the Queen, who resented the treatment which he received from the States-General at the Hague as an insult to herself. Indeed, of all her favourites, Leicester was the one who enjoyed her confidence and affection for the longest period. Upon the occasion when

No. 10.—POISONERS.

all England was alarmed by the Armada which Spain launched for the conquest of this country, Leicester was created Lieutenant-General of the kingdom, and recommended to the army and people by a speech from the Sovereign's own lips. The English army was assembled at Tilbury; and Elizabeth, that she might encourage her subjects, went to review that army in person, and delivered the following short but memorable speech:—"Soldiers of England," she said, "I myself will be your general, judge, and rewarder, of every one of your virtues in the field. I know you already for your forwardness. You have deserved rewards and crowns, and we do assure you, on the word of a prince, they shall be duly paid you. In the mean time, my lieutenant-general shall be in my stead, than whom never prince commanded a more noble or worthy subject; not doubting but by your obedience to my general, by your concord in the camp and your valour in the field, we shall shortly have a famous victory over those enemies of my God, of my kingdom, and of my people."

Truth cannot endorse this character of Leicester bestowed by his sovereign. On the contrary, this once proud earl, whose word shook the council, and whose hand wielded the state, has his name execrated as a cruel, haughty, selfish and perfidious man. The foul murderer of the beautiful Amy Robsart—the poisoner of the Earl of Essex—the poisoner and would-be murderer of the Countess of Sheffield, and of many others whom interest or revenge might prompt him to remove from his path, must ever be regarded as one of those loathsome characters that flourish on the corruption of a royal court. His death was well worthy of the life which he led. Royal justice he could evade or defy; but heaven, unlike Queen Elizabeth, was neither to be purchased nor frightened by the mighty earl, who, after all his murders and poisonings, was himself poisoned by that which he had prepared for others. Wearied by his exertions, and disappointed of his expectations, he retired to his castle of Killingworth to repose himself for a time, and to gather fresh strength to climb the steep ascent on whose summit stood the glitering goal of his ambition. By this time he had become enamoured with the charms of his third wife—the widow of the earl whom Leicester had murdered: he therefore resolved to rid himself of her by that potion which he had found so apt an instrument for the riddance of other men and women who were dangerous or disagreeable to him. One day the countess complained of a sensation of faintness—Leicester told her that he had a sovereign and specific remedy for that complaint. This she received, but for some reason did not use, but laid it by. One day the earl returned home somewhat fatigued; and his lady, thinking that the cordial which he recommended to her could not be injurious to him, administered a portion of it in some wine, without, however, letting him know that she had done so. In a few minutes Leicester was seized with excruciating spasms, which recurring at regular intervals, terminated his life in about five hours after he had partaken of the fatal draught: thus affording a most striking exemplification of that even-handed justice which commends the ingredients of the poisoned chalice to our own lips.

This event took place on the 4th of September, 1588. Such was the end of the haughty Earl of Leicester, the Queen of England's richest subject and most favoured lover. His character is, with slight abatement, truly set forth in the following satirical epitaph, composed by one of the court wits of the time:—

> "Here lies a valiant warrior,
> Who never drew a sword;
> Here lies a noble courtier,
> Who never kept his word;
> Here lies the Earl of Lei'ster,
> Who governed the estates,
> Whom the earth could never, living, love,
> And the just heaven now hates."

CHAPTER XXIII.

WILLIAM DOVE.

IT will not be out of place here to give a brief account of that poison which this year has attained to such fatal celebrity in English jurisprudence.

Strychnia is a vegetable alkali, obtained from the *strychnos nux-vomica*, in which it exists, combined with the igasuric or strychnic acid. Strychnia is colourless, inodorous, crystalline, unchangeable by exposure to the atmosphere, and extremely bitter. It requires more than 6,660 times its weight of cold water, and 2,500 times its weight of boiling water, to effect its solution. In absolute alcohol, or in ether, it is insoluble; but in diluted alcohol it is to some extent soluble; and this solution, by spontaneous evaporation, yields crystals in the form of octohedrons, and of a square prism terminated by four-sided pyramids.

It acts like other alkalis on vegetable colours, and neutralizes and forms salts with acids. It is extremely poisonous—one-eighth of a grain is sufficient to kill a dog, and a quarter of a grain produces a decided effect on a man. As usually obtained, which is by a tedious and complicated process, it is probably mixed with some *bruscia*, another very powerful vegetable alkali.

Strychnia is composed of 16 equivalents of hydrogen, 180 equivalents of carbon, 3 equivalents of oxygen, and 1 equivalent of azote.

Strychnos is from a Greek word, applied by Theophrastus and Dioscorides to a kind of night-shade. The name was adopted by Linnæus for a particular genus of plants. This genus is composed of trees or shrubs which do not yield a milky juice. The species are not numerous, and are found principally in the tropical parts of Asia and America.

Strychnos nux-vomica—poison nut or ratsbane—is characterized by its oval, shining leaves, 3-5 nerved, and its round smooth berries, containing many seeds. The flowers are small, and of a greenish white colour, and terminate in a series of clusters. The fruit, when ripe, is of the size and colour of an orange. Although the seeds of this plant yield an alkaloid which is a deadly poison, the pulp of the fruit is greedily eaten by many kinds of birds. The wood of this plant is very hard and durable, and on that account is applied to many purposes by the natives on the coast of Coromandel, and other places where it grows.

The genus strychnos consists of about twelve species, and is remarkable for containing among these some which possess only mild or beneficent properties, while others are endowed with more potent and destructive powers than almost any other members of the vegetable kingdom. This extraordinary difference is presumed to be owing to certain species containing only an extractive which is tonic and febrifuge, while others contain one or two alkaloids which are extremely poisonous. This is true, as far as the S. Nux-Vomica, S. Ignatia, S. Colubria, and S. Tieute are concerned, all of which contain either strychnia or bruscia, and some both of these alkaloids; but it does not refer to the S. Toxifer, in which alkaloid has not been detected. It must be admitted, however, that the S. Toxifera, though equally fatal with the others, produces death in a different way. Those possessed of an alkaloid produce death by causing tetanic spasms; whilst the *wouralli*, or *worary* (prepared from the S. Toxifera), produce diametrically opposite effects, as the muscles of voluntary motion are paralysed by it. The only species strictly officinal is the nux-vomica (poison nut) or ratsbane, the seeds of which are employed.

Strychnos nux-vomica is a native of Coromandel, Malabar, Ceylon, and other parts of India, growing in sandy places, and attaining the size of a tree, but short, crooked, and sometimes twelve feet in circumference, flowering in the rainy season. The fruit is about the size of a St. Michael's orange, with a bitter, astringent pulp, and containing from three to five seeds. The pulp may be eaten, but the seeds are poisonous.

Nux-vomica seems to exert a deleterious influence, alike over vegetables and animals; there is, however, a difference of susceptibility to its action in different classes of animals, since a much larger quantity is necessary to destroy herbivorous than carnivorous animals. The degree of effect varies with the quantity employed; but it seems to be the same in kind, being confined to the ganglionic system of nerves and the spinal cord, extending as high up as the medula oblongata, and, according to Flourens, influencing the cerebellum, but certainly not directly affecting the cerebrum. Hence, in fatal cases, the intellect is not disturbed till the extinction of life. The decapitation of animals does not hinder the characteristic action of nux-vomica; while, on the opposite hand, the removal of the spinal marrow completely prevents its peculiar agency, even though artificial respiration be maintained. From some experiments of Segælas, it appears also to exhaust the irritability of the heart; for, in animals, he found that organ could not be stimulated to contract after death, and life could not be prolonged by artificial breathing. Nux-vomica differs from all narcotic poisons, by not exhausting the sensibility. During the intervals of the fits, the sensibility is, on the contrary, heightened, and the faculties acute.

In cases of poisoning by nux-vomica, the most prompt treatment is necessary; and still more so, if any of the soluble salts of strychnia shall have been taken. Nux-vomica is occasionally made the instrument of voluntary death, although no poison causes such torture. The stomach-pump should be instantly had recourse to when nux-vomica has been taken in powder, and, as it adheres very obstinately to the coat of the stomach, it must be perseveringly used, with plenty of water. Emetics are too tedious in their action to be depended upon. M. Donne has recommended, where strychnia or any of its salts has been taken, to endeavour to form an insoluble salt; and for this purpose he proposes chlorine, bromine, or iodine. The tincture of iodine may be procured promptly; but if ten minutes elapse before it is administered, it is unavailing. When the quantity of strychnia taken is not large, nor the symptoms very urgent, vital stimulants or sedatives are often found to be sufficient; and for this purpose wine, brandy, or a mixture of acetous ether and laudanum, or laudanum alone, will remove the immediate danger. Conium or its tincture offers probable means of counteracting the effects of strychnia, as suggested by Dr. Pereira. It must ever be remembered that the danger is not entirely removed, though the spasms may have subsided, and the respiration become easy. Inflammation of the stomach may supervene, which will require the usual treatment, or secondary asphyxia may creep on, and destroy the patient. To prevent this last occurrence great watchfulness is necessary, especially during the night, and the patient should be frequently awakened, and made to drink freely of green tea. But perhaps the most potent and efficient antidote to the other poisonous strychnias would be the urari poison of South America, as suggested by Dr. Morgan.

On account of the very decided character of its symptoms, and the great perfection of modern analysis, no poison is more easily detected than strychnine; and no poisoner is more certain of being found out than the wretch who employs it for the murder of a fellow-creature.

Having given this brief description of the origin and properties of strychnia, we now proceed to relate the trial and conviction of William Dove, who made use of this dreadful poison for the purpose of committing one of the most horrible crimes of which a human being can be guilty—namely, the murder of the woman whom, before God and man, he had sworn to protect to the uttermost of his power.

This most wretched and guilty man was born at Leeds in the year 1818. His father was a highly-respectable man, and a currier by profession. By his unremitting attention to his business, which he carried on in Leeds, Christopher Dove amassed a very handsome independence. William Dove was one of several brothers and sisters who enjoyed a slight independency, bequeathed to them by their father. Upon the death of Christopher Dove, which took place in 1854, the infamous subject of this sketch came into the possession of a legacy of 90l. a year. His education had been carefully attended to. He was placed under the tuition of several schoolmasters

of unquestionable standing and ability. But fortune was kinder to Dove than nature. His intellect was o so very inferior an order, that all the care and labours of his instructors proved unequal to the task of making of William Dove a sensible and well-behaved member of society. As he was notoriously unfitted for any profession demanding an uncommon amount of learning and intelligence, it was resolved to make a farmer of him. He was therefore placed under the charge of a respectable agriculturist; and when it was thought that he was qualified for the undertaking, a farm was taken for himself. Here, however, as might be expected from his character and habits, he proved unsuccessful; and about the time that he was engaged in the murder of his wife, he was a candidate for the office of pay-clerk to the board of guardians at Leeds.

The circumstances of the murder we gather from the speech of the prosecuting counsel. Mrs. Dove, who was about his own age, was the daughter of a Mr. Jenkins, a most respectable person, who carried on the business of a leather merchant at Leeds. Mrs. Dove's brother married the prisoner's sister, and thus the two families became doubly connected. The prisoner became acquainted with his wife in the year 1851, at the house of a friend residing at Appleby-bridge. He continued his addresses until they were married in the following year. The prisoner, it would be shown, was of dissipated habits, and his wife endeavoured to repress them. This led to much domestic unhappiness; the prisoner having been often abusive, brutal, and violent to his wife; whilst on other occasions, it was due to him to state, he treated her with great affection. It would be shown by the evidence of Elizabeth Fisher, the servant who lived with the family, that the prisoner was often drunk—two or three times a week; that he flung chairs at the head of his wife, who on more than one occasion was obliged to fly from the house and seek the protection of a neighbour. These repeated quarrels at length induced the mother of Mrs. Dove to interfere, and it was agreed that they should separate, the prisoner allowing his wife a stipend of 20l. a year out of his income. This arrangement was not, however carried into effect, and unfortunately for Mrs Dove some friends induced her to alter her intention of leaving her husband on his solemnly promising not to relapse into habits of intoxication. It seemed, however, that this resolution was never realized, for the prisoner shortly afterwards broke out into his former habits, and, on being remonstrated with by his wife, he said to her, "Never you mind, I will do your job one of these days." On another occasion he threw her down, and brandished a carving knife over her, using the expression, "You are a d—— w——, and you were so before I married you," a slanderous accusation, for which there was no possible ground. It would also be proved in evidence that in January in the present year, when the prisoner obtained some money from his father's executors, he got drunk, and on his wife upbraiding him he was heard to say, "I will give you a pill one day, that will settle you." That Mrs. Dove apprehended foul treatment at the hands of her husband was to be gathered from an expression which she used to her servant, to this effect— "Elizabeth, if I should die at any time, and you are near me, it is my wish that you should tell my friends to have my body examined." It was believed that the chief motive which induced the prisoner to undertake the murder of his wife was his desire to marry a very respectable lady named Witham, who lived next door to him, and to whom he said on the night of the day on which the inquest was held on his wife, "When all this is settled, I hope you will allow me to come and see you, in consequence of your kindness to Harriet." On the 4th of January he sent for a person named Harrison to a public-house, and read to him an account in a newspaper of the coroner's inquest on Cooke, murdered by William Palmer, at Rugeley, to the effect that Dr. Taylor had not been able to find strychnia in the body of Cooke. The prisoner then said to Harrison, "Can you make me, or get me any strychnia?" Harrison replied that he could not, and then the prisoner said, "Never mind, I can get it elsewhere." Later in the same month he went to the surgery of Mr. Morley, of Leeds, and entering into conversation with the assistant, referred to strychnia, and said that it was the only poison which could not be traced. He also said, pointing to a bottle of strychnia, "That is the stuff that Palmer killed Cooke with." The assistant told him that Mr. Morley had traced strychnia in the body of a woman, but the prisoner said he did not believe it. In about five weeks afterwards he again called at Mr. Morley's surgery, and saw another assistant, named Elliotson. They had a conversation about Palmer's case, and the prisoner then said that his house was infested with rats, and that he wished some poison to kill them with. Mr. Elliotson then gave him ten grains of strychnia, having previously written the word "Poison" on the paper in which it was enclosed. The prisoner took the poison home, and the servant saw him put something on a piece of meat, and expose it on a dog-kennel in the yard. He mentioned the fact of his having the poison (enough, he said, for six people) to his servant, and to Mrs. Witham, the lady who lived next door. The poison was purchased on the 10th of February, and in a day or two afterwards he gave Elizabeth Fisher, the servant, a piece of poisoned cheese, which she placed under Mrs. Dove's bed. On the following day, a mouse was found dead in the room, and then the servant swept up the remains of the cheese and threw it and the sweepings of the room into the fire and burned them. A dead cat was also found in the yard, and the prisoner accurately described the manner in which the cat had died, saying, "It seizes them in the back, and they die." Some few days afterwards, he again (for the third time) went to the surgery of Mr. Morley, saying that he had killed one cat—that the rain had washed the rest of the poison away, and that he wanted some more. Mr. Elliotson on that occasion gave him four or five grains more, and that quantity had not been accounted for, except by the supposition that it was given to the prisoner's wife. The prisoner stated that he kept the poison in his razor-case, and that he had cautioned Mrs. Dove and the servant not to meddle with it. On the Wednesday, before the death of Mrs. Dove, which occurred on the Saturday, the groom of Mr. Morley detected the prisoner in the surgery of that gentleman alone, and apparently much confused at being found there. He said he had come to light his pipe, and then went away, but the groom would state that he had been twenty minutes alone in that room—that the gas was lighted to the full—so that he could have helped himself to any of the contents of the bottles. It should be stated that Mrs. Dove was an ailing woman, and that the prisoner had often complained of the great expense to which she had put him for doctors; but her ailments were not of a dangerous character, and the symptoms which would be described as preceding her death were admitted by medical witnesses to be inconsistent with any known disease. On the 25th of February last Mrs. Dove was first seized with illness, immediately after partaking of her breakfast, which consisted of bread and butter, fried bacon, and tea. The prisoner went for Mr. Morley, and told his assistant that his wife had been ill all night, and that he must come to see her at once. He at the same time asked whether, if she died, there would be a coroner's inquest, and whether Mr. Morley would make a post mortem examination. Mr. Scarfe (the assistant) said that coroner's inquests were only held in case of sudden death, or death by poison. The prisoner then said he would not allow his wife's body to be opened, and that her friends would never allow it. Mr. Scarfe prescribed some sedatives for Mrs. Dove, and, about four o'clock, Mr. Morley himself called, and found her much better, although some of the muscular twitchings continued. The presence of strychnia was suggested to that gentleman, but, considering the respectability of the prisoner's family, he banished the idea from his mind. On the evening of that day the prisoner wrote to his wife's mother, telling her that her daughter was seized with a violent attack of illness, and that she had better come and see her at once. Mrs. Dove was again attacked with the same symptoms (pains in the legs, tightness of the jaws, and twitchings of the feet and hands), and Mr. Morley was again sent for. The prisoner appeared much concerned, and expressed his conviction that his wife would die. Mr. Morley reasoned with him, and told him there was no danger, but that, if he feared she would die, he had better have additional advice, suggesting that Dr. Hod-

son should be sent for. The prisoner said he was satisfied with Mr. Morley, and wrote him a note to that effect in the course of the following day. On the morning of the 1st of March the deceased appeared to be much better. Mr. Morley called in the course of the day, and told her she might get up, and eat a mutton chop. She did so, and Mrs. Witham came in and took tea with her, leaving about eight o'clock. Shortly afterwards the prisoner called at Mrs. Witham's, and asked her to come and sit with his wife, as he was going to Leeds. The prisoner was then rather worse for liquor, and appeared much excited. Before he left the house, Mrs. Dove asked him to give her her medicine, and he then left the room, and returned with a glass containing something, which she drank off. The prisoner then washed out the glass, and observed, "I always wash out the glass—physic is such nasty stuff." He then left the house in a state of excitement, and did not return for some time. Shortly after he left Mrs. Dove was again taken ill. The symptoms were more aggravated than usual. Mr. Morley and Dr. Hodson were sent for by Mrs. Witham, but at eleven o'clock she died in great agony, calling upon the persons round her to turn her or move her in the bed. After she was dead the prisoner kissed the body, and appeared overcome with grief and despair. He told Dr. Hodson, who was present, that he would not allow the body to be opened, as his wife had the greatest horror of dissection. Half-an-hour after the death of the prisoner's wife he went to a public-house and told the people that his wife was dead, and that the doctors had told him she could not live. He afterwards called at the house of a friend, who accompanied him home, and prevailed upon him to go to bed. He was then very drunk. As soon as Mr. Scarfe heard of the death of Mrs. Dove, he for the first time mentioned to Mr. Morley the sale of strychnia; and that gentleman calling to mind the symptoms which the patient had exhibited, and which he had been unable to account for before, at once suspected the administration of poison. On the Sunday morning Mr. Morley received a note from the prisoner, stating that "it would be very harrowing to his feelings that one he loved should be cut open;" but later in the day the same gentleman received another letter, signed by the prisoner and his mother jointly, consenting to a post mortem examination of the body being made. A post mortem examination was made, and an inquest ultimately held. The contents of the stomach were submitted to a most careful analysis, and strychnia was found in large quantities. Animals were poisoned with the strychnia thus extracted, and it would be proved that a little dog which had licked up some of the blood on the floor of the room where the post mortem examination had been held, was shortly afterwards seized with spasms and died. The body of the animal was opened, and strychnia was found in the stomach.

For this most foul and abominable crime, William Dove was, on the morning of Wednesday, the 16th of July, 1856, arraigned in the Crown Court, at York Castle, before Baron Bramwell.

As may be supposed, the trial excited a great deal of interest, and before eight o'clock the passages to the court were thronged with persons anxious to obtain admission. The galleries appropriated to the grand jury and the acting justices were filled with ladies and gentlemen, and the other portions of the court were crowded to excess. At nine o'clock the judge took his seat on the bench, and, after a number of less heinous criminals had been disposed of, William Dove was placed in the dock. In the indictment he was described as 38 years of age, and "well educated." His person is of a slight build, his face was much embrowned, the result of great exposure to the sun. The keen spectator might observe a restless expression in his eye and about his eyelids, and slight spasmodic twitchings, which imparted a sinister and unfavourable expression to his face. When ordered to plead, he replied "Not Guilty" in a firm voice, and declined to exercise his right of challenging the jury.

The counsel for the prosecution were Mr. Overend, Q.C., Mr. Hardy, and Mr. Bayley; the prisoner was defended by Mr. Bliss, Q.C., Mr. Sergeant Wilkins, Mr R. Hall, Recorder of Doncaster, and Mr. Middleton.

Mr. Overend, in a calm and lucid speech, opened the

AMY ROBSART.

case, and described the circumstances of the crime, as we have given them above. Every one of the allegations were fully substantiated by the witnesses called on behalf of the crown. The examination of those witnesses, together with Mr. Overend's speech, occupied two days. On the third day Mr. Bliss replied for the prisoner. The facts of the case were so clear from the beginning, that it was at once perceived by the prisoner's attorney that it would be useless to deny them. Accordingly the whole of the defence was rested on the plea of insanity. William Dove, it was contended, was not a responsible agent. Ample preparations had been made for demonstrating the truth of this proposition. Witnesses were summoned and examined, who knew the prisoner from his childhood. His schoolmaster, his medical attendant, his brother-in-law, and friends of his family, all testified that his words and actions were generally of that description which proved that, if not insane, he was decidedly of an eccentric and imbecile cast of mind. It was testified that his temper was irritable; his disposition was suspicious and revengeful; his religious notions superstitious and extravagant; his language frequently wild, irrational, and incoherent; and his acts generally foolish and purposeless. Mr. Bliss made the most of this material; his appeal to the jury was earnest and pathetic. He admitted the fact of Mrs. Dove having died of the effects of strychnia, and that her husband was the person who administered the fatal poison. But that husband, he contended, was not a responsible agent. In addition to the testimony of the witness who had deposed to the prisoner's weak intellect and eccentric habits, Mr. Bliss adduced the con-

duct of Dove since his committal to prison, in order to show that the wretched man was insane. Among other extraordinary acts of behaviour referred to by the learned counsel in support of his position, was a letter which Dove had written in prison, and addressed to no less a personage than the Devil. The following is a copy of this unique production, the reading of which in court excited a sensation of pain and disgust in the minds of the auditors :—" Dear Devil,—If you will get me clear at the assizes, and let me have the enjoyment of health, wealth, and tobacco, beer, more food and better, and my wishes granted, life till I am sixty, come to me to-night, and tell me.—I remain your faithful subject, WILLIAM DOVE. Written in blood."

But the efforts of his counsel were unavailing to procure the acquittal of the prisoner. On the fourth day of the trial, the jury returned a verdict of " Guilty," with a recommendation to mercy, on the ground of the prisoner's weak understanding. But the recommendation of the jury, backed though it was by the representations of those who had known the criminal from his childhood, had no effect upon the Secretary of State. Sir George Grey firmly declined to advise the Sovereign to exercise the royal prerogative in his behalf. Accordingly, on the 9th of August, at York, the wretched murderer underwent the extreme penalty of the law. Dove himself fully and frequently admitted the justness of his sentence; and when informed a few days previous to his execution, that the efforts of those who had endeavoured to procure a commutation of the sentence had been unavailing, he declared that it was nothing but what he had expected. He made a full confession of his crime, and attributed the foul deed partly to the suggestions of a "fortune-teller," in Leeds. During the interval between sentence and execution, he evinced on the whole no small degree of fortitude, but on the day before his death a very fearful change overtook the unhappy culprit. He had comparatively many visitors during the day, and either from excitement or exhaustion he appeared to be breaking down under the constant contemplation of his fast and irresistibly approaching doom. He evidently was suffering great agony of mind, and doubts began to be entertained as to how far he would be able to face the gallows with that cool, indifferent, imperturbable air which characterized his demeanour in so marked a manner during the whole of his four days' trial.

In illustration of the distress of mind felt by the convict, we give the following sentence, which he appears to have recollected as having been addressed to him years ago by a dear friend, and which he has committed to paper:—" William, if you are *determined to go to hell*, you shall wade through *seas of tears*, and over *mountains of prayers*." The words in italic are underlined in Dove's own manuscript.

The convict repeated a confession of his guilt, and of the justice of the sentence of the law, in the presence of Mr. Noble, on the day previous to his execution. Dove avowed the fact freely that he administered the poison to his wife, and that he knew at the time that what he was administering was poison! Then he added, " I execrate and abhor myself, in dust and ashes, for the crime I have committed; and I am astonished only that any one could take an interest in, and be so kind to, so dreadful an offender as I have been."

When the high sheriff had his interview with the wretched man, he inquired of him if he had any request to make? Dove replied, " I hope you will not allow any cast to be taken of my head;" and the high sheriff assured him that his wish should be complied with. We believe that the relatives and friends of the criminal have been exceedingly anxious upon this point, and they have also begged that his clothes may not be disposed of, as is too frequently the case, for the purpose of public exhibition, to satisfy a morbid and most deprecable curiosity. This request was also complied with, Mr. Noble having given a positive undertaking that Dove's clothes should not pass into the hands of strangers, either for the above or any other purpose.

Such was the end of the poisoner, William Dove; and it is to be hoped that he is the last Englishman to whom the foul crime can ever again with justice be imputed.

THE END.